THE CONSCRIPTS

'Tough and true to life . . . the taste of raw violence'

Aberdeen Evening Express

'Brilliantly realistic n… verve and wit . … new but this …

…elegraph

'Thro… re-time woma… z'

… Supplement

'Excelle… novel . . . conveys extremely well the attitude of the regular Marines to their National Service counterparts'

Grimsby Evening Telegraph

'How well his barrack room dialogue comes over'

Scarborough Evening News

'Vivid and convincing . . . adept at conveying the tragic pointlessness of war; he can describe heroism without indulging in false heroics . . . a highly satisfactory novel'

The Scotsman

'A believable, racy lookback at those two years we cursed but probably wouldn't have missed. Those that lived, that is.'

Northern Echo

By the same author:

THE SUCCESS

(*to be published in 1970*)

THE CONSCRIPTS

Walter Winward

UNABRIDGED

PAN BOOKS LTD : LONDON

First published 1968 by Cassell and Company Ltd.
This edition published 1969 by Pan Books Ltd.,
33 Tothill Street, London, S.W.1

330 02340 3

The characters in this book are imaginary, although the incidents depicted are largely based on fact

Printed in Great Britain by
Richard Clay (The Chaucer Press), Ltd.,
Bungay, Suffolk

For

Charlotte Eleanor

This day is called the feast of Crispian.
He that outlives this day, and comes safe home,
Will stand a tip-toe when this day is nam'd
And rouse him at the name of Crispian.

Shakespeare: Henry V.

And he who does not come home?

PART ONE

ONE

Riordan paid for his coffee, and sat down on a stool by the window. As he unbuttoned his raincoat he caught sight of the unfamiliar gleam of a white shirt. It reassured him. It made him feel as good as anyone.

It was cold outside. January cold. The early evening traffic poured inexorably into and out of the West End. New cars, second-hand cars, ancient cars – apotheoses bought on HP by suburban commuters, and flanked by lorries and buses, grotesque and noisy. Motorized beetles heading God only knew where. In the centre of the plexus Eros frowned at the untidy scrimmage, while on both sides of Piccadilly marauding tarts ignored the temperature to earn the rent.

Riordan sipped his coffee. He appeared older than his twenty years. He was tall, with the body of a man who has always worked with his hands. There was no padding in his raincoat; the bulges were sinew and muscle, the end-product of five years' hod-carrying and pick-swinging. His nose had been broken long ago in a fight with someone whose name he had forgotten.

The door of the café opened and two girls came in; pert, well scrubbed, fresh from their typewriters. He followed their progress to the counter. One of them noticed him and nudged her friend. They eyed him saucily, and giggled.

Stupid bitches, he thought. He had been with their sort before. They were all right in the dance-hall and not bad on the way home. But get them inside the house, try to put your hand anywhere near their private property – and Jesus, did they yell. Ask them who they were saving it for and they'd answer their husband or the right man; although how the hell they could tell if he was right before trying him was a mystery. But he knew what they meant: they meant men who had 'good' jobs, who wore a collar and tie as a matter of routine and not just on special occasions, who opened doors for them and gave up their seats on trains. They did not mean labourers who dressed up for the evening, who usually wore sweaty shirts and dungarees, whose fingers were calloused and nails broken. They did not mean nobodies. They did not mean him.

Bitches.

They were nothing special. They might keep their mothers happy by staying out of trouble, and they might wear fancy frills that no one ever saw; but underneath it all they were scrubbers, and no different from the rest. They'd get married, have a few kids, then start cheating on their good-jobbed husbands with the postman or the milkman, or anyone else who'd give it to them on a long, hot afternoon.

Bitches. All bitches. He knew. He'd seen it. In Notting Hill, where he lived.

Notting Hill.

He was not sorry to be leaving it behind, not sorry to see the back of the tiny flat he shared with his father, not sorry to see the last of building sites, lay-offs, casual work, twenty pounds one week and zero the next, the Labour Exchange. It could rot in hell, so far as he was concerned. For two years, anyway.

He checked his watch: five minutes to opening time, five minutes to the start of his last drunken night as a civilian.

His friends, he knew, could not understand why he was so anxious to do his National Service, why he was so willing to subject himself to the regimentation of the Marines.

You're nuts, Tom. Lissen, I'd rather cut me bloody leg orf than join that lot.

You mean you wanna go in? You're a loony.

Two years' square bashin'. And you could get your 'ead shot orf. Not me. Not bleedin' likely.

You shoulda come to me, Tom. I could've given you the name of a guy who'd've supplied you with a bottle of stuff that 'ud convince any doctor in the world you'd got diabetes. Honest.

He only partly understood it himself, but it had something to do with a second chance, an opportunity to do something with his life – or two years of it, at least. He was a nothing in

Civvy Street, a builder's labourer, a number to be called out at the end of the week. He needed to be more than that. He needed to be . . .

And here he would give up the difficult process of trying to analyse himself.

One of the typists came over. 'Do you mind if I borrow the sugar?'

'Take it.'

'Haven't I seen you at the Streatham Locarno?'

'No.' He did not look at her.

'Oh, well, be like that.'

She tossed her blonde hair and clicked away on her stiletto heels. Pink. Pure.

Stupid bitch, he thought. But no more of that for him. Finish Notting Hill. Finish London. Tomorrow was a new day.

He drank the remainder of his coffee and buttoned his raincoat. He left the café without a backward glance, and vaulted the railings on the north side of Piccadilly. He ran across the road. The lights from Snow's Bar beckoned.

'The Marines will make a world of difference to him, sort him out, you mark my words. I'm all for youngsters doing a two-year stint away from home. Teach 'em something about life. Bound to.'

Michael Porter opened the sitting-room door a fraction. He waited, his hand on the door knob, for the conversation between his parents to continue.

'But he's only nineteen, dear. He's far too young.'

'Nonsense. You're too protective, always have been. He's not a child. And don't forget a lot of them go in at eighteen.'

'Well, I don't see why he couldn't have gone to university first. He could easily have been deferred until he'd taken his degree. It makes last summer seem such a waste. He worked and worked for his A-levels.'

'They'll come in useful sooner or later. Besides, they might help him get a commission.' Mr Porter shut his eyes and allowed himself a moment of fantasy. He saw his son, *his* son, in an officer's uniform. The Sam Browne gleamed in the sunlight. Men were saluting him. His son. 'Anyhow, he's doing what he wants to do and I admire him for it. He's no conchy, Michael, I'm glad to see. Mind you, there was a time . . .'

In the hall Porter moved away from the door and sat on the stairs. He had a good idea what his father was going to say, and he had no wish to hear it. It was an old lament, a familiar litany. *There was a time when I had reservations about Michael. I thought there was something peculiar about him. You know, he doesn't act like most lads of his age. He hardly ever goes out, he hasn't a steady girl. It's strange, to say the least.*

Yes, he'd heard it all before. He was the peculiar one, the funny one, the one who had no particular ambitions, the boy who had never been caught, not once, reading a dirty book or magazine, who had never brought a girl home. An oddity. But now the old man was satisfied. He could tell the other fathers in clubs and pubs that his son, *his* son, was doing his National Service in the Royal Marines. *Not the REME or the Pay Corps or any of those other soft regiments, but the Marines. My God, do those lads go through it.* It was as though a single stroke of the pen, a simple decision, had made him respectable in the old man's eyes. National Service was to be the panacea which would cure all ills, the catalyst that would change him. In two years he would emerge looking like a Wagnerian hero or the 'after' photograph in a physical culture advert. He would then be fit to take his place in the family line-up – cleansed, a new man, a son to be proud of.

Hallelujah.

Take his place where? In the green fields of Surrey, last bastion of civilization? Or in the City, perhaps, alongside the million other bowler-hatted automata. Or perhaps merely in a house like his father's: all flower-beds and double garages and central heating and grandfather clocks and phoney antiques and three telephones and meticulously cared for golf clubs and a name on the gate instead of a number and charge accounts with all the local shops and two bank accounts.

No. Not that. Anything but that.

'Michael? Are you out there, Michael?'

He got to his feet and went into the sitting room.

His mother glanced up from her knitting. She smiled her usual inoffensive smile. 'Oh, there you are, dear.'

'Drink?' said Mr Porter.

'Please.'

'Whisky do?'

'Oh, not whisky, dear. Not before dinner.'

'Let him decide for himself, for goodness' sake. He's old enough to know what he wants. Whisky?'

For a second Porter was tempted to say, No, that he'd have sherry, but he decided against it. He would soon be away. In a day or so there would be no more idiotic fights, no more points-scoring.

'Whisky's fine.'

'Good. Help yourself to soda.'

Mr Porter watched his son add twice as much soda as there was whisky, and he sighed inaudibly. Why, when he was nineteen he had taken double the quantity neat. There was something faintly womanish about drowning good Scotch. No, not womanish, he mustn't think that because then the other word, effeminate, would spring to mind, and he'd vowed never again to think of Michael in those terms. Perhaps his hair was too fair, his shoulders too slender, his hands too . . . too artistic, and his features all too regular, but that was neither here nor there. In any case, the Marines would put some muscle on him.

Unobtrusively Mrs Porter studied her son and husband from behind a half-knitted sweater, and wondered if it were her fault that the pair had never got along together. She suspected it was, up to a point. Michael was the third and last child and the first boy, and his father had had great plans for him. A top-class public school, Oxford, the Blue her husband had just missed, a legal or business career. Wishful thinking. At the time there hadn't been enough money to send him to any sort of public school, and they had been compelled to settle for the local Grammar. As for the Blue, that would always be out of the question. Even as a child Michael had been completely apathetic about games, and she had not encouraged him to be otherwise. She had molly-coddled him, probably.

Of course, it wasn't only her fault. Nature had played its part. With her husband away on business most weeks her son had grown up in the company of three women. Not the best environment for a boy who was expected to mature into his father's ideal son.

And now the Marines. To prove something? Impossible to tell. She would cry, anyway, when he left.

'Isn't it almost time for dinner, dear?' said Mr Porter pointedly.

'Dinner? Oh, yes. Yes. It is getting rather late. I'll see to it.'

She went out. A rehearsed exit, thought Porter, and prepared himself for a speech from his father.

'Well, tomorrow's the big day, Michael,' began Mr Porter. 'Soon be in uniform. Any regrets?'

'None.' Liar. The new, the unknown and unexplored – it frightens you. Metuo, ergo sum.

'Excellent. Glad to hear it. Be over before you know it, in any case. Mind you' – he gave what he hoped was a mildly salacious chuckle – 'mind you, there'll be one or two things you'll have to be careful of.'

'Such as?'

'Such as women, for instance. Uniforms and all that.'

Porter felt his stomach heave. Here it comes, he thought – the man-to-man bit. He sought refuge in his drink. His father was at his most odious when trying to be friendly.

Mr Porter stood with his back to the fire. 'We've never really talked about . . . women . . . Michael. I mean, I've no idea whether you've ever . . .' He faltered. God, how unbelievably difficult it was.

'What, had a woman?' Porter was surprised at how easily the words came out.

Mr Porter coughed uncomfortably. 'Well, yes.' He paused, waiting for chapter and verse.

There was a long silence, which Porter enjoyed. It wasn't often he had his father on the defensive.

He had never had a woman, but he could not tell the old man that. Too much like a confession. He rarely thought of himself as a virgin, but he supposed that was the technical term. Nineteen and a virgin. Intacta. (Or was it intactus?) It often disturbed him. It would disturb him more to reveal the secret to a man who, deep down, hoped his son was paying one or two paternity suits.

'You're not listening to me, Michael.'

'Sorry. What did you say?'

'Nothing. It doesn't matter.' Mr Porter shook his head. Michael never listened to him. There was no level on which they could communicate.

Mrs Porter returned, timorously. She smiled at her son and he smiled back, fondly.

The urgent clangour of the door-chimes invaded the privacy of his shallow sleep with the sudden indifference of an electric shock. He sat up with a start, willing away the cobwebs. And his first thought was, as it always was: Where the hell did I put my pants?

The woman beside him stirred. She said, her voice husky and tired with recent sex, 'It's awright, honey, it's awright, Roy. Let it ring. Husband's got a key an' won't be home 'til six. Go to sleep, Roy.'

She turned over, tugged at the blankets, and was soon breathing evenly.

Webster looked down at her, at the several creases in her neck, just below the hairline, at the mole on her left shoulder, at the purple mark on her throat made half an hour earlier. A cool one, he thought. Bloody cool. He made a silent wager that she had spent many an afternoon tucked up in bed next to a comparative stranger.

Bored housewives. Easy pickings.

The chimes rang again, but with less authority. He stretched lazily.

He had made a study of housewives during his two years as a door-to-door salesman, and had come to the conclusion that they fell into three broad categories. There were the young-marrieds, who were still starry-eyed and prone to showing off their wedding photographs: this group was virtually unassailable unless they lived in an area where there were no garden walls to chat across or Bingo halls to visit. Then there were the mothers of very young children: they were usually too busy to think of anything but their kids' snotty noses or scuffed shoes or dirty knees or torn shirts and frocks. Finally there was the thirty-five-to-forty age group with teenage children – the easiest defences to penetrate. Frightened of approaching middle age, they would try anything to convince themselves they were not growing old. Pushovers, most of them.

The woman next to him, whose body had given him a pleasurable if energetic hour or so, was about thirty-eight. Thirty-eight and disillusioned. The gold leaf had worn off her marriage and she could now see what lay underneath. Greyness. Menopause. Corsets. Diets. Glamorous grandmother contests. A couple of gin-and-its with hubby on a Saturday night. Bills to pay. Clothes to buy. Gone were the youthful days of hope, and future was a word which spelled less than half a lifetime. Only the television to escape to now. Or sex.

He had known he was on to a good thing the moment she opened the door. He always watched their eyes. When they were on heat something happened to the pupils; they dilated, shone, in anticipation. She hadn't even wanted to see his samples, which was an agreeable change. Most of them liked to pretend that they were genuinely interested in what he had to sell, and that the rest was purely accidental. But not her. (My name's Cathy, honey. What's yours? Well, Roy, would you like a drink?) A couple of drinks, a bit of patter. (You can't be old enough to have children that age, Cathy.) And that was all there was to it, with the exception of the three Ws: When does your husband get home; Where's the back door; What time are the kids due in from school.

Easy pickings.

Silly cows.

He reached for his cigarettes. Through a V-shaped chink in the partly-drawn curtains the afternoon light made the bedroom seem cold and unfriendly. Bedrooms were always like that – afterwards. A heap of clothes slung over a chair, a shoe without a partner, rumpled sheets, the faint smell of sweat, fluff on the carpet, breath on the window, a holiday snap on the dressing-table. *Cathy, Jim and the kids at Blackpool. June 1952.*

He held the flame of his lighter towards the alarm-clock. Three PM. In bed at three-bloody-PM. At the rate he was going he'd be dead before he was forty.

Mrs Edwards, he thought, blowing smoke at her, you are a slut. S.L.U.T. But at least you're honest with it. Well, as honest as you can be. And you'll be the last for a while because I hear they put bromide in our tea for the first few weeks. Bromide. Jesus, that's a hell of a way to keep a man down.

She sensed him leave her side, and turned over quietly. She watched him dress, and the knowledge that he was unaware of being watched excited her.

She shuddered. He was a good-looking bastard. Too good-looking. All that black hair. And those slim hips and that firm belly. And the way one corner of his mouth dropped when he smiled. He'd been around, too, but he was nowhere near twenty-six, as he claimed. Not by a long chalk. Twenty or twenty-one perhaps. It was easy to tell the young ones: they kept going even when they were exhausted, which was what made them so attractive.

Roy. She had forgotten to ask his surname, but she could find that out another day because there would be other days – unless some woman's husband caught him on the job and beat him to pulp. He wouldn't be much of a fighter; no lady's man ever was. He wasn't a weakling, but his strength was reserved for what he was good at. Underneath he was brittle.

He finished dressing and she closed her eyes. She waited for him to whisper her name or kiss her, but all she heard was the sound of the bedroom door closing.

The bastard. The ungrateful bastard.

Downstairs Webster helped himself to a large rum from a bottle on the sideboard and scooped up a handful of cigarettes from a box close by. Near the bottle was a photograph of two girls in school uniform. How old had she said they were – twelve, thirteen? Something like that. Not old enough to know their mother was a whore, anyway.

Aloud he said: 'Kids, your mother's okay.'

He picked up his sample case and let himself out into the street. It was bitterly cold, and he walked quickly.

It was raining in Manchester; dull, grimy rain, heavy with dirt from factory chimneys and carbon from car exhausts. It ruined the young girls' Saturday hair-dos, drove the home-going football crowds into doorways, spattered the businessman's shoes, filled the cinemas and pubs with steaming people, emptied the parks, drenched cats and pigeons, and made bronchitis sufferers cough fluidly. Lorries hissed on wet tarmac. Newspapers sellers covered their wares with awnings of tin and canvas. Hot-dog vendors abandoned their barrows.

At the corner of Deansgate and Blackfriars Street a youth in a dark-green anorak and faded blue jeans waited impatiently to cross the road. He was eighteen or nineteen, thin and wiry, and a fraction under average height. Clutched on his chest was a carrier-bag which bore the legend: Benson's Off-licence. Protruding from the bag were the necks of half a dozen quart bottles of brown ale.

At the first gap in the traffic he made a dash for it, ran down the east side of Deansgate and turned left into St Ann Street. Several minutes later he stopped before a terraced house and opened the door by barging it with his shoulder. He went along the hallway and into the kitchen.

'What kept you, George?' grinned one of the three youths sitting around the table.

'The angels did. They're havin' a right old pee out there.'

George Thatcher put the carrier-bag of beer on the floor, and unzipped his anorak. 'I'm gonna get out of these wet duds,' he said. 'Shuffle the cards and don't guzzle all that bleedin' ale. I won't be a sec.'

In the bathroom he peeled off his shirt and jeans, and emptied his pockets. Some silver, a roll of notes, a bunch of keys, and a buff envelope. The envelope was wet and the ink smudged, but he knew it contained a call-up card and a train warrant. 'Bastards,' he muttered. 'Just when the barrow was startin' to make a nice profit, too.'

He dried his hair and combed it in front of the mirror. He talked to himself while he combed, as though appealing to his reflection for sympathy.

'Bastards. Rotten flamin' Government. Wouldn't believe me when I told them I had an old mum and dad to support. Not them. Had to check up and find out they'd been dead for donkeys'. Wouldn't believe me when I said I was helpin' the export drive. Not them. Sellin' fifteen bob clocks and china dogs from a barrow in the market isn't an exempt class, they tell me. Can't get away with anythin' these days. Why me? I mean, why me? It's bloody unjust.'

'You comin', George? Can't play three-handed poker.'

'Two minutes.'

One of his friends started whistling a military march as Thatcher took his place at the table.

'Bloody funny, Fred, bloody funny. But they'll get you, buddy-boy, you wait. Come on, deal. The only thing that's gonna cheer me up is to take you blokes.'

He felt better when he saw that his first three cards were Kings.

'Five and up five.'

'I'll stay.'

'And me.'

'Pass us a bottle.'

Thatcher poured himself a glass of beer. The other card players, he was sure, would not be sorry to see him go. They owned barrows themselves, but he was the one who did the most business. He was quicker than they were, sharper. He knew where to buy cheap and sell dear. He'd had it made – until now.

He drew two cards, both sixes.

'Your five and up ten.'

'Suits me.'

'What are you going to do with your stock, George?'

'Never mind what I'm gonna do with my bloody stock. Play poker. Ten bob to stay.'

Fred had a point, though. What was he going to do with his stock. And his barrow. Sell? To the trade, stock and barrow weren't worth more than sixty quid. But that sixty was worth three hundred in the right place.

'Come on, George. Stop scratchin' your balls. A quid to keep goin'.'

Thatcher eyed the player who had bet a pound. He took out his roll of notes and counted them.

'What are you doin'?'

'I'm seein' how much I can afford to lose, d'you mind?'

'What's to see? And what's to lose? With your sort o' luck you just need a shovel to pick up your winnings. Come on, bet.'

'Okay, a tenner.'

'Tenner! Ten quid! Are you off your bleedin' 'ead!'

'Are you chicken?'

'Am I hell! There's my ten. Pick the bones out o' that.'

'That clears me.'

'An' me. You two barons can fight it out.'

Thatcher licked his upper lip, white with beer froth.

'I'll see you, Jim.'

'Full house, Queens on top.'

Thatcher grinned with relief. 'Hard bloody cheese. Me too. Kings over sixes.'

He chuckled as he shuffled the notes into a crisp green heap. And then he had an idea.

'Tell you what,' he said, in between mouthfuls of Benson's Brown Ale, 'who wants the barrow, stock an' all?'

'You sellin'?'

'I'll have it. Fifty quid.'

'Fifty-five.'

'Fifty-five nothin'. Look, I'll do a deal. The stuff's worth three ton on the market. If you blokes pool your money I'll bet the barrow against whatever's in the kitty. One card. All right?'

'You're on.'

There were one hundred and twenty pounds in the kitty. It wasn't much, he thought, but he couldn't take the barrow where he was going.

'Cut.'

The cards were cut.

'You, George. Mugs away.'

Thatcher tapped the pack, prayed, and drew a Jack. He blew a C-major raspberry. 'Beat that, jug-ears.'

The others, after hesitating, drew a Queen. Thatcher knocked over his beer in disgust.

'It's just not my bloody week,' he moaned, as he listened to the winning trio squabble about who was to have what of the spoils.

Earth.

Good earth. Brown earth. Fertile. Yielding as a woman. Furrowed. Earth that is all things to all men. Master. Mistress. Slave. Overseer. Earth as weather-beaten as Tim Rourke himself. As strong.

Earth.

It was dark now, but once in a while the headlamps of a car on the Dorchester road illuminated the snow-covered landscape and enabled him to pick out everything he knew and loved. There was the barn at the end of the yard, where he had seen his first calf born – a damp bundle of legs and innocence; the old tractor, due to be pensioned off shortly, which he had learned to handle like a veteran almost before he could read and write; the quarry where he had played as a child; the elm he had climbed for a dare. The fields, the trees, the distant hooting of a predatory owl. It was part of him, and he was leaving it for two years in the care of his elder brother. In a way, Ken was lucky to have had TB as a young 'un. Bloody lucky.

He would miss it all.

The smell of the night.

The wind in the thatch.

The clear, crisp winter mornings with their million diamonds of frost.

The crack of a twelve-bore.

The warm loving of his wife of seven months.

Especially that. Especially Mary. Especially the way she nuzzled him.

(Oh, Tim, I didn't think anything could be like that. Is it the same for everyone? Is it like that for you? Do all girls feel like this? Mollie told me that Ken . . . But I'd better not tell you that. We don't talk about it. Girls don't. I expect men do. I've read in books that they do. Will you talk about me? Will you tell them what I'm like? What will you say? Don't tell them everything, will you? I never want to leave you, darling. Never ever. I want a child. A boy. When can we have a child? We'll try and try, won't we? Oh, Tim. Put your hand there, Tim. Put it there. Oh, Jesus. Sweet Jesus.)

Especially that.

The cross-beam of the doorway in which Rourke was standing was six feet from the ground, but he had to lean to one side and bend his knees a little to avoid grazing his head on it. His shoulders were broad and his forearms as thick as a sapling, and he had the easy if vacant smile of someone who finds it too much trouble to follow the substance of an argument or debate. He was twenty-two and joint tenant, with his brother, of the farm.

His wife came up behind him. He put an arm around her.

'Supper's nearly ready,' she said. 'Aren't you cold out here?'

'No. I'm fine. Have you got a cigarette on you?'

She gave him one from the pocket of her apron. He lit it.

'We'll go to bed after supper – will we?'

He grinned. 'Last night blues?'

She looked hurt.

'Sorry, love,' he said. 'You bet we'll go to bed.'

She squeezed his hand. Only a few more hours – twenty-four, thirty-six. It wasn't fair. It wasn't fair at all. It would be different if they'd been married for years, but they hadn't. Seven months, seven short months. Thirty weeks. Two hundred days. Not long.

The cottage would seem empty without him. Desolate. Dead. It was strange how dependent a woman was, a wife was. A wife spent her life doing things for her husband, helping him, comforting him, until he became her life. But she was never part of him; or rather she was a very small part. A wife had to share her husband: with his job, his friends, his hobbies, his ambitions, his thoughts. Yet without him, she was incomplete. If anything were to happen to him ... But she wouldn't think that; that was silly. He wasn't going far, only to Devon. But where after Devon?

'You're shivering,' he said.

'I'm all right.'

'Better go in.'

'And you?'

'In a minute. Another minute.'

She understood, and left him to the trees, the fields, the night air.

'No more, Ed. You've had enough.'

'I can take it.'

'I don't care. You're supposed to be working here, not drinking the profits. Anyway, I want you sober. There's a couple o' boyos over there who look like disaster with a capital D. Keep an eye on 'em.'

Mr Goldstein walked off, shaking his head. That Ed, he was a case. You hire someone like him and he gives you ulcers. You don't hire him, you get smashed up, and still you get ulcers. There ought to be laws . . .

Sure, Mr Goldstein. Anything you say, Mr Goldstein. Up your pipe, Mr Goldstein. Jew gett. 'A double, Max,' said Ed Shaw to the barman.

'Can't do it, Ed. You heard the boss.'

'Screw the boss.'

'Take it easy, Ed. It's more than my job's worth.'

'Okay, okay. You don't have to plead. You're not in the Old Bailey.'

The club was full of night people and early-morning people and let's-have-another people and find-me-a-girl people and we're-on-the-town people and high-as-a-kite people and God-is-it-that-late people and flotsam-and-jetsam people who disappear, into holes or burrows, during the day and only emerge when the pubs are closed and the street-lamps extinguished and the policemen patrol in pairs and the cats make love in the bushes and the breath makes tiny white clouds in the silent streets. Tom Collins, John Collins, Sidecar, White Lady, cheap wine masquerading as champagne under the guise of an outrageous price – the nomenclature of insomniacs, of those too scared to sleep.

'Hey, Maggie,' called Shaw, 'you coming home with me tonight?'

'Not this night or any other night.'

'You don't know what you're missing.'

'I know what I'm missing.'

'It's my last night in town.'

'It wouldn't worry me if it was your last night on earth.'

'Clever girl, clever girl. You should get a job in music hall. That's dead, too. She doesn't like me,' he complained to Max.

'You gave her a rough ride the other week.'

'She went for my wallet.'

'Yeah.'

'You don't believe me?' Shaw leaned across the bar, his fists half-clenched, smiling with his mouth but not his pale-blue eyes.

Max cleaned a glass nervously. Ed Shaw was a rough customer. The neatly pressed dark suit and the girlish wave in his blond hair were fronts. Underneath the elegance he was as mean as a hungry dog. He was only twenty or so, but a man twice his age could have taught him nothing about in-fighting.

'. . . Believe me, Max?'

'Sure, Ed, I believe you. Look, I gotta serve.'

Shaw chuckled. Fear. What it was to see fear like that. 'Then serve, Max, serve. I'm not stopping you.'

'Attaboy.'

'You're all right, Max.'

'Thanks.'

Shaw swivelled on his stool. He leaned back, his elbows resting on the bar.

He appeared to have drunk more than he actually had, which was the impression he wanted to give. The degree of success he achieved in his job as Goldstein's bouncer, he reasoned, depended on how much quicker he was than the next man. And if the next man thought him a lush, that was an advantage. The troublemaker would expect his reactions to be slow, and instead he would discover, a fracture or two later, that they were fast. He would be out in the street before he knew it; which was why Goldstein paid a high wage.

'You off tomorrow, Ed?'

'Yeah.'

'Don't shoot too many civvies.'

'Try not to.'

Shaw munched an olive and flicked the stone at Maggie, who scowled and ignored him. She remembered how, the week previously, he had caught her going through his pockets in the small hours; how he had calmly, without a trace of anger, selected a towel and soaked it under the tap; how he had beaten her with it; how he had grunted peculiarly as each stroke fell; how she had not wanted him to stop; and finally how they had made love with a terrible fury.

'You're on, Ed,' said Goldstein. 'In the corner. The two I told you about are coming it.'

Shaw nodded.

As he got near to the table where the argument was taking

place, he noted that the man in the loud suit was carrying too much weight around the belly. One good punch . . . The second man, younger, was a different proposition and would have to be dealt with first.

'Anything wrong?'

Loud Suit glared at him. 'You the manager?'

'Assistant. Assistant manager.'

'Then I'm not talkin' to you. Fetch me the manager.'

'Why?'

'This waiter's cheatin' us. I give him a fiver and he hands me change for a quid.'

'That right, Frank?'

'No, Ed. He gave me a pound. I haven't had a fiver for an hour.'

'You're a liar,' said the younger one. 'A bloody liar.' He raised his voice deliberately. The room took notice.

'Leave us, Frank,' said Shaw quietly. Then: 'Piss off, you two.'

'Don't tell me to piss off. I'll have your teeth.'

'You've got half a minute.'

Shaw counted the seconds. He was relaxed. He liked an audience.

'. . . Twenty-nine, thirty.'

The younger man lunged, but he was handicapped by being seated. Shaw jabbed him between the eyes with an elbow. He staggered back, blinded. Loud Suit opened his mouth to protest, but the only sound he made was an agonized bleat as Shaw hit him twice in the belly, and spat with satisfaction as his fist sank several inches into soft flesh.

'Get them out of here!'

Goldstein bought him a drink. 'You deserve it, Ed. We're gonna miss you.'

'Yeah.'

Maggie came over. 'You hit the fat one too hard.'

'Just thank Christ they weren't your guts. You on your own?'

'Yes.'

'What happened to the guy you were with?'

'He left in a hurry; couldn't stand the sight of blood. I always pick heroes.'

'Then it looks like you're stuck with me.'
'Looks like it,' she said, after a moment.
He was surprised. 'You're a sucker for punishment.'
She shrugged philosophically. 'I know it.'

. . . . .

The night trains splutter and cough, hiss impatiently.

Riordan takes a bottle of beer from his suitcase, removes the top by using the carriage ashtray as an opener. Drinks quietly.

Mr Porter grips his son's hand. Firmly. Slender fingers. (Good luck, Michael. You can do it.) *Do what?*

Webster ogles the pretty Wren. God, he could find a use for her. His regular girl, Jenny, feels apprehensive. The Wren has long slim legs.

Thatcher toys with a cheap wristwatch. A sailor offers to buy it for three pounds. With apparent reluctance, Thatcher sells. He has paid twenty-five shillings for the wristwatch the day before.

Mary Rourke kisses her husband again. He holds her, wills her not to cry, knows he is asking the impossible.

Shaw sits in a corner seat. He stares out of the window, thinks of the rifle they will give him in a day or so.

There are others, too. Barker, Bailey, Carter, Davidson . . . Jones, A., Jones, P., Kelland . . . Martin, Owen, Pearson . . . From: Aberdeen, Aldershot, Barnsley, Dorking . . . Liverpool, London, Merthyr Tydfil . . . Rochdale, Rotherham, Torquay.

Different names. Different cities. One destination.

The night trains shudder, lurch off into the darkness.

TWO

A fall of new snow covered the camp. It crackled underfoot like broken walnut shells, freezing already. It had swept down from the hills, south-east to Exmouth, south-west to Okehampton, and on south to Dartmoor, forming drifts en route, collecting in hollows, trapping sheep, isolating cottages, snapping telephone wires, and finally blanketing Alpha, Bravo, Charlie, and Delta Companies' lines, the Officers' Mess, the Sergeants' Mess, the Naafi, the other ranks' canteen, the assault course, the parade ground, the guard-room, and the grey-green trucks lying dormant in the MT Pool.

In Charlie Company the new arrivals, perched uncertainly on wooden benches and suitcases and bunks, waited for instructions. Townsmen, city men, village men, countrymen. Some with straw in their hair and a predilection for draught cider, some with the cool, hair-oil arrogance of industrial communities, some wet behind the ears. They offered each other cigarettes, and introduced themselves.

And they thought:

If this is the Marines I should've joined the Brownies.

When do we eat?

It never looked like this on the recruiting posters. What about the sun-tanned corporal quaffing beer, and the women in bikinis? And all those goddam ciné-cameras.

It's only for two years.

The next guy to say, It's only for two years, gets a punch in the mouth.

Eight o'clock? You mean it's only eight AM? Christ, I feel buggered already.

And they said:

I'm married a week. I'm married a week and my papers come. Registered delivery on a Saturday morning while I'm having a quick how's-your-father with the wife. So I send 'em back, Not Known at this Address. But they got me anyway.

The doc says I was VIP. Yeah? says I. Yeah, says he. Venereal infection positive. Oh Jeeze, says I.

Me too. I told the doc I had one ball that hung lower than the other. So has everyone, he said. It was a relief, I can tell you. It's worried me for years.

I thought I was joining the RAF. Honest.

You know what Naafi stands for, don't you? No ambition and fug all interest.

Never volunteer for anything. My brother volunteered for a driving course at Aldershot, and ended up as a cook in Malaya.

I don't care where they send me as long as it's London.

If I like it I'll sign on, but I don't reckon I'm gonna like it.

It's my missus I'm sorry for. She needs it, if you know what I mean.

I'm gonna work bloody hard and maybe make corporal. Then when I've made corporal I'm gonna go for a commission. Then . . .

There was this dame on the bus, see. It was obvious she had hot pants. Well, there was no one on the upper deck apart from me an' her . . .

And they heard:

The far-away crack of a low calibre rifle; the hoarse commands of the drill NCOs; the rattle of supply trucks; the sound of marching feet; the grunts and curses of a Squad back from a dawn run.

And they growled: Roll on demob.

They studied Sergeant Hayter and they did not approve of what they saw. He looked too keen, too efficient, too fit, the personification of the professional Marine from the top of his close-cropped head to the tips of his highly polished boots. A man who would take a cold shower in the morning for the hell of it, and expect everyone else to do the same.

Hayter toyed irritably with a pencil and waited for the last of the recruits to settle down. National Servicemen, he thought with disgust. National bloody Servicemen. Fifty of them. Fifty lumps of soft living, and sixteen weeks to turn them into fighting troops, teach them how to march until they dropped and then march some more, teach them that a rifle was designed to kill, teach them how to throw grenades and climb ropes and ford streams. Teach them how to obey as a body. Fifty part-timers who'd spent their adolescence in coffee-bars and dance-halls. Christ, it was a bit much. After ten years in the Corps he deserved more than the end of the stick the dog shat on. Trust the Adjutant to pick him. Trust Captain bloody Useless to cancel his overseas posting and leave him in England while the rest of the Brigade were sunning themselves in Malta, making hay with the matelots' wives. Officers. And National Servicemen. Jesus Christ.

'All right, cut the chatter,' he said. 'Cut it! You're bootnecks now, not civilians, and bootnecks do as they're told.'

He got the silence he asked for. An apprehensive silence.

'Right,' he went on, 'what I'm going to do first is call your names. Say Yes, sergeant or Here, sergeant, then give me your religious denomination. C of E will do for Church of England, Catholic for Roman Catholic, and so on. I need this information to divide you up for church parades. When you've told me your denomination, I'll give a serial number. Write it on a piece of paper or scratch it on your bums, but remember it. It'll be yours for the rest of your days in the Marines.' He paused. 'Bailey.'

'Yes, sergeant. C of E.'

'421838. Barker.'

'Yes, sergeant. C of E.'

'421839. Carter.'

'Yes, sergeant. Catholic.'

'421840. Davidson . . .'

His voice droned on, and after a while the litany became automatic. There were no cranks so far, he thanked God. No Buddhists or Pancake Tuesday Adventists.

'Klein.'

'Yes, sergeant. Jewish.'

Everyone stared at the sallow-skinned youngster with the incredibly black eyes. Most of them had only read about Jews, and connected them vaguely with Germany, concentration camps, property, banking, and the Old Testament.

'Jewish,' repeated Klein, adding with a shy grin: 'And I eat bacon and eggs for breakfast and roast beef on Sundays.'

'Good for you, Klein. 421851. Lowrie.'

'Here, sergeant. C of E . . .'

Squatting on the floor, wedged between Rourke and Davidson and panting for a cigarette, Thatcher began to fidget as his name drew nearer. For him, church was no place to be on an icy morning after a drunken Saturday night. All those bells and priests and hymns. Hypocritical old sods. Not on your life. Not on anybody's life. Besides, what had God ever done for him?

'. . . Shaw.'

'Yes, sergeant. C of E.'

'421887. Thatcher.' There was no response. '*Thatcher!*'

'Yes, sergeant. Er . . . atheist.'

'4218 . . . What did you say, Thatcher?'

'Atheist, sergeant.'

'What d'you mean, atheist? You mean you don't believe in God?'

'Yes, sergeant.'

Hayter grunted with annoyance. There was always one clever one who thought he could work the system to his own advantage. Now why the hell couldn't he have said C of E like the other liars? It would have made things a lot easier.

'If this is a gag to get out of church parades, Thatcher, you've made the biggest mistake of your young life.'

Thatcher was all innocence, a sideburned cherubim.

'It's no gag, sergeant. I've never believed in God. It's not logical.'

'Okay, Thatcher, have it your way. But don't think you'll be lying in bed while the others are playing Christians. Your number's 421888, and you can report to the corporal i/c canteen every Sunday at 0900 hours.'

Thatcher knew by the triumphant don't-try-your-tricks-here leer Hayter gave him that he'd made a mistake by disavowing God, but he hoped for the best and asked: 'Why, sergeant?'

'Because that's where we hold the special atheists' parade. It's called scrubbing out.' He pencilled a circle around 421888. 'Webster.'

'Here, sergeant. C of E.'

'421889. Anybody's name I haven't called? Good.' He closed the notebook and took out his cigarette-case. 'Smoke if you like,' he said, and gratefully the recruits lit up.

'Rotten sod,' muttered Thatcher, in between puffs. 'Rotten sod.'

'It was your own fault,' said Rourke, not unkindly. 'You shouldn't have tried it on.'

'Now you tell me. How was I to know the gett would act like that? Interferin' with religious liberty, that's what he's doin'.'

Hayter rapped on the floor with his pace-stick.

'Let's have your attention,' he said. 'I'm going to fill you in on a few details. Not a lot because you'll be getting lectures on Corps history and so on later this week.

'First, you're 428 Squad and you're in Charlie Company. Those two things and your serial numbers are part of your address, part of your soul, for that matter. If you happen to die in the next two years, St Peter'll want to know who you are and where you're from. So don't forget. Second, you'll be here for four months, and it'll seem more like four years before you're through. For twelve weeks you'll do basic training, and then you'll do a four-week Commando course – those of you who haven't already broken their necks, that is. Third, you're confined to camp for six weeks, which means you won't see a civvy woman until you've forgotten what to do with it.'

He smiled mirthlessly at the reaction this produced.

(Jeeze, I'll never last. What are we, monks? But it's food and drink to me. I haven't been without it since I was ten. I'll have to tie mine in a knot. Mother, come and get me. What are we gonna do?)

'You know what you can do,' he continued crudely, 'but if anyone faints on parade he'll be in the guard-house. You're not kids, so don't play with yourselves. Six weeks isn't that long.'

(Speak for yourself. Is he nuts or sumpin? Six weeks is for ever. And I'd set myself a target of three a fortnight. Oh brother, the laundry's gonna be busy.)

'All right, can it. Most of you have probably never had it, anyway. Which reminds me: there are two girls in the Naafi, but that doesn't mean they're tarts. Keep away from 'em. It's worth ninety days if you as much as say hello.'

He checked his list.

'Fourth, you'll be getting jabs in the next day or two; anti-tetanus and smallpox. You're not compelled to have them, but anyone who refuses is on a charge. Fifth, you're all in for a haircut this afternoon. And I mean a *haircut*. Some of you look like bloody schoolgirls, and we don't want any of your hut-mates making up to you in the middle of the night, do we?'

(After six weeks on my Jack Sloan, who cares.)

'Sixth and last, you get paid on Thursdays. Thirty bob, and don't spend it all in the one shop.'

(How much? Thirty bob! He's crazy. Does he mean thirty bob a day? That won't keep me in french-letters. We need a Union. And they wonder what's wrong with the British Army.)

'Questions?' asked Hayter.

'When do we get our rifles, sergeant?'

'When you can handle them without killing yourselves or me.'

'And our green berets, sergeant; when do we get them?'

'You in the Reserve?'

'Yes, sergeant.'

'When you've completed the Commando course – if you survive.' The inevitable question, thought Hayter; the one the Reservists always asked. The green beret, the Commando's head-gear, symbol of manhood and achievement. Anyone would think it added a couple of inches to their choppers.

'What about leave, sergeant?'

'You only just got here, for Chrissake. Two months, three months.'

'And when do we get demobbed?'

Hayter let them laugh. They could have their jokes today. After today, they'd find nothing to joke about for a long time.

'No more questions? Okay, you can get back to your huts now, but I want you outside the Company Office in half an hour. You're going to get kitted out this morning.'

National Servicemen, he thought, as the last of the recruits disappeared. It was a hell of a way to earn a living.

Hut 8 was smaller than the others but equally austere. From end to end it measured fifty feet, and from side to side twenty-five. It contained six iron bunks, opposite one another in pairs and bare except for a straw-filled mattress apiece. At the head of each bunk was a locker, khaki coloured. In the centre of the hut stood an ancient coke-fired stove which did not give out enough heat to melt the stalactites of ice on the windows. Near the stove was a trestle table, scrubbed white, and a pair of backless benches. The wooden floor was uncovered, the electric light unshaded, the overall atmosphere redolent of Sparta or Parkhurst or Auschwitz. All that was missing was a bed of nails and half a dozen hair shirts.

'Scrubbin' the canteen,' grumbled Thatcher, sitting at the table. 'Bloody hell, I didn't even get the chance to become converted. I'll bet that's how Christianity started, with guys like Hayter crackin' the whip. It was either come to Jesus or scrub the Roman lavs. Bloody hell.' He brought out a well-thumbed pack of playing-cards. 'Anyone for a quick game o' poker?'

'I don't mind taking your money,' said Webster, putting a handful of loose silver on the table. 'Anything to warm me up.'

'You can deal me in,' added Shaw.

'No one else? Okay, three-handed draw it is. Cut for deal.'

From his bunk Porter listened to the card players' laconic bids and counter-bids, watched how they smoked nervously, inhaled deeply, whenever they were losing, and realized he had a lot to learn. His education, his upbringing, his environment, had been designed to turn him into a first-class citizen, a pillar of the community, a potential executive, a neatly-dressed robot capable of talking the Queen's English flawlessly. It had not been designed to teach him the difference between a Full House and a Straight – essential knowledge now.

Insular and insulated, that summed it up. Isolated from reality by the stupidity of a father; wrapped in cotton wool and handled like Dresden by a mother who wanted the best for him but who had been unable to define 'best'. He had wasted the good years, the fat years, the years when he could have been, should have been, scrumping apples, puffing furtively at

Woodbines, discovering how little girls differed from little boys. A complete waste, a futile decade that had left him rudderless, unprepared. He didn't want to be the only man in the hut who pronounced bath as barth, who had spent his youth reading Schopenhauer instead of Spillane. *God, how inadequate the philosophers were when confronted with the problem of living.* He didn't want to be the solitary non-smoker. He didn't want to be the only one who couldn't boast, truthfully, about a conquest on a double-decker or behind a hedge. He wanted to belong. He wanted to be *free* to belong.

Freedom.

Freedom to act, freedom to shout, freedom to curse and swear, freedom to masturbate, to fornicate, to drink and sing; freedom to develop. Freedom from the claustrophobia of home. Freedom from the miasma of pointless ritual. Freedom: the word was relative, not absolute. To the prisoner it simply meant casting off old shackles, old ties, old allegiances.

Old loves.

The umbilical was cut now – well cut. It would remain cut. He was on his own. He could do whatever the hell he liked.

'Three lovely sevens.'

'Jesus, again.'

'That's how the game's played, buddy-boy.'

Riordan unpacked his canvas hold-all. He placed his shaving-brush, razor, shaving-soap, toothbrush and toothpaste in a neat row on the top shelf of his locker, and nodded, satisfied. Orderliness; that was one of the things that would count in the Marines. That and obedience. If a bloke was to get on, if he was to be a Somebody, all he had to do was as he was told, and do it better and quicker than anyone else. It didn't matter that he hadn't had much schooling, it didn't matter that he'd been a labourer in Civvy Street, a zero. Everyone was equal here – to start with.

'Where you from?' asked Rourke, who had the bunk next to Riordan's.

'Notting Hill. London. Ever been to London?'

'Once. About eight months back. Never again. I got taken.'

'Where to?'

Rourke grinned. 'Not where to. Just taken. By a woman in a

whadyacallit, a clip-joint. Jesus, those women know all the tricks.'

'Not half.'

Not half, echoed Rourke silently, remembering the sleek professionalism of the teenage whore, the smoothness of her skin, the rustle of her dress. And it had happened a week before he married Mary. It was funny how a man could love one girl and yet sleep with another – and love her too, for a while. Love her with all his heart and body for ten or fifteen minutes on a narrow bed in a dingy third-floor room. Love her until she said, 'That's your lot, darlin'. Don't bang the door. I've had a long day.' Love her until he was out among the bright lights again. And love her, a bit, while he was caressing his wife and his wife was thinking, 'He's mine. See how he kisses me, see how he touches me, listen to what he's saying.' Of course, maybe wives thought nothing of the sort. Maybe wives remembered too. Other hands, other bodies.

Maybe.

'Five bob.'

'I'm in.'

'Me too.'

'Did you hear the one about the kuckakuckakucka bird?'

'Your five and up three.'

'Check.'

'Raise five.'

'Jesus.'

'This kuckakuckakucka bird lives in the Arctic, and it spends its whole life sliding up and down icebergs on its arse saying, Kuckakuckakucka Christ, it's kuckakuckakucka cold.'

'Are you in this game or not?'

' 'Course I am. Raise three.'

'Check.'

'I'm out. I don't reckon a pair of sixes.'

'You an' me, buddy-boy. An' I think you're bluffin'.'

'Try me.'

'Okay, I will. See you for three.'

'Chicken liver. Two pair, Johns and fours.'

'Jesus wept.'

'*Outside, 428 Squad. Outside at the double. I said half an hour, not thirty-one minutes. You're in the Marines now. Last man out is on a charge.'*

It had begun to snow again.

'Get yourselves sorted out,' barked Hayter. 'Tallest on the right, shortest on the left. You – Rourke, isn't it? You're the biggest so you plant your fairy feet on the far right. You, Thatcher . . . No, not there, Thatcher. You married to Rourke or something? You're a short-arse. Get on the left. My God, this Squad's going to need some shaking up before it's much older. In threes. You're not in threes, Klein. Can't you count? Do you want me to say it in Yiddish? You – Davidson, isn't it? – straighten your back. You deformed, or what? You're not Quasimodo or whatever he calls himself. Now keep still. Still, Webster. Stop holding your whatsit. If it drops off we'll buy you a new one. Stand still, Thatcher. I've got my eye on you.'

428 Squad stood motionless. They faced the front and tried not to blink. Snow collected in their hair and on their eyebrows.

'When I give the command right turn, pause and then turn. Right . . . Wait for it! Right . . . turn. One two. That's not your right, you fool. Ask your girl friend. Let's try it again. Left . . . turn. Steady. Stand still. Right . . . turn. Quick . . . march. Left right left right left right . . . Keep your arms straight. Fists closed but not clenched. Bags o' swank. You're gonna be the best goddam Squad on the camp. Aren't you? Come on, let's hear it. We're gonna be the best goddam Squad on the camp.'

'We're gonna be the best goddam Squad on the camp.'

'Louder! What are you, a bunch o' sopranos? Somebody got hold of you between the legs? Split your lungs. Now!'

'*We're gonna be the best goddam Squad on the camp.*'

'That's more like it. Left right left . . . You're out of step, Barker. Rourke, see the camp cobbler and get him to make you two left boots. Wipe that grin off your face, Thatcher. Oh brother, you and me are gonna fall out. You, Ginger, button your coat. You're not pregnant, are you? Left . . . left . . . left right left . . .'

Large pack, small pack, pouches, shoulder-straps, waist-belt, anklets, denims, cap badge, beret, peaked cap, boots, two pairs, socks, khaki, three pairs, shirts, three, shorts, blue, two pairs, tin mug, knife, fork, spoon, blankets . . .

To the recruits the list seemed endless.

'I feel like a bleedin' Christmas tree,' said Thatcher, staring stupeficd at the mountain of kit on his bunk. 'What are we supposed to do with this lot?'

'Put it in your locker,' answered Rourke. 'What you can't get in your locker, leave in your kitbag.'

'And fold your shirts and socks,' added Riordan. 'I heard Hayter say he's having an inspection this afternoon.'

'Fold this, fold that, march here, march there. Jesus.'

'There's worse to come,' called Shaw. 'You see all this khaki webbing; well, it's got to be black by the end of the week.'

'Black? What d'you mean, black?'

'Boot polish. It's got to be blackened and polished.'

'So why do they give it to us khaki when they want it black?'

'Because that's how the Marines work,' said Webster. 'I'm only just getting the picture. There are two ways of doing everything: the easy way and the bloody awkward way. The Marines do everything arse about face.'

'Screw me.'

'No thanks. Come back in a fortnight.'

The day wore on. They were shunted from hut to stores, from stores to canteen, from canteen to barber's shop, from barber's shop to hut, from hut to stores . . . Everywhere they went they were accompanied by Hayter. Hayter the shepherd, Hayter the good shepherd, Hayter the watchful shepherd, Hayter the shepherd with the voice reminiscent of a thunder-clap and an atom bomb transmitted simultaneously through an amplifier at a range of one yard. They were treated like moronic children because, to the Marines, they were moronic children. They had to unlearn everything they had ever been taught. They had to make themselves as empty vessels ready to be filled with the wisdom of the universe. 'I can't help it if the boots don't fit, mate; they're the biggest we've got.' 'The cap badge is placed at the front of the beret, like so. It is not placed at an angle.' 'The brown brush is used for polishing boots. The grey brush is used for polishing buttons. Only when there are no grey brushes available will brown brushes be used for polishing buttons.'

They had to begin again.

Gradually they got to know each other better.

'You a student, Porter?' asked Shaw.

'I was.'

'University?'

'No, school.'

'Going for a commission?'

'I doubt it. Waste of . . . bloody energy.' He inserted the 'bloody' after hesitating, deciding it took some of the honey from his voice. 'What did you do before you came in?'

'I worked in a night-club.'

Webster pricked up his ears. 'Night-club? Bags of talent there, I'll bet.'

'Enough.'

'I was a salesman – door-to-door. I got on okay so far as crumpet was concerned, but I had to graft for it sometimes. There was one married scrubber who . . .'

And at the other end of the hut.

'It's a healthy life,' said Rourke. 'Keeps you fit. There's nothing like getting up at the crack of dawn on a summer morning.'

'Ugh,' said Thatcher. 'Give me the city every time. All that fresh air in the country could kill a guy brought up on smog. Right, Riordan?'

'Perhaps.'

'Perhaps arseholes. Look, what have you got in the country except for a few cows and pigs and randy old milkmaids?'

'You live longer.'

'You call that livin'! Not me. You wanna come up to Manchester one day. There's a bit of excitement there.'

'Manchester,' scoffed Riordan. 'You could lose Manchester in Hyde Park.'

'Balls. You Londoners are all the same . . .'

And in the canteen.

'This is supposed to be stew? My dog would take my hand off if I gave him this.'

'Jesus, Mary and Joseph, what's in the bleedin' tea?'

'Bromide.'

'What's that?'

'It stops you getting the urge.'

'Then I'm not drinking it. I want mine to function when I next get hold of a woman.'

'You'll have forgotten what to do with it by then.'

'Not me. I could find my way there blindfold. It's a sixth sense.'

'With a mug like yours you'd have to blindfold her.'

'Listen, boyo, with the ammunition I carry I don't need no face. One quick shufti and they're dancing like round a maypole . . .'

And in the barber's.

'Christ, take it easy.'

'What were you before you got called to the faith, a sheep shearer?'

'Hey, Webster, you look like a bleedin' brush.'

'If I catch pneumonia you'll be sued. I got friends . . .'

And in the hut.

'No, Porter, the blankets must be taut. I want to be able to bounce a coin on them.'

'You call that shirt folded, Rourke? Here, watch me.'

'Okay, Thatcher, start again. And we'll keep doing it until . . .'

And in the latrines.

'Jesus, I've heard of communal living but this is ridiculous. How's a bloke supposed to relax with twenty others staring at him?'

'They do it all the time in Israel.'

'That's a bright remark. Who the fug's in Israel?'

And in the stores.

'Listen, corporal, the tunic's too big. I keep telling you.'

'And I keep telling you we ain't got no smaller.'

'So what am I supposed to do?'

'Grow.'

And back in the hut.

'Is that your locker, Riordan?'

'Yes, sergeant.'

'Not bad, not bad. Okay, you're hut orderly. I'll tell you what your duties are later on.'

'Yes, sergeant.'

'Jesus, Riordan's got promotion awready. Giz a kiss, Riordan.'

'Lights out, Hut 8,' yelled the duty corporal. 'Come on, get them lights off. You need your beauty sleep.'

Darkness. Hot coals glowing amiably in the primitive stove.

'Bugger Hayter,' muttered Thatcher.

Webster stretched. G'night, Jenny, he thought dozily. G'night, all you lovely Devon cream-cakes that I can't have for six weeks; all you slim-hipped, round-breasted darlings. No; mustn't think about that. Drive a guy mad. Must think of other things. The shoulder-strap is attached to the pouch like so . . . The Corps motto is Per Mare Per Terram. By Horse By Tram? The small pack is fitted to the slim-hipped . . . G'night, Jenny.

Shaw smoked another cigarette. Two years was a hell of a long time to spend in the company of Rourke the Farmer, and Webster the Lech, and Riordan the Keen, and Thatcher the Crafty, and Porter the Schoolkid. Porter. Christ, what had persuaded a pouf like Porter to join the Marines. The Intelligence Corps, yes, or the RAF, but not the Marines. He was too frail. But it took all sorts . . .

Riordan lay awake. It was his job, Hayter had said, to see that the hut was swept every morning, the windows cleaned, the table scrubbed. He would have to make a list, give each man a task to do and make sure it was done properly. Hayter was relying on him. The men were his responsibility.

His responsibility. Jesus, he was off to a good start.

. . . . .

Everything in Notting Hill stinks of old clothes and garbage. This is one of the things that Tom Riordan, aged eight, becomes aware of very quickly. Not far away is Hyde Park, where he can play and run and shout and watch the cars going up and down Park Lane at breath-taking speeds. Nearby, too, are the flats and houses where the rich live. The rich are always smiling. No one smiles without irony in Notting Hill, and there the air is heavy with the smell of furnished rooms and failure.

Tommy!

His father calls him, and he obeys the imperious command immediately.

Yes, Dad?

Go down to the off-licence and get me two big bottles of pale ale. Big bottles, mind you.

He watches his mother. He waits for her to protest that they cannot afford it, but she says nothing. He sees she has been crying.

Dirt. Always dirt. His father drunk and his mother weeping over a tub of laundry.

I'm getting out of this some day, says his elder brother Joe.

Where'll you go?

I dunno. But I won't be staying here.

But he does stay, caught in the gin-trap of environment.

Old clothes.

Tom goes to secondary school. The eleven-plus has defeated him, and he takes his place in a long line of silent rejects. The other children laugh when they see his blazer is leather-patched at the elbows. He resents their laughter and opts to fight one of them. His mouth bleeds, and he wishes he were bigger.

His mother dies. She has been ill for months. She weighs less than five stones and the pall-bearers lift the coffin as though it were paper. His father is drunk and remains drunk until long after the funeral.

He walks the streets. His mother is dead. Gone. Buried. He chokes back his tears. There is no time for crying. Crying never got anyone anywhere. Instead, he picks up a stone from the gutter. There are red curtains in the house opposite. New curtains. He throws the stone through the window, and runs.

He comes home, at fifteen, to an empty house. He has grown accustomed to making his own meals. His father is in the pub, and his brother is frequently away – some say in prison. The emptiness of the room is three-dimensional. He can almost touch it. He sits down. He would like to sit in the same chair for ever.

Adolescence. The painful process of growing up without guidance. Emotions that have no outlet – except in violence.

The surgeon resets his nose. That's a nasty one, he says to his nurse. Very nasty. Is my tea ready?

He stares at his reflection in the mirror, and touches the broken bone gingerly. I'll get that bastard, he vows.

And he does.

Hey, how about it? he asks the girl.

She tosses her head. She is dressed in her elder sister's nylons and high-heels, and feels superior. Besides, she is fed up with being asked, How about it. It's crude. She wants to be courted.

In Notting Hill?

He touches her dress. It is silk. How about it? he repeats.

You're not old enough.

Try me.

It'll cost you ten bob.

He waves a ten-shilling note in front of her, and she is bought.

She leads him into an alley, and they mate furiously on a piece of sacking which carries the warm stickiness of her last client.

He gives her the ten shillings. It was worth it, his first. Wait till he tells his mates.

Garbage. Unending.

Different jobs. Different women.

A pint and a game of darts at the weekend.

No one remembers his eighteenth birthday, as no one had remembered his seventeenth and sixteenth.

Furnished rooms and failure.

. . . . . .

Riordan turned over. The hut slept.

THREE

Six AM. Inert bodies breathing evenly. Frost on the windows. The silence of darkness.

In the guard-room a senior NCO gulps scalding tea and gives a curt nod to a bleary-eyed youngster, who puts a bugle to dry lips. He wets the mouth-piece with his tongue, and inhales.

The wail of reveille is deafening. Dead-raising. It is relayed to each hut by Tannoy. The bugler reaches the final cadenza, and . . .

The door of Hut 8 was flung open with a hinge-splitting crash by the duty corporal. He snapped on the lights.

'Wakey, wakey, rise and shine, the morning's fine, get up, you lazy bastards! Drop your shoots and grab your boots!'

He went from bunk to bunk, pulling off blankets, prodding shoulders, pinching toes, while the recruits tried desperately to shut out consciousness for a few more seconds.

'Lea' me alone,' pleaded Webster, groping blindly for the blanket the corporal had tossed to the floor.

'It's still the middle of the bleedin' night,' mumbled Shaw.

Thatcher threw a tin mug at the Tannoy. 'Stick your trumpet up your arse!'

The corporal warmed his hands by the stove. 'You got two minutes to get your feet on the deck. Anyone in bed when I come back goes twice round the assault course. Dress of the day is denims, boots, and berets. No belts or anklets. Who's i/c this hut?'

'I am,' wheezed Riordan, from behind a cloud of cigarette smoke.

'*Corporal*. These tapes aren't Scotch mist.'

'I am, corporal.'

'Then get these sleeping beauties up before I have your guts for garters. This isn't Butlin's. You've got a parade at 0800 hours. Get the hut cleaned. Sweep the deck, scrub the table, ditch the gash.'

'Gash, corporal?'

'Rubbish, dirt, filth. The sort o' manure horrible little men like you leave about. Bloody civilians,' he muttered, and stomped out.

Riordan yawned. Jesus, it was cold. 'Hey, Porter, come on, get up.'

Porter buried his head deeper in the pillow. 'I'm getting up. Give me a minute.'

He had been having a dream, a glorious dream, and he was loath to abandon it. It involved a woman, a young and pretty woman, sprawled on an enormous rock in the middle of a lake. She was beckoning him, calling him. *Try, Michael, try. There's nothing to be frightened of. You can do it.*

He had not found out what it was he could do. The moon-faced corporal had woken him up too soon.

Blast him.

The hut came alive slowly, like the opening scene in a modern ballet. Tousled-headed figures sat up blinking, cigarettes were lit, coughs renewed, goose flesh born, denims donned. Within a few minutes everyone was on their feet with the exception of Thatcher.

Riordan stood over him. 'Shake it up, Thatcher,' he begged. 'You'll have us all going round the assault course.'

'Go stuff yourself.'

'You heard what the corporal said.'

'Stuff him too, noisy sod.'

'You can tell him that yourself, here he is.'

Thatcher leapt from his bunk. 'I'm up, corporal,' he chirped, but all he saw was Riordan grinning at him. 'You rotten liar!'

In twos and threes – yawning, cursing, groaning, moaning, and shivering – the recruits of 428 Squad made their way to the ablutions. The early risers, shaved and washed, passed them, going in the opposite direction.

Steam obscured the mirrors. Bare feet padded cat-like on the wet floors. Queues formed for wash-basins.

'Did you see the stars outside?' growled Webster, finding

himself next to Porter. 'Stars in the *morning*, for Chrissake. This is a hell of an hour to get a guy up.'

'It could be worse,' said Porter mildly, carefully lathering the point of his chin, the only part of his face that required regular attention.

'Worse! You must come from the back of beyond if you reckon anything could be worse than having a trumpet stuck in your ear at six o'clock. Me, I'm beginning to think I should've joined the RAF.'

'Those fairies,' put in Thatcher, rinsing his razor; 'they're all bum-boys. I knew a bloke in Manchester, an ordinary bloke, who went into the RAF likin' a bit o' skirt as much as the rest of us. He came out as queer as a nine-bob note.'

'It must have been in him anyway.'

'It wasn't, God's truth. An officer got at him.'

'Screw officers,' said Webster, who had never met one in his life.

'Lend us your soap, Thatcher. Somebody's had mine.'

'Comin' over.'

'Anyone got a spare blade?'

'What for?'

'Whadyamean, what for? I'm gonna circumcise meself, what else?'

From the door Riordan called, 'Hurry it up, lads. We've got the hut to clean before breakfast.'

'That Riordan seems to like throwing his weight about,' murmured Shaw to Rourke.

'He's got a job to do. He didn't ask for it.'

'But he doesn't have to have such a big mouth about it, does he?'

In the hut Riordan drew up a list. Thatcher, table; Shaw, sweeping; Webster, windows; Porter, gash; Rourke, coke for the stove. At the bottom he added: Riordan, spare man. He tacked the list to the door.

Webster spotted it first.

'Have I got to wash all the windows every morning?'

'No, give 'em a going over with a duster during the week. You can wash 'em Saturdays.'

'Where do I get the coke?'

'From a bin behind Hut 5. I noticed it yesterday.'

'I see you've given yourself a soft touch,' drawled Shaw.

Riordan coloured. 'We'll do it turn and turn about. Each man moves up one every week. I'll be on coke next week and Thatcher'll be spare man. Okay, Shaw?'

'Natch, you're the boss.'

Bastard, thought Riordan.

It took them half an hour to finish the hut, and by the time they arrived at the canteen the tea was no more than lukewarm. But it did not taste so bad as it had the previous day. Even Webster forgot about the threat to his virility and had two mugfuls.

Hayter inspected the parade. His comments were brief.

'Did you shave this morning?'

'Yes, sergeant.'

'Did you use a mirror?'

'Yes, sergeant.'

'Use a razor blade tomorrow.'

'You, those denims are too small. You look like a hundredweight of coal in a pound bag. Get 'em changed.'

'Yes, sergeant.'

'You, close your mouth. I can see your breakfast.'

The inspection over, he stood the Squad at ease.

'Right, you start work today. At 0830 hours you get your jabs in the sick-bay. At 1100 hours you've got a lecture by the Company Commander, Captain Leigh. L.E.I.G.H. You call him sir. You call all commissioned officers sir. The only non-commissioned officer you call sir is the RSM. Got that? Okay, now brace yourselves. Squad . . . 'shun. Left turn. By the left quick march. Left right left . . .'

'Next.'

Webster paled as the MO's hypodermic disappeared with the force of a pile-driver into the arm of a recruit three places ahead of him.

'You can go before me if you like,' he said to Riordan.

'You scared?'

'Me? Scared? No, not me. But he might run out of stuff,

and I wouldn't want to stop you getting your shot of anti-whatever-it-is.'

'I'll go in front of you,' offered Porter.

Gratefully, Webster made a space for him.

'Injections don't bother me, you know,' he went on. 'It's just that hospitals give me the creeps. It's the smell, I guess. Some people can't stand the smell of fish – with me it's hospitals.'

'Next.'

Shaw stepped forward. '421887, Shaw.'

'Ever had an anti-tetanus or smallpox jab, Shaw?'

'Smallpox, sir, about two years ago.'

'Roll up your sleeve.'

'What the hell's tetanus?' whispered Thatcher, who was next in line.

'It's like lock-jaw,' explained Porter.

'And what's he squirtin' into us?'

'I don't know about tetanus, but with smallpox he gives you a dose.'

'A dose o' what?'

'Smallpox. You get a minor dose, and then if you catch it, it's not fatal.'

'Bugger me, germs. That's a funny way to keep a bloke healthy.'

'Next.'

'I don't mind waiting, you know,' said Webster to Riordan.

'Neither do I.'

'What about you, Rourke?'

'I'm okay where I am.'

'Next.'

'421884, Porter.'

Webster wiped his damp palms with a handkerchief, and shut his eyes as Porter was immunized.

'Next.'

'421889, Webster.'

'Had either of these before, Webster?'

'No, sir.'

'What, not even smallpox?'

'No, sir. Is that bad, sir?'

'You'll live. Sleeve, please.'

Timidly Webster bared his arm and clenched his teeth. He started to count to himself. One two three . . . Come on, come on. Four five . . . Christ, what was the bloody fool up to? He'd heard tales about military doctors. Useless buggers, most of them. Only joined up because they couldn't get a decent job in Civvy Street. Seven eight . . .

'Move, Webster, you're holding up the queue.'

'Eh?'

'Move it. You're done.'

'Done? You mean I'm finished?'

'Unless you want a second helping.'

'No, not me.' He rolled down his sleeve. 'Nothing to it,' he beamed. 'There's nothing to worry about, Riordan.'

Captain Leigh's limp was a legacy from Korea, and at times he was proud of it. It added a touch of distinction, a soupçon of dash, to an otherwise undistinguished and undashing career. It made him feel less a cipher and more a useful officer – some days.

But there were other days when it saddened him to reflect that his youthful dreams, in which he had visualized himself commanding a brigade, would crystallize in a couple of years with only a majority. After that, soon after, he would be placed on the retired list, given a bowler, relegated to the scrap-heap reserved for men of limited ability and no connections in the Ministry. With his gratuity he would buy a farm, a small one, and spend his retirement with his wife and his dogs. Once in a while, perhaps in the local, he would permit himself the luxury of bragging about the MC he had won outside Seoul. No, not won, awarded; awarded was more accurate. An award like his permanent home posting – a gift from a benevolent master to an industrious servant. An award for cripples. A tin crucifix for an inch off the left leg; a desk job for a good chap.

Patronage, that was all it was. A robot could do his job and probably do it better, because then the lecture would never vary in pitch, tone or content. A robot could blast forth with esprit de corps and propaganda and hooray-for-our-side. A robot could satisfy the requirements of the Book. It could tell them jokes, bully them on occasions, punish the malingerers. And a robot would not have to live the lie, act out the charade, pretend it was superior because of the three stars on its shoulder, which was what the Corps demanded of a man. It was the Book's way of saying: We know we're bloody fools, but for heaven's sake don't let them see it. Tart up, shout your slogans, wave your polished sword, be God. The Symbol is greater than the individual.

No doubt.

'428 Squad all present and correct, sir.'

'Thank you, sergeant. Sit them at ease.'

He scanned the immature faces, some eager, some already bored. They were pretty much the same as the last lot, and the next lot would be similar. Putty. Plasticine waiting to be moulded. Children aping Ghengis Khan, dying to swop their toy pistol for a real one, asking to be taught how to kill. The youth of the world was a robot, too; one that could be harnessed to the right kind of violence – the kind that took succour from Rule Britannia and the Star-spangled Banner.

Or the Red Flag.

He glanced at his notes, numbered and underlined with different coloured inks. Green for seriousness, blue for jokes, red for history.

'I won't be keeping you for very long,' he began briskly. 'You have a great deal to do and not many weeks in which to do it. The main purpose of this talk is for you to meet me, and for me to tell you that I'm always available if you have any problems. By this I don't mean you're to come to my office with complaints such as, Sir, my boots don't fit, or, Sir, Jones has stolen my toothpaste.' Blue ink. 'Change your boots and punch Jones.' He paused for the expected laughter, and got it. 'If, however, you have home worries, domestic troubles, then that's what I'm here for. Come and see me. Don't take matters into your own hands and go over the wall. We'll catch up with you sooner or later. If your mother's ill, you'll get compassionate leave. If your girl friend's pregnant, we'll help – which is not to say we'll perform an abortion.'

More laughter.

'He's all right,' whispered Webster.

'A prick,' muttered Shaw. 'A prick trying to be one of the boys.'

Green ink.

'Most of you will find many things to grumble about – the Marines is not a rest home. But grumble to your heart's content. It's healthy and a fine safety-valve, and it's one of the rights you have as a Marine. Grumble about the food, the officers, the NCOs, and the drill – but remember that everything is done for a reason. Cleverer men than you and me have planned the training programme, and we stick to it whatever the weather. Wars are not always fought in grassy fields on sunny afternoons.

'The discipline is rigorous because discipline is an essential part of a Marine's equipment. One day you may be called upon to react instinctively, and discipline will sharpen your reactions, make you worthy members of the finest body of fighting troops in the world. You'll hear a lot about the Parachute Regiment – mainly from the Parachute Regiment – but you can dismiss them. The Royal Marines, especially the Commandos, are the cream.'

Red ink.

'The Corps was founded in 1664 by Charles the Second and originally known as the Duke of York and Albany's Maritime Regiment of Foot . . .'

The Squad listened: to how the Marines won the Laurel on their colours at Belle Isle; to how, in 1802, they were given the prefix Royal by a grateful Hanoverian; to an outline of the campaigns in Egypt and the Sudan in the late nineteenth century; to tales of the Corps' valour during the Boxer Rising; to stories of bravery, and implicit lunacy, at Gaba Tepe, Jutland, Zeebrugge, Crete, Dieppe, Normandy, Sicily and Korea; to flag waving, cheer leading, and death before dishonour; to shades of Henry before Agincourt, Richard before Bosworth Field, Leonidas at Thermopylae, and, tacitly, God at Armageddon; to achievement squared, heroism cubed, and glory to the power of 4.

At the rear of the lecture room Hayter counted off the minutes on his wristwatch. Par for the talk was fifteen minutes, and it never failed to raise his bile that he had to sit through it three or four times a year. It was typical officer chat. Come on, chaps; that's the spirit, chaps; well done, chaps. A load of balls. Leigh could pump esprit de corps into National Servicemen until he was black in the face, but it did no real good. When the chips were down it was how fast the lads could reload and how much stamina they had that mattered. It was no use knowing about Charles the Second or Crete when confronted with a thumping great Russian or German or gook with a naked bayonet. Jesus, no. But officers would never understand that. Officers still thought the men fought out of pride and loyalty and patriotism, whereas they fought because they were scared bloody stiff of having their goolies sheared. All that Charge of the Light Brigade stuff was so much crap.

Five minutes to go, if he was on schedule.

It was just as well the NCOs ran the Marines, because otherwise every battle would be the biggest cock-up since the Flood. Of course, officers gave the orders, but it was the corporals, sergeants, and colour-sergeants who made sure that everything went smoothly. If the last war or Korea had been left to officers – well, they'd have been shouting 'Well done, chaps' while Hitler's little lot were jackbooting up and down Leicester Square, or the gooks arriving by the boat-load in Melbourne.

Thank Christ for NCOs.

Two minutes.

Thank Christ for sergeants. Not many medals handed out in that division – just kicks in the arse if things went wrong. But a sergeant had to know it all. The lot. If an officer made a mistake there was always someone higher up the ladder willing to say, 'Never mind, old man – went to school with your father. We'll sort it out.' But if a sergeant made a mistake it was back to the ranks at the double.

Thirty seconds. And Leigh, thank God, was on schedule. Like a bloody alarm clock, the Company Commander.

'We'll treat you hard,' intoned Leigh, 'but we'll treat you fairly. You cooperate with us, and we'll cooperate with you.' He paused. 'I think that's all, Sergeant Hayter.'

Hayter stood up. 'Very good, sir. Carry on, sir?'

'Certainly.'

'Sit to attention, 428 Squad!'

The recruits stiffened. Leigh acknowledged Hayter's salute, and limped out.

'Right,' said Hayter, 'you've met the Company Commander and this afternoon you're going to meet the parade ground. Outside in three ranks, at the double.'

There was a rush for the door.

FOUR

And in the beginning was the Word. And the Word was Movement.

Keep them moving. Give them something to do. Chase them from dawn to dusk. Never permit them to be idle, not even for a minute. An idle Marine is an inefficient Marine. Marching, saluting, polishing, scrubbing, listening, learning. Take a handful of men and erase the qualities that make them individuals. A Marine with a working knowledge of classical Greek is useless. An idiot who can shoot straight or make a button gleam is revered. Keep them occupied. Keep their thoughts away from home and women and comfort and comparative sanity. They must be moulded. They must become part of the machine. The machine will not function if the cogs are inadequate. Destroy their idiosyncrasies. There is no place for the non-conformist. The man is part of the Squad, the Squad of the company, the company of the battalion, the battalion of the brigade, the brigade of the army. The machine is omnipotent. The machine is always right. The Russian peasant is our enemy. The Chinese peasant is our enemy. The German is our friend. Shifting sands. Ours not to reason why, ours but to stay out of trouble. Lectures on this, lectures on that: lectures on the bren gun, the sten gun, the rifle, the grenade, night fighting, day fighting, gas, crawling, camouflage, cover.

The killing range of the two-inch mortar is . . .

Achilles' wrath, to Greece the direful spring . . .

Teach them how to survive. Abuse them, scream at them, swear at them. But above all keep them on their feet. When there is nothing else to do, drill them. Saluting to the right, saluting to the left, slow march, quick march, right turn, left turn, right wheel, left wheel, mark time. Puppets. An endless puppet show. Fatigue is not in our vocabulary. A Marine does not tire. Do you hear that? We hear it, sergeant. We understand, captain. We will obey, colonel. Obedience is the great lesson.

And he saw that the Word was good.

It was their second day on the parade ground.

'Rourke, right *marker*.'

Rourke brought his heels together with a painful thud and marched forward. He wondered how often the exercise would have to be repeated before Hayter was satisfied.

'... Four five six ... Ten eleven twelve. Halt. One two. Stand still!'

Hayter filled his lungs. Tiny purple veins in his forehead pulsated rapidly.

'428 Squad, in three ranks, fall in. One two three ... Seven eight ... Eleven twelve. Halt. Twelve paces, Barker, not thirteen. That's gonna be your unlucky number, my lad, unless you're careful. Right ... dress. Arms up in line with your shoulders, heads sharply to the right. Quick now. Don't shuffle, Kelland, you're not Victor Silvester. Eyes ... Wait for it, Riordan. Eyes front. Bring those arms down like a machine-gun. Ratatatatat! Now hold that. What's the matter with you, Webster? Your arm came down like a fairy's.'

'It aches, sergeant.'

'Aches! All you had were a couple of pin-pricks. You're not in the Girl Guides, Webster, though God knows that 'ud be too much for some of you. Okay, we'll do it again. My way this time. Ay-bout turn. Quick march. Left right left ... Halt. Ay-bout turn. One two. Stand at ease. Don't lounge, Shaw. Stand at ease doesn't mean curl up in a heap. Rourke, right *marker*. One two three ...'

They had been drilling for two hours without respite, and their bodies were empty of sap. Their boots, new and stiff, hurt, and the icy, snow-bringing wind from the north stung their faces and wrung reluctant tears from their eyes. To a man they hated the parade ground. Yesterday it had been no more than a few acres of distant tarmac. Today it was a hard reality which numbed their feet. Hayter, too, the instrument of their discomfort, was an object of their rancour. Hayter of the permanent scowl and lungs of leather, Hayter the tireless and pitiless, Hayter who stood before them not because he had to, not because he had been conscripted, but because he chose to.

'When's the bastard gonna let up,' hissed Thatcher to Klein. The pair were next to one another on the extreme left of the Squad.

'Search me, mate, but he could go on for ever at this rate.'

'I'd like to get him up a dark alley one night.'

'He'd have you drilling on your tod before you could say kosher.'

'Shut up, Klein. I'll tell you when you can talk, which is never.'

Hayter checked his wristwatch and decided there was time to practise the exercise again before the Squad were due on the assault course.

'Rourke, right *marker* . . .'

Porter wondered why he did not collapse. His breath came in short, discordant shudders, the straps of his pack bit deep into his narrow shoulders, his eyes were misty with exhaustion and anger. 'Fug 'em,' he managed to mutter, not even aware of the profanity. 'Fug 'em all.'

The assault course was three-quarters of a mile from beginning to end. It was littered with man-made and natural obstacles, brain children of some devotee of de Sade. A plank nine inches wide and thirty feet long straddling a yawning trench; a slack rope suspended between two stanchions fifteen feet from the ground; a brick wall the size of a double-decker bus; a tank-trap bulging with nettles; a fast-flowing stream twenty feet wide; and finally a run-in of two hundred yards to a sixty-foot rope.

Cross the plank, swarm the slack rope, surmount the wall, ignore the nettles, wade the stream, and climb the vertical rope – all in full fighting order.

Ahead of Porter was the wall. It had steel stakes driven into it at irregular intervals, designed as toe- and hand-holds. He grasped a couple above his head and tried to lever himself higher. But his untrained muscles would not respond. He hung limply like a hunk of meat.

'Move it, Porter,' yelled Shaw, coming up fast. 'I haven't got all bleedin' day.'

'You . . . first.' He couldn't do it. It was impossible. He'd gone as far as he was physically able.

'Get over that wall!' screamed the instructor.

'Take hold of me!' snarled Shaw. 'Come on, give us your fuggin hand.'

'I can't . . . over that.'

'You can and you're bleedin' going to. If you don't the bastard'll have us all round again.'

Schoolkids, thought Shaw. Jesus Christ.

Slowly and painfully, pausing at each rung for air, they made the top and sat astride the wall. Porter looked down. There were no stakes on the other side. He scarcely recognized his own voice as he mumbled, 'How?'

'Jump. Forget about your neck. Just go. Like this.'

Shaw hit the ground with a sickening thud.

'Jump, Porter, blast you!'

Porter jumped. He felt sure he would break his spine and it did not worry him. He was beyond worry, through the pain barrier.

Everything went red and black. Then white.

Shaw helped him up. 'You okay? Then move your arse.'

The stream reached their waists and threatened to sweep them off their feet, but they forded it and ran on, with only instinct and the fear of punishment to keep them going.

'Me . . . rope . . . before you,' gasped Shaw, and Porter nodded gratefully.

Just the rope now, he thought, just the rope. Another minute and he'd have done it. It would be easier next time. Jesus, it had to be.

Shaw dropped beside him. 'Greasy. Half-way. Careful.'

Porter climbed blindly, thinking of nothing but the next step, the next arm-wrenching, thigh-chafing step.

Christ Almighty, how much further. How much further. Fingers numb with cold. Pack heavy as lead. And at school they talked about preparation for life. What preparation? All that mattered was the ability to get up a rope. That was all. Quod erat . . .

How much further, for Jesus' sake!

His head grazed a branch, and he knew he was there.

There.

Shaw was waiting for him at the bottom.

'You did all right.'

'You helped . . . Thanks.'

'Balls.'

Shaw shrugged off the gratitude. It made him feel uncomfortable.

Evening.

Thatcher dabbed iodine on a heel blister the size of a penny. He winced as the antiseptic penetrated the raw flesh.

'A bleedin' sadist, that's what Hayter is,' he grumbled. 'No one but a sadist would have kept us out there for two hours with the assault course to come. He likes to see us suffer, d'you know that? I reckon he was born givin' orders. "No, that's not right, doctor. Try again. You'll stay here until I'm satisfied, doctor." Christ, I pity the bird he marries. He'll have her doin' it by numbers. "At the command One, remove your dress, Two, lie down, Three . . ." '

'Quit talking about women, can't you,' pleaded Webster. 'It's bad enough not being able to get at one without you reminding me of what I'm missing.'

Thatcher grinned. Webster and his women. 'What d'you mean you can't get at one? There's a Naafi bird outside the window.'

Webster leapt up. 'Where, where?'

'Sorry,' said Thatcher, 'made a mistake. It was that fat corporal from A Company.'

Webster threw a towel at him.

'You rotten bastard, making me get up like that. I'm sore all over, and I've got a swelling on my arm as big as a football.'

'You're lucky to have any sort of a swellin'. That bromide's doin' me no good. I spotted it this mornin'. Nothin'. Absobleedinlutely nothin'. And I usually wake up with one that 'ud knock your eye out.'

'Pressure,' said Webster knowledgeably. 'Pressure on the bladder.'

'Who has?'

'You have. That's why you wake up like that.'

'Crap. It's virility, mate. Virile George they used to call me.'

'Virol, more like. Virol for bouncing babies. Talk about the midget with the frigid digit . . .'

Thatcher threw the towel back.

At one end of the table, his belt stripped of its buckles and brasses and laid across a sheet of newspaper in front of him, Riordan smoothed polish on to the toe-cap of one of his boots with the convex side of a spoon. They were coming along nicely, his boots, as was his belt. His equipment would soon be the best in the hut. No, the Squad. It would be the best in the Squad.

'You can do mine while you're at it, Riordan.'

'I'll wash your back for fourpence.'

'Here's a tanner. You can have the change.'

'Up yours.'

'After you with Webster's.'

At the other end of the table Porter wrote in a cheap note-book, bought from the Naafi stores: 'I have decided to keep a diary. The idea, prompted by Webster, came to me this evening in the canteen. Webster said: "We'll probably laugh at all this in ten years." I wondered if this was true, and I decided to find out by recording the present for the future. By the ghost of Rupert Brooke!

'First thoughts. The human body is a remarkably resilient contraption. This afternoon, after the assault course, I wanted to pack up and go home. Now, however, though tired, I feel marvellous. I made it, bruises and all. I proved something – a little something, maybe, but something. Perhaps that's what yesterday's dream meant.

'I like the people I'm with. I like Thatcher because he's funny, and Webster because he's such a braggart, and Rourke because he says little but thinks a lot, and Riordan because of his determination, and Shaw – I'm not certain about Shaw. He's a strange fellow.'

'You writin' your memoirs already?' said Thatcher.

'Could be.'

'Am I in them?'

Porter smiled. 'Of course. Opening chapter's devoted to you.'

'Attaboy.'

In the ablutions Rourke sang softly as he showered. It was a love song, a sad song made sadder by the caterwauling of the current pop hero who had driven it into the rarefied atmosphere of the hit parade. Where Rourke had forgotten the words, he da-dummed.

Take me as I am or don't take me at all,
Don't try to change me, da-dum-dum-dum fall . . .

He thought of home, of his wife, and, like all men who are ninety-nine per cent certain of their wife's faithfulness – which is every man – found himself dwelling on the odd one hundredth. In the past, this was the time of night when he and Mary had had a drink of something before going to bed. Sometimes tea, sometimes cocoa, sometimes whisky. After whisky, even one tot, Mary was a tiger in bed. It was as if she didn't know him, as if he were merely the instrument of her pleasure. Perhaps it was just a man she needed, any man. Supposing she took a tot with someone else, just out of friendship. With her husband fifty miles away she could . . . No, not Mary. But why not? Men played around – he had – so why not women? Good answer to that: it was different for a man. With a man – well, the stuff left his body. With a woman, it entered hers, became part of her. That made it different.

No, not Mary

We used to be lovers until that day
You met another and sent me away.

No, not Mary. Other guys' wives, yes, but not her. She wasn't the type. Not Mary.

He lathered himself more vigorously, erasing his nascent and groundless fears with carbolic.

Outside Hut 6 Shaw collided with Klein. The little Jew was heading at speed for the latrines.

'Sorry, mate,' he grinned. 'All this Gentile grub.'

Shaw did not reply, but walked on.

Jews, he thought. Blimey, they were everywhere.

He had only the vaguest idea why he disliked Jews. It was an emotional as opposed to a rational dislike, and it had something to do with his past, with an incident he could never quite remember – or chose to forget. But it was also connected with the fact that Jews lived well. As a child he had stared enviously at their big cars and bigger houses, and asked himself the unanswerable question: Why? Why them, not me? And when, as an adolescent, he understood and practised bitterness, he discovered in Jews a ready-made target, an outlet for impulses which needed direction. It was some years before he transferred part of his loathing to the new immigrants with their black skins.

'Lights out.'

He pushed open the door of Hut 8.

'Lights out, Hut 8.'

'Jesus, already.'

'I won't tell you again, Hut 8!'

'Yes, Dad. D'you wanna tuck me in, too, Dad?'

'Shut up, Thatcher. You'll drop us all in it.'

'Balls.'

Bromide, bromide everywhere . . .

I'm gonna be the best bloody Marine in this Squad.

We've only got seven hundred and twenty-eight days more to do.

Why don't you celebrate?

Jews.

Aching legs.

G'night, sergeant, g'night, sergeant, it's time to say g'night.

Lights out.

The assistant MO, a junior lieutenant with very pink cheeks, was nervous. The venereal disease talk always gave him an unpleasant itch around the groin. Association, he supposed. The MO suffered from the same ailment, which was why the MO never lectured on the subject nowadays.

'Don't,' he went on, 'take up with any of the local girls without protecting yourselves. I know what can happen in a moment of passion . . .'

Does he now.

Bit of a lad, isn't he.

The next time he has it will be the first.

'... and it's madness to be unprepared. The necessary preventives are available free in the sick-bay, and all you have to do is ask the duty SBA.'

I'll take a gross.

I wonder if there's a market for them in Exeter.

They're not rejects, are they?

'Now I'm going to show you a slide to illustrate what can happen to a man's – well, a man's private parts if this disease is not caught in the early stages.'

He selected a slide from a box and put it in the projector. The screen lit up. Three men in the front row passed out immediately, and half a dozen others rushed outside to be sick.

About average, mused the lieutenant, switching off the projector.

'Any complaints?'

'Yes, sergeant. There's a nail in my rice pudding.'

'What sort of a nail – a human nail or a nail you knock in wood?'

'A nail you knock in wood, sergeant.'

'Then what are you worrying about? It'll put iron in you. Any other complaints?'

They were introduced to unarmed combat.

'The weakest section of a man's anatomy is his testicles,' said the corporal instructor. 'If you catch him there, you send for the cleaners. Has anyone ever done any judo?'

Carter, of Hut 5, raised his hand. 'I have, corporal.'

'Good, you can assist me in the demonstration. I want you to aim a kick at my crotch. Don't mess about and don't be surprised if you finish up on your behind. I'll go easy on you, though.'

'Yes, corporal, but . . .'

'No buts, lad. Just do it. I've got the rank. A hefty kick, now.'

Carter took a long run, checked as he approached, feinted as he kicked, and the corporal became a writhing grey-faced heap on the floor of the gym.

'Do you think I should have told him I was a brown belt?'

They practised bayonet charging on dummies.

'Make like you mean it, Riordan. It won't hit you back. Come on, Jones, you're not conducting an orchestra. Stop mincing, Porter; that's a rifle, not a rolled umbrella. In, boot, out, run on – that's the pattern.'

'I can't get it out, sergeant.'

'I won't answer that Porter. I won't answer that. You show 'em, Webster. A hard lunge, now.'

Webster lunged to the left as the dummy, swaying from an earlier thrust, swung to the right. Webster spat out a mouthful of earth.

'Fug it,' he said.

'I bet you couldn't even do that properly.'

And so it went on. Bayonet charging, unarmed combat, drill, lectures, polishing, more drill, cleaning, eating, sleeping – until:

Saturday.

'You're sure it's not a gag?' said Thatcher. 'You mean we haven't got a parade or anythin'?'

'Nothing,' answered Riordan.

'It's a bloody miracle, that's what it is!' exclaimed Shaw. 'A bloody miracle.'

In the evening they went to the Naafi. The small bar was was crowded with other recruits who were confined to camp, but they managed to squeeze into a corner.

'Keerist, beer!' Webster licked his lips. 'Lemme taste it. Jee-SUS. I feel like a civilian. And will you get a load of the cakes on her.'

He jerked a thumb at one of the Naafi girls, who, if less than pretty, was the first woman any of them had seen for a week.

'Bet you don't make her,' said Shaw.

'No bet. She's prob'ly reserved for sergeants and above. Anyhow, tonight, who needs it? Not me. Get the ale in, Thatcher.'

'Move your bum, then, and let's get at the bar.'

They drank slowly for an hour or two, and then the evening became an endless procession of glasses and songs and jokes and noise and quick dashes to the latrines and green gills.

There was an old man of Dundee, who climbed up a very large tree . . .

Where are the heads?

You gonna be sick, Porter, don't be sick over this kiddy.

Who's gonna – going to – be sick?

Four-and-twenty virgins came down from Inverness . . .

And reminiscences and women they had known and places they had been and towns they had lived in and pints they had drunk and films they had seen and books they had read.

Liverpool's the greatest city in the world. It's got the largest dry dock and . . .

She was a nympho. A fifty-year-old nympho, for Chrissake. I swear to God . . .

And the corn's like yellow hair . . .

So this guy rides into town and says to the sheriff, You and me, sheriff . . .

All the good bits were marked in biro. You didn't have to read it at all . . .

I didn't believe it. She – I mean he – looked like a bird and dressed like a bird, but when I got her – him – home . . .

An' Liverpool's got the largest clock-face in England, you know that?

You get up in the morning and you take a deep breath and you think, Jesus, this is mine, I own it . . .

Married women are all scrubbers . . .

That's balls. Not all married women . . .

Listen, my wife . . .

So the Irishman said to the Jew . . .

Whose round? Whose bleedin' round is it?

They say that the camp is a wonderful place,
But the organization's a bleedin' disgrace . . .

Keep it down, lads. Ladies present.

Ladies, my bum.

There's corporals and sergeants and RSMs too
With their hands in their pockets and sod-all to do . . .

Easy, lads. It could be your sister.

My sister wrote the song.

Laughter.

Drink and laughter, the serviceman's twin escapes. Out of the intolerable and into a dream. Away from regimentation and a world without women, and into a beer-coloured Shangri-la where everything comes right in the final reel. God bless Bass and Truman's and Watney's. May their barrels never run dry. Bless 'em all. Bless everyone. Comrades in booze, sharing the same frothy glasses and empty beds. Eternal friendships struck over a bottle of Guinness. Be merry. Gone is Friday, and Monday's a light year off.

They stand on the square and they bawl and they shout,
They shout about things they know sod-all about . . .

Hey, Porter, twice round the assault course if you don't get the next round in.

Up yours.

Porter, what would your mother say!

Riordan's gonna make corporal yet, corporal yet, corporal yet. Riordan's gonna make . . .

I'm the best goddam Marine in this Squad.

You've got the biggest mouth, that's all.

Get you, Thatcher. With a gob like yours you'd make a fortune trapping stray elephants.

D'you smoke, Shaw? (Yes.) Then lend us a fag.

Hey, where's Moisie Klein? Where's my Yiddisher brudda?

The name's Jacob, Thatcher.

That's not a name, it's a cream cracker.

It could be any Saturday in their local pub. Over there is Molly, a barmaid who's worked here for twenty years. Usual, Molly. And that's Jim on the dart board. Never misses a double-top, old Jim. What about the match this afternoon . . . Did you see the goal young Billy got . . . Worth every penny they paid for him . . . Hello, love, you look lonely. Got a friend . . . Anyway, this geezer says to me . . .

Time, ladies and gents.

Already? Jesus.

Sup that or I'll sup it for you.

For all the good they are they might as well be . . .

God bless you, Bass. See you tomorrow, Fred. You gonna give the missus a bang tonight, Fred? 'Course. It's Sat'day, ain't it?

Beer the great liberator. Laughter the wine of fools and the homesick.

Drink and laughter, laughter and drink.

Time.

Thatcher hurled the long-handled brush to the floor. He was annoyed. It had taken him three hours to scrub the canteen, whereas the church parade had been over by ten o'clock. The rest of the Squad were by now reading the Sunday papers or chewing the fat. It was a bastard.

'Finished,' he announced to his overseer, a lance-corporal.

'Done the tables?'

''Course I've done the fu . . .' He stopped. Oh no, his mouth had got him into enough trouble. 'Yes, corporal,' he said meekly.

'Okay, you can go.'

Thatcher put on his beret. 'Where can I find Sergeant Hayter?'

'Try his hut – 27, Delta Company.'

'Thanks.'

Hayter was lounging in a canvas-backed chair, picking his teeth with a match-stick and listening to Family Favourites.

Thatcher knocked timidly, although the door was ajar.

'Yes? Oh, it's you, Thatcher. What is it?'

'Can I speak to you, sergeant?'

'What about?'

Thatcher cleared his throat. 'D'you remember the other day when I said I was an atheist?'

'And I put you on fatigues.'

'Yes. Well, I've been thinkin'. I mean, it's not that I don't believe in God, not exactly. It's just that . . . What I mean is, I never went to church, I never got the chance when I was a kid.' He made a valiant attempt to look under-privileged. 'But I'd like to give it a shot now. Maybe I'd see the point if I listened to a few sermons. You understand, sergeant?'

Hayter understood. 'Okay, Thatcher, next Sunday you can join the Christians. Shut the door on your way out.'

'*Yes*, sergeant. Thanks, sergeant.'

The door clicked shut. Hayter grinned to himself and turned up the volume.

FIVE

The weeks pass. A metamorphosis occurs. From placid and hedonistic butchers, bakers, and candlestick-makers they become tough, suspicious, and hard. They discover that their friends are of their own kind, men without rank, and that their enemies are officers and NCOs. They learn new rules, primitive ones, such as how to escape fatigues and how to strangle an adversary with a length of wire. They remember that there were once better things in life than lying face down in March slush or eating cold chow at midnight, but their recollections are vague, like a dream five minutes after waking. They now realize that it is useless to complain if unfairly treated. Here the code is different, definitions of right and wrong more absolute and rigid. Ignorant men can and do wield power and are protected by the more powerful. They accept this, as they accept the fact that deceit, cousin of dishonesty, is tacitly encouraged because it is only the cunning who avoid hardship. Do not get caught, that is their sole maxim.

The plasma of change flows through their veins, altering their values. A photograph of Bardot, a cigarette on a Thursday morning before pay parade, a pornographic book: each is worth more than a sackful of gold or a PhD.

Their job is called duty, and duty implies obligation. But what do they owe, and to whom? Who can claim them: their country, their Queen, their Corps? No, these abstractions are for academics. Separately and silently they conclude that their foremost allegiance is to themselves.

It was a cold, dull afternoon. The grass was wet from a recent fall of rain, and a light mist was beginning to descend upon the firing range, which faced the sea. In the distance a pair of sailing-dinghies ignored the red flag which warned them of danger.

Riordan lay flat on his belly, his legs wide apart in an inverted vee. He adjusted the back-sight of the Lee-Enfield until it read 300 yards. The bloody thing was slipping, he thought. That was the third time he'd had to check it. Easy, Tom, he cautioned, raising the rifle to his shoulder.

He pressed his cheek against the butt, and took aim.

Crack!

The recoil jarred him and his ears rang from the percussion, but instinctively he jerked back the bolt to eject the empty cartridge-case, then slammed it forward again, forcing another round into the breech.

He waited. An arrow-headed pointer appeared beneath the target and indicated that he had scored a bull.

'Good shot, Riordan,' said the instructor.

He grunted with satisfaction. Six bulls out of six and four rounds to go. He would get ten out of ten today, beating his previous best by one. Nobody in the Squad had achieved a maximum as yet, and he was determined to be the first.

He concentrated, squinting along the barrel.

Crack!

Seven out of seven.

'How the bloody hell do you do it?' demanded Webster, who had never scored more than five out of ten.

Riordan shrugged, and said nothing. It was a mystery to him, too, the reason why he could shoot with such accuracy. It was just one of those things. The rifle was an extension of himself, another arm, and he spent many of his leisure hours cleaning and polishing it. He was as familiar with its manifold parts as he was with the palm of his hand.

Check back-sight. Find the target. Exhale. Squeeze the trigger, don't snatch.

Crack!

A long pause. Jesus, had he missed? No, there it was, the pointer. Eight out of eight.

To be the Squad's crack-shot had become an obsession with Riordan, because with this distinction invariably went the title of top recruit – an honour he wanted desperately. He was holding his own, just, in the other tests – map reading, drill, and leadership – and it was touch and go, Hayter had hinted, between himself, Barker, from Hut 5, and Owen, from Hut 7.

A succession of high marks on the range would decide it. The award was simply a rectangle of blue cloth sewn on to the left sleeve, but it stayed with a man throughout his two years – proof that he had made the grade.

Crack!

Christ, they were slow in the butts. C'mon, c'mon, put the bleedin' pointer up.

It went up.

Hell, that was a close thing. Low right. A good six inches below the previous eight rounds. Must be a breeze somewhere or the back-sight's slipping again.

He tested the wind with a wet forefinger. Virtually zero. Concentrate. Concentrate, you bastard.

Crack!

He yelped with delight. Ten out of ten. Ten out of bloody ten. Beat that, you bums.

'Nice shooting, Riordan,' said the instructor. 'What's your number?'

'421885, sergeant.'

The instructor made a note on his pad.

Riordan jerked the bolt backwards and forwards half a dozen times to make sure the magazine was empty. He flicked on the safety-catch.

Webster stared at him in awe. 'I'm glad you're on our side,' he said.

Porter wrote in his diary: 'Two-fifths of a soldier's vocabulary is derived from his anatomy and bodily functions; a further two-fifths from a woman's anatomy; the remaining fifth from what happens before, during and after the two anatomies fuse. And I am learning.'

'You ready?' said Webster, struggling into his greatcoat.

'Yes.'

It was almost four AM and they were in the guard-room, about to take over the last picket-watch.

Webster yawned and rubbed his eyes. 'I don't know how you can write at this time of the morning,' he said. 'Me, I can hardly see. And my mouth feels like it's full of feathers.'

'Keep the chat down, Webster,' said the guard commander. 'Others are trying to get some sleep.'

'Sorry, sergeant. Is there any tea in that urn?'

'Not for you. And shake it up, you're a minute late.'

On their way out they met Rourke and Thatcher, whom they were relieving.

'The duty officer's done his rounds,' advised Thatcher, 'so you can relax. Keep your legs closed though, or your nuts'll freeze off.'

A sliver of waxing moon lit the camp as side by side and slowly they walked the predetermined route. It was their third guard together, and they now knew each other well enough not to talk unless they had something to say.

Porter thought about the entry he had just made in his diary. It was true that he was learning, changing. Before joining the Marines he had rarely blasphemed, but these days every other sentence drove another nail into God's coffin or contained a four-letter noun, verb, or adjective. His vocabulary, he mused, was getting to be as colourful as an American's tie. About as aesthetic, too. And the mutation did not end with the spoken word. He now smoked a hundred cigarettes a week, he could drink a maximum of four pints of beer without throwing up, and lately he had begun to think of women less as remote goddesses who needed to be wooed from alabaster pedestals, and more as sexual outlets. Receptacles. Of course, he had yet to be initiated into the practical mysteries of coition, but he was less apprehensive of this than he used to be. At least, he presumed he was less apprehensive; the proof of the pudding would come with the mating.

All in all he was pleased with the transformation. His parents would hardly recognize him when he went home on leave. He had left their house a skinny youth; he would return in the summer with an extra stone in weight, with once white fingers nicotine stained and cut, with the outlook of a man. A man? Well, almost.

'Roll on Saturday,' muttered Webster.

'Roll on.'

Saturday marked the end of their sixth week, and they would be free from noon until midnight. Webster had his campaign planned already – a train to Exmouth, find a lively pub or coffee-bar, choose the best-looking woman in sight, head for the nearest secluded spot, bring the time-proven Webster technique into play, and finally chalk up another notch on his belt.

'What are you doing Saturday?' he asked.

Porter shrugged. 'Dunno.'

Webster debated whether or not he should invite Porter to make a twosome. It was a risk; Porter looked as green as mouldy bread. On the other hand, women usually hunted for it in pairs, and a guy was in trouble if on his own. He didn't stand an earthly of splitting them up. That was a funny thing about women: they didn't mind doing it providing their mate was doing it. Collective security or something.

'How about teaming up with me,' he said. 'We could pick up some of the local talent and head for the sack. How about it?'

'Suits me,' answered Porter. 'Suits me fine.'

They walked on in silence.

After a quarter of an hour had gone by Webster said, 'Look, this is daft, both of us losing our kip. I'll toss you for who gets his head down in the boiler house.'

'Okay.'

'You call.'

'Heads,' called Porter, and lost.

'Wake us up at ten-to-six.'

Webster disappeared in the direction of the boiler house, but he was back within minutes.

'Occupied,' he said laconically, with a faint shudder of disgust.

'Occupied? Who by?'

'A couple o' cooks from HQ Company.'

'At this hour? What the hell are they doing?'

Webster gave him an old-fashioned look. 'What do you think they're doing?'

'Christ,' said Porter.

In the guard-room Thatcher unfastened his boots and kicked them off. His feet made sweat stains on the stone floor. He wiggled his toes. Stink like a mangy old tom, he thought, lighting a cigarette. He was tired, but he knew from experience that if he slept until reveille he'd suffer for it all day.

A glossy magazine lay open on the table, and he flicked through it. Apart from the pin-ups, which some joker had decorated with beards and moustaches and biologically improbable organs, there were advertisements for hair-oil which guaranteed to turn the weediest of runts into a combination of Casanova, Charles Atlas, and Pan overnight, and advertisements for beer which implicitly promised the drinker an Aston-Martin, a fairy princess with a penchant for sex in the raw as a girl friend, and a sun-tan that would have made Othello appear pure Caucasian. There was also one which read: 'It's a Man's Life in the Regular Army'. Above the caption 'It's not all work for Corporal Edwards' was a photograph of a blonde in a bikini lolling lustfully against the fortunate corporal. Thatcher broke wind.

'You sittin' up?' he said to Rourke.

'Might as well. You?'

'Yeah. Want some tea?'

'Thanks, George.'

Thatcher padded across to the tea-urn. Rourke loosened his tie.

The pair had been on Christian-name terms, and close friends, for a month. It was an odd David and Goliath friendship, born of an empathy which begins somewhere in a similarity of chemistry, is weaned on mutual respect, and matures because of propinquity, of shared guards, of wading through ankle-deep mud together, of beer bought by the one when the other is broke.

'Here y'are, Tim, hot and wet.'

'Thanks. What day's today?'

'Wednesday. No, Thursday. Why, you plannin' your summer holidays or somethin'?'

'Or something.' Rourke winked one bloodshot eye. 'Mary's coming over on Saturday. It's easier for her to do that than for me to get home. She can only make it for the one day, mind, but even that's something.'

'You bet it is, you lucky ol' sod.'

'You can say that again.'

And again. And again. Sing it, for that matter, thought Rourke. Jesus, just to touch her. Just to smell her own, her very own, personal smell of soap and scent and clean hair and country. Just to lay beside her. Just to love her. They would have a few drinks first, and then they'd go to an hotel. They'd pull the blinds, draw the curtains, shut out the rest of the world for half a dozen hours, lose themselves within themselves.

His loins stirred.

Easy, boy, he warned. Easy.

'I want you to meet her,' he said to Thatcher.

'I'd like to.'

'I've written and told her about you. It's all fixed. You come with me to Exeter, then the three of us go to a pub, and after that . . .'

'Hold it, hold it! When are you talkin' about, Saturday?'

'Sure.'

Thatcher shook his head. 'Not me, Tim, not on your bleedin' life. I'm not playin' goosegog. Your wife 'ud kill me if I tagged along. No, thanks, some other time.'

'Don't be wet, it'll only be for an hour or so. After that, I'll get rid of you, don't you fret.'

'You're a mug. I wouldn't do it if it was my wife.'

''Course you would. 'Course you would, George.'

From one of the guard-room bunks Riordan called, 'Will you two guys make up your mind what you're doing on Sat'day, because I'm trying to sleep.'

'Go crap in your hat,' muttered Thatcher.

Shaw's task on the night exercise was one he relished: unaided, he had to cross a mile of wooded, hilly country and simulate the destruction of a pill-box. The pill-box and the approach routes were being guarded by the remainder of the Squad. So far he had covered three-quarters of the distance undetected.

It was being alone that pleased him. He enjoyed his own company best. He had no one to answer to, no one to make decisions for him. It was like playing Cowboys and Indians as a child, except that as a child he had rarely played with other children – or they had rarely played with him.

Solitude. Glorious solitude. No lousy people.

He stopped and peered into the darkness. Over to his left he saw the glow of a cigarette. The fools, the bloody fools, he thought. Now if this was for real . . . He lifted the bren to his hip and in his mind fired a long burst. Dead. Send for the undertakers. A War Office telegram to the next-of-kin. 'Your son-brother-husband got his because he could not do without a fag.'

He moved forward, stealthily, quietly, keeping to the narrow path. They would probably have a couple of men, perhaps three or four, somewhere ahead of him, he figured. The main body of the Squad, though, would be at the foot of the hill, below the objective, about three hundred yards up front by his reckoning. It was getting through them that would present the greatest difficulty.

He walked on. Five minutes passed before a cough entered the arena of night noises. It was followed by a hissed, 'For Chrissake, Les!'

Shaw sank to the ground.

'Sorry,' said a second voice. 'Anyway, I'll bet he's long gone by now.'

'Naw, not him. He's gotta stick to the path. Hayter's fixed trip-wires on either side of it.'

'He could go up the far side of the hill.'

'No can do. Some of the lads did a recce. He'd never make it. It's three hundred feet of brambles and gorse to the top. He's not an idiot. He'd cut himself to ribbons.'

Flat on his belly Shaw crawled back the way he had come. Trip-wires. Up the far side. Three hundred feet of brambles and gorse. Cut to ribbons. Don't bother, part of him said; it's just an exercise. But another part of him said: You scared of a few scratches? Scared, Ed?

It took him half an hour to skirt the hill, and he paused only to catch his breath before beginning to climb.

Brambles and nettles tore at his denims, and his hands and calves bled in a score of different places within minutes. Rivulets of sweat ran down his forehead and dropped from the end of his nose. The gradient mocked his puny efforts, pulled relentlessly at his leg muscles, forcing him to bend almost double. His heart pounded painfully in protest. Sometimes his feet slipped on the clay-like soil, and he fell on his face. Once he let go of the bren and had to slide back twenty hard-won yards to retrieve it.

Climb, you gett, climb. What's the matter with you? It's a heap o' rock. Are you gonna be beaten by a heap o' rock? You're supposed to be tough, Ed. You're a schoolgirl if you let this lick you.

Keep going, that's all, keep going. Head down. Don't look up. *Don't look up.* And don't leave go the bren. Think of something else. Don't think of the top. What's the killing range of the two-inch mortar? Three hundred yards. Four hundred. Can't remember. How many rounds does a bren take? Come on, answer. Twenty-eight. Right. *Don't look up.* Why does a sten fire 9 mm ammo? Dunno. *Think.* Captured stuff. Second war. Right. How many men in a Commando? Six hundred. Right, right. Keep it up, it can't be far. Can't be far.

Can't be far.

Can't be far.

There are sixty-five men in a Commando Company. No, not Company – called Troops in the Brigade. Four Rifle Sections and a Support Section. Higher, Ed, higher. The sten is usually used for house and street clearing and it functions best in a confined space. Jesus, Jesus. Seven Troops in a Commando. Can't see. Can't fuggin see. No more. No more.

No more.

He covered the last twenty yards on his hands and knees, crawling like some sightless marine animal thrown up on the shore. The gorse and brambles thinned, and his fingers caressed the coolness of thick, lush grass. He wiped his face on his sleeve.

He lay supine for a long time. Thoughts came and went. Hayter had said it couldn't be done. He'd done it. Done it. By himself. Nothing was impossible with will power. Nothing.

. . . . .

Birmingham.

The orphanage is cold and grey. It stands in its own grounds and is surrounded by a high wall. The gates are locked at sunset; the authorities do not want the children to escape. It's for their own good. Of course.

Poor lamb, he's not very big.

Illegitimate?

What else? His name's Edward Shaw. Shaw's the mother's name. The father's a Jewish businessman – marked unknown on the birth certificate. Can't take the scandal. Mother's been bought off.

Honestly, some of these mothers.

Hardly a mother. A tart, more like.

He grows to hate the orphanage. Outside, where he goes to school, the other children have homes and families.

Please, sir, why am I here?

That's not an easy question to answer, Edward.

Didn't my mother want me?

It's not as easy as that . . .

When he is ten a childless couple decide to adopt him. He is chosen from a dozen others because of his blond hair. He lives with them for a month.

You mustn't do that, Edward. It's not nice.

Do try and listen when we talk to you. You're very lucky we took you away from that place.

You like being here, don't you? Well, say something, boy!

Do you know what I found in his room, Ann? Dirty books. Filthy things. Where did you get them from? Tell me.

Whack!

I'll teach you not to fill your evil little mind with filth. You'll learn, my lad.

Whack! Whack!

He lies on his bed. His would-be parents are downstairs. They don't want me, he thinks. Not me.

He tears a sheet to shreds, and then another. Systematically, he destroys everything in sight.

Whack!

We can't do a thing with him, Matron. God knows we've tried and tried, but he doesn't appreciate us. We can't keep him, I'm afraid.

The wall again. He stares at it. Caged.

Eddie's father's a Jewboy. Eddie's father's a Jewboy . . .

Don't say that.

It's true. I heard Matron talking. They kill Jews in Germany. They put them in big ovens and fry them. You're gonna fry, Eddie, you're gonna fry. Friiieee!

He has bad dreams. The child psychiatrist says: It's quite common. He feels deprived. Does he get on well with anyone?

He seems to like Mr Stone, his teacher. I'll have a word with him.

At school he is considered bright. He is Mr Stone's favourite pupil.

Stay behind after class, Edward. I've got something to show you.

Mr Stone puts his hand near the boy's genitals. He retreats.

There's no need to be frightened. I'm not going to hurt you. Look.

The teacher unfastens part of his clothing. Edward picks up a steel ruler.

Don't come any closer.

Please, Edward. Please, now.

The boy hits out with the ruler. Mr Stone appears surprised to find that he is bleeding. Edward hits him again and again. He shrieks with delight, and is only prevented from doing murder by one of Mr Stone's colleagues.

. . . Without provocation. He just went for me.

Is this true, Edward?

Silence. He would not be believed, anyway.

Speak up, this is very serious.

Silence. Then punishment.

There are other incidents. A maid at the orphanage complains that he tried to assault her.

What, a lad of thirteen?

He knows what it's for.

Don't be disgusting.

I took pity on him, too. I told him he could call me Mum. He seemed to need someone, always hanging around with his big hurt eyes. But it's not a mother he wants . . . Why, before I knew where I was he had me pinned across the table . . .

Of course, intones the child psychiatrist, he was acting out his complex. You see, in his unconscious he blames his mother for deserting him. He substituted the maid for her and tried to take revenge in the only way he knew how, by raping her – or possibly by trying to re-enter the womb. It's not an uncommon phenomenon.

His dormitory window overlooks the front drive, and each night he stares out. The whole world hates him, he thinks, but one day the world will pay for that. Oh, yes. There won't always be a wall.

. . . . .

After a while Shaw sat up. Below him, just visible, the Squad waited. Stupid bastards, he chuckled, pulling the bren towards him. He cocked it and aimed. They were in his sights. One magazine and they'd be dead. Jesus, if only he had real bullets . . .

SIX

To Webster and Porter, quietly proud in their khaki uniforms, Exmouth was Aladdin's Cave. The pearls were pubs, the rubies freedom, and, most precious and iridescent of all, the diamonds were short-skirted, pert-breasted girls who either smiled indulgently or tossed their curls truculently at each searching glance or low whistle of appreciation. Like gluttons outside a sweet-shop, primarily they devoured with their eyes. Tall girls, small girls, fat ones, thin ones, diamonds uncut and diamonds polished were all acceptable for the moment. Soon they would enter the sweet-shop and reach into a tempting jar. But not yet. A glutton, however hungry, does not gorge himself immediately. First he likes to savour the smells, walk round the table for a while.

'This is going to be easy,' said Webster joyfully, half to Porter and half in the direction of a busty eighteen-year-old, who flashed him a black I-know-what-you're-after scowl that would have withered lesser men. 'Well, easy enough, anyway. All we've got to do is find a pair who don't look as though they're married to bloody great coal heavers, who don't look as though they've got a couple of screaming kids at home, and who don't look as though their idea of a good time is watching the telly. Rich, poor, young, old, anything else goes. Okay?'

'Okay,' agreed Porter, prepared to let Webster do the leading. This was unexplored territory and best left to the expert. 'When do we start?'

'Right now. It's two o'clock. By four o'clock we should be half-way to somebody's bed.'

But at four o'clock they were sitting in a coffee-bar, and alone. Outside it was raining, and the streets were nearly empty.

'It's not fair,' lamented Webster. 'It's not bloody fair. Trust the weather to screw us up. We picked the wrong town. I'll bet the sun's cracking the flags in Exeter. Jesus wept.'

'Probably.' Porter sugared his third cup of foamy coffee. 'Maybe it'll clear up,' he added.

'You kidding? This lot's here to stay. They'll already be issuing wellingtons to the ducks. We'll be lucky if it goes off by eight.'

'That'll still give us a couple of hours.'

'What use is that? Chatting up birds takes time. You can't just go up to one and say, "My name's Porter, get your skirt off." It can take hours, even days. I once spent a week chasing a teacher in Liverpool. Mind you, it was worth it.' He licked his lips at the memory, then dismissed the irrecoverable past. 'No, we've gotta face it; the rain's screwed us up. They'll all be home drying their fannies in front of the fire.'

'So what do we do?'

'Pray. Or go to the pictures. Pray preferably.'

Webster stared lugubriously at some ash which had fallen from his cigarette into his coffee. The earlier hosannas had disappeared from his stomach, and their place taken by the cement of disappointment. Heavy cement. The day was a failure.

Porter tried prayer. Dear God or Dear Whoever it is who deals with these things, send two angels instantest. Webster's can be anything in a skirt that appears vaguely female – excuse the ambiguity – but make mine blonde and soft and not too old...

The door opened with a ring of the warning bell. Webster nudged him.

'Were you praying?' he said excitedly.

They were out of breath and giggling, the two girls: out of breath because they had been running to cheat the rain, and giggling because their efforts had been for nothing. They were wet. They stood in the doorway and shook themselves like dogs after a swim. Drops of rain flew everywhere.

'Take it easy, loves,' said the man behind the counter.

'Sorry.'

The elder of the two, the one who had apologized, took off her head-scarf and ran her fingers through her dark-brown hair. She was about twenty-three, and pretty in a lean and hungry fashion, the fashion of too many late nights and snatched lunches, of worry, perhaps. The head-scarf was followed by her plastic raincoat, which she hung on a peg near the door. Her floral dress clung to her legs damply – legs slim and white. The younger girl was eighteen or nineteen and plumper. But not too plump, Webster noticed, already selecting and rejecting a dozen opening gambits; not too plump at all. Comfortably plump. Plump as a cushion. Small too, small and compact. And if he was any judge that fleshy lower lip, moist with fresh lipstick, promised a thousand and one tricks to some fortunate guy, which could be him if the jeep bounced right, and if Porter didn't object.

'I'll take the little one, okay?' he murmured.

'Okay.'

'Good. Let's move in.'

They got up from the table.

She was standing near the ticket barrier, dressed in her Sunday-best. The train came to a halt with a hiss and a gurgle, and disgorged scores, hundreds, of uniforms, all identical. She experienced a spasm of panic: would she recognize him? The uniforms clattered past her, hell-bent on enjoyment. Some of them studied her licentiously, others gave epiglottal mating noises. She tried not to blush.

Was he there, was he there? Perhaps he'd missed the train. Perhaps she'd got the time wrong. God, where was his letter? She'd left it at home. Fool. Fool.

And then she saw him.

'Tim!' She waved frantically. 'Tim!'

'Oh, Tim,' called a uniform, in a high falsetto.

'Be mine tonight, Tim.'

'Get it in there, boy.'

'You don't want him, missus, you want me.'

'I'll wait over there,' said Thatcher.

Rourke took his wife by the arm and led her into the nearest thing to a quiet corner. He kissed her on the mouth and pressed his body close to hers. For upwards of a minute he thought only: She's mine and she's here.

'Hello,' he said eventually, smiling the easy smile of the contented.

'Hello yourself,' she answered, breathless. 'God, it seems like years.'

'For me, too.'

They looked at each other, both thinking the same thought and both embarrassed because the thought could not be banished by action. Not yet.

'You've put on some weight.'

'I know, about half a stone. Did you have a good trip down?'

'I had to stand part of the way, until a soldier gave me his seat.'

He grinned. 'You shouldn't talk to soldiers.'

'Why ever not?'

'They're only after one thing.'

'And what about Marines? Does that include Marines?'

'It does for this one. In fact, if we were anywhere but on this station I'd . . .'

'Don't.' She squeezed his hand. 'Save it for later or you'll drive me mad. Where's your friend?'

'Friend? Oh, George. Hell, I'd forgotten about him. There he is, the little bloke by the cigarette kiosk. Hey, George.'

Thatcher shuffled across, smiling bashfully, feeling very much the intruder.

'George, this is Mary. Mary, George.'

They shook hands formally.

'Hello, George. I've heard a lot about you.'

'And I've heard a lot about you.'

'And I'm gasping for a pint,' put in Rourke. 'Let's find a pub.'

They found a pub, and amid an atmosphere of Marines and wives, Marines and girl friends, and Marines and beer, they drank steadily for an hour. Inevitably, the camp was the prime topic of conversation. It was a kind of catechism.

Mary: How do you manage on thirty shillings a week?

Rourke: We don't do anything.

Thatcher: When I was a civvy I used to make a tenner a day.

Mary: What's this Sergeant Hayter like?

Thatcher: Oh, great. He's got the sort of face I'd never get tired of kickin'.

Mary: Do you have to peel potatoes and things, the way they do in films?

Rourke: You bet.

Mary: Why? What's that got to do with being a Marine?

Thatcher (thoughtfully): That's a good question. I'll take it up with the CO next time he invites me to tea.

Mary: What do you miss most? I'll send it to you.

Rourke (with a leer): What I miss most you can't send.

Mary (shocked): Tim!

God, he's changed, she thought. The change disturbed her because she could not control it, while simultaneously the mild suggestiveness of his remark excited her. It added fuel to the warm fire that was already burning deep down inside. A fire impatient for attention.

'I like him,' she said, on one occasion when Thatcher had gone to the bar to refill their glasses. 'But he seems a lonely kind of boy.'

'Boy? He's not much younger than you are. As for being lonely, can't say I've noticed.'

'Men never notice anything.'

'They notice their wives.'

'Do they? And do they know what it means when their wives touch them – like this?'

'It means they want their husbands to take them to bed, which is what this husband is going to do before long. So don't drink too much. You're going to need your energy.'

'Huh, the pot calling the kettle black. You've had three to my two. And you know what they say about beer.'

'Don't worry about me. I've been in training.'

She arched her eyebrows. 'Have you, now. Who with?'

He chuckled.

They had got as far as first names. The younger girl was Brenda, the elder one Carol. Brenda was a clerk with an insurance company. Carol was a quiet, apparently disinterested, enigma.

Webster had done most of the talking. Apart from asking the girls if they would like a cigarette or a second cup of coffee, Porter had said nothing for twenty minutes. His was the unhappy silence of uncertainty, and if some benevolent fairy had offered him a single wish, he would have wished for Webster's power of banter.

'But where's the harm, Brenda?' Webster was saying. 'We take you out and buy you a few drinks, or we go to a dance. Where's the harm in that? What can you lose?'

'Plenty,' answered Brenda saucily. 'We know you Marines.'

'We're not all like that.'

'Like what?'

'Like – well, like whatever you're thinking.'

'You don't know what I'm thinking.'

'I can guess.'

'Guess, then.'

'You're thinking that we, my mate and I, are two of the best-looking blokes you've ever seen. And you're thinking how lucky you are that you chose this coffee-bar.'

'Fancy yourself, don't you?'

'That's not all I fancy.'

'I can believe that.'

Brenda took a mirror from her handbag and repaired her lipstick for the third time. Carol smoked a cigarette and listened to the musical pit-a-pattering of the incessant rain. Porter sipped, wet palmed, a cup of lukewarm coffee. And Webster waited for the Look.

The Look was a phrase of his own coining and it had flashed between many a female duo since the day he discovered that little girls were not made simply to give pleasure to little boys. It could take one of several forms: a blink of an eyelash, a nod of the head, a shake of the head, a hitherto forgotten appointment. It could be interpreted as: Yes, I will or No, I won't or I will if you will or Let's get to hell out of here. And it could mean a barren wilderness of an evening or bonanza.

He almost missed it when it came, and it came from Brenda. It said: I'll play along for a bit. Carol's response was: Count me out.

Tough on Porter, he thought.

Brenda stood up. 'Well, rain or no rain. I've got shopping to do.'

'I'll help you,' offered Webster.

'Who asked you?'

'Nobody, but you'll need somebody to carry your bags.'

'I've got arms.'

'You'll strain them.'

'That's my problem.'

'And mine. I want you in one piece for tonight.'

'I didn't say I'd go out with you.'

Webster gave his best darling-this-is-inevitable smile. 'And you didn't say you wouldn't.'

Porter sighed. That was how it was done.

'How long will you be?' asked Carol.

'Half an hour. Are you staying here?'

'Yes. I can't afford to ruin my hair altogether. No more than half an hour, mind,' she added pointedly, and Porter knew what she meant: Thirty minutes is as much as I can stand by myself with this guy.

Webster held the door open. 'Where to . . .'

Alone with Carol, Porter wiped his hands on his trousers. Christ, he was sweating like a pig. What the hell was wrong with him? She was a girl – only a girl. Say something, he ordered himself. Say something. Anything.

'Would you like another coffee?'

'No, thanks.'

'Cigarette?'

'I've just finished one.'

'Do you mind if I do?'

'It's a free country.'

She watched him strike a match and light his cigarette at the second attempt. Another lonely kid, she thought. Another one. So young, too.

'How old are you?'

'Twenty-four,' he lied.

'I don't believe you. You're – well, twenty.'

'I'm twenty-four,' he insisted.

She shrugged. 'Please yourself, but it's no crime to be twenty.'

She fell silent then, and he tolerated the silence for as long as he could before blurting, 'Can I take you out tonight?'

'No.'

'Why not?'

'Because I don't want you to.'

'Why?'

'I don't have to give reasons.'

'But I'd like to know.'

'And I'm not going to tell you. In any case, you don't know anything about me. I might be . . . married.'

'That doesn't matter.'

'It matters to me. Look, if it's just a woman you want . . .'

'Oh, for Chrissake, it's not just a woman!' he snapped, annoyed at being patronized.

'Then why me – because I'm here?'

'No. Because . . .' Jesus, how would Webster answer that one? 'Because you're attractive.'

'Thank you.'

'I meant it.'

'I'm sure you do.' She laughed. It was a pleasant laugh. 'You're funny.'

'Am I?' he demanded, hurt. 'Am I funny because I can't say the right things, because I haven't got the gift of the gab like Webster? Okay, I haven't, but that doesn't make me funny. I don't want to be laughed at, all right?'

'All right.'

Poor kid, she thought, poor bloody kid. God, how many nineteen- and twenty-year-olds had she seen pass through the camp, all concealing their vulnerability beneath arrogance. It must be hundreds. They strutted around town in their bright new uniforms, pretending to be grown up, missing their homes like hell but refusing to admit it. And it was peculiar that a lot of them ended up at her side. Too many of them – far too many lost sheep who were merely looking for a few hours in bed or a breast to nuzzle or a good lay to brag about. But there'd be no more of that. She was nobody's whore, not any longer. The little lambs would have to find their mothers elsewhere.

'I wasn't laughing at you,' she said.

'It sounded like it.'

'In that case, I'm sorry.'

'*You're* sorry.'

'I'm sorry.' She glanced out of the window. The rain had eased.

He guessed what she was thinking. 'You said you'd wait for Brenda.'

'Yes, but . . . Yes, I suppose I did.'

'Then what about that coffee?'

Refuse, something told her, but she said, 'Thanks, I will.'

She took out her compact. Don't be a fool, she warned herself. Drink the coffee and go. Remember the others and don't be a fool.

At each of the several hotels the Rourkes tried they were greeted by the frozen eye of self-righteousness. You cannot expect us to sully our RAC-bestowed reputations by admitting a Marine in uniform and his picked-up girl, said the eye, while the mouth tightened into a prim, striped-toothpaste smile and the voice intoned, 'Full house.' After the third Sorry-we're-full-up they returned to the pub. Thatcher was where they had left him, in the enthusiastic process of demolishing his fifth pint.

'What kept you?' he said.

Mary, practically in tears of anger and frustration explained, concluding with: 'God, you should have seen their expressions. I felt dirty, really dirty. Have you got to carry your marriage certificate in this country? My God!'

Thatcher bought them a drink. 'There must be somethin' you can do,' he said. 'What about phonin' the camp? Leigh 'ud tell them you were married.'

'Oh, yes, that would be a fine thing, wouldn't it! Do you think I want permission from some officer to book in to a hotel with my husband? No, thank you.'

They searched for the solution in the bottom of their glasses. It was five minutes and five suggestions later that Thatcher had his idea.

'How much were you plannin' to spend on a hotel?'

'What?'

'What's that got to do with it?'

'How much?'

'About a couple of quid or so, I expect,' answered Rourke.

'Let's have it.'

'Let's have what?'

'The two quid. Come on, half the day's gone already.'

'Why do you want it?'

‘I’m not gonna tell you, not until I know if it’ll work.’

‘Give it to him, Tim.’

Thatcher pocketed the two pounds. ‘Stick around,’ he said, and went out.

In the street he walked as briskly as five-eighths of a gallon of best bitter would allow. Occasionally he lurched, but the passers-by avoided him with a skill they had originally imbibed with solid food. To them drunken Marines were a residential hazard, and they swore to do something about it one day, complain to the Council. But they never did. They were English.

On his way from the station to the pub earlier, Thatcher had noticed a row of warehouses. He had paid them particular, if cursory, attention because, as a civilian, a lot of his business had been transacted in warehouses: warehouses which specialized in the distribution of cheap Japanese knick-knacks or, more often, in goods which had somehow fallen from the backs of lorries. Anyway, he now reasoned, all warehouses had storerooms, and in one of those storerooms, with luck, the Rourkes would spend their evening.

The first three warehouses were locked and shuttered, but outside the fourth an ancient dwarf of a man in overalls was polishing a brass plate. The plate read: Johnson and Son.

Thatcher spoke to him. ‘Where’s the gaffer?’

‘Not here, son. Sat’day afternoon.’

‘Who’s in charge, then?’

‘Nobody. I’m just the caretaker.’

‘Are you the only one here?’

‘Ay.’

‘Then you’re in charge.’

‘Not me. I’m the caretaker.’

Thatcher grunted with exasperation. ‘Who the bloody hell would I see if I wanted to buy twenty-seven thousand blue teddy-bears, eh?’

The dwarf glared at him. ‘Now don’t you come using that sort of language here. Do what you like in barracks, but not here. Anyhow, what would a youngster like you do with all them teddy-bears?’

Thatcher counted slowly up to ten, then shifted his tack. He rustled the two pound notes. 'How'd you like to make yourself a deuce?'

The dwarf sniffed suspiciously. 'Doing what?'

Thatcher explained. The dwarf sucked his false teeth and hummed and hahed. It was more than his job was worth if he was caught, but none of the guv'nors would be in before Monday. And two pounds was two pounds.

'I'll do it,' he said eventually. 'They'll have to be out by ten o'clock, though. I get me head down then.'

'Aren't you the night-watchman?'

' 'Course I am. You want me to lose me sleep or something?'

Thatcher grinned. 'Let's have a dekko at the storeroom, eh.'

The Rourkes had given him up for lost by the time he got back. He stood over them, beaming with satisfaction.

'Well, that's that settled.'

'That's what settled?'

'I'll show you. It's not the Ritz, mind you, but it's not bad. There's a mattress on the floor and a wash-basin. There's even a gas-fire, for God's sake. Come on, this is your second honeymoon.'

The storeroom was twenty feet square but it appeared smaller because of the profusion of junk with which it was littered. Boxes, packing cases, moth-eaten carpets, a score of toy rabbits, a dozen plastic ducks, a chestful of books, a dilapidated stove. Whatever Johnson and Son's business was, no one could accuse them of putting all their eggs in one basket.

'This,' announced Thatcher, proud as the owner of a stately home, 'is your bedroom. It's your whole bloody house, for that matter.'

'But . . .'

'No buts. It's yours till ten o'clock. There's no lock on the door but the old geezer downstairs won't bother you.' He shook hands with Mary. 'Look after yourselves. S'long.'

The door closed with a creak.

'What a guy,' said Rourke. 'What a guy.'

Mary slipped out of her coat, and together they tested the mattress. It was as hard as a ship's biscuit but they were beyond caring about such trivialities. He unbuttoned her blouse and cupped her small breasts in his hands. She shuddered. Her fingers travelled the length of his body and stopped near his groin.

'Thanks, George,' he murmured.

'Forget about George.'

'He's – aah – awright.'

She stroked him. 'I know, but I'm glad I'm married to you and not him.' She giggled softly. 'He wouldn't be very big, would he?'

'But I am.'

He touched the silky smoothness of her thigh. She moaned.

'Now,' she whispered. 'Now, love.'

Webster peered through the windows of the coffee-bar. There was no sign of Porter or Carol.

'Do you reckon she gave him the heave-ho and he's gone off in a huff?' he said to Brenda.

'Go in and ask.'

Webster did so.

'Went out about five minutes ago,' replied the counter-hand.

'Together?'

'Yes.'

'Any message?'

'No.' The man winked. 'Your pal knew he was on to a good thing, Royal. Best o' luck to you, too.'

'Thanks.'

'Well?' said Brenda.

'They've gone off together and didn't say where to. It looks like you're stuck with me for the night.'

'The *evening*,' she corrected him. 'I'm not that sort.'

'What sort?'

She pursed her very red lips. 'The sort you spend nights with.'

We'll see, he thought. We'll see.

SEVEN

The rain had cleared by dusk, drifted south with the fat black clouds, leaving a legacy of sidewalk puddles and cigarette-packet boats sailing leisurely along the gutters. The street lights came on suddenly and in a hurry, as though as an afterthought, and cast pale bruises on the ground. Pubs opened their evening doors.

Shaw was bored, and annoyed because he was bored. He had been in Exeter since one o'clock, and had done nothing. The trouble was, he thought, doing things cost money, and his pay wasn't designed to stretch to a bottle of whisky or an expensive meal.

He stood on the corner of Queen Street and listened to the sounds of an early-start party coming from the house opposite. A honkey-tonk piano belted out a tune of the Twenties. A score of glasses clinked in time with the music. A dozen laughs greeted a dozen jokes. A solitary baritone sang drunkenly. Shapes flitted past the half-curtained windows. Elegant shapes. Men in tailored dinner-jackets and women in flowing gowns.

Bloody rich, he thought resentfully, and walked on.

A group of students went by on bicycles. Cocoon-like and insular they called to one another with the cheerful cries of youth – youth which had yet to face a world without cloisters and academic panaceas. The girl students' dresses were high on their legs, but Shaw was unmoved. It wasn't a woman he wanted. Even so, a little later, he spent twenty minutes in the shadows watching a dolled-up teenager waiting for her boy friend. And he wondered, in passing, what she would be like in bed and whether her mother knew she was out.

Six-thirty found him in the High Street. He paused before a tobacconist's and read some of the postcard advertisements. *Woman cleaner required three mornings per week – 4/6d an hour. Spanish lessons given by Spaniard. Are you a serviceman and lonely? Join our Friends of the Forces Club. Massage relaxes. Miss Jean Craig supervises personally.*

I'll bet, he thought.

'Hello,' said a soft voice.

He turned.

The queer was in his forties and immaculate in a camel-coloured overcoat, dark suit and suede gloves. Hatless, his iron-grey hair appeared to have been dyed.

'Hello,' he repeated.

Shaw saw red. Christ alive, he was being picked up. *He* was being picked up. He opened his mouth to utter a string of obscenities, but restrained himself. A queer, he reflected. A rich queer too – as rich as the party-goers. Maybe this was the answer to his boredom. Maybe. Queers were generous. And they could be handled.

'You're from the camp, aren't you?' said the queer, with a suggestion of a lisp.

'No, I'm in the Salvation Army.'

'The Salvat ... Oh, I see – very good. How long have you been in?'

'Six weeks.'

'So this is your first pass.'

'Yes. You seem to know all about it.'

The queer smiled sweetly. 'I have a few friends in the camp. Well, one or two. Are you on your own?'

'Yes.'

'I am too. I was supposed to meet someone but I got let down. Perhaps we could have a drink together.'

Shaw played dumb.

'Why should you want to drink with me?'

'Oh, this reason and that rcason. Let's simply say I'm doing my bit for the defenders of our country. Let's also say I'm someone with an hour to spare – and a little money.' A repeat performance of the sugar smile. 'Would you like a drink?'

Shaw nodded innocently.

'Good. I know a splendid tavern not far from here. We could go in my car. It's parked by the Guildhall. My name's James Pascoe, incidentally.'

'Shaw. Ed Shaw.'

Her flat was no more than a large bed-sitting-room, but it was cluttered and cosy with worn cushions and china ornaments and posters from the Costa Brava. Porter felt relaxed. Nothing bad could happen to him here. The forces of destruction, of fear, lay outside the window, beyond the closed doors, somewhere in the incipient darkness of the night. Inside, all was warmth.

He took off his belt and hung it over the back of a chair. As he sat down he noticed an envelope on the mantelpiece. It was addressed to Carol Fuller. *Mrs* Carol Fuller. But it didn't matter. It didn't matter.

The traffic signals changed to green. Pascoe revved the engine.

'What do you think of the Marines?' he asked.

'Not much,' answered Shaw.

'The discipline?'

'Something like that.'

'I sympathize with you. I was in the army during the war, and being treated like a recalcitrant child wasn't my cup of tea at all. Where do you come from, by the way? You don't have an accent.'

'Birmingham.'

'Really? I have a sister who lives in Sutton Coldfield. Do you know it?'

(*Smack!* Do as you're told. *Smack!* I'm going to teach you . . . *Smack!* We're sending you back to the orphanage.)

'I know it,' said Shaw.

Pascoe brought the Daimler to a smooth halt.

'Well, here we are. That didn't take long, now did it? Ready?'

Shaw made no attempt to get out of the car.

'Look, this is a mistake,' he said, with feigned embarrassment. 'I can't afford to buy you a drink.'

Pascoe chuckled. 'My dear boy, no one's expecting you to pay.'

'But I have to get my round in.'

'Nonsense. However, if it worries you – here.' From a pigskin wallet he selected three one-pound notes. 'Here, take them.' His hand rested briefly on Shaw's knee. 'We understand each other, don't we?'

'We do, Mr Pascoe, we do.'

Shaw pocketed the money and unlocked the passenger door. 'Well, thanks for the lift. Good night.'

'*Good night*. What on earth do you mean, good night?'

'What I say. The game's over, Mr Pascoe. I like my meat sliced a different way.' He grinned unpleasantly.

'You little bastard!' hissed Pascoe slowly. 'I've a good mind to . . .' He raised a gloved fist.

'Why don't you?' taunted Shaw. 'Why don't you take a swing and see where it gets you? I'll beat the bejesus out of you and then send for the law. I'll bet you've had dealings with them before. Try your luck. Go on.'

Pascoe lowered his fist. 'Get out of my car.'

Shaw put one foot in the road, but before getting out he reached across and removed the ignition keys. 'I'll keep these as a souvenir.'

'Give me those keys.'

'Come and get them.'

'*Give them to me!*'

'Come and get them. No, half a sec.' Shaw left the car and stood in the middle of the road. 'You wanted games, I'll give you games. How's this for openers – hide-and-seek.' He hurled the keys as far as he could. 'I've hidden them, you find them. Good night.'

He walked off whistling. His earlier boredom had vanished.

The pub was almost empty. The after-the-match drinkers had gone home, and the professional boozers were as yet elsewhere, stuffing themselves with a nostrum of sandwiches and milk in preparation for the weekly Bacchanalia.

Riordan was enjoying the quiet until Thatcher staggered in. It was not that he disliked Thatcher; it was just that Thatcher was still drunk from his afternoon excesses, and Thatcher drunk meant Thatcher trouble. Riordan was anxious to avoid trouble. One blot on his copy-book would put paid to his chances of being made top recruit.

Thatcher blinked in the doorway. The clock on the wall read seven-ten, and he wondered where he had been for the past three and a half hours. He had a vague recollection of lying on a bench near the river and attempting to be sick. The rest was a blank.

He saw Riordan at the bar and lurched over to him.

'Hey, Riordan, how's ev'ry li'l thing, eh? How are you, boyo? Christ, did I have a skinful.'

'Keep it down,' hissed Riordan.

'Eh?'

'Keep your bleedin' voice down.'

'Wha'? Oh, yeah, yeah. Sorry. Sorry,' he said to the barman. 'Don' mean no harm.'

'Where the hell have you been?' demanded Riordan. 'You've got crap and stuff all over your tunic.'

'Crap? Where? Oh that, that's nothin'. A good scrub'll bring that out. Guess I fell over or somethin'. Christ, did I have a skinful.' He paused. 'I awready told you that, didn't I?'

'Yeah.'

Riordan drummed nervously on the counter. Problem: Thatcher's as drunk as an Irish navvy on St Patrick's Night. Solution: He must be got back to camp. Method: Take him to the station and stick him on a train.

'Look, why don't you go back to camp, sleep it off?'

'Me? Not on your bleedin' life. This . . . my first run ashore. Gonna make the most of it. Gonna live it up.'

'Then for Chrissake sit down before you fall down.'

'Get me drink. Wan' Guinness. Wan' bottle o' Chateau Dublin. Fed up with bitter. Get me Guinness, huh?'

'Yeah, but you park yourself, okay.'

'Sure. Sure, I'll siddown.'

He made a nearby table with difficulty. Riordan signalled the barman.

'Bottle of Guinness.'

'Not for him, he's had enough.'

'I'll get him out in a minute. One Guinness and we'll be off.'

'Okay, but you're responsible for him. If he breaks the place up, it's you I'll be reporting.'

Jesus, thought Riordan.

Thatcher took a long swallow. 'Goo' stuff, this. Used to call it iron filin's back in Manchester.'

'Get it down you.'

'Yes, colonel.' He started to chuckle. 'Hey, you know Rourke, Tim Rourke? Boy, did I fix him up. He'll be bangin' away like an ol' ram by now. Goo' ol' Tim. Got a smart li'l wife. Fancied a piece o' her myself.' He frowned. Something was wrong. He shouldn't have said that about Mary. She was no bag. 'Didn't mean that,' he said. 'Didn't mean I'd like a piece o' Mary. She's nice . . . She wouldn't lay it on for anyone. Saves it for Tim. That's goo' isn't it? Don't meet many like that. You gotta a fag? Lost mine.'

Riordan gave him a cigarette, and lit it. Crazy bastard, he thought. Crazy drunken bastard.

'Listen,' he said, 'after that fag we go, all right?'

'Go where?'

'Home. Barracks. Camp. Hut 8.'

'Not me. No, sir. When I've had another couple I'm gonna find me a piece o' tail. Plenty of it around. Hey, how's about you an' me teamin' up, Riordan. You're not a bad-lookin' bastard. We might do okay. Whadyasay?'

'Suits me. But there's nothing here. We'll have to move on.'

'Sure we'll move on. You an' me.'

Riordan got up hopefully. 'Now?'

'Naw, not yet. Relax, can't you, for Chrissake. You got ants in your pants? Siddown, Riordan siddown.'

Riordan sat down. Behind him the barman kept a cudgel handy.

She stood at the window for a while after drawing the curtains. The inevitable question presented itself: Why? It didn't make sense, inviting him home, not in view of the promises she had made to herself. It would be different if he was all man, but he wasn't. From the looks of him he hadn't got what it took to satisfy a girl, and she was already beginning to loathe him, the way she loathed them all sooner or later. It was one thing to be sorry for him – or was it sorrow? – and another to let him make love to her. She could have put him off. It would have been so easy. But she hadn't, and he was here, waiting. She didn't want to go to bed with him, but she would. She always did. That was the horrible part, the part she never understood. She loved them with hate and fear, but she loved them nevertheless. She gave them what they came for, and then she cried herself to sleep, with new promises. They said she was a slut. All of them. But only when it was over. Only then.

The swine.

'You're married,' said Porter.

'How —?' He pointed to the envelope. 'Oh, that. Well, I as good as told you in the coffee-bar.'

'I suppose you did. Where is he, your husband?'

They had to have an answer to that one. They had to be certain they weren't biting off more than they could chew.

'He won't walk in on us if that's what you're worried about,' she said sarcastically. 'He's overseas, in the navy – a PO. He left me.'

He got sick and tired of climbing into a warm bed.

Why do you do it, Carol, why?

I don't know. It won't happen again, honestly.

It will. I could kill you.

Kill me, then. Kill me.

'It doesn't bother you, does it, that I'm married, was married?'

'No.'

'I didn't think it would. You're all the same.'

'All?'

'All. You didn't think you were seducing an innocent, did you?'

I can't explain it. It's something to do with how they stare at me. Lost. I never start off with it in mind. I never do. Believe me.

I can't believe you.

You must. I just want to hurt them. It sounds crazy but it's true. They stare at me and want me and – I want them. But I have to hurt them. They must suffer.

Hurt them. They must suffer, suffer as she would suffer later.

'Perhaps you're the innocent,' she said, and he coloured. Her eyes shone. 'I'm not right, am I?' she said eagerly. 'You don't mean to tell me you've never had a woman? Good God, you haven't.' She laughed. It was a curious laugh. 'I pick them, don't I. I certainly can pick them. What do you expect me to do, teach you what it's all about, show you the positions? Is that what you expect?'

He did not reply directly. 'Why?' he said.

'Why what?'

'Why this? Five minutes ago you were a girl drawing the curtains. Now this.'

'If you don't like it you know what you can do, don't you?'

'Yes.'

He reached for his belt.

She panicked. He was leaving. He was leaving without . . .

She got to the belt first and held it to her, taut across her breasts.

'Oh no you don't. You came here to dip it – isn't that what they call it? – and that's exactly what you're going to do. So come on, Mike, let's see what you're made of.'

'The belt.'

'You'll have to fight me for it. Come on, take it. You're a man, aren't you? Oh, I was forgetting.'

He moved towards her. 'The belt,' he repeated quietly.

She backed away from him, her face flushed. Her voice rose. 'Take it, come on and take it,' she jeered. 'Take me. You want me, don't you? You want me badly. Well, I'm here. But you'll have to fight me. *I want you to fight me.*'

'You're ill,' he said. 'You need a doctor.'

He lunged at her and grabbed the belt. She struggled and spat at him. And then she began to scream.

He hit her, once, with the flat of his hand. Her mouth dropped open and her knees buckled. She fell heavily on to the carpet. Her tears, when they flowed, were those of a very young child who has been punished for no reason.

He crouched beside her, horrified.

'I'm sorry. I didn't . . . It was an accident. Please don't cry. Please.'

He held her by the shoulders and tried to sit her up, but she shook her head violently.

'Leave me! For God's sake, leave me!'

Her flowered dress was above her knees. He touched her, and she squirmed, moaning. Her thighs were cool and strong and firm. White firmness. She stiffened as his hand moved higher, and he experienced a sharp stab of delicious pain. Christ, she was his. This was the way it had to be.

He kissed her clumsily. She faced him, her eyes misty with tears and longing.

'You're beautiful.'

'Don't talk. Don't.'

He lay beside her. She fumbled frantically with his clothing. He felt her slim fingers caress him. Christ, she was beautiful. Christ in Heaven, why had so many years been wasted. Christ in Heaven . . . Christ . . .

Her lips found his. She covered his mouth with hot, demanding kisses, and moved her position to take his weight.

'Now, sweetheart, now, darling, now, love . . .'

She cried out involuntarily as he entered her, before surrendering to the pulsating tremolo of approaching orgasm.

Two sailors, a three-badge gunner and a youthful AB, came into the bar. They ordered rum.

'Bleedin' matelots,' muttered Thatcher, glassy-eyed.

'Now don't start anything,' warned Riordan.

'Me start anythin'? You've got the wrong boy, Riordan. I'm just havin' a peaceful drink . . .'

'Let's keep it that way.'

''Course. 'Course.'

In a shelter near the sea-front Webster said: 'Look, why don't we go back to your place?'

'Can't. Dad's in.'

'Haven't you got a front room?'

'Dad wouldn't let us use that.'

'Why not?'

'He wouldn't, that's all.'

'Then can't we go somewhere quieter?'

'It's quiet enough here.'

'You mean that?'

'Maybe I do and maybe I don't.'

God save us, thought Webster.

'Stop looking at your watch, Tim.'

'I've got to keep an eye on the time. You wouldn't want me to miss the train, now, would you?'

'I wouldn't care if you missed that train and every other train.'

'Yes, you would. We'd better get dressed.'

'Not yet.'

'We haven't got that long.'

'Not yet.'

'All right.'

Riordan had been away for less than a minute, but when he returned Thatcher was at the bar, arguing with the two sailors.

'Bleedin' matelots all the same. Do nothin' but sit on your bums. Call that work? Get paid for nowt. Marines do the graft, the real fightin'.'

The three-badge gunner grinned tolerantly. 'Yeah? And how much fighting have you seen, shorty?'

'Well, not a lot,' admitted Thatcher, supporting legs of jelly by holding on to the counter. 'But that's got sod all to do with it. When it comes, I'll be there. And where'll the navy be? At the back o' the bleedin' line.'

'That's right,' said the AB. 'We let you heroes win the medals. Now get lost, short-arse.'

'Short-arse! Who you callin' short-arse?'

'You. Now beat it before you get hurt.'

Riordan grabbed Thatcher by the arm. 'Okay, let's go.'

'Not 'til these bleeders 'pologize.'

'Out!' said the barman.

Riordan put a half-nelson on Thatcher and pushed him towards the door. Thatcher wriggled and squirmed and lashed out with his feet. His steel-tipped boots connected with the AB's shin, and there was a sickening crunch as metal met bone. The AB went white.

'You little bastard!'

Riordan threw open the door. 'Run, for Chrissake!'

Thatcher tried to, but he covered no more than a dozen yards before falling. His cap rolled into the gutter. He lay on his side, chuckling.

'Get up. Get up, you daft bastard!'

'Lea' me alone. I'm awright.'

'Get up!'

'Bollocks.'

'Oh, Christ.'

It was always the little guys who stirred it, thought Riordan miserably, as the two sailors came up behind him. It was always the little guys who wanted to take on the world.

'Move your arse, mate,' said the AB, limping to a standstill. 'I'm gonna do 'im.'

'Look, he's drunk. He didn't know what he was doing.'

'He'll know next time. He bloody near broke my leg. I've got no beef with you, but he's gonna get his head booted.'

'You'll have to go through me first.'

'Suit yourself, Royal,' said the gunner.

They rushed him. He snatched off his cap and hurled it. It hit the AB between the eyes. He leapt forward, seizing his advantage. The gunner chopped him twice – quick, professional chops picked up in a hundred bars from Hong Kong to Alex. The pavement came up to meet him. It stank of urine and dogs and orange-peel. A kick landed on his shoulder. He grabbed the ankle and twisted. The gunner sprawled in an untidy heap and struck his head against the wall. Blood oozed.

Faces peered out of the pub windows. Faces interested only in the outcome. Somewhere a transistor radio disgorged hot music.

The AB raided a crate of empties and gripped a bottle by the neck. He smashed the broad end with a wrist flick. The jagged edges gleamed in the half-light.

'You an' me, Royal.'

'For Chrissake, Thatcher!' shouted Riordan.

Thatcher snored contentedly.

'Let's see how tough you are now,' said the AB.

As he drew back his arm to deliver a thrust that would have cut Riordan to shreds, he was caught by the throat from the rear. He dropped the bottle and clawed at the fingers that were slowly and inexorably choking him.

From the pavement Riordan could just make out the silhouette of a Royal Marines cap, and then he heard Shaw ask: 'Who's that on the deck?'

'Me, Riordan.'

'Fug me, it would be. Can't you handle a lousy matelot?'

'Two of 'em.'

'Eh? Oh, yeah. Well, thanks for saving me one. I haven't had any fun for an hour.'

He released his hold on the AB's windpipe, spun him round, and brought up his knee. The sailor collapsed with a shrill scream, and retched.

Shaw dusted himself. 'Who's that over there?'

'Thatcher. Drunk as a bastard. Give him a hand, will you, while I get some of this crap off me.'

Thatcher opened one red eye as Shaw pulled him to his feet.

'Hiya, Shaw,' he grinned. 'Boy, am I glad to see you. Ol' Riordan, it's no good goin' ashore with him. All he ever wants to do is fight. Let's find a pub, eh, Shaw? Whadyasay, eh . . .'

The gas-fire flickered blue and yellow. Specks of charcoal glowed. Porter knotted his tie with difficulty. His mind was elsewhere. He had made it. He felt elated and depressed simultaneously. Elated because there was, at last, a notch on his belt; depressed because he suspected she had not enjoyed it half so much as he had. His actions had been free and spontaneous; hers had been calculated, ritualistic: an old game with a new opponent. But that was only to be expected. It was odd, though, to think that others had heard her whisper, during that brief, too brief, flood of excitement, the same things he had heard. And how many others: two, four, a dozen? Too many. One was one too many now that he wanted her all to himself.

From the narrow single bed she watched him dress. Another face. Another body. Another second of pleasure. Another boy with a memory. Another hour gone.

What do you mean, hurt them?

The pain comes later – when they're unprepared.

'You'll miss your train,' she said.

'I'll run.' He paused. 'Can I see you again?'

'Yes.'

'Tomorrow?'

'Yes.'

'About three o'clock.'

'I'll be in. Will you be able to find the flat?'

'Easily.'

He kissed her.

'Good night.'

' 'Night.'

He closed the front door quietly. It was some time before she began to cry.

'But why not, Brenda? I don't get it.'

'I told you, I'm not that sort of girl.'

'Everybody's that sort.'

'I'm not.'

'I'll bet I wouldn't be the first.'

'Don't be dirty. You go on and on, you Marines. You buy a girl a couple of gin-and-tonics and you think she'll do it all. Well, I won't.'

'You won't miss it if it's gone.'

'Of all the filthy things to say! No one's ever talked to me like that before. I'm going.'

'Don't!'

'Leave me alone.'

'I'm sorry.'

'Goodbye!'

She strutted off into the darkness, wearing her indignation like a badge. Webster swore solidly and without repetition for upwards of a minute.

'You'll catch your own train okay?'

'Yes, Tim. I've got an hour yet.'

'Careful while you're waiting.'

'I'll be careful. Write to me, won't you? Write every day.'

'I will.'

'And think of me often.'

'I will.'

'And take good, good care of yourself.'

'I will, I will.'

. . . . .

In ones and twos and groups they make their way back to the station. Some are drunk, some sober, some quiet, some noisy. Saturday has gone, but there is always Sunday. The rigours of a new week do not have to be faced yet.

They boast and brag and swear and sing.

'For Chrissake give us a hand with this bum, Shaw.'

'Jesus, did I have a skinful. I can't remember nothin'. Hey, Riordan, you been in a scrap? Four-and-twenty virgins came down from Inverness . . .'

'. . . And when the ball was over there were four-and-twenty less . . .'

'Don't encourage the bum.'

'Did you click for anything, Bailey?'

'Naw. I went to the pictures. I got a steady at home.'

'You're crazy. You don't reckon she's knitting socks on a Sat'day night, do you?'

'So this bloody great para corporal says . . .'

'. . . The village conjuror he was there, doin' his favourite trick . . .'

'Shut up, Thatcher.'

'Who are you talkin' to? . . . Doin' his favourite trick . . .'

'Belt up.'

'. . . He put the head in. You should've seen the mess . . .'

'Jeeze, I feel sick.'

And on another train.

'How'd you get on, Porter?'

'Not bad.'

'Come off it. That Carol was frigid. I spotted that as soon as I saw her.'

'Oh, yes.'

'Yeah. You can't kid me. I had the time of my life, though. I tell you, I've been with some but she knew it all. Talk about French. Christ!'

'Oh, yes?'

'Yeah. You don't believe me? Now listen . . .'

And when the ball was over . . .

EIGHT

Spring becomes summer. Black trees turn green. The recruits are issued with salt tablets, and in the canteen there is an abundant supply of iced water.

They curse the heat as much as they did the cold. More so, in fact. In the winter they had to move to keep warm. Now, however, they would rather sit in the Naafi with a jug of ale than march or shoot or run. Grey skies are infinitely preferable to blue when the order of the day is motion. Their packs weigh heavier in the sun. The parade ground saps their strength. But there is no respite. Someone, somewhere has decreed that they will be fully trained in sixteen weeks. And fully trained they will be. If the cost is measured in broken bones, bruises, exhaustion, this cannot be helped. We have dominions to protect, bases to guard. We may not rule the waves these days but, by God, no one can lick us when it comes to putting on a show.

Their uniforms have lost some of the newness. They are battle scarred without ever having seen a battle. They no longer look like civilians masquerading as soldiers. The alchemists have done their work. The metamorphosis is almost total. Soon they will be ready.

'When have you got 428 next, Stan?' asked Hayter.

'Wednesday. Grenade range. Why?'

Hayter grinned knowingly. 'Oh, nothing.'

'Bloody liar. Let's have it.'

'Well, it's just that I see you lost your girl to one of the lads.'

'Girl?'

'Mrs Fuller. Saw 'em together in Exmouth on Saturday. Very pally.'

'So what.' Sergeant Bell, the weapons instructor, shrugged disinterestedly. 'That was over weeks ago. There must have been two or three between me and whoever's keeping her happy now. Who is it, anyway?'

'Porter.'

'Porter? Oh, yeah. Kid with the mouthful of washers.'

'That's him. What happened to you and her?'

'Wife got suspicious. Had to pack it in.'

Like hell, thought Hayter. You were given the shove.

'Porter, you say.'

'Yeah. Christ, look at the time. Leigh'll be chewing the carpet. See you, Stan.'

'See you, Bill.'

'Sergeant Hayter's here, sir.'

'Send him in.'

Hayter stood to attention in front of Leigh's desk. The Company Commander flicked through a batch of documents, scrawling his initial perfunctorily at the foot of each.

'Relax, sergeant. Pull up a chair. I'll be with you as soon as I've finished this bumph. Smoke if you wish.'

'Thank you, sir. Would you like one?'

'No, thanks. My wife's been complaining that I smoke too much, and I promised I'd cut down.' He smiled absently. 'Wives. Always worrying. The day mine stops giving me advice will be the day I die. However, you don't have that problem. Free 'n easy, eh?'

'Not exactly, sir. I just came to the conclusion that having a husband in the Forces was no life for a woman.' He coughed. 'No offence, sir. What I meant was . . .'

'No need to apologize, sergeant. I understand and, up to a point, agree with you. Mrs Leigh certainly does. A woman should have a permanent home, a secure base. Married to a soldier she's likely to hang one set of curtains in Aldershot and the next in Hong Kong. Mind you, Mrs Leigh and I have been fortunate. That is, if you can call a game leg and a home posting fortunate. It's worse for those who can't have their wives with them. I often wonder how our National Servicemen feel. We've got several married men in 428, haven't we?'

'Four, sir. They cope.'

'Of course.' Leigh tossed the last of the documents into the out-tray. 'That's that, thank God. Now, what can I do for you?'

'Weekly report on the Squad, sir.'

'Read it out.'

Hayter produced his notebook.

'428 Squad successfully completed Phase Three of the training schedule by the end of Week Thirteen. Training included the dummy grenade, the rocket-launcher, the two-inch mortar, cliff climbing, a night exercise under battle conditions, and unarmed combat. Casualties were light: four slightly injured and one seriously.'

'Who was that?'

'Kelland, sir. It was on the cliff climbing exercise. He was about twenty or thirty feet from the bottom when he panicked and let go the rope. Broke a wrist.'

Leigh grunted. 'We've had worse. No danger of him being incapacitated for ever, I trust.'

'No, sir.'

'Good. Trying to get a disability pension is a dreadful business. Carry on.'

'That's more or less it, sir. Phase Four begins this afternoon with the fifteen-mile route march, and 428 pass out two weeks on Thursday.'

'And you won't be sorry to see them go, I'm sure.'

'Dunno about that, but I'll be glad to get abroad again. Has anything come through on my posting yet, sir?'

'Not yet, but it shouldn't be long now. And if you go back to 49 Commando, you'll have company. Most of the Squad have been posted there. I received the Movement Order this morning.'

'Won't bother me, sir. You can't beat Malta in July, and Mellieha Bay is big enough to take this Squad and ten others.'

Leigh nodded, and wondered whether he should tell Hayter it was an even money chance 49 would not be in Malta in July. Better not, he thought. It was only a guess.

'I envy you,' he said, after a moment's consideration.

'Envy me, sir?'

'Yes, you and the others. Here am I stuck behind a desk, and there are you off to Brigade. I had some grand times in Brigade.'

'Yes, sir.'

'Really grand. There's a certain camaraderie in Brigade that you never find in a training unit. Every day was different, if you follow me. We had our problems, true, but we solved them together, the officers, NCOs, and men. Here – well, here nothing changes. Smith has gone over the wall, the CO wants a Squad for the Earl's Court Tattoo, there's too much salt in the stew. I'm not an officer any more; I'm a marriage guidance counsellor and maitre d'hotel rolled into one. Damn' leg.'

'Yes, sir.'

Yes, sir, no, sir. Cobblers, sir, thought Hayter. Camarad-something-or-other was undiluted crap. And so was that bull about officers and men working together. Officers could believe what they liked, but in Brigade or the UK the NCOs and the men wanted nothing other than a quiet life. So stuff it, sir, stuff it.

'Yes, grand times,' repeated Leigh, dreamily. 'But enough of that. Is there anything else, sergeant?'

'Just one item, sir – this business of top recruit. You've only got a fortnight.'

'Quite. Well, I'll take your advice on it. I've read your recommendations, naturally, but there doesn't seem much to choose between them. Riordan has an excellent record on the range, but his interpretation of an ordnance survey map leaves a lot to be desired. Barker has had a good education, but he's nowhere near a first-class shot. Owen appears to be above average on the range and educationally. But where do we go from there? Have you a preference? You're closer to them than I am.'

'It's between Barker and Riordan, as far as I'm concerned.'

'But which?'

'I don't know.'

The telephone rang and Leigh picked up the receiver. He stiffened when he heard the COs drawling baritone. A call from the CO was of a somewhat higher order than God summoning Samuel.

'Yes, sir. Yes, sir. Immediately, sir.' He replaced the receiver. 'CO wants me,' he said, adjusting his Sam Browne.

Hayter stood up. 'And the top recruit, sir?'

'Oh, toss a coin, man, toss a coin. It's not that important.'

Leigh left the office at the trot. Hayter took out a half-crown, and spun it. It landed tails up on a folded newspaper. He made a mental note of the winner.

As he pocketed the coin he noticed a short item in the newspaper which Leigh, or someone, had ringed in green ink. It read: 'Nicosia, Cyprus. Sunday. A further act of violence was perpetrated here today near the Pancyprian Gymnasium. A home-made bomb was thrown at a car containing two British civilians. Both were slightly hurt. The leaders of the Turkish community have made a formal request for more British troops to be sent to the island.'

Go stick your fez up your jacksie, thought Hayter.

They had been marching for two hours. The afternoon sun, white and oppressive, beat down on their exposed necks. Their shirts were dark with sweat, their boots made of thorns. The earth beneath their feet was hard and uncompromising. Their cheeks were drawn and pinched, their eyes dull with fatigue. No one spoke. The air was silent except for grunts. They had begun the route march with songs and jokes, but now they conserved their remaining energy. Earlier, before starting, they had been confident of their ability to see it through. Now they had doubts. The pace was murderous, far too fast, and they had covered less than two-thirds of the distance. A third to go. Five or six lonely, agonizing miles. They could expect no help. Each man was alone with his aching lungs and weary limbs, and each man kept his gaze fixed firmly on the waist-belt of the man in front. No one wanted to look up because that would mean seeing the next hill, always bigger than the last, and despairing. It was better to let the mind go blank or, if that proved impossible, to think of anything but the task at hand. Some counted, silently, from one to hundred, and then began at one again. Others muttered nursery rhymes or told themselves familiar stories. Still others visualized a foaming glass of beer.

Crunch. Crunch. Steel-tipped heels on desiccated soil.

At the head of the column someone stumbled, causing the man behind to check his stride and break his rhythm. An oath shattered the quiet. 'Pick your bleedin' feet up, you bastard!' The man who had stumbled and the one who had cursed him were, ordinarily, great friends. They drank together and swopped girls. But here things were different. Here a man's best friends were his own muscles and will. If a mother had begged for food from the edge of a field, she would have been ignored. If a whore had spread-eagled herself naked on the brown earth, she'd have been stepped on. They had no compassion now, or desires. They were required to have neither. The object of the route march, like the object of all their training exercises, was to weld fifty individuals into a co-ordinated whole. And in this it was succeeding. They might hate their NCOs and each other, but no one wanted to be the first to collapse. If Bailey could do it, Barker could do it. If Barker could do it, Carter could do it . . .

Esprit de corps. Die Tat ist alles.

Crunch. Crunch. Across fields. Through gorse. Over ditches. Up hills. Shoulders hunched. Backs bent. Hearts thumping. Newly ploughed furrows that bar the way. Gradients which destroy. Thorns that cut. Ditches impassable. Blind with sweat.

Jesus, another hill. Where's the camp? Where the fug's the camp? It must be somewhere. Should be able to see it from here. One two three four five . . . Little Jack Horner sat in a corner . . . A bleedin' big glass of beer. With froth an inch thick. Pick your bleedin' feet up. Eating his Christmas-pie. Jesus, Christmas. Christmas and snow. All that lovely snow. Twenty-eight. Twenty-nine . . . Must be able to see the camp from the top of this bastard. Must be. And when I've drunk that I'll have another. And another. Gonna drink beer 'til it flows out of my asshole. Snow. Remember snow? You put it in your mouth and it melts. Goes down your throat and cools your insides. Cold as an Eskimo's bum.

Crunch. Crunch.

Soon the numbness would come and they waited and prayed for it. Sweet numbness. Five minutes. Ten minutes. Three hundred yards. Six hundred yards. A blinding flash, a snap in the brain, then peace. Grey peace, hanging like a soothing fog before the eyes. Drowning the mind. Anaesthetic peace. Hypnotic greyness. They would soar above the ground – over the ditches, over the furrows, over the bushes – and run. Yes, run – because their legs would be light and their heads lighter. Jesus, let it happen quickly.

Seventy-eight. Seventy-nine.

Little Bo-peep has lost . . .

Drain it to the bottom. Drink the barrel dry.

Pray for rain, lads, pray for rain.

A mile. Half a mile. Not far. Not far. Hayter's a bastard, Hayter's a bastard, Hayter's a gett. Bastard, schmastard, custard. Gett, let, bet, met, net . . .

Ninety-nine. One hundred. One two . . .

Hey diddle diddle the cat did a piddle . . .

Hayter's a gett. Hayter's a gett.

Arthur Guinness for King.

And then there were no more hills, no more fields. They were on a road, and the road was flat. The melting tar burned, but it didn't matter. They knew instinctively that this was the last road. Around that bend or around the next was the camp. Those at the head of the column quickened their pace, and those at the rear responded. It was nearly over and not one had fallen by the wayside. By Christ, they were a bloody good Squad. By Christ, they were.

One more bend. Just one.

They straightened their backs and glared defiantly into the sun.

Sergeant Bell tossed the grenade from hand to hand. He was a big man with a deep hairy chest and the close-set eyes of someone who has been short-changed on brains and liberally endowed, by way of compensation, with mean streaks. It had taken him twelve years to make sergeant and, short of a major war, he had reached the end of the promotion trail.

The Squad were on the grenade range, in the larger of the two covered dug-outs which connected with an open six-foot-deep trench via a narrow passage. Some thirty yards from the trench, on level ground was a painted circle five feet in diameter, and in the centre of this a red pole.

'You've handled dummy grenades before,' began Bell,

'but this isn't a dummy. It's for real. If you drop it after removing the pin – kaput. They'll never find the pieces. So no mistakes.' He paused, then: 'Catch!'

He flung the grenade at Webster, who missed it. The Squad scattered.

Bell hooted.

'Jesus, Webster, I'd hate to be with you in a tough spot. Chuck it back.' Webster did so, gingerly. 'It's harmless,' explained Bell, 'until it gets a fuse. To insert the fuse you unscrew the screw-cap, like so, put the fuse in and replace the cap. What happens now if I pull the pin?'

'We all go to hell,' muttered Shaw.

'Wrong. I can sit here for an hour without making any widows – as long as I keep hold of the grenade. But once I let go, once the spring-clip flies off and activates the fuse, I've got four seconds to vanish. Got that? Okay, each man will take a grenade but he won't prime it until I give the word. You'll throw from the trench, and I want every throw to land in the circle. As soon as you've thrown and the grenade's exploded, come back here. And don't let me see any wise guy pulling the pin with his teeth. That sort of stunt can be left to Warner Brothers. Right, you're nearest, Owen, you can go first. Grab a grenade and follow me.'

After Bell and Owen had gone, there was a scramble for the khaki boxes stencilled WD. Rourke emerged with two grenades and handed one to Thatcher.

'Thanks.' Thatcher fingered the segmented, egg-shaped object. 'Not much to look at, is it? Feels like chocolate. Four seconds did he say?'

'Yes.'

'Seven,' corrected Webster.

'What d'you mean, seven?' demanded Thatcher. 'He said four. We all heard him say four.'

'He said seven,' insisted Webster.

'My arse. You weren't listenin'. What's the use of havin' a seven-second fuse? The bloke you're heavin' it at could have his dinner and still have time to chuck it back.'

'I'm sure he said seven.'

'Well, he didn't cloth-ears. Tell you what, though,' added

Thatcher, with a wink at Rourke; 'I'll bet you a week's pay you don't keep your turnip up for six seconds after you've thrown. Deal?'

'Not likely. You think I'm daft?'

'You guessed it.'

There was a hollow explosion and a whine of flying metal from outside the dug-out, and a moment or two later Bell and Owen reappeared.

'Next one,' said Bell.

Rourke shuffled forward. 'That's me, sergeant.'

'Come on, then. No, wait a sec,' he said thoughtfully. 'Where's Porter?'

'Here, sergeant.'

'You're next, then.'

Puzzled, Porter tracked Bell into the trench. He selected a fuse and primed the grenade.

'How's that girl of yours?' asked Bell, as Porter prepared to throw.

'Girl?'

'Yeah. Carol Fuller.'

Porter was surprised. 'Do you know her?'

'Not half. We're old friends, Carol and me. Been seeing her long?'

'A few weeks.'

In fact, he had seen her every weekend since their first meeting, but she had never mentioned Bell. Of course, he thought, there was no reason why she should. Then again, they had often talked about the camp.

'Yeah,' Bell went on, 'a right little whore, our Carol. Been wife to half the Sergeants' Mess at one time or another. Never made the Officers' Mess, though. Funny, that. They're choosy, I suppose. Do you get it regular?'

'That's my business.'

''Course it is, lad, 'course it is. I just don't want to see you make a mug of yourself. She's a great lay but she spreads it around a bit. She likes variety.' He smirked: that'd teach him a thing a two. And her. 'Well, carry on. There are others waiting to throw.'

But Porter stood motionless. The sickness he felt in his

stomach showed in the sudden pallor of his face. Christ, Bell. Bell was one of them. How could she. How the hell could she with a stupid, unfeeling bastard like that. And there was something else: when?

'When did you . . . When were you last with her?'

Bell shrugged. 'I can't remember dates.'

'*When*, sergeant?'

Bell looked at him. 'Last week.' The lie came easily.

'*Last week!*'

'Yeah. Wednesday, I think. What difference is it to you? You can't expect her to sleep by herself just because you're locked up in camp. She's a hot piece, Carol. She needs it. Me during the week, you at weekends.'

'You're a liar!' spat Porter. 'You're a bloody liar!'

'Watch it!' snarled Bell. 'Watch your mouth or I'll have you inside before you can say knife. These stripes aren't cornflakes. I'm not takin' any crap from you, bird or no bird. She's a tart, so wake up.' He held out his hand. 'And you'd better give me that grenade. You're not in a fit state to throw. You hear me? Let's have the grenade.'

Porter made no attempt to comply.

'I hear you,' he said, his voice ominously quiet. 'And I'm throwing.'

'I'm ordering you not to!'

'Why, scared I might let go of it in the trench?'

'You wouldn't be such a fool.'

'Sure, sergeant? Absolutely sure?'

He pulled the pin and let fly. Bell winced, and ducked. The explosion sent up a cloud of earth which fell, like hail, into the trench.

'THAT WAS TOO FUGGIN CLOSE!'

'No, I scored a bull,' said Porter calmly, and walked back to the dug-out.

It was Riordan who noticed Porter was missing. Last Post had been sounded half an hour before and Hut 8 was settling down for the night.

'Anyone seen Porter?' he called softly.

'I saw him before Lights Out,' said Rourke.

'Where?'

'By the Naafi. He was heading in this direction.'

'He had a dust-up with Bell this morning,' offered Shaw.

'What about?'

'Dunno, but it was pretty fierce.'

The same thought struck all of them simultaneously. Webster put it into words.

'D'you reckon he's gone over the wall?'

'No,' scoffed Thatcher. 'I mean, why should he? So what if Bell had a go at him. That's no reason to go over the wall. Well, is it?'

No one answered.

'I'd better report this to the duty officer,' said Riordan, sitting up.

Shaw disagreed. 'Why? The least you can do, if he's gone, is to give him a start.'

'That's bloody daft. When they catch him, and they will, he'll be in the rattle.'

'So? It's his neck.'

'I guess you're right,' said Riordan eventually. 'I guess you're right.'

A few hundred yards away, at the southern edge of the camp, which backed on to the Exeter-Exmouth railway line, Porter cautiously pulled apart the middle strands of the barbed-wire perimeter fence. He climbed through and began to walk. Behind him, except for the guard-room, the camp was in darkness.

It was six or seven miles to Exmouth and he estimated he would not be there much before two AM. The last train had not yet left the local station, but he could not risk travelling on that or using the roads. It was too dangerous. He might be seen. The regimental police were always on the look-out for deserters.

He coughed, and the sound split the night.

He did not think of himself as a deserter, although he realized that this charge, or the lesser one of AWOL, would be brought against him. The minimum penalty was seven days' detention, and the maximum a military prison. Colchester, more than likely. But he had to take the risk. It was essential that he saw Carol. Now. Tonight. He could not wait until Saturday.

Carol. Jesus, sweet Carol. She couldn't have done that to him. She wouldn't sleep with Bell during the week and then casually change lovers at the weekend. Not her. Not any woman. But especially not Carol. She knew how much he needed her. And he did need her. Not only because she was his first, but because she was Carol. She wouldn't do it. She wouldn't, she wouldn't, she wouldn't.

. . . . .

But you must go to Sunday school, Michael.

I don't want to.

You're not old enough to know what you want.

Of course he isn't. Don't argue with him. No more nonsense from you, Michael, or you'll feel my belt.

Don't talk to him like that. He's young. Run along, dear.

His mother kisses him fondly. He likes being kissed by his mother. She never shouts.

He takes off his cap and stuffs it into his pocket as soon as he leaves the house. This single act of rebellion pleases him.

None of the other boys go to Sunday school, he thinks. Well, not many. Why should I? I won't go.

But he does. He fears his father's anger.

All things bright and beautiful . . .

He does not sing, but instead annoys the little girl beside him by tugging at her hair.

Stop that, she says indignantly. Stop that, Michael Porter. This is God's House.

God's soft.

Michael Porter! I'm going to tell. Please, Michael Porter's just said that God's soft.

The other children giggle.

Did you, Michael? Did you say that? Well, answer me, Michael, or must I take your silence as an admission of guilt? Very well, if you won't answer you can go. Go on. I'll be talking to your father about you.

On his way home he deliberately scuffs his shoes. He chuckles delightedly at the scratches on the new leather.

His mother and father are not expecting him so early, and they are making love in front of the fire. He peers through the sitting-room window and presses his ear to the glass.

Hurry, dear, the children will be in shortly.

The children won't be in for hours.

But dear . . .

For heaven's sake, woman.

He is horrified. His father is hurting his mother. He must be. And he can't help. He is locked out.

Don't let him hurt you. Don't!

No use. No use.

School report: Michael is an exceptionally intelligent thirteen-year-old, but he does not participate in as many activities as we would wish. The school is noted not only for its academic achievements, but for the number of County players it has produced in the last decade. Therefore . . .

What's all this, Michael?

What's all what?

This report. You have excellent marks in most subjects, but your games record is lamentable.

I'm not keen on games.

But you should be, you should be. Games are an important part of growing up. They help prepare you for the rigours of industry and commerce. Anyway, the headmaster has carte blanche to give you as many extra games sessions as he deems fit.

Run, Porter, run with the ball. It won't explode in your face.

Not like that, Porter, like this. Hold the bat like this. Heavens, boy, don't you understand anything!

Keep going, Porter. If you run like blazes you'll just about be last.

Laughter. Mocking laughter.

His mother sits on his bed at night and sympathizes.

Your father's only doing what he believes to be best, darling.

I wish he wouldn't. I'm no good at games.

You will be, darling, you will be.

She hugs him and he clings to her. Desperately.

Soon he takes an interest in girls, but he lacks the courage to strike up conversations. In any case, they flock around the school athletes. It matters not to them that he is top of the class in Latin, English, and History.

His sisters make jokes about him.

I saw Michael with Jenny Robson today.

You didn't!

Well, you were ogling her.

I was not. She's ugly.

They're all ugly, he decides in self-defence. And they're always giggling and sniggering and making sly remarks.

Unconsciously he compares them with his mother. Not one has her kindness, not one her understanding. Not one will listen when, on rare occasions, he needs to talk.

He feels very lonely. In a houseful of people he feels quite alone.

It's about time we decided on a career for you, Michael, m'boy.

Don't rush him, dear. He has years yet.

He does not have years. A boy should know what he wants to do by the age of sixteen. What about it, Michael? Law. Insurance. Banking. Good opportunities for men with degrees.

I'm not sure.

Well, you'd better make up your mind soon. You won't be young for ever, you know.

He knows it. He sees his parents age and his sisters marry. He is leaving his childhood behind, but he is not yet an adult.

Perhaps I never will be, he thinks. Perhaps I'll never grow up. Never.

All things wise and wonderful,
The Lord God made them all.

. . . . .

Porter slid down the embankment. Above him an express thundered by, its carriage lights throwing a pale, evanescent glow on to the road. He glanced at the luminous dial of his wristwatch: one-forty. Not long now. Her flat was less than five minutes' walk.

He was weary. Weary and apprehensive. He had no idea what he was going to say to her.

He turned right along a familiar street, and then left. He passed landmarks he recognized: the tobacconist's, the dairy, the pub where they drank; and he was outside her flat almost before he realized it. He glanced up. There was no sign of life. He pushed the bell with his forefinger. It rang, and kept on ringing.

NINE

The flat was not as he remembered it. It had that just-woken-up look of rumpled bedclothes, unwashed supper dishes, unemptied ashtrays. Worse, the warmth had gone. The gas-fire burned brightly, but the warmth had gone.

He had sat in the same position for fifteen minutes, leaning forward on his elbows, his head resting on clenched fists. The cup of coffee on the table in front of him had gone cold. A wafer of scalded milk covered its surface. There had been questions and answers, and more questions. He had heard her say, No, he wasn't here on Wednesday; he hasn't been here for weeks – and he believed her. But that was only the beginning. He knew a name now; a name that would serve as a constant, leering reminder of what she had been – what she could be.

'Why him?' he said. 'Why him?'

Away from him, kneeling before the gas-fire, a dressing-gown slung loosely about her shoulders, she replied: 'He was there when I needed someone. What difference does it make? I told you there'd been others. I can give you a list if you like, if it'll make you feel better. John, Gerry, Bill, Tony . . . It's a long list.'

He lit a cigarette. 'Bloody long.'

Too long. Far too long. Bell and the others had slept with her in that bed. That bed. Their bed. His and hers. Bell knew what it was like to make love to her. He had touched her body and she had touched his. It was useless and irrelevant for her to imply that it had happened before she met him. It *had* happened, that was the point. It could happen again, while his back was turned. He'd be none the wiser. He'd always be uncertain because he couldn't be with her every hour of every day. Watching. Guarding.

She understood. Somehow she understands his thoughts. She had played the scene before.

If you weren't abroad so much . . .

But I am. It's my job.

You could get another job. I want my man with me.

You want any man.

That's not true.

It is true. Any man. Any man. Isn't it? Isn't it?

'You want to own me, Mike. You want to own me brand-new. Because I was your first you think you should have been my first. I've let you down, haven't I?'

'Don't be stupid.' But she was right. When they were in bed together there were always doubts – nagging, probing doubts whether he was as good as the last one or the one before that or the one . . . 'Stupid,' he repeated, with less conviction.

'It's not stupid. You're jealous of men you've never met, never will meet. But you can't own me. Nobody can. I'm not for sale.'

She wrapped her dressing-gown more tightly around her, shielding herself, perhaps, against an empty tomorrow.

It was over now whether he realized it or not. Over because he was falling in love with her. And she wouldn't have that. Not love. Not again. It was too complicated, too painful. It made life unbearable. It was better to finish it tonight. Quickly.

'You remind me of my husband,' she said.

'How?'

'Oh, in little things. Like labels. He wanted to put a label on me too, a label that read: Mine. This woman belongs to me. Hands off.'

'What's wrong with that?'

'Nothing to a man. Nothing to most women. But I didn't like it.'

'You married him.' It was almost an accusation.

'Yes. Yes, I did. I was eighteen. Do you want to hear about it?'

'No.'

'No, I don't expect you do. I couldn't tell you, anyway. It was just one of those things – like you and me, a mistake.'

He looked at her, acknowledged her with his eyes for the first time in half an hour.

'Are we a mistake?'

'Of course. We're a mistake because I'm twenty-three and

you're nineteen. We're a mistake because you're in the Marines and soon you'll be on your way to God knows where. We're a mistake because I've slept with a dozen men and you can't forgive me for it; because you're frightened I'd sleep with a dozen more.'

'Would you?'

'Yes. If the mood took me, yes.'

'You bitch.' He levered himself up from the table. 'Christ, you bitch. Bell was right. You'd lay it on the line for anyone, anyone at all. What's the matter with you – are you ill or something? You must be. And I must be, risking my neck to come and see you. You're not worth it. You're not bloody worth it!'

You're cheap and dirty. You're a prostitute but you don't take money. You live between your legs. That's all you live for.

I know.

'I know, Mike, I know. You'd better go now.'

His anger became self-pity as he picked up his cigarettes and put them in his pocket. He paused by the door, willing her to call him back, wake him up, tell him it was all a bad dream.

She was looking the other way.

He slammed the door behind him, and the noise of wood against wood made her start. She bit her lip. She would cry tonight, cry and get it over with. New tears, old tears, temporary tears. Temporary tears. There'd be other Mike Porters, Stan Bells. Oh yes, there'd be others.

In the street he started to walk. Aimlessly. A light mist drifted in from the river, and he shivered. His thoughts were a kaleidoscope of fact, fiction, and self-deception.

No more Carol. Finish Carol. Christ, well out of that. Little tart. Little whore. Meant nothing to her. Nothing. Everything she said was lies. All those other bastards. A dozen. *Dozen.* More like a hundred. Get it in the neck when I get back to camp. Right in the neck. *Chop.* Stupid bugger. She'd have it off with anyone. Anyway, had one woman. One notch. Got to begin somewhere. Wonder if I can hitch a lift. Jesus, don't even know which direction the camp is. And I'm tired. Dead tired. Christ, the bitch. The bitch.

He dismissed the faint voice at the back of his mind which

jibed: But that's what you were after, a bitch, a tart. You and Webster, remember? You weren't looking for a wife or a sister or a mother. Remember? Don't blame her for being what she is.

After a while he sat on a low wall. His eyes were heavy with sleep, and he dozed. He was muttering quietly to himself when the policeman tapped him on the shoulder.

Webster broke the news to the others the following morning.

'Guess what, I've just seen Porter being wheeled into Leigh's office. Hayter's there too.'

'Is he under arrest?'

'Hayter?'

'Porter, you daft sod.'

'I should say he is! He's got a bloody big RP on either side of him.'

'Why's Leigh dealing with it? AWOL's a CO's offence.'

'CO's away,' said Riordan. 'So is Major Rowe. Leigh's senior captain.'

'Lucky bastard, old Porter,' said Thatcher. 'Rowe would've put him inside for a month.'

'Dunno about lucky,' murmured Riordan. 'Cells is cells. He's shit it in Spades whichever way you look at it.'

Queen's Regulations. Para this, Section that, Sub-section the other. RSM with a countenance like the wrath of God. Leigh listening to the charge. Impassive.

A boy in uniform cannot plead youth and inexperience in mitigation.

The charge, is it understood?

Affirmative.

The accused has rights. The accused may call witnesses. The accused can opt for trial by court martial. The accused must bear in mind, however, that a court martial can mete out heavy punishment.

Understood?

Affirmative.

The accused may speak in his own defence.

Negative.

What, the accused has no excuses?

Negative.

AWOL is a serious charge.

Understood.

Then excuse your conduct.

Silence.

A nuisance. A damned nuisance. Truth will be punished more severely than an effective lie.

Sergeant Hayter will testify as to the accused's previous record.

Excellent.

He is a good Marine?

He has worked hard.

Thank you.

The accused will step forward. Seven days' detention.

Thank you.

Carry on, RSM.

Pris'ner an' escort, right turn. To the guard-room, dismiss. Left right . . .

Post-mortem:

Why do they do it, RSM?

Lord knows, sir. Lack o' discipline at home.

Perhaps.

A signature scribbled at the foot of an indictment sheet. A record blemished.

Next case.

The detention cells are small. Suffocating. Whitewash covers the walls. Here and there previous inmates have drawn lewd pictures in pencil. A single naked bulb, permanently lit, casts pale shadows. The light seems inadequate during the day, but at night it burns the eyeballs. In the door is a grille. It squeaks when it is opened, but the guard is too lazy or indifferent to have it oiled. In one corner stands a bed. When unoccupied, the sheets and blankets must be folded and stacked at the foot. Near the bed is a locker, inside which are the prisoner's uniforms and equipment. Each morning the uniforms and equipment must be taken from the locker and laid neatly on the floor. The duty officer inspects this kit-muster. If he is not satisfied, if an item is dirty or unpressed, the prisoner is ordered to re-lay his kit within the hour.

The lavatory is at the end of the detention block. For permission to relieve himself the prisoner must tap on the cell door. A guard accompanies him, and watches. Some of the guards make crude remarks, but the prisoner learns to live with this. Ignominy is the least of his worries, and at night he is given a bucket.

The prisoner's day begins at five-thirty AM. The rest of the camp sleep while he washes and shaves and scrubs his cell with an inadequate brush.

Before breakfast he is drilled for an hour by an instructor who resents this early morning imposition, and who vents his anger on the prisoner. The regulations forbid the prisoner being forced to march with his rifle held out, at arm's length, in front of him. It is also forbidden to double the prisoner for more than five minutes, or to make him stand to attention for long periods. The regulations are invariably breached. The prisoner is in no position to protest.

At breakfast he is flanked by two RPs whose job it is to see that he gets the minimum possible time to eat his food. Afterwards he returns to the parade ground, where he marches and counter-marches until he is ready to drop. When he is not marching he is cleaning, and when he is not cleaning he is marching.

Throughout the day he is required to wear four or more different uniforms. All must be spotless. He is inspected regularly.

In the evening, within the confines of his cell, he is permitted to write a letter or read a book. For the most part he does neither, but instead sits and stares at the wall, sometimes smirking at the sight of a cleverly etched woman's organ. Occasionally he listens for outside noises: laughter, chatter. He hears little. The cells are isolated. He thinks about his guards and wonders why a man chooses to become an RP. Is it a calling like the Church? If it is, what is it about the novitiate's chemistry that makes him quickly learn how to punctuate an order with a blow to the kidneys?

Soon he will be instructed to undress and go to bed. There

he will toss and turn, hug his warmest parts, pray perhaps, resist the temptation to masturbate for fear that he will be discovered. He has heard stories of what happens to prisoners caught masturbating. Cruel, sadistic stories.

In his solitude he longs for a friendly voice, a reassuring word. But he knows he is alone. Inevitably he remembers happier times.

Tomorrow the pattern will be repeated, a pattern designed to punish. Detention is not intended to rehabilitate. The reformers are in another world.

Scrub. Clean.

March. Drill.

And let that be a lesson to you.

And the next day will be the same.

And the next . . .

Thatcher and Webster were alone in Hut 8, playing cards, on the evening Porter was released. When he came in, he nodded briefly but did not speak. They watched him cross to his bunk and unpack his large kit-bag.

'What about a game of cards?' called Thatcher.

'No thanks.'

'What was it like?' asked Webster, and winced as Thatcher kicked him on the shin.

Porter smiled vacantly. 'I've lived in better places,' he said.

And that was as much as any of them ever got out of him.

The Thursday of their passing out dawned. It had been a hell of a week. Hayter had vowed, at the beginning of their training, that they would be the best Squad ever, and he seemed determined to live up to his promise in blood. Their blood.

From Monday they drilled for six hours a day. They sloped arms, ordered arms, fixed bayonets, slow marched, quick marched until their bodies throbbed. But they no longer minded the weariness. They accepted the sweat and the blisters. They cursed, true, but their oaths were simply the ritualistic grumblings of the trained Marine. They were a unit now, and they had their own particular pride. To them their webbing was the cleanest, their backs the straightest, their boots the shiniest, and their drill the most precise. Not one of them thought of himself as a butcher or baker or candlestick-maker any more. They were Marines, fighting troops, members of a corps d'elite. They had green Commando berets which bore witness to the fact that they could run faster and further than the ordinary soldier, climb mountains like Sherpas, shoot the eye from a fly at two hundred yards. Their powers of endurance were indisputable, and other, lesser, men would stare at them with awe.

Übermensch.

At two o'clock on Thursday they were on the parade ground. The sun was high and white, the trees motionless, and from a distance, in their dark-blue dress uniforms, they resembled a child's playthings. Immobile aluminium figures awaiting a five-year-old general. To their left stood the reviewing party: The CO, the Adjutant, Captain Leigh. Solemn faces perspiring genteelly, panting for a large gin and angostura with ice.

'428 Squad . . .'

They stiffened as Hayter's stentorian voice pierced the quiet of the afternoon. Each man gripped his rifle more tightly, squared his shoulders, and waited for the first command.

'. . . 428 Squad – 'shun. Open order maarch. Raight dress. Salope aarms. Pree-sehnt aarms.'

Hayter marched to within four paces of the CO, and saluted.

'428 Squad all present and correct and ready for inspection, sir.'

'Very good. Carry on, sergeant.'

'Thank you, sir.' He turned. '428 Squad – salope aarms. Order aarms. Second and third ranks, stand at ease.'

The CO began his inspection at the extreme right of the Squad, with Rourke, and made his way slowly down the front rank. Every so often he stopped and had a word with one or another of the recruits. His questions were purely automatic, however; a well-worn routine. He scarcely listened to the answers – that was not his function.

'How have you enjoyed your time here?'

'Very much, sir.'

And:

'What were you in civilian life?'

'A fitter, sir.'

And, unfortunately, to Thatcher:

'Ever thought of signing on?'

'*No*, sir.'

Thatcher's negative was emphatic enough to bring a smile to even the Adjutant's face. But Hayter was not amused. The scowl he gave Thatcher said: Just wait till I get you alone, my lad.

'Second rank – 'shun. Front rank, stand at ease.'

In the middle of the third rank Riordan could hardly contain himself. This was it. He would soon know whether he was top recruit.

The CO barely gave him a second glance when, finally, the third rank was inspected, and his heart sank. He'd missed it. It wasn't him. The bastards. All that work for nothing. The lousy bastards.

The inspection complete, Hayter asked the CO for permission to drill the Squad.

'Carry on, sergeant. But no more than five minutes. It's a warm day.'

So for five minutes 428 Squad executed a variety of drill movements – almost unobserved. The officers had things to talk about.

'Seen the Movement Order, John?' said the CO.

'Yes, sir. I wish I was going with them.'

'To Cyprus? Not with your leg. In any case, it's not exactly a pleasure resort and it'll get a damn' sight worse before long.' He stroked his thin moustache with a fore-finger. 'I'd like to tell them about it if you've no objections.'

'By all means, sir.'

'Good. Oh, who's your top man, incidentally?'

Leigh gave him a slip of paper on which was typed a name – a name decided a fortnight earlier by the toss of a coin.

'Riordan, eh.' He glanced at his wristwatch. 'Try to catch your sergeant's eye, will you? I said five minutes and he's taking ten. Oh, don't bother, he's got the message.'

Hayter brought the Squad to a standstill.

'Stand them at ease, sergeant. I want to have a few words with them.'

'Yes, sir. 428 Squad – stand at ease.'

The CO cleared his dry, gin-starved throat.

'First, the award for the top recruit. 421885 Marine Riordan, T.'

'Marine Riordan!' bawled Hayter. 'Two paces step forward maarch. Left turn. Quick maarch. Left right . . .'

Riordan, unable to believe his ears, came to a halt and presented arms. Jesus, they'd picked him. Jesus Christ.

The CO handed him the rectangle of blue cloth. 'Well done, Riordan. I expect to see you a corporal before you leave the Corps.'

'Thank you, sir.'

Riordan rejoined the Squad, grinning fiercely.

'There'll be no holdin' him now,' muttered Thatcher.

'Secondly,' the CO went on, adopting his best land-of-hope-and-glory voice, 'your training is at an end. You are Royal Marines now, not raw recruits. And as Royal Marines your duty will be wherever there is trouble. You have earned your green berets, and the time has come to show your mettle.'

Somewhere, someone whistled Colonel Bogey, inaudibly.

'Most of you will read the newspapers and you will have observed that during the past weeks the island of Cyprus has figured prominently. So has the world's latest terrorist organization, EOKA, whose sworn policy it is to unite Cyprus with Greece. Greece, of course, has never had a valid claim to Cyprus. The island belongs to Britain. It is vital strategically.

'Until a few days ago EOKA was no more than a nuisance. It had dynamited power stations and the like and terrorized a lot of harmless villagers, but it had not actually killed anyone. But since last Tuesday it has started to kill, and the Royal Marines have been given part of the task of stopping and smashing it. 49 Commando is already on its way from Malta, and you, all of you, will join 49 immediately after embarkation leave. I know you'll do a good job.' He paused. 'March them off, sergeant.'

'Yes, sir.'

The Squad left the parade ground for the last time.

'Fine set of chaps,' said the CO. 'Fine set of chaps. Now I think we've earned that drink.'

The grape and the grain reigned supreme in the Naafi that night, and leave pay was spent as though tomorrow were a lie. In between unsteady trips from tables to bar and back again, the talk centred on Cyprus.

'Bunch o' bleedin' wogs,' jeered Shaw, emphasizing his sanguine hypothesis by thrusting his beer mug under Thatcher's nose and belching loudly. 'Bunch o' gollies with pitchforks.'

'Zat so. So how do you dynamite a power station with a pitchfork, eh? Answer me that. They got modern weapons, boyo, and don't you forget it.'

'He's right,' agreed Webster. 'I read it in the papers. They've got rifles and brens. There's a real war going on out there.'

'Well, we'll handle 'em, rifles or not. Just lead me to 'em. Wogs don't know anything about fighting.'

'What about Joe Louis?'

'Eh?'

'Joe Louis. What about him?'

'That's different.'

'You're nuts.'

'Who is?' Shaw recalled New Street and Corporation Street and coffee-coloured hands on the wheels of brand-new motor-cars. The injustice of it all. 'Who's nuts? Look, what have the gollies ever done for the world? They're only good for poncing and bumming. You should live in Birmingham, Thatcher, you'd sing a different tune then. A white bloke can't walk a dozen yards without seeing a crowd of them propped up against a street corner. They do sod all. Sod all. So don't talk to me about gollies.'

'Okay, okay,' said Thatcher, anxious not to start anything.

Webster ran his fingers through a pool of beer and wiped them on his tunic.

'Well, I'm not looking forward to it,' he said. 'I'm too young to get shot at. A guy could get killed.'

Thatcher grinned wickedly. 'Aah, they don't aim for your head, these Cyps. They aim for your goolies.'

'Crap.'

'It's true. It's a trick they've picked up. I heard about it on the news. And with goolies like yours, Webbo, it'll be like shootin' at a barn door from three feet with a cannon.'

'Crap and double crap. You're a bloody liar, Thatcher, you always have been.' He chuckled. 'But if that's how it is, they'll need telescopic sights and a guided missile to hit yours.'

'Ya cheeky sod! Quality counts, mate, not quantity. Anyway, quit yappin' and get the drinks in. It's your round.'

Webster collected the glasses.

At the other end of the table Riordan murmured for the fiftieth time, 'I never thought I'd get it.'

He had the strip of blue cloth in an empty match-box and every two minutes, like a programmed robot, he opened the match-box and gazed wide-eyed at his prize.

'I never thought I'd get it,' he said for the fifty-first time.

'You earned it,' said Rourke.

'Oh, I dunno 'bout that. I loused up the ordnance survey test, and Barker and Owen were in with a chance.'

'You earned it,' reiterated Rourke, and added to himself: Now for Chrissake knock it off.

He sipped his beer and wondered how he was going to tell Mary that he'd soon be en route to Cyprus. She'd throw twenty fits when she found out. Malta would have been bad enough, but Cyprus – Jesus.

'How d'you tell your wife you're going to Cyprus?' he asked Porter.

'Search me.'

'You're a big help.'

'Do a Kitchener, then.'

'A what?'

'A Kitchener. Your Country Needs You.'

'Oh, that. Wouldn't wash – she'd say she needs me more.' He shook his head: sometimes it was a bastard, being married. 'You're lucky, you unmarried blokes.'

'Lucky?'

'Dead lucky.'

Lucky, thought Porter. Well, yes, that was one way of putting it. Lucky to have got seven days instead of fourteen. Lucky to have the sort of father who wrote: 'Your letter distressed your mother and me more than I can ever explain. When you were called up I had great hopes. Now these are so much dust. Didn't you consider us when you did what you did? Have you no feelings for your parents? And why write to us about it, anyway? You could have kept us in ignorance.' Lucky to have a father who preferred the blissful pink-iced, green-lawned ignorance of Surrey to the truth – even if that truth had been revealed deliberately to hurt. Lucky to have that kind of home to go to for embarkation leave. Lucky – yes, it was possible.

'Oh, balls!' he ejaculated suddenly.

'Balls what?' said Rourke.

'Balls to everything. Come on, let's have your glasses.'

The evening wore on and the Squad got more and more drunk. Sentences were left unfinished as speaker or listener disappeared slowly, like a stone in quicksand, under the table. The two Naafi girls who usually served behind the bar had been given the night off because the camp authorities could not guarantee their safety or chastity when a Squad passed out. And 428 were passing out in style.

'They get their weapons from the Russians, you know,' yelled Webster, peering through the haze at Thatcher, who was standing on a chair, a mug of beer balanced on his forehead.

'Shurrup! I'm conencrat . . . consten . . . Shurrup!'

Webster turned to Shaw. 'They get their weapons from the Russians.'

'Who do?'

'The Cyps. The bloody Cyps.'

'That's crap.'

'It isn't.'

Webster underlined his argument by thumping Thatcher's chair.

'Ya clumsy bugger, Webbo! Watch it.'

'Webster says the Russians supply the Cyps with guns.'

'I'm right too.'

'You're daft, Webbo. You're just anti-commie.'

'And I suppose you're for them.'

'That's right.' Thatcher spread his arms and sang at the top of his voice. '*Though cowards flinch and traitors fear, we'll keep the Red Flag flyin' here.* I learned that from me dad. He was as Red as an Indian's bum.'

They say that the camp is a wonderful place,
But the organization's a bleedin' disgrace . . .

'Come on, lads, sing up.'

There's corporals and sergeants and RSMs too . . .

'Hey, Porter, cheer up.'

'Get knotted.'

'And you. Where's Riordan? Riordan should stand us all a drink.'

'Listen, I'm right about those Ruskies . . .'

'Bang, bang, bang. That's three Cyps dead. Can I have a golly-killing medal, sir?'

''Course you can. VD and scar for Shaw. Hip-hip hooray . . .'

'*A married man's got problems, and his problem's in his bed. A married man's got a load of bills, but he ends up just as dead.*'

'I never thought I'd get it. I never thought it'd be me.'

I grabbed a knife and the missus grabbed a broom,
And we chased the bloody lobster round and round the room,
Singing Ro-tiddli-o . . .

'Watch what you're doing with that beer, Thatcher!'

'Balls! This is a good trick.'

'Pull his pants off.'

'Touch me, Webbo, and I'll have you. I swear I will.'

'Get the drinks in, Riordan.'

'Bar's closed.'

'Already? Jesus!'

They staggered back to Charlie Company, singing and shouting, happy that they were going home in the morning. They passed a couple of recruits from 430 Squad, doing guard duty, and they laughed and catcalled. No more of that for them.

'There's just one thing,' hiccuped Webster, as Shaw and Riordan carried him into the hut. 'Where the hell's Cyprus?'

PART TWO

TEN

It was hot. Sticky heat. Down on the plains it would be worse, a hundred-plus, but that was no comfort. Winged insects that a second or two before had been sleeping or reproducing congregated about his face. He brushed them aside. They buzzed angrily and regrouped. A rock lizard poked its brown-green skull out and thought better of moving. Somewhere a snake dozed.

He crawled forward on his stomach to the top of the ridge and peered through his field-glasses to scan the valley ahead. Nothing stirred. The stillness was absolute.

He switched on the 88-set.

'Sunray to 3 Section, Sunray to 3 Section. Quiet as a graveyard. Come up. Over.'

The earphones crackled. '3 Section. Wilco. Out.'

He turned, and several hundred feet below saw his Section Sergeant, Hayter, emerge from the undergrowth and deploy the men with the swift, accomplished gestures of someone who has seen it all and done it all before. And he wondered, momentarily, how long it would take him to acquire that kind of easy professionalism.

He took a cigarette from a packet marked Duty Free, Forces Only, and lit it. Two keen blue eyes watched the smoke billow skywards; eyes that occasionally glittered with a quality that would be called fanaticism by some and be overlooked by others. The August sun burned down, but somehow he remained incongruously pale. Like the rest of the Section, he had been in Cyprus for two months.

Back at base camp they had a dossier on Second-lieutenant Langley. It was filed between Hargreaves, L. S., Lieutenant, and Mayhew, F., Captain. Part of it read: Langley, Brian Keith. Age 22. Cambridge. Second in History. Father,

Brigadier (Ret'd) R. E. W. Langley, VC, DSO and Bar. Mother dec'd. Personal remarks: A promising if sometimes impetuous officer.

It might have added that he graduated from Officers' School in the middle of his class, and that he had been a fully-fledged second-lieutenant since May.

He puffed at the cigarette. It tasted good. Damned good. It was his first for two hours.

From where he lay, high up on the southern slopes of the Troodos mountains, he could see mile after mile of Aleppo pine, and the sweet, fresh smell of the trees hung heavy in his nostrils. Above him towered Mount Olympus – sinister, forbidding: a composite of ten thousand polygonal crags hewn by the chisel of some son of Zeus an eternity before God was born. Its six thousand feet sheltered imperial eagles which now and again left the dark flanks of home to soar and wheel overhead. Majestic predators dinner hunting. In the valley a clear stream bubbled and chuckled over grey shale. Further south the foothills and vineyards stretched almost to Limassol, while to the north, out of sight, the mediaeval bastions of Nicosia guarded the central plain.

And in the streets of Nicosia – the narrow, dusty, fly-blown streets – and on the waterfronts of Limassol and Famagusta, the EOKA gunmen mixed with the crowds. They were youngsters, most of them; youngsters with brilliantined hair and white gigolo's teeth and sudden death under their armpits. Their faces were as yet unfamiliar to the police and the Security Forces, and they were able to strut and plan with impunity. They killed when they got an Order. They killed quickly and pitilessly from behind: a son from Bradford, a brother from Cardiff, a husband from Glasgow. And then they ran.

The villages of the middle slopes grew the reddest apples and cherries, bred a race that cared little for progress, and spawned hundreds of tiny cafés whose terraces were permanently occupied by bearded coffee-sipping officials of the Greek Orthodox Church.

And from the villages the mountain gunmen, the hard core, demanded protection and food. They took what they wanted in the name of patriotism: wine, bread, the prettiest of the village girls.

No one argued with them. It was useless to oppose someone whose voice was a pilfered Browning or a captured sten. In any case, the young men were fighting for liberty, weren't they? For liberty and prosperity. The Church said so.

On the tortuous roads from the mountains to the plains shepherds, looking like extras in a Bible movie, tended small flocks of hardy sheep, and women, all in black and toothless, with faces as old as suffering and as creased as parchment, accompanied dwarf donkeys on unknown errands. Barefoot girls, who would have been at school had there been enough schools, herded skulking goats and sometimes smiled at the soldiers. But not often these days. They were learning how to hate.

I swear in the name of the Holy Trinity that:

I shall work with all my power for the liberation of Cyprus from the British yoke, sacrificing for this my life;

I shall perform without objection all the instructions of the organization which may be entrusted to me, and I shall not bring any objection, however difficult and dangerous these may be;

I shall not abandon the struggle unless I receive instructions from the leader of the organization and after our aim has been accomplished;

I shall never reveal to anyone any secret of our organization even if I am caught and tortured;

I shall not reveal any of the instructions which may be given to me even to my fellow combatants;

If I disobey my oath, I shall be worthy of every punishment as a traitor, and may eternal contempt cover me.

Signed: Dighenis.

Langley looked round as someone came up behind him. It was Hayter. The sergeant stared curiously at the officer's cigarette.

'Are we taking a break, sir?'

'We are, sergeant. It'll be dark in a couple of hours. We might as well eat now. Tell the men they've got thirty minutes then rejoin me here. I want to discuss tactics.'

'Very good, sir.'

Hayter scrambled back forty or fifty feet to where he had left the Section. Tactics, he thought with disgust. Christ, anyone would think Langley was on the General Staff.

'You've got half an hour to eat,' he said, 'but that doesn't mean you can relax. Keep your eyes open and don't bunch. Riordan, you and Porter mount the bren over by that big rock.'

'Can we smoke, sergeant?' asked Webster.

'Yes. But bury your dog-ends when you've finished. This lot'll go up like paper if it as much as sniffs a spark. Is that set on, Klein?'

It was Klein's turn to carry the second 88-set.

'Yes, sergeant.'

'Then kill it. Those batteries have got to last a few hours yet.'

'Yes, sergeant. Bastard,' he muttered, as Hayter walked off.

The Section found the nearest thing to shade and mopped its corporate brow. Jesus, it was murder, the heat.

The Section was part of D Troop, 49 Commando, based at Platres, a village in the Troodos range. It comprised: Second-lieutenant Langley, Sergeant Hayter, Riordan and Porter, the bren team, Thatcher, Webster, Rourke, Shaw, and Klein, riflemen, and Costas, the interpreter. It was on a routine seek-and-destroy patrol, its seventh. It had seen action on four of the previous six patrols.

It had seen action in Amiandos, a mining village, where it had surprised an EOKA saboteur in the act of planting a home-made bomb in the main shaft. The saboteur had surrendered after one of Hayter's bullets had buried itself in his thigh. It had seen action on Olympus, where it had ambushed two teenage boys as they buried a case of stolen grenades. One of the boys had given himself up immediately. The other chose to die, and failed. He would simply never walk again, not with a splintered spine. It had seen action in Kyrenia, on a motorized mission, where it had arrived just too late to prevent the reprisal slaughter of two British civilians, a man and his wife, who had been dragged from their car. The woman had been raped and strangled; the man beaten and then shot in the stomach at point-blank range with a shotgun. It had taken him a long time to die, but his killers had paid for that with an eight o'clock walk to the scaffold. It had seen action outside Platres, where the fifteen-year-old mistress of an

EOKA gunman had witnessed the felo de se death of her noose-bound lover before pulling the pin of a grenade and holding it against her temple.

It had seen action, been sick at the sight of blood and decimation, asked itself the unanswerable question Why, and gradually hardened to inevitability. It chose not to think about the next time, when it knew that the conditioned reflexes of self-preservation would take the decisions and responsibility from it.

Thatcher broke open a 24-hour ration pack and held up a tin.

'Christ, Irish bleedin' stew again. They should try floggin' this in Dublin. What you got, Webbo?'

'Steak-and-kidney.'

'I'll swop you.'

'You bloody won't. That stuff runs straight through you.'

Thatcher tried Klein.

'What about it, Moisie? I'll swop you my beautiful Irish stew for your lousy steak-and-kid. As a favour to you. They eat stew all the time in Israel, don't they?'

'How should I know? I lived in Dalston all my life.'

'Bloody Cockney.'

Klein grinned. Thatcher was okay. He was not anti-Semitic, not like Shaw.

He had stopped marvelling and analysing men of Shaw's mould years ago. They existed, and that was that. It was something a Jew had to live with.

He recalled his father telling him about the pre-war days in the East End, where even intelligent men blamed the Jews for the world's misfortunes. Fascist banners, burning torches, smashed windows, looted shops, inflammatory speeches, parades. *Juden raus. Juden raus.* 'They call us usurers,' his father had said. 'We suck the blood of the Gentiles.' And then he would chuckle. 'Usurers. And me looking yet for next week's rent.' Well, at least all that was dead and gone. They had a country of their own now, a country he would see one day. It didn't matter in Israel that a Jew wasn't Orthodox. Everyone was welcome. They were crying out for immigrants. Hell, it would be great to walk along streets where no one spat,

Dirty Jew, where there were no Shaws. Well, one day, when he'd saved enough. One day.

Rourke speared a soggy potato with his fork.

'I reckon old Langley's picked a dud this time,' he said. 'I'll bet there are no EOKA for ten miles.'

'Could be,' grunted Thatcher.

'Bloody hope so,' murmured Webster.

'Tripe,' said Shaw, wiping his forehead with his beret. 'They're here somewhere. I can smell 'em.'

'Lend us your crystal ball, colonel.'

'Lend us your nose.'

'They invisible or something?'

'What d'you think they are, bloody elves? If they were here we'd see 'em.'

'Not if they didn't want us to,' said Shaw. 'There are dozens of places a bloke could hide. Over there, in those rocks, or down there, in the trees.'

They followed his pointing finger, and thought: Perhaps there is someone there, correcting his sights or clipping on a fresh magazine. They moved closer to their rifles.

Webster shivered. 'You give me the bloody creeps.'

'Doesn't take much to give you the creeps, does it?' sneered Shaw.

'What's that supposed to mean?'

'Just that if somebody sneezes you're doing it in your pants.'

'Crap.'

'That's it.'

'Now listen . . .'

'Stuff it, you two,' said Rourke, tearing the wrapper off a packet of hard biscuits.

'He can't talk to me like that,' complained Webster. 'I do my bit.'

' 'Course you do. Tell him he does his bit, Shaw, for Chrissake.'

Shaw grinned. 'Okay, so he does his bit.'

Bastard, thought Webster. Lousy bastard. Typical Shaw. Typical bloody Shaw. It was all very well for him because he didn't care if he copped it or not. He was a nut; always the first to let fly when the order came to open fire, always the last to quit shooting. The sort of nut who wouldn't be satisfied until he'd killed someone or got the rest of the Section killed. Well, that wasn't for ol' Roy. Jesus, no. There was nothing wrong in playing it cool, and to hell with Shaw.

Shaw gargled a mouthful of water, swallowed some, spat the rest into his cupped hands and soaked his blond hair. Webster, he mused with pleasure, was scared. Scared shitless, witless, and purple. It was a funny thing, that, but guys who had a lot to do with women, who made a religion of it, always had a yellow streak a mile wide. Guys like Webster. And Rourke too, in a way, though Rourke had his reasons now, what with the kid and all. But women turned a man chicken. A man got tied up with a wife or steady and straight off he had to think twice before he did anything. It wasn't worth it. A man should do whatever he wanted to do or chuck up his badge.

He recorked his water-bottle.

A yard or two away Rourke scooped out a handful of the hard brown earth, thought absently that nothing would grow here, and buried an empty steak-and-kidney tin. As he bent forward to wipe his fork on a tuft of yellowish grass, his knee touched the breast-pocket of his shirt, and he felt the reassuring crackle of Mary's latest letter. It was a week old and he had read it and read it, but he had not yet grown accustomed to the idea that he would be a father in a few months. March had she said, or was it April? He took out the letter: late March or early April. 'I didn't tell you before, darling, because I had to have some tests. It must have happened at the end of your leave.' He remembered his leave. Christ, they'd had a ball and a half. 'Is there any chance of you getting home? Will you ask? Even a week would be something. Please ask. You will, won't you?' He wouldn't. The answer would be No. They would only allow him to go home if there was a danger of Mary dying. Jesus, the bloody rules they had. His son – it had to be a boy – would be six or eight months old before he saw him. It was a sod.

He read on: 'Take care good of yourself. If anything were to happen . . .' Nothing would happen. He'd make sure of that. They needed him more than ever now – both of them.

'Read us a good bit, Tim,' cracked Thatcher.

'You don't get good bits in a wife's letter.'

' 'Course you do. Let's have a pash bit.'

'Okay, you read me one of yours and I'll read you one of mine.' He stopped. Thatcher never received letters. 'Well, I mean . . .'

'Skip it. Toss us your matches.'

'Catch.'

Thatcher lit a cigarette and lay back, shielding his eyes with his beret. It would be all right, he thought, to get a letter once in a while – from one of his brothers, maybe, or one of his mates. He'd like to know what was going on up in Manchester. But you had to write one to get one. In any case, they didn't have time, his brothers. They'd never had much time.

Over by the big rock Riordan cleaned the back-sight of the bren with a match-stick.

'Where d'you reckon we're heading?' he said.

'North,' answered Porter, checking the bren magazines to ensure that none of the shells had jammed. He was Riordan's number two on the bren, which meant that while Riordan did the actual shooting, he, Porter, carried and reloaded the magazines.

'That'd be my guess, too. That's where they'll be. Jeeze, a guy could get lost for ever in that forest.'

He polished the barrel of the bren with his sleeve. It was the best damned bren in the Troop, the most accurate. He'd spent hours zeroing it on the base range.

Porter sat in the shade of the rock, leaning against it. It was cool on his neck. The sky above was blue, like a lake, a cloudless canopy. He thought how glorious it would be to dive in and disappear.

'Don't go to sleep,' warned Riordan. 'Hayter's watching us.'

'Up Hayter.'

Disappear. Leave the world and its cousin to the stupid business of killing each other, and abdicate. He sucked his teeth. Students' thoughts. No room for academics out here. You didn't worry about the greater glory of mankind when someone was pointing a gun at you. You simply said to yourself: I've got to get him before he gets me. And that was the trouble. You could get used to anything in time, even killing. You threw up when you saw your first dead man; you looked the other way when you saw your second; and after that it didn't bother you. The good old human race. Great people.

Question: Why is it always the nineteen- and twenty-year-olds who do the fighting in every war? Why are the casualties in the forty-plus category infinitesimal?

Answer: Because everyone over forty is a politician.

Question: What's wrong with politicians?

Answer: Nothing, except that they lounge in chairs by Chippendale, stroke their dewlaps, eat breakfast at nine and barter lives at ten, and urge: 'Get on with it, lads. We'll come to an honourable settlement when the blood covers our spats.'

Question: Makarios, you mean?

Answer: And Eden and Eisenhower and Mao and Kruschev. They're all in the game for what they can get out of it: Power, prestige, the right to have their memoirs made compulsory reading for university entrance in a hundred years.

Question: Hasn't it always been like that?

Answer: No. Not a few centuries ago or in a fairy tale. A fairy tale, for starters. There the dragon is evil and the knight virtuous. And up to circa 1900 the sovereign was right and his enemies wrong. Harold was good and the Conqueror wicked. Now, today, black is white and white is black. You can't tell the difference.

Question: But you've got to believe in something, even if it's only your own side. Haven't you?

Answer: Right. So bloody right. We are Just and they are Not. It's called self-deception.

Question: So why don't you desert?

Answer: Are you crazy? Nobody stands up for his principles any longer.

'Ten minutes,' shouted Hayter.

Behind Porter, Costas, the Greek-Cypriot interpreter, ate alone. He wore a khaki bush-jacket several sizes too large over the upper half of his body, and on his head perched a workman's cloth cap. He rarely spoke unless spoken to, and when he answered a question he did so with his sad eyes as well as his voice. He was forty and had been his village's schoolteacher until one of the local police had discovered that he refused to indoctrinate his pupils with Enosis.

His pupils. Eight- to ten-year-olds who could scarcely write their names.

He knew that one day he would be killed. It was a fact as inevitable as the winter snow on Olympus. Grivas or Drakos or Afxentiou or Ashiotis – one of them would kill him, as they had killed his brother; a brother whose only crime had been to call Grivas a power-drunk fool, a fool who was attempting to emulate the Hitler he had helped defeat. They had left him in the street for a whole day as a warning, and no one had dared bury the body or comfort the widow.

To EOKA he was a traitor. To himself he was a teacher who had been barred from teaching, a brother who had lost a brother, a father who had powerlessly witnessed a priest administer the EOKA oath to his eldest son Doros – a more than eager twelve-year-old who longed to do greater things for the cause than just spy on his parents – and a man who had acquired the habit of hating the smouldering hatred of the bereaved. He had no solution to Cyprus' problems. He was a simple man who knew only one thing: that God was not on the side of the priests and the plunderers and the glory-seekers; that God was on his side.

O Theos ine me to meros mas.

'Five minutes.'

Up on the ridge Langley had a map spread out in front of him. He stabbed a forefinger at a spot shaded dark-brown.

'About there,' he said. 'That's where the intelligence report put them.'

'It'll mean losing wireless contact with Platres, sir,' said Hayter.

'We've already lost it, sergeant. I tried them on the 88 an hour ago. Dead as Memphis.'

'Sir?'

'Dead as . . . Never mind. Dead anyway.'

'They might send out a search party.'

'Not them. I told Captain Miller he probably wouldn't hear from us until tomorrow morning. He won't worry before then.'

Hayter studied the map. His training and experience told him that losing contact with base was lunacy, but he kept quiet. He was only an NCO. The officers had the brains. Huh.

'By road or across country, sir?'

'By road, I think. It'll take longer but it'll be less tiring on the men.'

'The men are fit.'

'No doubt, sergeant, no doubt. But we'll do it my way. We'll go down either side of the road. You'll lead one column and I'll lead the other. I'll take the bren team and Costas. You can have the remainder. Who's got the other 88-set?'

'Klein, sir.'

'Okay, he'll bring up the rear. I'll keep to the right-hand side. The two groups will stay about one hundred yards apart.'

'A hundred yards, sir? That's a hell of a gap for half a Section. You could be cut off and we'd never get to you.'

'A hundred yards,' said Langley, firmly.

Hayter shook his head. 'I don't like it, sir.'

'No one's asking you to like it. Just do it, sergeant.'

Hayter reddened under his sunburn at Langley's imperious, don't-argue-with-me tone.

'Yes, sir. I'll get the men on their feet.'

'Do that. We'll join the road about a quarter of a mile beyond the stream. Arrowhead formation until we get there.'

'Yes, sir.'

Bloody swine, thought Hayter, as he yelled at the Section to get ready. Bloody half-witted, straight-out-of-school swine.

Langley folded his map and returned it to its case. He glanced skywards and then at his wristwatch. It would be dark in less than an hour and a half.

'Hurry it up, sergeant.'

'Right, sir. Get the lead outa your pants, Klein.'

He thought of his plan. It was a good plan. Uncomplicated – and better kept to himself. Hayter would not understand that it was necessary to split the Section in order to draw the terrorists' fire. Hayter would object to the risks. Fool. Any war entailed risks, and the winner invariably took more than the loser. That was the essence of victory. His father had taught him that much.

London. Night before embarkation. The fanciest of fancy restaurants. Champagne. Heidsieck '47, and dry.

Congratulations, Brian. I know you'll do the family name proud. Do my best, Father. *You'll have to do better than that. They'll be watching you, you see – son of a VC and all that. They'll expect great things from you. They won't mind chopping you down, either. That's human nature. But stand no nonsense – not from your superior officers, or your NCOs, who always think their stripes give them wisdom. Use your head. Forget about the book. All officers worth their salt are individualists. Can't win battles without flair. Take Monty, for example.* Yes, Father. *Monty once said to me . . . But that's another story. Just do your best, as you said. So long as your best's damned brilliant. You've got a lot to live up to.*

'Ready, sir,' called Hayter.

'Okay, let's move off.'

At the rear of the formation Thatcher pointed to the 88-set and said to Klein: 'Can you get Luxembourg on that?'

'Only if you've got big ears.'

'He's got the biggest bloody ears since Dumbo went out of business,' gagged Webster, and Thatcher blew a raspberry.

They made their descent at a point where the gradient was not too acute, and crossed the valley. They forded the stream and pressed on at a good pace, through the tall, phallic trees, and beyond. Soon they reached the road.

ELEVEN

Except for the crunch-crunch of vulcanized rubber soles on old gravel, all was quiet. They had been on the tortuous road and climbing for half an hour. To their right the ubiquitous pines stretched towards the late-afternoon sky and formed a natural fence to Olympus. To their left the valley had dropped away – several hundred feet to more pines and the silver stream. The sun had become a crimson ball low in the west, and the temperature was less suffocating.

Langley checked his map. They were closer now to the brown-shaded portion, and he approached each bend in the road with caution. If it was going, it could happen at any time.

Beside Langley walked Costas, and behind Costas Porter and Riordan with the bren. Farther back came Hayter and the others, strung out at ten-yard intervals. The altitude had begun to trouble Klein, and occasionally Thatcher slowed down to offer help.

'Okay, Moisie?'

'Sure.' *Grunt*. 'Touch o' bleedin' asthma.' *Grunt*. 'Comes of livin' on smog for twenty years.'

'Take your rifle?'

'No. C'n manage. Thanks.'

At the head of the left-hand column Hayter had understood for a quarter of an hour that Langley was deliberately exposing the Section, and he cursed his luck for getting assigned to an officer who still thought terrorists were coloured discs on a classroom blackboard. Every man was a sitting target for a sniper. One shot and somebody could kiss goodbye to demob. Screw him, the irresponsible, glory-hunting bastard. Screw him and double screw him.

Up front Langley started at the sudden rustling of a small animal foraging for its supper, and he was looking the other way when Costas touched him on the arm.

'Lieutenant. See.'

Langley saw. Coming towards them, bent double under the weight of the enormous bundle of firewood slung across his shoulders, was a wizened old man.

Langley tightened his grip on his pistol and snapped into the 88-set: 'Get up here as fast as you like. Out. Cover us,' he added to Riordan.

The old man shuffled to a halt as Langley held up his hand. Two frightened eyes peered out from beneath heavy, blue-veined lids. His face was gnarled and red-baked, his beard grey stubble, his baggy trousers and flannel jacket in rags. Sandals, held together by string, covered his feet. He tried to smile, as if to reassure himself. His gums were toothless.

Langley circled him slowly, examining the bundle of newly-cut wood.

'Ask him who he is, where he's going and why, and where he's from,' he instructed Costas.

Costas repeated the questions in Greek and translated the croaking reply.

'He is called Orfanides, lieutenant. He is from near Platres and he is returning there. He has been to collect wood.'

Langley frowned. 'From near Platres? He's come a hell of a way for fuel. Tell him I don't believe him.'

'O axiomatikos lei oti les psemata.'

The old man protested that he was telling the truth.

'He says he has no cause to lie, lieutenant,' said Costas, and added: 'This man is a simple peasant. Sometimes they will walk a great many miles to a place where the wood is best. Their lives are their own. Time is not important when there is nowhere to go.'

'I'm going to search him anyway,' said Langley. 'Tell him that.'

Costas did so, and solemnly the old man lowered his bundle to the ground. The fear in his eyes had disappeared and in its place was the patient resignation of the aged. Resignation that is almost a philosophy: of men who have witnessed but who do not understand why the world has changed.

Hayter and the rest of the Section came running up.

'What have you got there, sir?'

'I'm not sure.' Langley gave a shudder of disgust as he

caught a whiff of the old man's breath. Orfanides or whatever his name was hadn't rinsed his mouth for days and had probably never taken a bath. He smelt dreadful. 'Here, you search him, sergeant.'

Hayter grimaced. 'Me, sir?'

'You, sergeant.'

'Not exactly bristling with concealed weapons, is he?' muttered Webster. 'Any bloody idiot can see that all he wants to do is bugger off home and watch the Cyp telly.'

'Could be Grivas in disguise,' grinned Thatcher.

'Yeah, and I'm Old Mother Riley.'

'He's clean, sir,' announced Hayter, finally.

'Hardly clean, sergeant, but I take your meaning. Costas, ask him if he's seen any strangers recently.'

Costas translated. The old man held out his hand and ignored the question.

'Cigarettes?' he said, in Greek.

'He asks for cigarettes, lieutenant.'

'And I want information. Ask him again.'

'The lieutenant wishes to know if you have seen any strangers.'

'Cigarettes? The officer has cigarettes?'

'He asks again for cigarettes, lieutenant. It might make him talk.'

'To hell with that,' snorted Langley. 'I'm not a travelling shop. But if he's got information, I want it. Make sure he understands that.'

'The lieutenant insists that you answer his questions,' said Costas, patiently.

The old man shook his grey head. The negative of the rustic: no cigarettes, no information. 'Kanena ektos apo tous horikous thio vthomathes tora.'

'I am sorry, lieutenant. He will not talk. He says he has seen no one but the villagers for two weeks.'

'Oh for God's sake?' Langley scowled his exasperation. These people, these bloody people. No wonder they had never governed themselves.

'A cigarette might do the trick, sir,' said Hayter. 'It's what he's after.'

'Then give him a couple, Costas. For heaven's sake, give him a couple.'

Costas took a crumpled packet from his bush-jacket, but the old man would have none of it.

'Tsiyara Eglezous. Eglezous.'

'He will not accept these, lieutenant. He wants English cigarettes.'

'Oh my dear Lord,' said Langley wearily, acknowledging defeat. 'All right, try him with these.'

He passed over a near-full twenty-five packet of Players, and the old man's face broke into a delighted, gum-revealing smile.

'Efharisto, efharisto.'

He grasped the cigarettes with one hand and Costas' wrist with the other, and began gabbling in Greek at nineteen to the dozen. Every so often he pointed – north.

'What does he say?' demanded Langley.

'He says, lieutenant, that he saw two men, two strangers, earlier this afternoon. They were searching for something and stayed only a few minutes. But he heard one of them say that they would return.'

'Where? Where did he see them? Show me.'

Costas indicated a spot on the map, in the valley, not half a mile from where the intelligence officer had reported a sighting. Langley smacked his palm against his thigh. This was it.

'Good,' he said. 'Good. Tell him he can go. He's to mention to no one that he's spoken to us.'

Costas translated, and the old man picked up his bundle of firewood and juggled it on to his pitifully thin back. Before leaving he looked at each of the Section in turn: a calm, studious look that seemed to challenge their very existence, that compelled them, if momentarily and perhaps unconsciously, to ask themselves what the hell they were doing thousands of miles from home, bribing an aged peasant with a packet of duty-free cigarettes. A peasant who was not concerned with politics and strategic bases, who had never voted or driven a car, who had never heard of Eden or ICBMs, who had not been enmeshed in the minutiae of civilization, who knew only the best place to collect wood. And for an instant they saw that the politically conscious, the would-be world-changers and drum-bangers, were just little men with loud voices and fancy uniforms caught up in the self-destructive maelstrom of acquisition and power.

The instant passed.

'Go on, beat it,' said Hayter.

The old man left them, clutching his packet of Players as though his life depended upon it. He was soon out of sight.

'Let's move it, sergeant,' said Langley. 'Same formation as before. If my map is accurate there's some kind of track up ahead. We'll make our descent there.'

It was dark now, and cold; the sort of contrasting cold that comes on suddenly in the Mediterranean. The wind blew in from the east, causing the smaller pines to rustle and sway in a contiguous dance. Once in a while the moon poked its head above the clouds and cast an ephemeral light over the clearing. A pale light. Yellow. Yellow on green. At such times it was possible to see the outline of figures skulking amongst the trees. Amorphous shapes. Indistinct. Like cardboard cutouts. Artemis the Huntress prowled the sky. Vigilant.

The Section had been posted singly and in pairs around the perimeter of the clearing, to the north of which the omnipresent stream gurgled its way icily down to the sea. There was only one definable entrance and exit: a narrow path beaten out by some long-dead hunter or animal. Rourke had been given the job of covering this.

'Everyone in position, sergeant?'

'Yes, sir.'

'Good.'

Very good. It was going to be a long night, thought Langley, but with any luck at all the patrol would make a strike, perhaps take a prisoner. God, that would be something, a prisoner. One in the eye for the other subalterns and a leg up for him.

To Langley's left crouched Shaw, a bullet in the breech of his rifle and the safety-catch off. He waited, patiently, for the chance to kill. They would come, something told him, and in his mind he saw the look of terror on a swarthy face the second before a bullet, his bullet, reduced that face to a mass of bone and gristle.

Beyond Shaw, squatting cross-legged, Riordan made himself comfortable behind the bren. He stroked its barrel lovingly. With this in front of me, he thought, I'm the best.

'Spare mags ready?' he whispered.

'Ready,' said Porter.

'Tracer?'

'One in ten.'

Riordan grunted, satisfied. Porter was okay. You could rely on him.

'Cut the chat,' hissed Hayter. 'You wanna tell the whole world you're here?'

Christ, he lamented, National Servicemen. It wasn't right that the whole Section should consist of National Servicemen and one pretty green regular officer. It was dangerous. He'd have to mention it to Captain Miller when they got back to Platres. Not that Miller would listen to him, of course; he was only a sergeant. *Only* a sergeant. Hell, where would the Marines be without sergeants? Up the bloody Swannee, that's where. Up it without a paddle. An officer spent twelve months in school and came out with a commission. But an NCO had to spend years in the ranks before he got anywhere. It was bloody unfair. And stupid.

On the far side of the clearing Webster was jumpy. The short hairs on the nape of his neck tingled, and he had an overwhelming urge to relieve himself. You're a mug, he told himself. A real mug. You could be sitting in an office, in the Pay Corps, typing memos and wages sheets. But not you. You had to be a hero.

'Thatch,' he called, keeping his voice low.

'Yeah.'

'How'd you like to have Bardot right now? Eh, Bardot under a groundsheet?'

'I'd settle for a fag,' muttered Thatcher.

'And me,' said Klein.

'A fag an' a steak an' a pint,' drooled Thatcher. 'That's what I'm gonna have when we get back. The biggest bleedin' steak ol' Fillipedes can find. None of that cookhouse horse. How about it, eh, Moisie? You and me and Tim Rourke. Fillipedes' Bar.'

'Suits me. Christ, I could use a pint of Watney's, though, and not that Cyp piss. How d'you reckon they make it, Thatch? They pee in it?'

'Naw, their goats do.'

Klein chuckled. He was glad he had been paired off with Thatcher.

'There's a pub in Stoke Newington High Street,' he said, 'that peddles the greatest beer you've ever tasted. Strictly from kosher. When I get home I'm not going to move from that place for a month. They'll need a squad o' cops to get me out.' He smacked his lips at the Saturday-night image of pals and booze and barmaids with heavy breasts. 'And after I've been stoned out of my mind for a month, I'm gonna open a shop, that's what I'm gonna do.'

'What kind of shop?'

'Are you kidding? With a hooter like mine. Clothes, mate. Second-hand clothes. There's a fortune to be made. After that, the big time: tailoring. Got a cousin in the business. I'll go shares with him.'

'I'll buy my first civvy suit from you,' said Thatcher.

'An' you can have it at cost,' said Klein, feeling warm and generous in the glow of comradeship.

From within the trees on the left of the path, a dry twig snapped. Rourke jerked at the bolt of his rifle.

'It is I,' whispered Costas, urgently.

'*Don't do that, for Chrissake. I might've killed you.*'

'Excuse me. Where is the lieutenant?'

'Back there somewhere. Did you see anything?'

'No. I must make my report to the lieutenant.'

He moved off down the path and Rourke heard him call, 'It is I, Costas.'

Then silence.

Rourke stood in the shadows. The absence of night sounds unnerved him. No birds, no animals, just the wind and its swishing song. It made him think that the world was dead. Shaw dead. Thatcher dead. And Langley and Hayter. And

Mary. Mary dead. He would never see any of them again. They had gone. He was alone on a dead planet.

Our Father, which art in heaven, hallowed be Thy Name. Thy Kingdom come, Thy will be done . . .

The first few lines of the Lord's Prayer were mumbled without thought as the cold slime of fear crept up his spine. He knew he was scared; not of death but of loss. To die was never to see Dorset again, never to love Mary, never to cuddle his unborn son, never to dig a ditch or trim a hedge, never to do the thousand and one things that being alive meant. To die was to lose.

He felt a sharp stab of pain in his bowels, and he longed to shout to his friends, to reassure himself that they had not left him. I don't want to die. I don't want to lose. I've got a lot to live for. A wife. A child. God help us. God help us all. Thy will be done, on earth as it is in heaven. Give us this day our daily bread . . .

. . . . .

As a boy he spends much of his time in the fields. His brother is ill. He has been ill for many months, and his father has grown dependent on his younger son.

He likes working beside his father, who can lift a bale of hay as though it weighed nothing. His father's brown arms, his thick neck, his blue eyes, and his laughter: these things he notices.

They eat their lunch under an oak tree. A tractor snorts and belches dragon-like in the distance. The sandwiches are wrapped in a red polka-dot cloth. They taste delicious, and he is hungry.

Is this our farm, Dad?

No, not yet, son. It will be one day, though. Yours and Ken's.

His and his brother's. He dreams about it.

They work until dusk and then his father carries him home on his shoulders. He loves his father.

Green fields.

Yellow corn.

A skylark plummeting from out of the blue. Like a stone from the top of a cliff.

Long days. Golden days. Nothing will ever change, he thinks.

The gentleman who owns the estate holds regular shooting parties. Tim and his father act as beaters.

They've had too much to drink today, he hears his father whisper to another beater.

Ay, we'll keep well away when they're shooting the coverts.

The noise of the shoot excites him. Birds fly high, then fall. They fall, he observes, before he hears the sound of the gun.

One hundred and seventy-two head. A good bag.

We'll try for two hundred.

Not much light left, John.

Rubbish. Plenty of light. Rourke, you and three of the others take the west side. Beat towards the house.

His father tells him to stay where he is, that the shoot will soon be over.

He waits.

The beaters' shouts grow louder.

Bang! Bang!

Good shot, Henry.

Careful now, John. Careful.

There's a cock coming in low.

Careful, John!

Bang!

A scream of agony. Pandemonium.

Oh my God, you've hit someone!

Who is it? For God's sake, who is it?

It's Rourke, sir. I think he's dead.

He watches them carry his father up to the big house. There is blood everywhere.

Dead? How can that be? His father can't be dead. He was alive just five minutes ago. Not dead. Not dead.

Is that his boy?

Yes.

Look – Tim, isn't it? – there's been an accident, Tim. I'm afraid . . .

He begins to cry. Bitterly.

The compensation is generous, and he receives a brand-new suit of clothes.

After a few months his mother seems to forget. But he cannot. He remembers the blood and the coffin with its brass handles and the tears and the fields where there is no more laughter and the terrible finality of it all.

Please, God, don't let me die – ever. Please, God, don't let me die.

He grows up. The farm becomes his and his brother's.

He is tall and strong and several of the village girls indicate their willingness to make him a man. He tries it: in the hay, in barns, lazy love-making on sleepy afternoons.

He meets Mary Kent. Somehow she is different. Prettier, too.

They go for long walks together and for drinks in the local pub. They visit each other's houses. Their mothers nod wisely.

Once, while walking, they come across a bull serving a cow. For the first time in his life he is embarrassed by the sight.

Come on, he says gruffly.

They lie in the long grass at the edge of a cornfield, and kiss. She thinks of the bull and the cow, and she aches.

I don't mind, Tim. You can do it.

I mind. You're not like the others.

It's all right if we love one another. You do love me, don't you?

Yes.

Well, then.

No.

Please. Please, I want you to. I need you.

Her mouth is open. She is breathing hard. It is irresistible, and he takes her quickly.

Your first?

Yes. Can you tell?

Yes.

My first. You were my very first. Oh, I do love you and I want to marry you.

And why not? he asks himself. A man doesn't live for ever. It's better to enjoy life while you can.

We'll get married, he says, and is suddenly happier.

. . . . .

The wind and its song. The silent moon creeping nonchalant across a black sky.

Rourke hugged his rifle for company.

The sun rose at five-thirty, and by six AM the Section were becoming restless. The smell of their unwashed bodies pervaded the air, and there was an unpleasant taste in their mouths.

'Let's go, for Chrissake,' muttered Thatcher.

At six-fifteen Hayter left his position and crawled over to where Langley, red-eyed and disgruntled, was concealed.

'They won't come now, sir.'

'We don't know that, sergeant. There's still a chance.'

'The men are tired.'

Langley studied him coldly. 'So am I, sergeant. So, doubtless, are you. We'll give it another hour.'

'But . . .'

'Another hour, sergeant.'

'Yes, sir.'

Three-quarters of an hour passed slowly. The early-morning mist lifted. The sun climbed higher and dried the trees.

At the head of the path Rourke yawned and stretched. He closed his tired eyes and rubbed them. When he opened them he blinked and pinched himself, to dismiss what could only be a figment of his imagination. Coming down the path, less than a hundred yards away, were two Cypriots. They were young – eighteen or nineteen, so far as he could tell – and they were real enough. So were the rifles they carried. They walked as though out for a Sunday stroll.

He began to sweat. This was it. This was really bloody it. He had no method of warning the others without firing a shot or exposing himself, and the tortuous nature of the path meant that the Cypriots would not come into full view of the Section until it was too late.

Jesus Christ.

Seventy yards.

He could hear them talking. He prayed that Langley or

Hayter would hear them too and come to his assistance, but there was no sound from the clearing.

Fifty yards.

His fingers trembled as he released the safety-catch of his rifle. He could see them clearly. One was younger than he had previously supposed, a boy of sixteen or so. A boy with a man's weapon. His companion was two or three years older; swarthy, confident, a black moustache covering his upper lip. They could have been brothers.

He raised the rifle and trained it on the one with the moustache. The face, laughing now, would soon register surprise as an ounce of lead ripped into the brain. His finger tightened on the trigger. And then he froze. He couldn't do it. Christ, they mightn't be EOKA. They could be hunters. Anything. He had to be sure. There had to be an alternative.

There was, and he tried it.

'Halt! Stamata!' he yelled, stepping on to the path.

The Cypriots turned to salt. For a moment they stared, mesmerized, at the bulky figure in khaki confronting them, and then the elder one fired from the hip. The bullet whined past Rourke's shoulder. He fired back, and missed.

'Treha! Treha!'

They ran. Rourke dropped to one knee and squeezed the trigger a second time. Nothing happened. In his excitement he had forgotten to reload.

'*What the hell is it, Rourke?*'

'Two of them, sergeant. They took a shot at me.'

'Why the fug did you let them see you!'

'I couldn't help it.'

'Which way did they go?'

'Right, sir. Into the trees.'

Langley issued his orders calmly and efficiently.

'Sergeant Hayter, take one man and stay to the left of the path in case they try to double back. Cross it about a quarter of a mile up. Thatcher, you and Klein take the path itself. Join Sergeant Hayter where you meet and then break right. That's where we'll be. Maintain wireless contact. The rest of you follow me. Aim for their legs. I'd like a prisoner. Let's go.'

'Shaw, you come with me.'

'Yes, sergeant.'

The Section split up.

'What did they look like, Rourke?' said Langley, keeping up a steady trot.

'Young, sir,' panted Rourke. 'One of them was only a kid.'

'Automatic weapons?'

'No, rifles.'

'How many shots did you get in?'

'Er, just the one, sir.'

'Hit anything?'

'No, sir.'

'Never mind, we'll get 'em.' He called over his shoulder to Costas: 'Where does this lead to?'

'Nowhere, lieutenant.'

'Can they get out of the valley?'

'Yes. By using the track we used.'

'Good,' grunted Langley. That was bloody good. If the Cyps chose to climb, they'd be exposed for two hundred feet. If they kept on running, they would get nowhere. Heads or tails, they'd had it.

They pressed on, stumbling over hidden stones, crashing through the unarticulated and sprawling undergrowth, ankle-deep, on occasions, in bracken and fallen pine-needles. Low branches tore at their bodies.

At the end of ten minutes they heard shots from their left – six or seven of them; rifles and the thud-thudding of Hayter's sten. A moment later the 88-set crackled into life. Hayter's voice came booming through, jubilant.

'We've got them, sir. They tried to double back, like you said. I've got them pinned down in some rocks. I don't think they can get any farther because of the stream. They're on top of it and it's about thirty feet wide here. I can't get any closer without taking risks. Can you get round them? If you fire a shot to let me know your position, I might be able to give you a fix. Over.'

Langley fired twice into the air.

'Did you hear that, sergeant? Over.'

'Yes, sir. You're parallel with us as near as I can tell. Over.'

'Okay. Do your best to keep them where they are. We'll get

behind them. Out.' He consulted his map. 'Sergeant Hayter's got them cornered,' he explained, 'and we're going to cut off their only exit. The stream bends sharply to the left some two hundred yards up. We'll ford it there. They're quite close now so everyone be careful.'

They moved forward, quietly. The forest was thicker in this part of the valley, making it difficult to see clearly for more than a few yards.

Langley, as he walked, went over the manual in his mind.

When contact has been made with an enemy, the officer will make his dispositions with clarity and simplicity. He will at all times look to the safety of the men under his command, and he will not jeopardize their lives needlessly. He will, however, ensure that the task entrusted to him is executed, whether or not this engenders danger and possible loss of life.

The sum total of which, he thought, was: get results, no matter how. Well he'd get results, and a prisoner. It was all over bar the shouting.

He held up his hand.

'Riordan, we'll drop you and Porter here in case they make a run for it.' He checked his watch. 'We'll be behind them in ten minutes. Don't shoot unless you see anything. I've an idea they'll surrender, but you never can tell. Got that?'

'Yes, sir.'

Langley called up Hayter.

'Everything as it was, sergeant? Over.'

'Yes, sir. They're not saying much, but they're there. Over.'

'Fair enough. I've placed the bren team, as near as I can judge, opposite the spot where they're holed up. I'll let you know when I'm in position, then I'll get Costas to talk to them. They may give up without a struggle. In any case, don't recommence firing until I give the word. Understood? Over.'

'Understood, sir. Out.'

Hayter removed his earphones. From the shelter of the edge of the forest, Shaw, Klein, and Thatcher looked at him questioningly.

'The bren team's over to our right,' he said. 'Mr Langley's going to cross the stream and give us the okay when he's set. Don't shoot, unless you have to, until you're told. Got that?'

Thatcher and Klein nodded in unison, but Shaw growled, 'Trust Langley to grab all the bloody glory.'

'What was that, Shaw?'

'Didn't speak, sergeant.'

'Let's keep it like that. I know you want a medal, but a dead hero's no use to anyone.'

Shaw rubbed spittle on the smoking muzzle of his rifle, and said nothing.

'What d'you think they're doin' now, sergeant?' asked Thatcher.

'The Cyps? Christ knows, but I'd be praying if I was them. They're gonna need all the help they can get.'

'Poor bastards,' murmured Klein.

Hayter grinned. 'Don't waste your sympathy, lad. They'd have your head on a plate if you stuck it out. They nearly had your pal Rourke's. It's them or us, remember that.'

'I guess so.'

'There's no guessing about it. They're not carrying them rifles to shoot dickey-birds. Whether you like it or not, there's a war on.'

Well, almost a war, he added to himself, because a couple of Cyp kids weren't much to be reckoned with. Not much at all. It was a pity Langley wanted a prisoner; a grenade or two would soon sort them out. It wasn't more than – what, forty yards.

It was nearer fifty, and between the trees and the rocks was a stretch of open ground. For the Cypriots there was no means of escape. Behind them was the stream, and the stream was deep. It would take them upwards of a minute to wade it, and they would never make it alive. To their right and left the safety of the trees was close but not close enough. They were trapped and they knew it. Every so often it was possible to hear them talking. Their words needed no translation; they were scared.

'Won't be long now,' said Hayter.

They waited.

It was Thatcher who first smelt smoke.

'They cookin' their bleedin' breakfast or somethin'.' And then: 'What the hell . . .'

One of the Cypriots had bobbed up and thrown a torch of

burning brushwood into the trees. A tongue of flame leapt eagerly for the lower branches, and sparks showered. The timber was thirst-dry, and within seconds half a dozen pines were ablaze.

'The crazy bastards!' ejaculated Hayter. 'They'll kill us all. Keep your eye on them rocks. They'll try to cross the stream under cover of the smoke.' He snatched savagely at the on-switch of the 88-set. 'Hayter here. They've set fire to the forest. Over.'

Langley sounded unconcerned. 'I can see the smoke. How bad is it? Over.'

'It'll be pretty bad in a few minutes. This stuff's like paper. If it starts to spread we'll have to pull out. Over.'

There was a long silence before: 'No pulling out, sergeant. *I want that prisoner*. Hold your positions. Over.'

'But that's gonna be suicide, sir. If the wind shifts we'll get caught. Over.'

Langley's voice rose an octave. He was not going to be cheated of his prize at this stage of the game, regardless of the cost.

'I repeat, sergeant: you will hold your position. Out.'

The wireless went dead.

'Are we pulling out, sarge?' asked Klein anxiously.

'No, we're bloody not. And you keep watching them rocks.'

Five minutes, Hayter decided. He would give it five minutes. After that, Langley could go and stuff himself. He wasn't getting them barbecued.

The wind was blowing from the north-east, driving the fire slowly yet inexorably towards them. Dense grey smoke obscured their vision. The Cypriots could already have escaped and they would have been none the wiser.

'I can't see a thing,' shouted Shaw, coughing.

'Nor me. Let's go, sarge, for Chrissake!'

'Stay where you are.'

Four minutes.

More than a score of trees were now ablaze, and the sound of them burning was like hot fat frying. The flames sprang greedily from tree to tree, devouring the desiccated wood. Branches and pieces of bark fell to earth and started new fires. Sparks drifted in the wind, drifted in all directions, where they ignited the brush and beds of pine-needles. The heat was intense. White, suffocating heat which singed the eyebrows and clawed at the throat. Heat that left the air without oxygen.

Two minutes.

'Christ, look!' screamed Klein.

Hayter looked, and cursed. The forest behind them was alight and the fire was racing to encircle them. Soon, very soon, it would cut them off.

He switched on the wireless. 'Hayter here. We're getting out. Over.'

'*You're to remain where you are, sergeant. Over.*'

'We can't, sir. We've got to go or we'll be roasted. Out.' He tore off the earphones. 'Go right,' he bellowed. 'And run like bloody hell!'

They ran.

The forest in front of them was a tableau of red, and the fire was gaining in depth every second. Their hair and skin were scorched before they had covered twenty yards, and their eyes poured, but they blundered on, terror lending them speed and stamina. The noise of falling trees and branches was deafening, as though the world were coming to an end and all of them about to be cast into hell. Above them a flock of birds shrieked a warning.

'This way!' yelled Hayter, and made for a gap in the flames.

They followed him through, choking, oblivious of pain, blind with tears and sweat. And then they were knee-deep in the cold stream. Sightless, they waded to the opposite bank, and collapsed.

It was a long time before they noticed Klein was missing.

When Klein stumbled and fell his first reaction was to panic. Dimly, he saw the others run into the smoke and disappear. An instant later he heard Hayter call, 'This way!' – and then there was nothing but the terrifying crackle of the trees.

He struggled to his feet, his lungs filling with ash, and ran on. But the gap in the flames had gone. The inferno had completed its circle. '*Thatcher! Shaw!*' he screamed, and what he imagined to be a shout was no more than a croak. Desperately he took his rifle by the muzzle and hit out at the blazing trees. He only succeeded in burning his hands.

His knees buckled and he began to whimper. The whimpering became low, anguished moans and then coughing, insane half-talk.

'God help. Don't leave. Don't let me. Please don't let me. Die. I'll do anything. Anyth . . . I'll be good. Jew. I don't want to. Please help. Don't leave me. Please. Don't . . .'

And that was as far as he got before a tall pine, its roots weakened by the fire, fell and crushed him.

421851 Klein was nineteen.

TWELVE

Platres. August. A tiny village in the Troodos mountains which only flourished in the winter, when the skiers came, before the Emergency. But now the troops are here and trade is booming. Café proprietors and bar owners, whose smiles are broad, grow rich and cultivate paunches. They save their money carefully, fearing some day the killing will end and the troops leave.

Seven o'clock on a hot evening.

A dog yawns and stretches, and watches, out of the corner of one lazy eye, a sleek cat strut brazenly in front of it. The dog does not move. Its cat-chasing days are over. It has become fat.

Washing hangs from makeshift clothes-lines and on bushes. A tethered goat lies supine, dreaming goatish dreams. Flies make a restaurant of a garbage can outside the canteen. The dust from a passing convoy takes a long time to settle.

The sidewalks are raised wooden boards, like in an old cow town: Tucson circa 1860. The whitewash on the walls of the flat-roofed houses has peeled, and the window shutters are broken. Children squat in the gutter and pick their noses.

The main street is no more than a wide track. It cuts the village in two, and is pot-holed. The Platresians have never heard of tarmac or concrete. On either side of the street are the bars, cafés, and hotels. The hotels have been commandeered by the troops, and hoardings which carry names redolent of finer days, such as Best Hotel, Little Flower Hotel, Morgan's, and Pine House, now have addenda which read: D Troop, Y Troop, CO's Office, Adjutant's Office. The nomenclature of an occupying force.

On the west side of the street, near the Little Flower Hotel, is Fillipedes' Bar. The sign over the door has part of the F and one L missing. Fillipedes himself is plump and fifty and has long black sideburns. He wears a striped apron and resembles the barber from a comic opera, or a reasonably successful ponce. His bar is always crowded. He has a stack of Elvis Presley records and he makes the best and cheapest brandy sours in the village. Further down is Joe's Bar, but this is not so popular. Joe has no Elvis Presley records and he charges sixty mils for a brandy sour – a high price with the exchange rate at five hundred to the pound.

At each end of the village is a barbed-wire fence and a gate guarded by a pair of armed sentries. To the south, just outside the wire, live two whores, both in their thirties. In the old days their beds were permanently shared, but for them the Emergency has meant ruin and frustration. The skiers no longer come with their heavy wallets and bodies that need revitalizing by experienced hips, and the troops are forbidden to visit them. Occasionally Fillipedes, or one of the other bar owners anxious for a change from his wife's familiar technique, calls on them, but not often. For the most part they pass the time reading. It is a sad sight to see a whore reading.

To the north lies the Troodos Forest and, overlooking this, not half a mile from Platres, the Forest Park Hotel. It is rumoured that King Farouk stayed there regularly. But Farouk is deposed, and the rooms are empty except for mice.

Bars and hotels. Green berets and guns. Brandy sours and profits.

Seven-ten on a hot evening.

From the door of the CO's office a figure emerges. He wears the three stars and shoulder insignia of a captain in the Royal Marines. It has taken him an hour to persuade the Colonel not to deal personally or refer to higher authority the case of Second-lieutenant Langley; to persuade him that he, the captain, will handle it.

Captain Miller, OC D Troop, is an ambitious man who has worked his way up from the ranks. The son of a Yorkshire grocer his native accent has long since been diluted by the fancy speech of the Officers' Mess, but occasionally the broad vowels of Bradford reappear. In looks he is the antithesis of the sort of officer who is always being photographed next to horsey debutantes. He is thirty-one and an inch or two above average height. His shoulders and forearms are those of a stevedore, and his party trick is lifting a heavy chair by one leg using only his wrist muscles. His brown eyes are shrewd, calculating, and specked with yellow. His dark hair is cropped short, tropical style.

Once he was married to the daughter of a Bradford wool merchant, but the brief union had ended violently the afternoon he caught his wife in bed with a naval commander. He had broken the commander's jaw and beaten his wife's backside black and blue. The commander had been in hospital for two months. The wife had remarried, to a major in the Intelligence Corps, and now lived in Malta.

Seven-fourteen.

A Presley record screams its message from Fillipedes' Bar. A sentry hopes his relief will soon arrive. The two whores gaze wistfully at the barbed-wire kill-joy . . .

Seven thirty-two.

'Will there be an inquiry, sir?' asked Second-lieutenant Langley.

Miller turned on him.

'*An inquiry!* Is that all you can think about, a bloody inquiry? There's a Marine lying on a slab across the street. You haven't seen what they brought in yet, but I have. And what's left of his body is black and burnt and ghastly. His people don't even know he's dead, and all you can worry about is an inquiry. By God, lad, yer a callous 'un.'

'I'm sorry, sir.'

'Don't sorry me. It's Sergeant Hayter you should be saying that to. You left him holding the baby. Why the hell didn't you listen to him? He was the man on the spot.'

'I don't know, sir.'

'Well, I know. You saw a chance for a cheap success and you snatched at it. I know something else too. I'd throw you to the wolves like a shot if I wasn't short of officers and if your stupidity wouldn't reflect on me. So bear that in mind. You'll have to work twice as hard to get half as far now.'

'Yes, sir.'

Swine, thought Langley. Damned ex-ranker. It would have been a different story if he'd captured the Cypriots. Then it would have been a fair swop, two lives for one. But they'd got away. The patrol had been a miserable failure.

His failure. Damn and blast them all. But he wasn't callous, whatever Miller said. It was just that he could feel nothing for someone he had scarcely known. *Klein? Which one was Klein?* It was ridiculous but that had been his first reaction when Hayter had told him. It was such an ordinary face.

'You're going over there later on,' said Miller.

'Over where, sir?'

'To the mortuary. You're going to take a good look at Klein. And I'd advise a couple of stiff drinks before you go.'

A bottle if you can manage it, thought Miller, remembering with a shudder the terrible smell.

. . . . .

Apart from the orderly and Colour-sergeant Wilson from HQ Troop, Hayter was alone in the Sergeants' Mess. He swallowed a glass of Keo brandy and signalled for another.

'We're supposed to be closed, sergeant,' complained the orderly.

'Shut your mouth. I'm off duty. Pour.'

'It's against regulations, sergeant. If the RSM came in . . .'

'Screw the regulations, screw the RSM, and screw you. Pour.'

'Take it easy, Bill,' soothed Wilson. 'The lad's only doing his job. Okay, son, give him another. I'll carry the can.'

The orderly refilled the glass. Hayter grabbed it and reached for the soda syphon. He grinned drunkenly.

'Thanks, Charlie,' he said to Wilson. 'You're a pal.'

'Sure.'

'I mean it.'

'Forget it.'

'Forget what?'

'Forget the thanks and forget the other thing. It wasn't your fault.'

''Course it wasn't my fault.' Hayter looked for confirmation of his statement in the bottom of his glass. ''Course it wasn't my fault. I wasn't in command, was I? I don't give orders. I'm only a sergeant. 'Course it wasn't my bloody fault.'

'That's it.'

''Course it is.'

The brandy glowed in Hayter's stomach. Warm. Warm and anaesthetic. It deadened the senses, kept him from thinking. Tomorrow he wouldn't need it. But today he did.

'It's not my fault that they're sending out schoolboys to do a man's job. It's not my fault that Langley's a stupid gett. Leader of men. Jesus Christ, he couldn't lead a horse to water. They must be out of their minds back in England.'

'Sure, Bill.'

'*Sure, Bill.* Is that all you can say, Charlie? Wotcha tryna do, humour me? He's drunk but keep him happy. That's it, ain't it?'

'You've had enough.'

'I *have* had enough!' Hayter banged the bar with his fist. 'You're bloody right I've had enough. I've had a bellyful of this life. I don't wanna be responsible for the officers as well as the men. That's not my job. Listen, Charlie, I never lost a man ever, did I? Did I?' he pleaded. 'None. Not one. I been a Marine for – Chris', ten years or so – but I never lost a man. Not in Korea or anywhere. Never made a mistake 'til yesterday.'

'It wasn't your fault, Bill. We agreed that.'

'We didn't agree. 'Course it was my fuggin fault! You think I'm drunk, don't you? Well, watch.'

He walked the length of the Mess and back again. He almost fell twice.

'No, he's not drunk,' smirked the orderly.

'You take that grin off your face, lad!' hissed Wilson.

'I'm not drunk, Charlie,' said Hayter quietly. 'I've had a few, but that's not being drunk.' He paused. 'It was my fault. We both know it, we both know the rules. When you're out on patrol with a green officer, you're in charge. He's got the rank, but it's up to you to see nothing goes wrong. And I made a balls of it, Charlie. I could've done something, talked him out of it, not waited that five minutes. But I didn't. I didn't, Charlie.'

Wilson nodded slowly. It was all he could think of doing.

The orderly polished a glass. Hayter lit a cigarette but allowed it to burn without smoking it.

No one spoke for some time.

It was too early for Fillipedes' Bar to be uncomfortably full, but most of the tables were occupied by Marines and junior NCOs from D Troop, whose rest day it was. The air reeked of olive oil, cigarettes, and liquor. *Jailhouse Rock* shook the record-player and assaulted the eardrums.

Behind the counter Fillipedes busied himself with the preparation of steak, chips, fried eggs, brandy sours. He worked quickly but without enthusiasm. He had heard about the previous day's fire, and he was worried. The troops were in a violent mood, ready to turn on anyone whose skin colour differed from their own. It was for this reason that he smiled extra hard whenever he got the opportunity.

At a table near the counter sat 3 Section. They had been drinking steadily since five o'clock. Shaw's arms and Thatcher's arms and legs were covered with strips of sticking plaster.

The talk was aggressive. The nascent flames of hatred were being fanned by brandy and ouzo. They wanted an eye for an eye. They resented the enforced rest.

'I'd recognize 'em again,' said Rourke. 'I think I'd recognize 'em again.'

'Who cares if you do or you don't? Grab the nearest two, that's what I'd do. String the nearest two up.'

'Bloody right.'

'That goes double for me. By Christ, it'll have to be a pretty nifty golly who gets out of my sights next time.'

'You can say that again,' said Thatcher.

I'm gonna open a shop, that's what I'm gonna do. Second-hand clothes. There's a fortune to be made.

'You can't shoot every Cyp on the island,' said Porter. 'You can't go down to Nicosia or Lefka and shoot the first two you see.'

'Who can't?'

'Whose bloody side are you on?'

'If you're gonna come that holier-than-thou crap . . .'

'Okay, okay. I was just making a point.'

'Then don't.'

'No, don't. They're all the bloody same. They'd all knife us if they could. Treat 'em like dirt, that's my motto.'

'And mine.'

'And what about Langley? Don't forget that bastard.'

'Who could? He'll get the lot of us killed before we're much older.'

'Bastard.'

There's a pub in Stoke Newington High Street that peddles the greatest beer you've ever tasted. Strictly from kosher.

'Burn a few Cyp villages,' said Shaw. 'That'd smoke 'em out.'

'Listen, they're bein' hidden, you know. Some sod's hidin' them.'

'Lousy bums.'

'We're too bleedin' soft, the British. They kick us in the crotch and we offer them our teeth.'

'Not me, not any more. The next Cyp I meet'll find out how British I am when he picks the shrapnel out of his head.'

'Burn a few villages.'

'Hey, Fillipedes, six brandy sours.'

'Immediately.'

'What about ol' Fillipedes, then. You reckon he's one of them?'

'Not him. He likes our dough too much.'

'Don't they all. They're all the bloody same.'

'Serves Fillipedes right if we bust his place up.'

'Ay, it would.'

'Don't start that, for Chrissake.'

'Why not? He's a Cyp.'

'Bugger that. We'll end up in cells.'

'He's right. Webbo's right. If we wanna bust some place, we go to the other end of the village. They're the sort of sods who'd hide them Cyps if they got the chance.'

'When it gets dark.'

'Lob a brick or two through a window. Teach 'em a fuggin lesson.'

'They won't put me on a slab, not like Moisie.'

'He was a pal o' mine too.'

'He was okay.'

'Hey, Fillipedes, move your fat arse and chop-chop with them drinks.'

'Coming.'

'Pay the man, Webbo.'

'My round? It's not my round.'

''Course it is.'

'One hundred-eighty mils, perakalo.'

'You do okay, don'tcha, Fillipedes?'

'Leave him. He's just a steak hustler.'

'Listen, when it gets real dark. . . .'

'Cambridge, wasn't it?' said Miller.

'Yes, sir,' answered Langley.

'What was your subject?'

'History, sir.'

'Peculiar beginning for a regular officer, no?'

'My father . . .'

'Yes?'

'It was my father's old college. It's a sort of family tradition.'

'I see.'

There was a suspicion of a sneer in Miller's voice.

Oh yes, Brian, there'll be petty jealousies and sniping. They'll be looking to see how good the son of the father is. I'll cope. *I'm sure you will. Got my blood in your veins. Stands to reason. And it's up to you from now on. They retired me because of my heart – damn' doctors – otherwise I'd be commanding an army today. However, we'll cheat 'em. You'll command that army some day. You'll be a brigadier by the time you're fifty, my lad, or I'll be after you. I'll pull whatever strings I can, but from lieutenant-colonel upwards you're on your own.* I'll make it, Father.

'What do you think of sons following in famous fathers' footsteps?'

'Sir?'

'I said, what do you think of sons following in famous fathers' footsteps? Do you think it's a good idea?'

'It depends on the individual, sir. In my case, I was brought up with the knowledge that my career would be that of a soldier.'

'Of course. Yes, you would be. Well, as long as you don't try too hard.'

'Sir?'

'Never mind.'

Don't try too hard. What the hell did that mean? thought Langley. Was his ability being questioned after a single mistake? Just one. Good God, his father had lost half a regiment at Dunkirk and won the DSO into the bargain.

Dunkirk was a damn' sticky business, damn' sticky. But the top brass didn't understand that. I was only a half-colonel at the time and it delayed my promotion no end. However, Sicily was a different cup of tea. Got my Cross in Sicily. Did you lose many men there, Father? *Company or two, I don't recall. But losses are an essential part of war. It's like a game of chess, really, Brian. You sacrifice a couple of pawns early on in order to trap your opponent's King later. It's the last battle that counts, not the mid-field skirmishes. Remember that and you'll have learned a valuable lesson.* I'll remember.

'All right, Brian, you can go,' said Miller.

'Go, sir?'

'Yes. I've said what I wanted to say. You'll take that trip to the mortuary, won't you? It's an order.'

'I will, sir.'

Langley paused by the door.

'There is one thing, sir: the letter to Klein's parents. Will you write that?'

'Yes. It's my job.'

'Thank you, sir.'

Alone, Miller opened the centre drawer of his desk. He took out a bottle of whisky, three-quarters full. Langley worried him.

'Come on, Bill, time to get your head down.'

Hayter ignored Wilson. He was slumped forward on the bar, studying the label on the Keo bottle.

'You 'member Korea, don't you?' he said. 'Korea. Jesus wept, that was really something. Those gooks kept coming and coming. And those bloody bells they used to ring. Remember the bells. Their officer 'ud stand behind them with a pistol, ready to shoot them if they turned back. But they got shot as they came forward. Why did they do it, Charlie? What's the point of getting blown to bits?'

Wilson shrugged. 'Don't ask me.'

'But I am asking you. I am. I've gotta know. They committed suicide, those gooks. Why?'

'They're different out there,' said Wilson, as though talking to a persistent and inquisitive child. 'The Chinks are different. They don't value their lives the way we do.'

'Balls. Balls, Charlie. The officers were Chinks, but not many of them got killed.' He chuckled quietly. 'Officers – the same the world over. The pbi gets the chopper, but never the officer.'

'Don't worry about it. Korea's long gone. We've got other things to think about.'

'But what did it mean, Charlie? Thousands of their blokes got killed and so did thousands of ours. Where's the sense? What did it mean? We had two wars, Charlie – two wars that were gonna put an end to all wars. Then Korea. Now Cyprus. Where next? Russia, China, the Germans again? I don't get it.'

'Neither does anyone else, Bill, neither does anyone else. Wars are people. A war's just a pub fight on a larger scale. When there are no more pub fights, then there'll be no more wars.'

Hayter nodded. 'Yeah, I guess you're right. Ain't that a kick in the head.'

Fillipedes removed *Jailhouse Rock* from the turntable and replaced it with *Heartbreak Hotel*. He listened to the opening chords. The record was scratchy. He would have to get another from the agent in Nicosia. He did not wish to lose his customers.

'Let's go, then,' said Shaw. 'It's dark enough.'

'No, let's have another first.'

'You chickenin' out, Webbo? Say if you are.'

'I'm not. They deserve all they get.'

'Too bloody true.'

'You with us, Riordan?'

'Sure.'

'Rourke?'

'Count me in.'

'What about you, Porter?'

''Course I'm with you. I'm in the Section, aren't I?'

'Good lad, Porter. Let's go.'

'One more. Jus' one.'

'Yeah, we'll tank up. Them Cyps aren't goin' anywhere. Hey, Fillipedes . . .'

Captain Miller wrote: 'Dear Mr and Mrs Klein, There is no easy way of writing this kind of letter . . .'

He paused. Christ, that wouldn't do; stank of insincerity.

He crossed out what he had written, referred to Klein's dossier, and began again.

Across the street, in front of the mortuary, Langley braced himself. He could do it without drink, he thought. He was not afraid. It didn't pay to be afraid.

He went in.

'Lean on me, Bill. Lean on me. A few yards, that's all.'

'Thanks, Charlie. Jeeze, it's a hot night.'

'Yeah.'

'Langley's gonna get his one day, Charlie. Christ, is he gonna get his.'

'Yeah.'

They picked on two houses at the north end of the village. Houses that were in darkness. There were plenty of stones on the ground, and they smashed every window shutter in sight, ignoring the cries of fear from within. When they were finished with the shutters they started on the doors, and finally they killed a goat by sawing at its bleating throat with a penknife. The whole business took under three minutes, and they were well away by the time the RPs arrived to investigate the disturbance.

THIRTEEN

Throughout autumn and early winter they comb the Troodos, write letters home, receive letters from home, drink in Fillipedes', eat in the canteen, watch five-year-old films, listen to War Office-sent unfunny comedians and big-breasted blonde singers with voices like bronchial crows and extra-curricula favours reserved for majors and above. They curse each other for no reason at all, do a daily check on the casualty list to see if anyone they know has caught it, pine for a woman, and drink some more in Fillipedes'. They surround villages at night and raid them at dawn, use the butt of a rifle as the final arbiter in any argument with the locals, and learn that everyone is guilty until proved innocent. They shoot and get shot at, kill and get killed, and every day seems pretty much like the one before.

Elsewhere:

Nicosia. Ledra Street A REME sergeant is gunned down. His murderer escapes behin a barricade of willing Cypriot children.

Limassol. A grenade is thrown at a passing truck, and a soldier dies screaming.

Lapithos. In an orange grove four children under the age of nine find a home-made EOKA bomb. Not knowing what it is they begin playing with it. It explodes. One child dies and the remaining three are maimed for life. An EOKA pamphlet appears the next day. It reads: Greeks, liberty is won with blood. Blame the British for Lapithos.

Akrotiri. An RAF senior aircraftsman is reading in a hut. Close by three Cypriot labourers are working. On four separate occasions one of the labourers asks for a drink of water. It is a hot afternoon, and three times the senior aircraftsman obliges the sweating Cypriots. The fourth time he is shot in the back of the head as he enters the hut. The killers are caught and hanged. The Security Forces celebrate their deaths with an orgy of drinking.

Nicosia. Outside the Pancyprian Gymnasium a gang of youths and girls hurl stones and Molotov-cocktails at a platoon of troops. The troops have been ordered not to retaliate – the British do not fight children – but two of them, their patience at an end, hit out. A fifteen-year-old girl suffers a broken wrist. Eight members of the platoon have first-degree burns. The girl is given compensation. The two rebellious soldiers face a court martial.

A Labour MP, a woman, visits the island. She goes home protesting that the Security Forces are taking excessive and cruel measures against the civilian population. Her comments are widely reported. The troops are amazed and angry. Is the woman mad? Hasn't she seen Harrison, blind now? And what about Craig, for whom plastic surgery can do nothing? And Harding, who cries all the time?

The woman is not mad. She is a politician. By definition she is permitted to be an unfeeling fool.

Paphos. A young girl, six months pregnant, is tortured and killed.

Larnaca. The sixteen-year-old civilian son of an RASC captain is ambushed after taking a swim. He is shot in the kidneys and dies on the operating table.

Ktima. A priest threatens excommunication to all those who do not support EOKA.

And in the Troodos: On a cold November night, with the snow white on the slopes of Olympus, 3 and 4 Sections of D Troop take a prisoner.

They had stripped him to his underclothes and stood him in a bowl of water, in the courtyard behind the Platres guard-room. They had left his hands and feet untied. There was nowhere he could run to, and the wall around the courtyard was too high to climb. His teeth chattered like snaredrums and his eyes were dull with pain, but he managed, by some concentration of will, to keep his chin jutted forward and his head held upright. He was about twenty, and stubborn.

Ten o'clock. A fresh fall of snow on the ground. The thermometer registered 26 Fahrenheit.

Inside the guard-room Captain Miller, Langley, and

Lieutenant Reynolds, the rangy, bespectacled Commander of 4 Section, sipped scalding coffee. Close by lounged the Marines and NCOs of 3 and 4 Sections, joking and laughing, delighted with the successful conclusion to the patrol. On a table by the stove lay the rifle they had taken from the prisoner, together with a bandolier of ·303 ammunition.

'How long has he been out there?' asked Miller.

'Three-quarters of an hour,' answered Langley. 'It won't be long now.'

'I wouldn't bet on that, Brian. He's a tough one.'

'Nobody's that tough.'

'The SIB will break him if this doesn't,' put in Reynolds.

'That's no use to me,' said Miller. 'They won't be here until tomorrow, by which time any information this fellow has will be old hat.' He drained his mug. 'Here, get one of your lads to fill this up.'

'Webster.'

'Yes, sir?'

'Fill this up for Captain Miller.'

'Yes, sir.'

Miller peered out of the window. The prisoner was lit by a shaft of pale light. Talk, blast you, he thought. Don't be a bloody fool.

'Coffee, sir.'

Miller took the mug.

'All right,' he said, 'we'll have another word with him. Where's Costas?'

'Here, captain.'

They went outside, Costas, Langley, Reynolds, and Miller carrying his coffee.

'That's the way to treat those Cyp bastards,' chuckled Shaw. 'Captain Miller's got the idea.'

'Too bloody true.'

'Just remember that if *they* ever catch *you*,' said Hayter.

'They never will, sarge,' Shaw stroked his rifle.

In the courtyard it had grown colder, and despite what remained of his body heat, slivers of ice were beginning to form on the bowl of water in which the Cypriot was standing. But he showed no sign of wanting to capitulate.

'Tell him,' said Miller, 'that he'll stay here all night unless he gives us his name and the names of his accomplices.'

Costas translated.

'Then ehete to thikeoma. Ine paranomo,' replied the Cypriot, with difficulty.

'He says you have no right to do this, captain. It is against the law.'

'So is murdering women and children. Tell him I am the law here.'

'Eyo ime o nomos.'

The Cypriot said nothing.

'Ask him where his friends are.'

'Pou ine i fili sas?'

'Then ksero to les.'

'He says he does not know what the captain is talking about.'

'Like hell he doesn't. Like bloody hell.'

Miller held up the mug of coffee, held it under the Cypriot's nose so that the smell and the warmth lingered.

'Coffee,' he said. 'Kafethes. Hot coffee.'

The Cypriot's eyes flitted from Miller's to the steaming coffee and back again. He tried to lick his lips.

'Coffee,' repeated Miller.

The Cypriot raised one frozen hand – a laboured, agonized movement – and reached out for the mug. Miller allowed him to touch it before pulling it away. He poured the contents on to the ground, slowly. Langley and Reynolds exchanged glances; Miller was really pushing it.

'Tell him,' said Miller, 'that there'll be plenty of coffee the minute he gives me the information I want.'

Costas translated.

'Then borite na mas skotosete olous,' muttered the Cypriot.

'He says, captain, that you cannot kill them all.'

'We can try,' said Miller. 'We can try.' He looked at Reynolds and Langley. 'Any suggestions?'

'Leave him in the fridge for another hour.'

'Brian?'

'Same here, sir.'

Miller nodded. 'All right, I agree. It's ten-thirty now. I'll be back by eleven-thirty. Post a two-man guard. They're to call me personally in my quarters if he says anything, anything at all.'

'Very good, sir. Good night.'

'Hardly good night. It's going to be a long one.' He paused. 'Incidentally, if he doesn't talk and if there's any subsequent Geneva Convention nonsense, you're both to swear you were acting under orders and that you made the customary protests. Got that? No arguments now.'

'Yes, sir.'

'Got it, sir.'

He left them.

'He's a good officer, Miller,' said Reynolds.

'I suppose he is. Toss you for which Section does the guard.'

They tossed, and Reynolds won.

In the guard-room the Marines fell silent as Miller came in from the courtyard. He strode wordlessly through and disappeared into the street. Then they all began talking at once.

'Christ, I didn't think he had it in him, tipping that coffee.'

'Came up from the ranks, that's why.'

'He really put that bastard through the hoop.'

'Bet he cracks before twelve.'

'Bet he doesn't.'

'You're on. How much?'

'A hundred Seniors.'

'Oh, big spender, Riordan. Come on, a real bet. A thousand mils.'

'Five hundred.'

'Done.'

'I'll take five hundred.'

'You're on. Five hundred for the gentleman with the bruised shins.'

'I haven't got bruised shins.'

'You will have when you stop kickin' yourself after you've lost this bet. Anyone else wanna piece of the action? Roll up, roll up. Honest George is makin' book.'

'Shut up, here's Langley.'

Langley and Reynolds came in, followed by Costas.

'We'll be trying again in an hour, sergeant,' said Langley.

'In the meantime, a two-man guard. They're to report the minute the prisoner says anything.'

'Yes, sir. Right, I'll have two volunteers. You'll do, Webster. And you, Rourke.'

In the privacy of his quarters in the Officers' Mess, Miller uncapped a bottle of whisky and poured himself a generous tumblerful. He drank the whole of it undiluted and without drawing breath, then poured out another. Dutch courage, he thought wryly.

He sat at his desk and unlocked the centre drawer. He took out a folder, and opened it. Inside were his personal papers, and he thumbed through them until he found what he was looking for: a letter from his father. It was a letter of congratulations, and the date showed that it had been written eight years before, a week after he had received his commission. He had read it often, particularly the quotations with which it concluded.

He knew that the essence of war is violence, and that moderation in war is imbecility. And: *There is such a thing as legitimate warfare: war has its laws; there are things which may be fairly done, and things which may not be done.*

There was a postscript to the effect that while his father had no idea who was responsible for the first quotation, the author of the second was Cardinal Newman. And both were cautionary reminders that a man, any man but particularly a soldier, can choose one of two paths.

Miller smiled. Christ, how on earth had a Bradford grocer managed to read Newman in between ordering tins of beans and stacking boxes of biscuits?

He closed the folder.

Newman or Anon. That was it, as simple as that. Opposite viewpoints but each valid. On the one hand there was a job to do and the possibility of Staff College if he did it and continued to do it well. On the other hand was the sheathed sword of humanity and common decency. To kill was one thing, to torture another.

Which?

The CO had gone to bed. He wanted nothing to do with

the affair, and he would, as he had said, deny all knowledge of it if the crunch came. The decision was his, Miller's.

Staff College. Decency. Staff College. Humanity. Staff College. Total war . . .

Total war.

Did total war demand total commitment? If so, when did a war cease to be partial and become total? Did one count the dead? Or did one count the atrocities perpetrated by the other side? Did one have a debit and credit column like a book-keeper? Was that all he was, a book-keeper? Did three children maimed and a soldier blinded justify torturing a prisoner? Did the columns balance? Or did none of these things apply; were they extraneous to the art of war. *Art. Christ.* Would the British have gassed Germans if they'd known that Germans were gassing Jews? Where would Newman have drawn the line? Did one listen to reason and forget the consequences? No, impossible. One listened to one's superiors, who required only results. One fought to win.

Staff College. Job to do. Decency. Staff College. Humanity . . .

Christ, there wasn't a solution, just expediencies.

. . . *Essence of war is violence, and that moderation in war is imbecility . . . Things which may be fairly done, and things which may not be done.*

He emptied his glass with a single swallow and reached for the bottle. He was not conscious of either action.

In the courtyard Webster stamped his feet to keep warm. He jerked a thumb in the direction of the Cypriot.

'Reckon he'll be dead by morning unless he coughs.'

'Probably,' said Rourke.

'Doesn't make sense, does it? I mean, all he's got to do is talk.'

'He might be scared.'

'Of what?'

'EOKA. They'd make mincemeat of him if he talked.'

'Yeah. I'd forgotten about that. Still, he'll die anyway, so what's the odds? And this weather isn't going to do his pencil much good. Freeze it off, I shouldn't wonder.'

'Is that all you ever think about, sex?'

Webster was hurt. 'No, 'course it isn't. I think of lots of things. But sex is important, you've got to admit that. If there was no sex there'd be no people. If it didn't make them feel good they wouldn't do it. Then where would we be? Nowhere. Sex makes the world go round.'

'It makes your world go round.'

'What's wrong with that? We're all the same. There isn't a guy in the unit who wouldn't like to jump the wire and screw one of those tarts. Or both of 'em. Who cares if they're a bit past it. Not me.'

'Why don't you do it, then?'

'I might, one day.'

'You won't. You'd get ninety days.'

'It'd be worth it. Jesus, I've almost forgotten what it's like. It's funny, you know, but when you're having it – I mean, when you're actually on the job – you think it's the greatest thing since sliced bread. You tell yourself that when this one's finished you'll have it again. But you don't. You lie back and have a smoke, and ten minutes later you can't remember how you felt. Believe me . . .'

'Aah, knock it off, for Chrissake,' said Rourke.

'What's the matter with you?'

'I'm bloody cold, that's what. Go and take a dekko at the Cyp.'

'Okay.'

Webster walked across to the Cypriot, whose eyes were closed. His lips moved occasionally, as though he were praying.

'How are you, boy?' jeered Webster, and the eyes opened. 'How are you, eh? Cold enough for you? How's about a cup of coffee? Or brandy? Kafethes? Keo? Aah, you're crazy. And don't stare at me. I don't like it.'

Webster raised his rifle, butt forward.

'Leave him,' called Rourke.

'I'm not going to touch him. Might dirty my rifle. See you, Cyppy. Don't go away.'

Webster rejoined Rourke.

'You shouldn't have gone that near,' said Rourke, slyly.

'Why not?'

'Well, he won't forget your face, will he? If he ever escapes you're a marked man.'

'He won't escape,' said Webster uneasily.

'He might. And if he does, I wouldn't want to be in your shoes.'

'Stuff it,' said Webster. 'I'm not frightened of one lousy Cyp.'

'No?' smirked Rourke.

'No.'

No, he repeated to himself. I'm not frightened of one lousy Cyp. I'm not. I'm not.

. . . . .

He lives at the poorer end of a middle-class Liverpool suburb, near where the council flats have been erected to rehouse the families from the slum-clearance areas. He avoids the flats like a disease. The roughneck children have caught him before and hit him, and would catch him again. To them it's a kind of game.

Hey, there's that kid from up the road.

Grab him.

Pinch his cap.

Run. Run. Run. And keep on running. But no use. They are faster.

Got you!

What's your name, kid?

Roy.

Roy what? Didn't they give you a second name?

Roy Webster.

That's a daft name. Jump on him, lads.

They hit him and keep on hitting him. Once he fought back, but they only hit him harder. So now he cries. They let him go quickly when he cries.

Aah, yer a sissy, Roy Webster.

He races home.

His mother is a tired, harassed widow who supplements her late husband's life insurance by working in a shop. It is a step in the wrong direction, and she hates it.

At thirteen he becomes interested in his body with its black sprouts of curly hair. He often strips and struts before his bedroom mirror, admiring himself.

He buys a book from a boy at school, who bought it from another boy who stole it from his father's pocket. It has a picture of a naked woman on the front, and is well thumbed.

I'm almost a man, he thinks proudly, noticing his body's reaction to the picture.

Almost.

He is fourteen when he learns that his mother is to remarry.

You'll like him, Roy. He has a son and daughter about your age.

But why do you want to get married again?

A boy needs a father.

I don't.

Oh yes you do. I know what's best.

After a month he grows to like his step-father, and his step-sister, Janet, but he hates her brother, Peter. Peter is fifteen and a bully.

Hey, Roy, lend us your skates.

Buzz off. Buy your own.

I'll take them, then, if you won't lend them. Are you gonna stop me?

No.

A reluctant but inevitable No.

And:

Come on, Roy, I've borrowed some gloves. Let's box a few rounds.

Go to hell.

Box, or I'll thump you anyway.

They box, and he receives a cut lip. Peter laughs.

Janet sympathizes.

Don't mind Peter, the pig.

He talks to Janet often. She is a pretty fourteen-year-old with red hair. He likes being with her and with all girls. They are soft and smooth – when he is allowed to touch them – and never want to fight.

Their conversations grow more daring.

You know what Mum and Dad do in bed, don't you?

Don't, Roy. She giggles.

In, out. In, out.

Stop it.

There's nothing wrong with it.

Not when you're married.

And when you're not.

Then on a Saturday morning, when the house is otherwise empty:

Have a drink of this, he says.

What is it? she asks.

Wine. It was in the cupboard.

We shouldn't.

Of course we should. You're not a baby any more.

They drink. A quarter. A half. Three-quarters.

He feels giddy but not sick. More, he feels very strong and big. An adult.

If I touch you there, what would you say?

Don't.

I'm going to.

He does. She flinches but does not move away. He moves his hand higher. And higher.

We shouldn't.

'Course we should. We've got to.

I'll have a baby.

You won't.

Oh, it hurts. It hurts.

Shut up.

He leaves her when it is over and goes upstairs. He examines himself in the mirror, and he is pleased with what he sees.

It happens often after that, always when the house is empty. He learns to let her drink most of the wine, and once he watches while she does it with another boy from his school. He has given his permission. After all, she belongs to him.

He feels manly in the company of girls. They don't care whether or not he is the greatest fighter in the world. They like him for what he does to them, the older ones.

At eighteen, with Janet long forgotten, he gets a girl pregnant. He sweats it out for a week, but eventually it is proved that she has been with many others, and he is let off.

After that, he takes precautions.

. . . . .

The prisoner fell on his face. His nose split like a rotten apple. Blood mingled with the snow. Webster and Rourke went over to him, and Webster poked him in the ribs.

'Come on, get up.'

'Tha – sta – po – ola.'

'What the hell's he talking about?'

'Tha – sta – po – ola.'

'Dunno. But you'd better get Hayter. And quick.'

Miller glanced at his watch: eleven-thirty. It was time to go, time to put further pressure on the Cypriot.

There is such a thing as legitimate warfare: war has its laws; there are things whch may fairly be done, and things which may not be done.

Rubbish. Newman was writing about other, more civilized wars. Anyhow, what the hell did a Roman Catholic clergyman know about war? Nothing. In this case, the end justified the means: a Marine might live because a Cypriot died, and that was his job.

Anon was right. The essence of war *was* violence. The rules were immutable.

He stood up and buckled on his belt. There was a knock on the door, the urgent rapping of someone in a hurry.

'Come in.'

Webster rushed in, and saluted. Without taking a breath he gasped: 'Sergeant Hayter told me to get you immediately, sir, because Costas says the prisoner wants to talk.'

'*What?*'

'Costas says . . .'

'Yes, yes. Tell Sergeant Hayter to give the man brandy. I'll be right over.'

'Yes, sir.'

Alone, Miller sighed and shook his head. It was a pity Webster hadn't arrived a minute earlier. Then he might have been able to convince himself that he had intended to be humanitarian all along.

FOURTEEN

They fed him coffee and brandy and sandwiches, and he talked for half an hour, even with his mouth full. He had reached that stage of mental and physical deterioration where treachery and loyalty are meaningless, where survival is paramount, where the thought of pain terrifies. Patriotism had become merely a word that is discussed and defined in drawing-rooms.

Costas translated as they went along.

His name was Constantinides and he belonged to an EOKA group known as Beta. His profession was that of a clerk, and prior to the Emergency he had been employed in a Famagusta shipping office. He was unmarried. He had been recruited in June by a man whose name he did not know. He had taken the oath in Nicosia, and after a month as a courier and propagandist he had been transferred to a mountain gang. The chain of command within the gang was complex, but the name of his leader was Markos. Markos was at present hidden in a small village on the road to Limassol. It was there that he, Constantinides, had been heading when captured.

Miller checked the files on known EOKA killers. There was only one Markos: Georges – and his scalp carried a bounty of £2500. Constantinides' name did not appear; he was too small a fish.

'Georges Markos?' queried Miller, and produced the dossier photograph.

Constantinides nodded. 'Georges Markos.'

'Keep him talking,' said Miller. 'I'm going to wake the CO. We'll hit that place tonight.'

It was six-thirty AM before they had cordoned off the village.

The sky grew perceptibly lighter: from black to dark-blue to purple. And then a diffusion of blues and greys. Cold greys.

Swollen clouds hovered overhead, but as yet there was no snow at this level.

Silence.

The village slept.

The Marines blinked at one another and rubbed unshaven chins. They checked their rifles and spare ammunition clips, although they had been through precisely the same routine not two minutes before.

Somewhere a cock prepared to crow.

At the east end of the village Miller briefed his Section Commanders.

'Okay, we don't know exactly where Markos is, but a recce has shown that there can't be more than five hundred people in the whole place, so you shouldn't have much trouble. 2 Section will take the left-hand side of the street, and 1 Section the right-hand side. Your job will be to get everyone out into the open and herd them into the café, which is up on the left. Do nothing else – 3 and 4 Sections will do the actual searching. And don't shoot if anyone makes a run for it. A and Y Troops have got the village surrounded.'

'Give them a chance to dress, sir?'

'If they're naked, yes. Otherwise, no. They can chuck a coat over whatever they're wearing. 3 and 4 Sections will follow 1 and 2. 3 on the right, 4 on the left. Go through every house. Search rafters, cellars, the lot. I want everything covered. But be careful. Markos has already got three hanks of hair in his wigwam.'

'Politics, sir?' asked Langley.

Miller shrugged. 'I'll leave that to you. No rough stuff unless it's unavoidable, but crack a skull or two if anyone gets stroppy. Any questions?' There were none. 'Good. In one minute I'm going to drive down the street in the Champ. Costas will be with me on the loud-hailer. 1 and 2 Sections will move off as soon as they hear Costas' spiel. 3 and 4 Sections will follow in three minutes. Keep wireless contact on Channel A. Away you go and good hunting.'

The Section Commanders rejoined their Sections. There was a muttering of instructions, the easing back of rifle and sten bolts, the nervous cough of a greenhorn.

'Ten seconds,' someone whispered.

The Champ's Rolls-Royce engine burst into life with a roar, and simultaneously Costas flicked on the loud-hailer. In Greek he said:

'Attention! Attention! This is an alert. British troops have occupied the village. You are requested to leave your houses immediately. Immediately. Take nothing with you. No one will get hurt if they obey orders. Repeat: no one will get hurt if they obey orders. Attention! Attention! This is an alert . . .'

A rifle butt crashed against a flimsy wooden door. It burst open. A shutter was flung back and an angry and frightened face peered out. A man about to make love to his wife cursed the Father and the Son. Somewhere a baby cried.

'Come on, move your arses!'

'Chop-chop, lads and lasses, chop-chop!'

'Shake it up, shake it up!'

'Attention! Attention! This is an alert . . .'

Soon the street was filled with anxious and resentful men, women, and children. They huddled together for warmth and security, and trudged flat-footed before the rifles, like refugees. Many wore only their night-clothes, and the old struggled to keep up with the young. Unwashed urchins clung to their parents and, sleepily, asked questions to which there were no answers. A mother suckled a child at her skinny breast. One or two of the men protested, but their protestations were silenced by a jab from a bayonet.

'Get along there.'

'Do as you're told and you won't get hurt.'

'Chuck us a fag, Jimmy, I'm gasping.'

The rifles urged them on, and they realized the futility of resistance. They had done something wrong. They had offended the British soldier. It was better to obey. It would all be explained to them sooner or later.

Like animals en route to the abattoir. Helpless.

'Attention! Attention! This is an alert . . .'

'Time check, sergeant,' said Langley.

'Half a minute, sir.'

'Bet you a round of drinks my lot get him,' called Reynolds.

'You're on, Robert,' said Langley, adding to Hayter: 'We'll

save time by leap-frogging. You, Shaw and Porter can do house one, while Thatcher, Webster, and Rourke do house two. Then you'll go on to house three and the others to house four. And so on. I'll stay in the street with Riordan and the bren in case you need covering fire.'

'Very good, sir. Go now?'

'Yes.'

They ran forward. Hayter led his group into the first house.

'You two do downstairs and I'll do upstairs.'

'Right, sarge.'

Shaw kicked at a door and went into a room. He held his nose. The air stank of rancid cooking oil and dogs.

'Jesus Christ.'

'You've seen it before,' said Porter.

'Never this bad.'

'There's no National Assistance here, you know.'

'They can wash, can't they. Jesus.'

The room was small and sparsely furnished. In the centre was a wooden table, hand-made and unpolished, and around this three or four chairs, again hand-made. On the table were the remains of the previous evening's meal: some dry bread, a chunk of cheese made from goat's milk, an empty bottle of cheap wine. A cooking-pot hung over an open fire. The fire itself was dead, the ashes grey and cold. The floor covering was a series of wooden planks, and underneath was the bare earth. In one corner crouched a mongrel bitch and half a dozen puppies, their eyes closed. The bitch snarled and arched its yellow back as Porter went to stroke it.

Shaw pushed over a chair contemptuously and picked up the wine bottle by the neck.

'There's no need to do that,' said Porter.

'Up you. Who'd notice the difference in this pig-sty?'

He smashed the bottle. The mongrel whined.

'Here, give us a hand with these planks.'

'Are you going to move them?'

'No, I'm going to build a bleedin' shed. 'Course I'm going to move them. There might be a hide somewhere.'

Upstairs, in one of the two rooms that served as bedrooms, Hayter prodded the bed-clothes with the muzzle of his sten. A fat bug crawled out and he squashed it with his thumb. It squelched, and oozed blackly.

The bed was all the room contained. There were no dressing-tables or cupboards or chests or chairs, and a pair of men's trousers lay in a crumpled heap on the floor. For the occupants of this house being alive was a question of survival. There was no time for frills.

He went into the adjacent room.

He saw a baby's crib, and close to it, a chamber-pot, unemptied for days. He hung on to his stomach. Against a wall was a double-tiered bunk, capable of holding a couple of ten- or twelve-year-olds. The kids' room, but no toys, no pictures, no obvious signs of kids. The ceiling was running with damp and sprouting green-yellow fungi.

He felt sick. In Korea and elsewhere in Cyprus he had seen a lot of poverty, but never had it been a way of life. In Korea it had been a temporary affliction, caused by war or famine or both, and it would go when the war was over or fresh food supplies arrived. But here the people lived with it day and night, and had lived with it for hundreds of years. Maybe they didn't even recognize it as poverty. Maybe they believed everybody lived as they did.

Jesus.

'Finished, sarge,' called Shaw.

He went downstairs.

'What about the planks, sergeant,' said Porter.

He and Shaw had removed them but not replaced them.

'Leave 'em,' said Hayter gruffly. Then: 'No, put 'em back.'

And he stood there while they did.

Langley was waiting for them in the street.

'No luck?'

'No, sir.'

'Okay, try house three. The others are already in house four.'

They had searched a dozen houses before they found anything. And it was Webster who found her.

'Keerist,' he breathed, and shouted: 'Hey, come and get a load of this.'

The girl was in her early teens. She lay in bed, the blankets barely covering her shoulders. Her dark eyes followed Webster as he walked towards her, and she gave a tiny whimper as he touched her long black hair.

Who'd know? he asked himself, regretting that he had called Thatcher and Rourke and hoping that they had not heard him. Who'd know? He could tell them to go on, that he'd be along shortly, and then there'd just be the two of them. It would be all over in five minutes; he wouldn't worry about preliminaries. She'd probably scream, of course, but he knew how to stop that. And afterwards, she wouldn't be in a position to complain. If she did, he'd deny it. They'd take his word against hers. They'd take his word before a Cyp's.

The sweet smell of woman. Christ, he'd know that smell anywhere. Warm. Slightly sickly.

He listened. Was Thatcher coming, or Rourke? There was no sound on the stairs. Perhaps they hadn't heard him. He hadn't shouted that loud.

He stroked her face. It was like silk. Pure silk. She edged away from him and clutched at the blankets.

'Easy, sweetheart,' he murmured. 'Easy does it.'

He'd never had a woman who wasn't willing. Not really. He remembered one who'd fought him at first, but she'd submitted before it had become interesting. But here was one who'd fight and go on fighting. Christ. And no more than fourteen or fifteen. That was illegal back home.

He put one hand under the blankets. She flinched but did not cry out. He could not understand it. She was frightened, he could see that much, but it was as if she were frightened not of him, not of what he was about to do, but of something else. Maybe she won't scream, he thought, his excitement mounting.

He moved his hand down from her shoulders and under her night-gown. He felt her breasts. Jesus, they were like apples. Little apples. Firm and delicious and hot and smooth. And the nipples were hard. It wouldn't take long. Not long.

'You can forget whatever you're thinkin', Webbo,' said Thatcher from the door.

'Wha'!'

Thatcher reached him in three strides.

'I oughta knock your fuggin head off!' he snarled. 'What the

Christ in hell are you tryna do – get us all shot? There are laws, Webbo, laws! Ya stupid great gett!'

'I dunno what you're talking about. I found this one in bed and I was trying to get her into the street.'

'You were gonna have her. If I hadn't walked in you'd have been . . . Look, Markos could've been in this house. He could've come up behind you while you were screwin' her. You daft . . . Aah, what's the bleedin' use! Your goolies'll get you killed one day, Webbo.'

'Crap! I wasn't going to touch her.'

'Not much! All right, scrub it. Have you done this place?'

'Yeah.'

'Both rooms?'

'No, Major bloody Thatcher, not both bloody rooms. And I haven't looked under the bed or in the cracks, either. You can see there's nobody here, you dope.'

'Okay. Come on, love,' said Thatcher to the girl. 'You've got to get up.'

She seemed to know that Thatcher meant her no harm, and she slipped from the bed. Webster eyed her hungrily as she put on an old coat.

Thatcher led her away.

Webster kicked a mound of cigarette-ends which were on the floor beside the bed; butts of English cigarettes, Players and Senior Service. If she's old enough to smoke like a furnace, he thought, she's old enough for a bit of the other. Anyway, I wasn't going to do anything. I wouldn't have laid a finger on her.

He followed Thatcher down the stairs and out into the street.

They had completed the search by nine AM and Markos had not been found. Miller called up the Command Post on the wireless and spoke to the CO.

'One-zero to Sunray, One-zero to Sunray. Message. Over.'

'Sunray listening. Send your message. Over.'

'One-zero, hunt over but no sign of fox. Over.'

'Sunray – let's drop the wireless procedure, Richard; I don't think the locals are sophisticated enough to be tapping the line. What do you suggest now? Over.'

'Begin again from scratch, sir. We've missed him. I'm sure Constantinides wasn't lying. Over.'

'He could have been and gone, of course. Over.'

'I doubt it, sir. The way Constantinides told the story he was supposed to meet Markos here this morning. It seems reasonable to assume that Markos would have waited for him. Over.'

'Logical, Richard, logical.' A long pause. 'What about the villagers? He could be mixing with the crowd. Over.'

'I'd thought of that, sir, and issued my Section Commanders with a copy of the dossier photograph. They've taken a good look at all likely suspects without success. No, if he's here at all – and I'm sure he is – he's still hidden. Over.'

A longer pause.

'Fair enough, Richard, I'll give you four more hours. Then we'll have to call it off. I can't have three Troops chasing their tails. Over.'

'No, sir. Thank you. Out.'

Miller took off the earphones and handed them to his wireless operator. He signalled his Section Commanders.

'We've got four hours. We'll take a twenty-minute break now for the men to eat, and then we'll begin again. He's here somewhere. We'll tear every house apart if necessary.'

'What about the locals, sir – keep them where they are?'

'We've no choice. I'll get Costas to explain the position.'

The villagers were congregated in and around the village café. They stood, crouched, squatted, lounged, and sat in groups, muttering to one another in undertones and beating their hands against their sides to keep warm. They were a sadly comical sight in their night clothes; like characters in a Molière comedy who suddenly discover that what they believed to be a stage is, in fact, a public park. They were a depressing sight too, with their bare feet and matted hair and thin bodies. But above all they were pathetic. They had lost the power to resist. They were quiescent, resigned. A community survives as a community by virtue of its corporate will, and theirs was non-existent. Only three or four youths, sullen in front of a weather-beaten Coca-Cola advertisement, scowled and shook their fists when Costas told them over the loud-hailer that they were to be kept where they were until one o'clock.

3 Section sat on a wall and broke into their ration packs. From where they were they could see the whole village in detail. It was the identical twin of a hundred others they had been through and raided. Bigger than some, perhaps, smaller than others. Flat-roofed houses with the stucco peeling. An inefficient pump that supplied water and encouraged typhoid. A score of skulking goats which survived on garbage, when the garbage had not already been eaten by the people. A half-dozen tail-down dogs, patchy with mange. A narrow street that led nowhere. Pools of water in pot-holes. Pools that never drained because there was no drainage. An old, bald Michelin tyre from God knows where. And the lingering, belly-heaving, nose-filling, yellow-puke stink of the poor.

'Hoobloodyray,' growled Thatcher. 'Steak-and-kid at last.'

'I've got the Irish,' grumbled Shaw. 'There's a bloody conspiracy somewhere.'

The villagers watched them eat. Dear God, they thought, why is it that the British have so much and we have so little? One of their meals would keep us for two days. Will Makarios change that? Will he give us food where we have none, wine where we have only water, schools where our children can learn and grow wise? Is that what Colonel Grivas is fighting for? Is that why we are treated like cattle?

Shaw spat out a mouthful of stew and poured the remains of the tin on to the ground.

See – see how they waste their food. They know there will always be more. But us – us, Archbishop – what about us? You tell us we will be happier when we are united with Greece. But Greece is a poor country. Are you poor, Archbishop? Are you deprived?

Riordan munched contentedly on a biscuit.

We hate the British. You have taught us to hate them, and who are we to disobey the teachings of Mother Church. But hate does not prevent drought, hate is no substitute for bread. We are Greeks, Archbishop, we are Cypriots – but first we are mothers and fathers. You feed us slogans when we ask for wheat. You preach self-sacrifice when it's shoes we need. Shoes for our children. And a question, Archbishop: Why is it that you look so fat and healthy? Can't we ask? Is that not permitted? It's such a simple question.

'You've got company,' said Rourke to Riordan.

'What?'

'Behind you.'

The little boy was five or six. His trousers and shirt were in rags, and through the dirt his bare feet showed blue with cold. Flies had eaten part of one eye at some time, but he was smiling shyly.

'Ehete shokolates?' he said. 'Ehete biscota?'

'What?' said Riordan. 'What does he want?'

'Ehete biscota?'

'Biscota? What the hell's biscota?'

'Biscuits, you dumb bastard, Riordan,' grinned Hayter. 'The kid wants a biscuit.'

'Biscuit? Do you want a biscuit?'

The boy nodded. 'Biskee. Biskee.'

Riordan gave him the packet.

'Here y'are, then.'

'Efharisto. Efharisto.'

Delighted, the child ran back to the café, shouting, waving his prize.

'Now there's a big tough Marine for you,' gurgled Thatcher. 'Jesus, Riordan, if a kid's not scared of you, how the hell can you expect to flush out a grown man? You'd better give me the bren. I'll see you're issued with an apron back in Platres.'

'Get stuffed.'

'Hey,' said Shaw, 'maybe we can do some trading. I've got a tube of condensed milk here. D'you reckon that 'ud buy me ten minutes with a woman, sarge?'

'You'll have to put in a bigger bid than that with your mug.'

'Fags, then,' suggested Webster. 'These Cyps'll do anything for a packet of Seniors. Twenty fags for a short time. And I know the one I'd have – plump and fourteen.'

'You'd come a cropper,' said Hayter. 'Even if they had the money, they're not allowed to smoke at that age. In fact, until they're twenty-one or married, they're allowed to do bugger all.'

'Then some of them do it on the sly,' said Webster. He turned to Thatcher for confirmation. 'Remember that bird we found this morning? There were a dozen butts by her bed. English butts at that. Bloody chimney she must be.'

'*What was that, Webster?*' Hayter's voice was urgent, imperative.

'That girl, sarge; the one Thatcher and me found. She had a pile of dog-ends by her bed.'

'And you searched the house, you searched it thoroughly?'

Hayter got to his feet. They eyed him curiously.

'Yes, sergeant . . .'

'You're sure? Every room, attic, rafters?'

Webster did not answer. He recalled the girl, her hot body, his cursory search, the room he had overlooked.

'You struck dumb, Webster? *Did you look everywhere?*'

'Well, maybe not everywhere, sergeant, but . . .'

'*You bloody fool, Webster! You bloody fool!* Take a gander behind you. The men smoke pipes unless they can bum a fag, and the women don't smoke at all. Those butts could've belonged to Markos. He might have been hiding in the house. The girl could've been there to throw you off. Mr Langley! *Where the hell's Mr Langley!*'

They surrounded the house, taking cover in other houses, in the doorways and rooms. They had their orders. Costas was to make a surrender announcement. If that failed, 4 Section would fire two tear-gas grenades – one into the ground floor, one into the upper floor. Then they would wait and see.

'It doesn't seem possible,' said Miller, 'that a girl of fourteen could be shielding someone like Markos – if he's there.'

Costas tugged at the peak of his workman's cap. 'It is more than possible, captain. To many of the peasants the EOKA fighters are heroes and they are permitted to choose any one of the village virgins. It is considered a great honour – for the girl and her family.'

Close by, Webster grimaced. Jesus, they couldn't smoke but they could screw themselves stupid. Jesus, what a country.

'Carry on,' said Miller.

Costas picked up the loud-hailer and said, in Greek: 'You –

you in the house. You cannot escape. You have one minute to lay down your arms and come out with your hands above your head. One minute.'

A minute passed. There was no movement from within the house.

'Again,' said Miller.

'You – you in the house . . .'

No movement. No sign of life.

In an upstairs room of the house opposite Hayter chewed the tipped end of an unlit cigarette. Next to him Langley belched and excused himself quietly, while at the adjacent window Shaw squinted patiently along his rifle barrel. Downstairs in the same house Thatcher said, 'I'll be glad to get some kip after this lot,' and Rourke nodded.

In the street, behind the Champ, Riordan pulled back the cocking-piece of the bren.

'I can't see the front door,' he muttered to Porter. 'I'm moving out a couple of yards.'

'You'll be in the firing line when the shooting starts.'

'If it starts. Anyway, I can't see a blóody thing from here. You stay where you are. You can toss the magazines to me.'

'Right.'

Riordan eased over to his left, leaving the cover of the Champ's rear wheels.

Miller switched on the control 88-set. '4 Section, let's try some tear-gas. Out.'

Each tear-gas grenade found its target, and white smoke, like breath on a frosty morning, billowed out into the street.

'Bisley for that boy next year,' growled Miller, and a second later a burst of firing came from within the house.

'He's there! By Christ, he's there!'

Then everything happened so fast that no one, even later, could agree upon the sequence of events.

Somebody yelled: 'There are two of them!'

And somebody else: 'They're coming out!'

'I want Markos alive!' shouted Miller, but his words were lost in the fire power of fifty rifles and automatic weapons.

Two figures emerged from the house, from out of the smoke, shrieking like banshees, carrying rifles and shooting as they ran. One of them was cut down before he had taken a dozen steps. He collapsed like an empty glove puppet. The second ran on, towards the Champ, weaving from side to side. He was clutching something in his right hand. 'Grenade!' bellowed Miller, and ducked. Those near him ducked also, but Riordan, in the open, knew he had no chance. He cursed vilely, and as the figure raised its arm to throw, he aimed for its belly and squeezed the trigger. He shut his eyes and kept on firing. The grenade exploded with a roar and a whine of metal. Riordan screamed involuntarily as a segment of shrapnel entered his body, but he held on to the bren until the magazine was exhausted. Somewhere a girl, Markos' girl, sobbed.

Then silence. The smell of cordite. The smoke drifting leisurely up the street.

'Riordan's been hit, sir.'

'Check him.'

Porter crawled across to Riordan. 'Where did it get you?'

'Thigh.' He grinned weakly. 'Just missed me goolies.'

'He's okay, sir.'

'See to him. Field dressing.'

Miller stood up. The Troop subalterns left their positions and joined him.

'Let's take a look,' he said.

The nearer of the two figures was lying on his back.

'Markos,' grunted Miller. 'What about the other one, Robert?'

Reynolds loped across to the second figure. He turned him over with his boot. Most of his face was missing.

'Unrecognizable, sir, but he won't trouble us again.'

Langley put his hand inside Markos' shirt. He felt the warm stickiness of blood and the pump-pump of the heart.

'Markos is alive, sir.'

'Alive? Are you sure? Here, let me.' Miller pushed Langley aside. 'Christ, he is. Okay, let's get moving. Rig up some sort of ambulance. We'll take him back to Platres. And round up that girl and her family. The SIB will want to talk to them.'

'Yes, sir. Sergeant Hayter. *Sergeant Hayter!*'

Markos underwent an emergency operation in Platres. The

MO removed three of Riordan's bullets from his stomach and sewed up the wounds with forty-six stitches.

He remained in a coma for three days, but on the fourth day, although feverish, he sat up and drank some thin soup. A week later he was judged fit to travel and was sent, by road, from Platres to Nicosia, to a military hospital.

In the ambulance, in English, he twice whispered, 'You will never hang me,' but his guards took this boast to be a symptom of his recent fever, and ignored it.

He studied his captors for five miles. They felt secure – secure in the knowledge that he was helpless. Well, they would see.

Under the cover of the blankets, using all that was left of his strength, he tore out the forty-six stitches, one by one.

He became drowsy.

By the time the guards noticed the pools of blood on the floor and blankets, it was too late. He was pronounced dead on arrival.

FIFTEEN

It snowed heavily on Christmas Eve. From Fillipedes' Bar fingers of light stretched out into the street, illuminating the flakes and making them seem warm and friendly instead of cold and damp. Inside, the off-duty Sections slapped each other on the back, donned paper hats, cracked jokes, poured each other drinks, ate bacon sandwiches and plates of tinned turkey; while outside an occasional great-coated figure, unsteady, stumbled from barrack-room to bar or bar to barrack-room, carrying a bottle, mumbling a carol.

In the Officers' Mess they were having a party; a refined sort of party because it was too early yet for the imported whisky to have had much effect. The bonhomie was genteel, the laughter subdued, and the grunts that passed for conversation epiglottal. Christmas-cards hung, on twine, from the walls. The manufacturers' messages were curiously inept, and it was apparent that the sentiment-writers at Valentine's had never considered to whom the cards would be sent. *Peace and Goodwill to all men. Hope your holidays are happy days. God rest you merry, gentlemen.*

In the Sergeants' Mess, too, they were having a party, but there no one was much concerned about dignity or rank. After all, tomorrow could mean a bullet in the back or an unwary foot on a landmine. It had happened before; it would happen again.

Farther down the street even Joe's Bar was doing record business, and Joe congratulated himself on having had the foresight to buy a Frank Sinatra album.

In the canteen the Chaplain tuned the broken-down piano he had filched from one of the hotels, and counted the carol sheets. He had ordered two gross, and he was beginning to regret his rashness. It was unlikely that more than a dozen people would turn up, and half of them would be drunk. However, there was always the Watchnight Service.

They thought of home. Wherever they were and whatever their rank, they thought of home.

Riordan, self-consciously aware of the single chevron he had been awarded for his part in the Markos affair, thought of home. And so did Shaw, chuckling over a dirty postcard; and Webster, impatiently waiting his turn; and Rourke, reading a letter from his wife, now six months' pregnant; and Thatcher and Porter. And Langley, sipping whisky in the Mess, hoping the CO would buy him a drink. And Miller, arguing the merits and demerits of the Schlieffen Plan. And Hayter.

And they thought of other Christmases.

A boar's head stuffed with veal and pork. A jug in the local and a quick nibble at the married barmaid. Port after dinner. A crate of Guinness and a hand of cards. A pheasant shoot and the devastating power of a twelve-bore Holland and Holland. A night out in Pompey and the sleek expertise of the matelots' wives. A toast to the Queen. The shrill cackle and pink bloomers of the sixty-year-old widow doing *Knees Up, Mother Brown*. That shindig at Pat's place, in Chelsea. The nuts and raisins to soak up a bellyful of beer. Mother, wearing her age like a coronet, leaning on her stick and calling for another tot of brandy. Mum, with her hair still in curlers, up at six AM to cook the turkey. Father recreating Jutland with the aid of the salt, pepper, and mustard. Dad lying under the table, his flies wide open, and the girls picked up for the night giggling hysterically.

Gracious living. Easy women. Speeches. Bawdy songs. Toasts. Vomit.

Other Christmases.

Other places.

Other times.

It was Thatcher's idea to bring in the two whores from the other side of the wire. With the exception of selling a few hundred duty-free cigarettes at shop prices to the local Cypriots, he had not had a decent racket since joining the Marines. But where there were women there were profits, he reasoned. And anyway, it was Christmas, wasn't it? The men had money to burn, didn't they? And if they wanted to burn it on women, which they did, it was up to some Samaritan to give them the opportunity.

He solicited Fillipedes' help.

'But eet ees impossible, Meester Thatcher,' said the bar owner, who found it politic to address everyone as 'Mr', regardless of rank. 'You are not permitted to visit the girls. The rules are quite plain. I, myself, have read them. The girls – alas, eet ees sad – in their leetle house, they have no food. Eef eet were not for me' – he stroked his sideburns self-righteously – 'they would starve.'

'I didn't say we were gonna visit them,' persisted Thatcher. 'I said they were gonna visit us. That's the difference, see? There's nothing in the regulations about that, is there? We could set up in your back room, put in a couple o' bunks. Christ, we'd be doin' everybody a favour: the lads, the women, everybody.'

Fillipedes shook his head sadly. 'Eet ees impossible, Meester Thatcher. Eef the authorities discover, they send me to prison. I cannot take the reesk.'

'There's no risk,' said Thatcher. 'We'd keep it under our lids.'

'Pardon?'

'Under our lids . . . Never mind. It'd be a secret, anyway. Besides' – he played his trump card like a veteran – 'there'd be money in it for you.'

'Money?' Fillipedes' brown eyes became less apologetic. 'Money?'

'Sure.' Thatcher was all magnanimity. 'You didn't think I was askin' you to do this for nothin', did you? Not me. We'd be partners. We'll charge the lads four hundred mils a throw, give the girls two-fifty and split the rest between us. Fifty-fifty.'

'Feefty-feefty? Half each?'

Fillipedes did a rapid calculation. Seventy-five mils for him. In the name of the good God, that was two brandy sours. And all profit.

'Half for me?'

'Sure. All you gotta do is talk to the girls. A couple o' mates o' mine from A Troop are on guard tonight. There'd be no trouble gettin' 'em in.'

'You are certain?'

'One hundred per cent.'

'And the beds, the bunks?'

'Easy. I'll fix that. You just explain the deal to the girls.'

Fillipedes stroked several of his chins. There were six, perhaps seven, hundred men in the village. A lot of money, even if very few came. And they would drink while waiting.

'I will do eet,' he said eventually. 'I will talk to them.'

'That's the ticket. Good boy.' Thatcher rubbed his hands. Then came the sixty-four-dollar question. 'They're clean, aren't they?' he asked cautiously. 'I mean, they've got no diseases?'

Fillipedes looked pained. 'Meester Thatcher, of course they are clean. I go to them myself, do I not?'

'Yeah, yeah. 'Course. No offence. See you later.'

'Yes.'

Thatcher went out, whistling.

'*Fall Gelb*, Case Yellow,' Miller was saying to an audience of politely interested junior officers, 'was not in the same class as the Schlieffen Plan. Not until von Manstein got hold of it and improved on it, that is. You see, Manstein's idea was to concentrate his armour on the Ardennes . . .'

'I didn't know Miller was such an admirer of the Germans,' said Reynolds, sotto voce.

'And what's wrong with that?' demanded Langley. He put his fifth large whisky of the evening on a table and lit a fat cigar, one of a box he had received for Christmas from his father. 'Why shouldn't he be?'

'No reason, I suppose, except that they're born losers.'

'Nonsense.'

Reynolds shrugged and quoted: '"I have often felt a bitter sorrow at the thought of the German people, which is so estimable in the individual and so wretched in the generality." Goethe,' he said, in the manner of a lecturer to a dull student.

'You philosophers,' sneered Langley. 'To hear you talk one would think the whole damn' world revolved on an axis of ultimate reality. Next you'll be giving me the chestnut about the Germans having a corporate death wish.'

'Highly probable.'

'Tripe. Look, here's one for you. Does this sound like the words of a man hell-bent on self-destruction? "This policy cannot succeed through speeches, and shouting-matches, and songs; it can only be carried out by blood and iron." Bismarck.'

'Another loser.'

'Temporarily. The Germans will wake up to what he said one of these days.'

'Wake up?' Reynolds frowned. 'Deutschland erwache?'

'If you wish.'

'And you'd like to see it?'

'Why not?' Langley puffed magisterially at his cigar. 'Anyway, they're not going to accept the Oder-Neisse line for ever, and we've got to decide which camp we're in before they make a move.'

'We?'

'Britain. The West. If they march, we march.'

'Straight into a Russian ICBM.'

'Nonsense. They wouldn't risk it. But it's a chance we'd have to take, anyhow. We couldn't let the Germans down. We need them. We need their nationalism – any form of nationalism. It's the biggest and best weapon against communism.'

'Try telling that to the Jews.'

'It got out of hand last time. Look, finish your drink. I'll get you another.'

Reynolds watched Langley's slim figure cross the crowded Mess, and wondered. *It got out of hand last time. We need German nationalism.* God, what a notion. There was something faintly unstable about Brian Langley. Nothing one could analyse and define. Just a certain instability, a lack of cohesion, a part missing. The Troodos fire had demonstrated it admirably if the Sergeants' Mess gossip was to be relied upon. Sometimes he was fanatical about the most trivial of subjects and sometimes indifferent about the most important. It was as if he were two people – what was the word: dichotomous, schizophrenic? – and one was constantly at odds with the other. It was surprising that no one on his selection board had spotted it, although perhaps his father had pulled a few strings there.

Langley returned with the drinks.

'Going back to Bismarck,' he said, 'there still is a case, you know, for blood and iron. For example, if we were less inclined to treat the Cypriots as no more than naughty children, perhaps we'd all be sitting at home this Christmas.'

'The jackboot?'

Langley smiled at Reynolds' deliberate attempt to provoke him.

'Not quite, Robert, not quite. But harsher treatment, yes.'

'We're soldiers, we do as we're told.'

'Then we should be told something different. You've got to admit that slapping a fine on a village is totally ineffective. They simply plead poverty and forget to pay.'

'And you'd like to do what?'

'I'm not sure. More stringent measures, though.'

'Deutschland erwache,' said Reynolds, with heavy irony.

'Meaning?'

'Meaning that I think you're taking your admiration for the Germans a little too far.'

'Oh for God's sake, I'm not advocating firing squads or concentration camps. Although my father . . .' He broke off.

'Yes, your father . . .?'

'It doesn't matter.'

The British are growing effete, Brian. It happens to all great nations when there is nothing left to conquer. A nation should be on a permanent war footing in order to stay strong. We've lost our will to win, to be first. You can blame Attlee and his idiotic crowd for that, of course. The rot began with them. Six years of their Socialist drivel would have put the Roman Empire on its back. We had a spirit during the war, a real spirit. And now look at us! India gone, Africa going, and God knows where next. We need another Churchill. This man Eden – well, he's all right but they broke the mould after Churchill. Now the Germans . . . Good God, they lost, didn't they, but look at them today. If I'd had a regiment of German soldiers, my boy, Dunkirk would have been a different story. The German soldier and the British officer: an invincible combination. They usually say that the other way round: the British soldier and the German officer. *Well, they're wrong, Brian, wrong. The Tommy is too much of an individual. He thinks for himself. The German doesn't do that. He obeys.*

Obedience, my boy, obedience. That's what Germany has taught the world; that's why she's strong. We'd never have beaten them, you know, if it hadn't been for the politicians. Damned politicians cock up everything. Give me a nation of obedient men, Brian, and I'll build you a new empire. Too late now, of course. The Socialists are here. The old days have almost gone, but we'll fight 'em every inch of the way. We have to – to survive. Remember that. I will. *The army is the only place where a man can live under the old rules these days, where his rank entitles him to some respect, where there are no damned unions.* Yes, Father. *Be a good soldier, Brian. I'm relying on you.* And I won't let you down.

'Miller wants us,' said Reynolds. 'I think he's standing a round.'

'Coming.'

Langley tossed his cigar into the fireplace. It fell in a pool of beer, sizzled, and went out.

Hayter ordered another bottle of beer.

'Off the hard stuff, Bill?' said Colour-sergeant Wilson, appearing at his elbow with a tray of empty glasses.

'Yeah. It's playing hell with my guts. If I'm not on patrol I'm smoking, and if I'm not smoking I'm drinking. Something's got to go.'

Wilson chuckled. 'That's not the Bill Hayter I used to know. I remember you shifting a bottle of Marsovin in an hour flat down Floriana way. Let me see, that'd be back in '51 or '52. Remember?'

'Do I not. That was the night we gave Kingsway a belting. I had a mouth like a pair of Arab's underpants for a week.' Hayter's eyes misted at the recollection. 'Christ, Charlie, we had some times in Malta, didn't we? Remember the bars down the Gut: the New Life, the Bing Crosby, the Gyppo Queen? I wonder if they're still there.'

''Course they are.' Wilson handed his tray to the Mess orderly. 'Three brandy sours, two ouzos and two whiskies. 'Course they are,' he repeated. 'Catholics or not, the Malts are good businessmen. Close the Gut and the island 'ud be ruined.'

'Yeah. Yeah, that's true enough.' He sighed. 'Christ, I wouldn't mind being there right now, though.'

'Some day, Bill, some day. This lot won't last for ever.'

'I dunno 'bout that. It could last ten years at the rate it's going.'

'Well, don't think about it.' Wilson picked up his refilled tray. 'Not tonight. It's Christmas. You coming to join us later?'

'Ay, later.'

Hayter took a mouthful of beer. Jesus, it was as weak as cats' pee.

'Give us a brandy, lad.'

'I thought you were on the wagon, sergeant,' smirked the orderly.

'Do I have to ask you before I can come off it?'

'No, sergeant.'

'Then button your lip. I can get you transferred to a fighting Troop, you know.'

'Yes, sergeant. Sorry.'

'I should bloody well think you are. One brandy, a large one, and no cracks.'

'Yes, sergeant.' The orderly uncorked the Keo bottle. 'There you are, sergeant.'

'Put it on the tab.'

Hayter coughed as the brandy made the short trip to his stomach. That was better. Much better. He would go back on beer tomorrow. As Charlie had said, it was Christmas.

They were singing in Fillipedes' Bar.

So beat the drum slowly and play the pipes mournfully
We'll sing the Dead March as we carry him alonn . . . nng.
We'll stand by his graveside, fire three volleys o'er him,
He was a young Royal cut down in his prime . . .

Webster had to shout to make himself heard above the din. 'You mean it, Thatch?' he yelled. 'You've actually got the women back there?'

'Yeah, both of 'em. And keep your bleedin' voice down. We don't wanna riot. Are you in for a slice?'

'Am I? Lead me to it.' He jumped to his feet, then paused. 'Is there anything to pay?' he asked warily.

'No, they do it for love. 'Course you gotta pay, you dumb cluck.'

'How much?'

'Four hundred mils. And you pay me.'

'Why you?'

'Because I organized it, didn't I? I've gotta square Fillipedes and the women.'

'I'll pay you later.'

'Oh no you bloody won't! You don't touch the merchandise until I've got your money. Four hundred mils.'

Webster gave him a note and some silver.

'Through there,' said Thatcher, giving Fillipedes the thumbs-up signal. 'And try not to make a pig of yourself. I don't want 'em worn out.'

Webster disappeared through a door behind the counter.

'Anybody else?' inquired Thatcher. 'What about you, Shaw? Put hairs on your chest.'

'I'll wait and see what Webbo's got to say.'

'You're a cautious bastard, you are. Well, don't wait too long. Pluck 'em while they're fresh, that's my motto. They'll be dead beat in a couple of hours. What about the rest of you? Tim?'

Rourke shook his head. After a mixture of four brandy sours and four ouzos the responsibilities of marriage and prospective fatherhood weighed heavily upon his shoulders.

'Not me, George,' he said thickly. 'Married man.'

'Variety is the spice of life, Tim, but please yourself.'

'I'll have four hundred mils' worth,' said Porter, taking a note from his pocket.

'You're livin' it up, aren't you?' grinned Thatcher. 'They're not college girls in there. They bite.'

'Bollocks. Do you want my money or not?'

'Bloody right. Off you go, then,' he added, when Porter remained seated.

'Now? Webster's in there.'

'So? There are two of 'em.'

'Yes, but . . .'

'No one's gonna be doin' a Kinsey on your winkle, if that's

what you're worried about. The bunks are curtained off. Get goin'. You've got ten minutes. I'm not a charity.'

Porter left the table. Fillipedes smiled lecherously. He ignored him and pushed open the door.

'She'll eat him,' gurgled Thatcher.

'Let's just hope to Christ he doesn't get a dose or you'll be in it up to your ears,' growled Riordan, conscious that he was not doing his duty as a junior NCO by condoning this violation of the camp regulations.

'What's your beef?'

'You are, you mug. You'll get a hundred and twenty days if you're caught.'

'Crap. Anyhow, I'm not gonna get caught, am I? Not unless a certain actin' unpaid Lance-corporal Riordan puts the knife in.'

'Which he should.'

'But which he won't, will he?' Thatcher gave his best but-we're-old-pals-aren't-we smile. Riordan was authority, and authority demanded respect. 'He won't, will he?'

'I guess not.'

'That's the ticket. And if you're a good lad, Riordan, I'll let you have a buckshee one later on.'

'Go stuff yourself. I don't want an arseful of penicillin.'

'Penicillin!' protested Thatcher. 'For Chrissake don't start rumours. We're organized in there. Bowls of water, towels, the lot. I do things properly.' He leaned back in his chair – an embryonic tycoon. 'Christ, it's good to be in business again. Come on, let's have a song and another jar while we're waitin'. Two, three, after me. *Along the street she pushed a perambulator* . . . You're not singin', Riordan. Let's go.'

Along the street she pushed a perambulator,
She pushed it in the springtime and the merry month of May,
Hey, hey!
And when they asked her why the hell she pushed it,
She said it's for a bootneck, who is far, far away.
Far away, not far enough,
Far away, not far enough,
She said it's for a bootneck who is far, far away . . .

The Chaplain, his Carol Service a dismal failure, sipped a pink gin and complained, 'Fifteen people, Richard, that's all I could muster. And not a single officer or senior NCO among them. It really is most disheartening.'

'I suppose it must be,' said Miller, and thought: Why the hell tell me?

'Indeed it is. I had hoped that one or two of the younger officers might have found the time. After all, carols are essentially for youth.'

He peered through his bifocals at youth in the shape of Reynolds and Langley. Reynolds cleared his throat in noisy apology, but Langley was in the mood, after seven whiskies, to argue about Germany, theology, or anything else that came along.

'It's only to be expected, surely, sir,' he said. 'The men were out yesterday hunting terrorists. Some of them are out again tonight. Others will be out tomorrow. You can hardly blame them if they feel that God and *The Holly and the Ivy* have no place in their lives.'

The Chaplain seized with both hands the opportunity to defend his God, his views, and his wounded pride.

'God, young man, has a place in everyone's life, no matter what the circumstances.'

'That wasn't quite what I meant, sir, if you'll forgive me.' Langley pretended not to see Miller's don't-take-this-any-further-or-we'll-be-here-all-bloody-night look. 'I'm no theologian, but I can certainly understand the belief that God can't be very concerned with a man He allows to be shot in the back.'

'You needn't go on, Brian. We take your point.'

'No, no, Richard,' said the Chaplain, 'let him have his say.' And then to Langley: 'Your hypothesis is presumably based on the theory that God, if He exists and if He is all the Church states He is, should not permit murder.'

'Yes, sir.'

'Then you are correct in saying you are no theologian.'

He put his glass on the bar and flexed his ecclesiastical muscles. Miller foresaw a sermon and sighed a quiet sigh of desperation. Reynolds shuffled uncomfortably. Only Langley remained drunkenly interested and unruffled.

'Each one of us is searching,' the Chaplain intoned, 'for happiness and perfection. When we don't find it, it is convenient to blame God, even condemn Him. Why couldn't He have arranged things a little better? we ask ourselves. But why should He? What has God to do with happiness and perfection? We have given Him, in our ignorance, man-made qualities. We assume He will react as we do to pain and suffering. We have transferred our needs and dreams, our opinions regarding the way the world should be run, to Him. But why should His definition of happiness and perfection be the same as ours?'

'Quite,' said Miller, hoping that that was the end of it.

But the Chaplain had got the bit between his teeth.

'All we want from God is peace of mind. When He chooses not to give it, we say He is cruel, unfeeling, or, at the very worst, non-existent. We become atheists because He won't play the game by our rules. Yet He has given us the tools, intellect, to mould Heaven. It's just that most of us prefer Hell.'

'Absolutely,' murmured Reynolds.

Hallelujah, thought Miller.

'If a man wants perfection he must become perfect. God weeps when a child dies, but He will not interfere and save the child. Why should He? There is no perfection without suffering.'

'Yes, sir, I see that,' said Langley. 'But . . .'

'Good,' interrupted Miller. 'I'm glad you see it, Brian.'

Langley took the thinly-veiled hint. 'Yes, sir.'

'Come along to the service tomorrow morning,' said the Chaplain jovially, mistaking Langley's silence for lack of argument. 'I'll make suffering the theme of my address. You will come, won't you?'

'Er . . . of course, sir.'

'Excellent. I'll look out for you. Now if you'll excuse me, gentlemen . . .'

He left them and went out into the Mess to preach the Gospel.

'Serves you damn' well right, Brian,' said Miller. 'He's always like that after a couple of gins and a disappointment.

Never mix religion with pleasure, to coin a phrase. Especially when I'm around.'

'No, sir.'

'So this guy from A Troop decided to work his ticket,' Shaw was saying. 'Whenever he got an order he refused to obey it, and instead picked up things like his boots, his pack, his rifle, muttering, "That's not it, that's not it." Eventually they sent him to the head-shrinker, who asked him a load of questions. But he didn't answer them, see. He just picked up things from the head-shrinker's desk, like the ink-well, the pen-stand, and so on. And he kept on repeating, "That's not it, that's not it." Finally the head-shrinker decided the guy was definitely nutty, and he wrote out his discharge. The guy looked at it and grinned. "That's it," he said, and walked out.' Nobody laughed. 'It's a joke, for Chrissake.'

'Yeah, bloody hilarious,' said Thatcher.

He was worried. By now everyone in the bar had discovered what was going on in the back room, and a queue had formed. A queue of singing, shouting, drunken, paper-hatted Marines who had not touched a woman for months, and who were vociferously announcing their intention of making up for lost time.

'You've got to do something, Thatch,' said Riordan, already visualizing the scene in Captain Miller's office where Lance-corporal Riordan became Marine Riordan. 'You've got to.'

'Like what? If I close the shop I'll get lynched.'

'And I'll tie the knot,' said Webster, counting his money. 'I'll be ready for another bang soon. That Anna – Jeeze, does she know something.'

They scraped him off the tarmac like a piece of strawberry jam,
They scraped him off the tarmac like a piece of strawberry jam,
They scraped him off the tarmac like a piece of strawberry jam,
And he ain't gonna jump no more.
Glory, glory, what a helluva way to die,
Glory, glory, what a helluva way to die,
Glory, glory, what a helluva way to die,
And he ain't gonna jump no more.

'They'll have the bloody law in here,' groaned Thatcher. 'Hey, you guys, quit the singin'! Do you want the RPs in?'

'That's your problem, Thatcher. We're just the customers.'

'Sure we are. Shake it up in front. I'll be too old to enjoy it before I get there.'

They sent him home to mother in a piece of four-by-two,
They sent him home to mother in a piece of four-by-two,
They sent him home to mother in a piece of four-by-two,
And he ain't gonna jump no more.
Glory, glory . . .

'Somebody's gotta talk to them,' pleaded Thatcher. 'Come on, Porter, you're the bloke with the words.'

'What?' Porter raised his head from the table. It felt as heavy as a cannonball, and it ached.

'Talk to them, for Chrissake. Say somethin', anythin'.'

'Wouldn't listen,' mumbled Porter.

He lowered his head and tilted his glass. He spluttered, and a trickle of brandy ran down his chin. Drunk, he thought, and giggled silently. Then he remembered. He remembered the back room and the faded looks of the woman who had helped him undress. The peasant fingers and the smell of grease and cheap scent. The whispered: 'All right, Johnnee, all right, Johnnee. Good, Johnnee.' The moans and obscenities from Webster in the adjacent bunk. And then nothing. The woman had caressed him, toyed with him, tried to arouse some desire. No use. Nothing. But he wasn't incapable. He wasn't, he wasn't, he wasn't. It was Webster who'd put him off. Christ, how could anyone do it with Webster grunting and whispering like that. He wasn't impotent. He'd proved himself with – with . . . God, what was her name? He couldn't even recall her name. But he'd proved it then, in Exmouth. It had been spontaneous with her, unrehearsed, unplanned. But here . . . Christ! You gave your money to Thatcher, went through a door, got undressed, did it, and came back and carried on drinking. No one could do it under those conditions. Webster had, though. And Shaw. And Riordan. He'd soon forgotten about his bloody stripe. Rourke hadn't, though. Not Rourke.

'Rourke,' he said.

'Yeah?'

'Are you going in there?'

'What's that to you?'

'I just wondered.'

'Then don't.'

'Sorry I spoke.'

Nosy sod, thought Rourke. It was none of Porter's business what he did. If he wanted to do it he'd do it. And if he didn't he wouldn't.

He sipped his ouzo.

He could do any damned thing he liked, he said to himself. Anything at all. It was up to him. Just him. It was different for a man, married or not, father or not. A man did it and forgot it. It meant sweet f.a. to him. Now for a woman, that wasn't the same thing at all. Oh, no. A woman thought about it after it was over. Of course, if it would hurt Mary he wouldn't consider it. But it couldn't hurt her. She was thousands of miles away. And what she didn't know wouldn't upset her. 'Course it wouldn't. In any case, it was Christmas. It was Christmas and he was enjoying himself. Why shouldn't he? No reason at all. It was six to four there were other married men in the queue. They were using their heads. 'Course they were. 'Course.

. . . Glory, glory, what a helluva way to die,
And he ain't gonna jump no more.

Hayter stood in the doorway of the Sergeants' Mess, insulated against the cold by a lining of liquor. Across the street, beyond the swirling snow, he could see the lights of Fillipedes' Bar and hear the singing and the laughter. The lads were having a ball. His lads. The Section was his, not Langley's. He'd trained it – what, nearly twelve months ago. Twelve months. Christ, time flew. They'd enlisted as a bunch of scruffy civilians and he'd made them Marines, Shaw and the others. He'd drilled them and cursed them, and they'd made the grade. They were as good as anyone, regular or National Service. He could never tell them that, of course, but they knew. They knew the curses, the abuse, the fatigues, the endless patrols and parades were just part of being a Marine. They knew they were good. Langley knew it, too. He'd taken over a ready-made unit. All he had to do was push the correct button, and they'd respond.

His lads.

One day, if they ever got to Malta, he'd take them down the Gut, show 'em the sights. Yes, he'd do that for them.

He lit a cigarette, cupping the lighter in his hands.

Along the street she pushed a perambulator,
She pushed it in the springtime and the merry month of May . . .

The words of the song were indistinct, lost in the wind and the snow, but he recognized the tune. It was a familiar one.

His lads.

The room grew hotter, and Langley found it increasingly difficult to focus. Snatches of conversation came at him in waves.

'. . . Don't know what's happening up at Brigade. Honestly, all they do up there is play with themselves . . .'

'. . . There was a rumour, old man, that he was given a bowler for taking a thoroughly unhealthy interest in several of the Arab boys . . .'

'. . . Fifteen people. It's most disheartening, really it is . . .'

'. . . His wife, you know. Got the morals of a Cairo whore, and that's being tough on Cairo . . .'

'. . . I said to the officer concerned, you've lost what . . .'

'. . . Schlieffen was undeniably a genius, and a flexible genius . . .'

Langley swayed. Brigade. Arab boys. Fifteen people. You will be there, won't you? Serves you right, Brian. Cairo whore. Schlieffen. God, young man, has a place in everyone's life . . .

'Are you all right, Brian?' said Reynolds.

Langley blinked. What a question. Reynolds was evidently tight.

'Of course I am. Why do you ask?'

'You look pale. Still, you'll be okay when you've had something to eat. They're rustling up some pork sandwiches.'

Pork. Langley's stomach heaved.

'Excuse me,' he gurgled, and made a dash for the door.

He felt better after he had been sick, and the snow on his exposed neck and face was cool and soothing. Fresh air was what he needed, he decided, and began to walk, keeping close to the shelter of the buildings on his right.

A figure emerged from the shadows. 'Who's that?' it demanded.

Langley started. 'Never mind who this is, who's that?'

'It's me. Is that you, Mr Langley?'

'Of course it is. And who the hell's me?'

'Sergeant Hayter, sir.'

'Oh.' Langley joined Hayter under the portico of the Sergeants' Mess. 'Taking the air, sergeant?'

'Yes, sir.'

'Me, too. Damn' warm in the Mess.'

'I know what you mean, sir.'

'Do you? Yes, I expect you do. What's going on over there?' He pointed.

'In Fillipedes'? A party, I suppose.'

'Sounds more like a riot. D Troop?'

'That's their regular haunt.'

'Humph.'

They heard the sound of a plate breaking, and then another.

'Definitely a riot, sergeant.'

'On Christmas Eve, sir?'

'It has been known. Perhaps we should investigate.'

Hayter hiccuped. 'You think so, sir?'

'I do. And if I were you I'd get something for that stomach of yours.'

And on the wall her father keeps a shotgun,
He keeps it in the springtime and the merry month of May,
Hey, hey!
And when they asked him . . .

'Oh, Jeeze,' wailed Thatcher, as a third plate hit the floor and shattered. 'Oh, Jeeze, they'll hear that in Nicosia. For Chrissake take it easy on the crockery!'

'Then tell 'em to shake it up in there.'

'Yeah. We've paid as well.'

A fourth plate joined its three cousins.

Thatcher put his hands over his ears and shut his eyes. Five minutes, he thought. Five minutes and every RP in the camp'll be here. And then that's it. That really is bloody it. Finish George Thatcher. Oh, what a mug. What a bleedin' mug.

Riordan nudged him.

'Sod off.'

The elbow persisted in trying to bore a hole in his ribs. He opened his eyes. The queue had stopped singing. He took his hands from his ears. Not a sound. Not a murmur.

'Let's keep it like that!' he yelled.

'Keep what like what?' asked Langley from the door.

'Wha . . .!'

'Keep what like what?'

Covered in snow Nanouk and friend in the bodies of Langley and Hayter trod an unsteady path between the tables. They stood over Thatcher.

'I asked you a question.'

'I just – er – meant – er – keep the noise down, sir.'

'I see. And why are these men in a queue?'

'Pardon, sir?'

'Why are these men in a queue?'

'What queue, sir?'

'That queue. What's through that door?'

'What door, sir?'

'That one. Well, if you won't tell us we'll see for ourselves. Come along, Sergeant Hayter.'

'With you, sir.'

They went into the back room. The door closed with a click of utter finality. The queue dispersed.

Thatcher held his head and wondered what prison grub was like.

They waited. Five minutes passed.

'The bastard's only collecting evidence, isn't he,' growled Shaw. 'What a bum.'

A further five minutes went by before the door reopened. Langley came out first, his face red.

'Carry on, men,' he said, looking neither right nor left.

'*Pardon, sir?*'

'I said carry on, Thatcher. Carry on with your party. Ready, Sergeant Hayter?'

'I'm right behind you, sir.'

Hayter gave them a broad, drunken wink and followed Langley out into the snow.

Pandemonium broke loose.

'The crafty getts!' bellowed Webster. 'The crafty, lecherous old getts!'

Thatcher was almost crying with relief.

'You were born with a silver spoon up your backside,' said Rourke, standing.

'Where are you going?'

'I'm going to jump that queue, that's where. It's different for a man, isn't it?'

'It sure is. It sure as hell is.'

And on the wall her father keeps a shotgun,
He keeps it in the springtime and the merry month of May,
Hey, hey!
And when they asked him why the hell he kept it,
He said it's for a bootneck who is far, far away.
Far away, not far enough,
Far away, not far enough,
He said it's for a bootneck who is far, far away . . .

SIXTEEN

Winter left the Troodos and spring hustled in – verdant, fresh, hopeful.

A truce was called in March, and for a while there was a lull in the killing, the patrols, and the ambushes. The politicians, in London and elsewhere, with simulated frowns that were intended to convey concern to the waiting pressmen, debated, dispassionately, how the Emergency could be brought to an end. Flanked by hosts of civil servants all anxious to see their names in the next Honours List, they discussed policy as though they were rewriting Revelations. Casualty figures were exchanged, between a working breakfast and lunch, like postage stamps. Academic arguments flew across the conference table with the incisiveness of damp straw. Finally they failed to agree, and the word went out to recommence hostilities. Wearily the troops zeroed their rifles, polished their bayonets, drew extra supplies of ·303 ammunition from the stores, and reacquired the habit of glancing over their shoulders every sixty seconds.

Langley was injured in the middle of March. He was travelling in a Champ from Amiandos to Platres when a home-made grenade was hurled from the cover of a nearby copse. The grenade failed to explode, but the Champ's driver, in taking evading action, turned the vehicle over, and Langley suffered a broken ankle. He was sent to Nicosia to convalesce. Hayter assumed command of the Section during his absence.

On April 3 Rourke received a cablegram. It was from his wife and read: *Boy. Monday. Eight pm. Nine pounds. Both fine. Names, please.* Rourke cabled back: *Timothy George. Write with photograph soonest.*

In the evening of April 3 Rourke and Thatcher got very drunk in Fillipedes'. 'Named him after you, George. Bes' pal . . . ever had.' 'Thanks, Tim, thanks. Am I godfather?' 'Bloody right. When we get home . . . have proper party. You, me an' Mary.' 'An' Tim George. Don' forget Tim George. Chris', me a godfather.' 'Bes' goddam godfather ever. Knew that . . . moment . . . saw you.' 'What do I have . . . do?' 'Dunno. Teach him, 'xpect.' 'Teach him wha'?' 'Things.' 'Oh, things.' 'I'll help. Mary too. Big 'sponsibility.' 'You're a goo' bloke, Tim.' 'An' you. We'll stick together, eh, you an' me, George? You an' me. See it through. No goddam Cyp's going . . . get us.' 'Too bloody true. You watch my back an' I'll watch yours. Hey, Fillipedes . . .'

Later in April D Troop were given a week's local leave. They went to a rest camp near Larnaca, and for seven days lazed on a beach and swam in a blue sea. Stretched out on the white sands they tried to imagine themselves elsewhere, and sometimes they succeeded. But when they opened their eyes and saw the guns of the guards who protected the beach, they remembered that this was Cyprus. Soon their leave would be over. Soon they would be back on patrol. For one or more of them it could be their last patrol. They spent most of their leave pay on brandy and ouzo and cheap wine.

It was early in May when Porter killed the little girl. Riordan had sprained a wrist, and Porter was on the bren, with Webster as his number two. They had positioned themselves at the end of a street. The youth they were waiting for came out of a house and ran towards them. He was brandishing a pistol. He saw the bren and grabbed the little girl to use as a shield. She was ten or eleven, and Porter would never forget the faded yellow of her dress, her skinny brown arms. He had orders to shoot on sight, but he could not fire. Webster shouted: 'Let him have it, for Chrissake!' He hesitated, trying to angle his shot. The youth had slowed to a walk, confident that his hostage was his passport out. Porter was suddenly calm. He squeezed the trigger. The girl fell, followed by the youth. When they got closer they saw that the little girl was dead, and they were surprised at how much blood one tiny body could exude. The youth lived, and Porter often wondered at the terrible irony of it all.

Later that same month Davidson, of Y Troop, lost an arm. The humerus had been shattered by a dumdum bullet, and there was no alternative to amputation. He cried bitterly when he recovered from the anaesthetic, and no one could console him. He had been a first-class amateur boxer in Civvy Street and it was rumoured that he would have turned professional on completing his National Service.

He was given an honourable discharge.

At the beginning of June A and D Troops were called from Platres to deal with a dockyard riot in Limassol. Fighting had broken out between the Greeks and Turks. The Marines had orders not to shoot unless shot at, and they attempted to disperse the mob using only their entrenching-tool helves. The Greeks responded with sticks and stones and anything else that came to hand. An English journalist photographed the incident and somehow managed to smuggle the negative off the island. It showed Shaw, his face covered in blood, grinning and cracking skulls as though they were walnuts. It was published as anti-Government propaganda in the left-wing newspapers, but the move misfired. Instead of being at the centre of an indignant outcry, Shaw became a minor hero. He received one hundred and fourteen letters of congratulation. Some of the writers enclosed money, and 3 Section drank genuine Scotch for a fortnight.

In the last week of June B Troop raided a village close to Paphos. In one of the houses they unearthed a cache containing weapons, ammunition, and EOKA pamphlets. The occupants were arrested and the Troop Commander ordered the house to be razed to the ground. It was constructed of wood and caught fire instantly. Some of the villagers made threatening gestures as it burned, and the Marines hoped that they would try to interfere. They were tired of these peasants, who were for ever protesting their innocence and simultaneously giving food and shelter to the terrorists. They were not simple farmers but vicarious killers.

The peasants did not interfere, and spring, in its turn, left the Troodos.

. . . . .

Decoded, the signal read: Governor requests detachment of Marines special duties Nicosia one day only. Governor and Turkish VIPs making grand tour of City as Whitehall public relations stunt. Maximum publicity essential to show Greeks no intention of leaving Turks to their tender mercies. Maximum security also vital. Confirm soonest.

It was signed by the C-in-C.

The off-duty Troop Commanders drew straws for the mission, and Miller drew the short one.

The open one-tonner groaned and bounced along in second gear, throwing up clouds of dust. In the back 3 Section sat facing outwards, scanning the shops and houses for that telltale sudden movement which could send them to the mortuary. They were nervous and it showed. This was unknown territory. They were more accustomed to the mountains and the forest. Here, in the centre of old Nicosia, they felt vulnerable.

The truck turned right. Langley stuck his head out of the passenger window and called, 'Ledra Street.'

So this was it, they thought. Ledra Street. Murder Mile. The setting of a score of killings. A narrow, noisy, dirty, colourful street off which ran a confused warren of tiny straggling alleys, bolt-holes for would-be assassins: subsidiary veins of darkness and squalor.

As always, the smell was the first thing that struck them – or rather, in this case, a diffusion of smells, each faintly distinguishable in itself yet combining with others to hang motionless and heavy in the July heat: of unwashed bodies and sores that were slow to heal, goat's meat decaying in the sun, dogs, urine, animal droppings, rotting vegetables, oil fumes from ancient and battered Fords and Citroens. The all-embracing nose-fillers of the Levant. And the sounds: of a distant bell, tinny, motor-car horns, the raucous, alien cries of the fish sellers, beer sellers, clothes sellers, everything sellers; the jeers from the white-shirted youths. And the sights: of urchins lying on the sidewalks, in the shade, too hot and indifferent to worry about the flies which congregated around their nostrils and in their loose mouths – fat flies, some red with the blood they had sucked; beggars, dressed in the ubiquitous black, sitting cross-legged, their arms outstretched, their palms open, their eyes sightless; women with young babies slung at the waist in carry-straps, going about their business; one middle-aged white woman, floppy-hatted, fearless, a refugee from nineteenth-century India, evidently a believer in the theory of God taking care of the British.

Sweating, heaving, jostling people.

Businessmen. Clerks.

Housewives. Tradesmen.

Gunmen somewhere.

Priests.

And then came the children – suddenly, surprisingly. A slight bend in the road and there they were – adolescents, really, their ages ranging from twelve to sixteen. A hundred or more of them, they stood at the end of the street, blocking it. Curiously, the girls outnumbered the boys by some two to one. Tall girls, short girls, pretty girls, plain girls, their immature, unfettered breasts pushing gently at the thin cotton of their dresses. They made no sound as the truck approached, shouted no slogans. They were quiescent, passive, disciplined. They waved no banners, carried no leaflets. They seemed content merely to obstruct.

Langley ordered the driver to stop. He jumped from the cab and called over his shoulder: 'Stay where you are and keep me covered.'

He went forward.

A hundred pairs of hostile eyes studied his wiry ever-pale body, and he noticed something he had not seen from the cab. Every face wore the same expression: one of smouldering and bitter hatred.

'Stupid sod'll get himself torn to bits if he's not careful,' muttered Webster from the truck.

Langley walked the length of the front rank and then retraced his steps. He paused before a small boy and took a bar of chocolate from his pocket. It was sticky and melting, but still chocolate. He held it out. The boy gazed longingly at the bar and its silver-paper wrapper, but made no attempt to take it. He offered it to several of the others. No one would accept it.

'Please yourselves,' he said, forgetting that they would not understand him.

He turned his back on them, and as he did so a stone, flung

from the rear of the crowd, hit him on the side of the head. He staggered and put a hand to his temple. It came away red and a trickle of salty blood ran into his mouth. He reached for his pistol, more angry than hurt.

'Who did that?' he demanded, raising the pistol to chest level.

There was no answer. The children in front tried to retreat a couple of paces, but they were prevented from moving by those behind.

'Who did that?'

Silence. The hatred in the children's eyes had now been joined by fear.

From the truck Hayter saw the danger. It would take very little for the fear to become panic and the panic to become a riot.

'Get ready,' he cried crisply. 'If Langley keeps on waving that bloody pistol, this could be it.'

'How many rounds, sergeant?'

'A volley over their heads. If that doesn't work, as many as it takes to drop the front row.'

'Drop them . . .?' said Thatcher.

'That's what I said. Aim for their legs . . .'

'You mean we've got to shoot *at* them?'

'You heard me, Thatcher. I know they're kids, but there's a lot of them. They could make a dent even in your thick skull.'

'But *at* them, sarge. You can't . . .'

'*Shut your goddam mouth, Thatcher!* I don't see any stripes on your sleeve.'

'But kids . . .'

'*Shut it!*'

Thatcher shut it.

In the street Langley dabbed his head with a handkerchief, and holstered his pistol.

'You little bastards,' he said, and returned to the truck.

Hayter wiped his forehead. 'You okay, sir?'

'Yes,' said Langley. 'Home,' he added to the driver. 'Can you reverse here?'

'I think so, sir. The CP?'

'Yes.'

The D Troop Command Post comprised two three-ton trucks, two one-ton trucks, a supply truck, and Captain Miller's Champ, and was situated in a small square half a mile from Ledra Street. On arrival, Langley dismissed the Section and limped across to Miller to report.

'How's the ankle?' asked Miller.

'Not too bad, sir, thanks. Get's a bit stiff at times, that's all. Not used to the exercise.' He had been out of hospital a fortnight.

'And what happened to your head?'

'A stone, sir. There are a hundred or so children at the far end of Ledra Street. One of them decided he didn't like me.'

'What are they doing, demonstrating?'

'No, just blocking the street. They're organized, though. At least, they've obviously been given instructions to do nothing but obstruct.'

'That figures. They're going to be a bloody nuisance before the afternoon's out. Are they making any noise?'

'No, sir. Except for the little swine who threw the stone, they're simply standing there.'

'I see. Well, we'll discuss it later. I've called an O-group for two o'clock. In the meantime, I'd advise you to rest that ankle. There's some cold beer in the supply truck. Try not to let the men see you drinking it.'

'Thank you, sir.'

Langley limped off. Miller unfolded a street map and made several jottings in the margin. Ledra Street, he thought. Slap bang in the middle of the Governor's route.

'Kids,' said Thatcher. 'So now we're shootin' kids, are we.'

He was sitting on the tailboard of one of the three-tonners, a cigarette dangling from the corner of his mouth.

'He meant it, you know,' he said. 'Hayter bloody meant it.'

'Of course he did,' said Shaw. 'What else could he have done – given 'em a stick o' rock apiece? They could've ripped Langley to pieces. Not that I give a sod about Langley, but they'd've started on us after him.'

'But some of 'em were only twelve or thirteen, for Chrissake.'

'So what,' said Webster. 'If they're old enough to chuck bombs and run messages for bumface Grivas, they're old enough to get shot at. That's the way I read it. If they don't want to get shot they should stay at home, read dirty books and play with themselves. It's as easy as that.'

Thatcher spat into the dust. The saliva made tiny wet spheres.

'Well, I wouldn't have done it, Hayter or no Hayter.'

'You'd've done it,' chipped in Riordan. 'You'd've done it because that's what you're paid for, that's what you're here for.'

'Balls, lance-bloody-corporal, and double balls. I'm here 'cause I'm stupid. I'm here 'cause a little bloke up in Manchester eighteen months ago said, Sign here, son, and I signed. I'm here 'cause I hadn't got enough sense to catch TB or grow flat feet. I'm here 'cause nobody told me about the Pay Corps or REME. That's why I'm here – not to shoot kids.'

'You'd've done it,' repeated Riordan, 'because you'd've been court-martialled if you hadn't. That's why you'd've done it.'

Thatcher was silent for a moment, then: 'Yeah, I guess so.' It was a sorrowful admission. 'Yeah, you're right, Riordan, you're right. Christ, what a hell of a fuggin war.'

He slid off the tailboard and walked out of sight, round to the front of the truck where he sat on the bumper-bar.

'What the hell's biting him?' said Webster. 'Kids, adults, what's the difference? That's right, isn't it, Porter? You're the guy who should know.'

'Shut up,' said Porter.

'Eh?'

'Shut your bloody mouth.'

'Yes, shut your bloody mouth,' said Rourke.

'Fug me,' muttered Webster, 'everybody's a prima donna.'

On the bumper-bar Thatcher swatted a fly that had alighted on his arm. He wiped the resultant sticky mess on his shirt.

He wanted to be alone. His thoughts disturbed him. They were new thoughts and, through lack of vocabulary, he was unable to express them properly. But somewhere in the jumble he was troubled by the appearance of the children, with their appearance as a whole, with their clothes and shoeless feet.

Nicosia wasn't Manchester but it could be if he closed his eyes. Yes, it could easily be. There they were, the kids, parading up and down Market Street, not quiet now but singing. *The big ship sails through the Illy-ally-o, the Illy-ally-o, the Illy-ally-o, the big ship sails through the Illy-ally-o on the last day of September*. Soon the police would come and chase them; chase them out of the city centre and along the back streets, across bomb-sites, over rubble, into broken-down houses. Well-fed policemen and skinny children. Funny, you never saw a skinny copper. But the kids would win in the end. They always did. They were younger. They had age, if nothing else, on their side. And then they'd go home to tea. Not much of a tea: a couple of slices of bread and marg, a sardine maybe. Not much of a tea but something.

The kids of Nicosia were pretty similar to the kids of Manchester. Poor kids, kids without money, were the same all over the world.

Christ, the one you shot could have grown up to be a somebody.

. . . . .

Even in Manchester children have dreams. Even slum children.

I'm gonna be big one day. I'm gonna own this city.

Sure you are, George. Now be quiet.

His parents are dead. He lives with his two elder brothers, but they have no time for him.

He walks the streets at night. No one cares if he is out until midnight.

He loves the bright lights, the shining windows full of unobtainable goodies. He presses his face against the glass, squashing his nose out of shape, and counts all the things he will have. The bike, the red one. The train-set. A collection of toy cars. Hundreds of them.

Small dreams but very real. Dreams fed on deprivation. Fantasies nourished by neglect.

He watches a courting couple in a doorway, and giggles. He knows what they are doing. His brothers do it with their girl friends. He spies on them occasionally.

Sod off, kid.

Sod off, yourself.

I'll larrup your backside.

You an' whose army?

He runs, and from a safe distance pulls faces at the interrupted lovers.

During the day he plays on a piece of waste land. Bombed buildings tower above him. Skeletons. Fleshless. The war has been over a year, but no one seems anxious to rebuild the shattered, lifeless houses.

For a dare he enters a four-storey derelict warehouse. The stairs no longer exist and the only way to the roof is via a rickety iron wall-ladder in the lift shaft.

He climbs.

His arms ache after a dozen rungs, his legs feel weak, but he has to go on. His friends are below, jeering, betting he will not have the courage.

Thirty feet up he pauses. The stanchions which secure the ladder are rusty at this point. The brickwork in which they are imbedded is loose. He looks down. Hell, it's a long way to fall. He shuts his eyes and continues to climb, sweating.

A gust of cool air fans his hot, wet face. He grins and shouts, Come on up. It's easy.

But his friends decline.

He sits on what remains of the roof. Everything on the ground appears very tiny. Tiny cars, tiny houses, tiny people. At this height, despite his lack of inches, he is the equal of the whole world. There is nothing he cannot do.

He stays on the roof until it is dark, and then is unable to make the descent. It takes two firemen to get him down, and he cries – not because of fear but because he called for help.

The big ship sails through the Illy-ally-o,
The Illy-ally-o, the Illy-ally-o . . .

Clear off, you kids.

Get stuffed!

You cheeky little bugger. I'll give you what for . . .

He runs. They all run. They are always running. From one street to another, from one piece of ground to an adjacent piece, from policemen, householders, shopkeepers . . . Nowhere to rest, nowhere to play. Unwelcome in the street, unwelcome in the house. Delinquents, a newspaper terms them. A menace, says a councillor. Something should be done, say the parents, drinking in the local.

And something is done. A benefactor builds them a club. He installs a table-tennis room, a couple of dart-boards, a reading room, a wireless.

They wreck the club within a week.

Ungrateful little wretches, says the benefactor, and decides that his philanthropy would be more appreciated elsewhere.

They do not understand why they wrecked the club. It was a good club, a place to go. It would have been fine except for the rules about cleanliness and silence and discipline. People, they conclude, only give you things because it makes them feel better.

His thirteenth birthday passes unheralded. All day he waits for his brothers to wish him, Happy Birthday. But they only grumble as usual.

Got put on short time today. Three-day week startin' Monday. Bloody Labour Government. Fat lotta good it's done us.

Ay, they'll be layin' off in the maintenance shop next. Have to cut down on fags.

Yeah. An' grub. It'll be better when George is workin'. He's just a useless mouth right now.

Ay, that he is. All kids are the same. Catch me gettin' married, slavin' me guts out for some woman.

Or me. I can get all I want without makin' it legal.

They laugh.

He leaves the room and wanders out into the street.

Useless mouth? Him? Well, he'd show them.

The woman outside the cinema pays no attention to the scruffy teenager standing behind her. Her shopping basket is bulging with groceries, and on top is a purse. It'll be easy, he thinks. Dead easy.

He barges into the woman, apologizes gruffly, and leaves with the purse. He opens it and counts his haul: almost four pounds. A fortune. He wonders what he will do with the money, and while he is wondering a policeman takes him by the ear.

This him, ma'am?

That's him.

The Juvenile Court is crowded. He recognizes one or two of the children.

And then it is his turn.

The Chairman lectures him for ten minutes.

You children don't know how lucky you are. You have everything in this country. Your fathers fought a war to give you everything, but sometimes, in this Court, I doubt whether it was worth it. You have advantages your parents never had: free education, free medical treatment, a chance for a decent future. Hope for that future lies with your generation. And what do you do? You steal. If I had my way I'd have you birched. You'll never amount to anything, that's patently obvious. You promise you won't steal again, but I know you will. It would have been better for some of you if you'd never been born.

Later, when it is dark, he walks the streets. He longs to be a grown-up. At least grown-ups can do more or less what they like. Nobody wants kids; not in Manchester, anyway, and probably not anywhere.

Useless mouths.

However, he thinks, today's kids'll be tomorrow's grown-ups. Maybe things'll be different then.

And youth shall inherit the earth.

Maybe.

. . . . .

Thatcher brushed a bead of perspiration from the end of his nose, and glanced up as a shadow blocked out the sun. It was Porter.

'Hayter wants you.'

'What for?'

'I don't know.'

'Okay. Prob'ly to bollock me for this mornin'.' Thatcher got to his feet. He hesitated before saying, 'Porter . . .'

'Yes?'

'You were a student, weren't you? I mean, you'll have read a lot, won't you?'

'A bit.'

'Well . . . Oh, I dunno.'

'Go on.'

'Well, it's all a bloody great lie, isn't it? I mean everything – what you're told, what you read. I mean . . . Oh, forget it. Scrub it.'

He walked off, straightening his beret as he went, and Porter only partly understood.

SEVENTEEN

It was two-ten before the Section Commanders were assembled for the O-group. The heat was unbearable now – city heat – and the buildings on all sides of the square shimmered. A solitary tree in the centre of the square drooped like a hanged man.

Miller began by recapping briefly. He told them that they were acting as riot police for the day; that two leaders of the Turkish community and the Governor would conclude their grand tour by visiting part of the Turkish sector; that to achieve the maximum effect it had been necessary to give the tour a great deal of publicity; and that as a result of the publicity the top brass were scared stiff an assassination attempt would be made.

'Which is where we come in,' he said.

He pushed his green-tinted sun-glasses up on to his head, and opened the street map.

'The route will take the VIPs near the Pancyprian Gymnasium and, later, across the north side of Ledra Street. The Special Branch had received a tip-off, partly confirmed by Brian's recce this morning, that the Gymnasium students are going to hold a large-scale demonstration either in Ledra Street or outside the school.'

'That's hardly original,' said Reynolds.

'No, it isn't, Robert, but our problem is we're not sure of the reason for the demonstration. It could be the mixture as before – lots of huffing and puffing and little else. But I doubt that, and so does the SIB. We don't believe in coincidences. I'll bet my gratuity against a lance-corporal's pay that Grivas is up to his greasy neck in this. And I don't have to remind you what could happen if the students succeeded in halting the convoy for five minutes in a built-up area. A bomb from a window and we'd be minus a Governor, I'd become a second-lieutenant again, and you gentlemen would spend the rest of your service scrubbing the heads. The Turks wouldn't be very pleased, either. However, the convoy won't be stopped because we won't allow it to be.'

He took a cigarette from his case and indicated that the others could smoke if they wished.

'The convoy,' he continued, 'starts at four o'clock from the Governor's Mansion. Here.' He tapped a spot on the map. 'The party should be over by five. We set off at three o'clock and cruise the streets, paying particular attention to Ledra Street and the Gymnasium. ETA for the convoy at the Gymnasium is four-ten, and four-twenty-five at Ledra Street. We break up any mobs long before then.'

'Method, sir?'

'Fixed bayonets as far as possible. If that proves hopeless, tear-gas. After that, my discretion. I don't want to kill anyone, but neither do I want any of our fellows killed. We'll shoot if it can't be avoided.'

'Why three o'clock, sir?' someone asked.

'Useless to go any earlier,' answered Miller. 'We can't be in half a dozen places at the same time, and if we have to disperse a mob, it can re-form as soon as we've gone. Timing will be crucial. Ideally I'd like the streets to be empty two minutes before the V IPs arrive.'

'Then why not use more troops?' said Reynolds. 'Station them at all the potential flash-points.'

'Wouldn't work, Robert. Too many soldiers will scare off the locals, and it's for their benefit that Whitehall is putting on the show. For the same reason we can't impose a three o'clock curfew. Anyone else?'

There were no more questions.

'Okay,' said Miller, 'you can brief your Sections now. Be embussed by two-fifty at the latest. 1 Section in the first three-tonner, 2 Section and Support in the second three-tonner, 3 and 4 Sections in the one-tonners. We'll sandwich the supply truck between 3 and 4 Sections. Off you go.'

Alone, Miller consulted his watch: two-twenty-five.

'Are we in contact with the SIB?' he asked the Champ's wireless operator.

'Yes, sir.'

'Good. Get them for me.'

'Yes, sir.'

Miller lit a second cigarette from his first and inhaled a lungful of cool, nerve-soothing smoke. Security men, he thought. Idiots. It was begging for trouble to route the convoy via Ledra Street.

From one of the cafés on the east side of the square a half-dozen elderly, bearded Cypriots, leisurely sipping their afternoon coffee, watched with interest the hustle and bustle on the square itself. Such energy, they thought. And at the hottest time of the year, too. No wonder the British were a colonial power. No wonder they were rich. And no wonder they were always at war with one country or another: they had never learned to relax.

They sighed sleepily.

There was a lot to be said for not being British. Power created its own problems. Riches made few real friends. And too much energy eroded the tissues very rapidly.

Yes, there were chapters to be said for not being British. And for not being young any longer.

A driver pressed the starter of his three-tonner. The engine bellowed into life. The exhaust spewed out black smoke. The driver waited for the signal.

The lance-corporal i/c the supply truck wedged himself between a crate of 24-hour ration packs and several boxes of grenades. He puffed surreptitiously at a cigarette.

2 Section's senior NCO wrapped lengths of bandage around both hands and pulled on a pair of gloves. It was an old trick but one which had served him well in the past. At close quarters he would not get his knuckles broken.

In the passenger seat of the first one-tonner Langley eased himself into a more comfortable position, while in the back of the truck Hayter resolved to let Langley make his own decisions if it came to a fight. He resented Langley's return to active duty, his peremptory reassumption of command without so much as a word of thanks.

Behind Hayter 3 Section were quiet. They faced each other, three on either side of the truck. Like everyone else, they waited.

On the running-board of the Champ Miller raised his arm. 'Tell the SIB we're on our way,' he said to the wireless operator, and gave the signal.

How incredible it all was, he thought, as the convoy moved off to an accompaniment of head-shaking from the ancients in the café. How incredible that a phalanx comprising six vehicles valued at something like fifteen thousand pounds, sixty or so men whose training must have cost a hundred thousand, and equipment which was worth another ten thousand was cruising the streets of Nicosia, looking for a bunch of children whose immediate aim in life was to reduce that one hundred and twenty-five thousand pounds to so much dust. And then there was the time and effort taken to plan the operation, the Most Secret cables from Whitehall, the Governor's escort, the midnight oil burned by the SIB. Add how much for that? A further hundred thousand? Yes, easily. Two hundred and twenty-five thousand pounds. Round it off to, say, a quarter of a million. A quarter of a million on public relations. Christ, all Grivas had to do was wait until the British went bankrupt.

From the sidewalk a ragamuffin poked out his tongue at the passing vehicles.

Nicosia, thought Miller – in its mentality, at least – was not so very different from any smallish English town. In fact, the present operation was rather like invading Market Harborough or Bingley or Welwyn Garden City; like driving up to the Town Hall and saying to the astonished clerks and typists, 'You're under arrest. You will not go to the cinema tonight. You will not walk about the streets without an identity card. We are going to search your typewriters for propaganda leaflets and your sandwich-boxes for bombs.' Like that. Of course, the average typist in Market Harborough did not carry sudden death in her handbag.

A Royal Navy helicopter flew overhead. It was low enough for Miller to be able to see the pilot clearly, and he acknowledged the friendly wave, thinking: add two hundred and fifty thousand for the chopper.

'What speed are we doing, driver?'

'Twenty-five, sir.'

'Slow down to twenty. We're in no hurry.'

He studied the road ahead of him. A donkey, almost invisible beneath an enormous load, trotted out of the convoy's path at the behest of its master.

The sun on his neck and the slip-stream in his face and the soft monotones, the Rogers and Wilcos, of the wireless operator logging routine messages, made him drowsy, and he mused, It's not such a bad country, forgetting how, earlier, he had cursed the heat and spent most of the morning swatting flies. Of course, he thought, it wasn't really a country at all, not to a military man. It was a tiny smudge on a map, put there, it seemed, as an afterthought by the cartographer. A space filler, a frying-pan shaped blur coloured red and marked BC for British Colony. It had no people, only a strategic significance. It had no towns, no animals, no crops, no seasons; it didn't live and breathe; men and women did not make love on it, die on it; babies were not born in its houses and hospitals. It was simply an outpost of the Western Defence System. It could be removed from the map by a well-aimed ICBM. Removed. Annihilated. Sunk. A latter-day Atlantis which had served its brief purpose. And then, in about a million years, some boffin or other with a grant from the World Government would descend to the seabed and rediscover it. He'd find nothing but rock and sand, naturally, and maybe a few fossilized bones, but he'd get a mention in the Times and everyone would ask: 'I wonder what sort of individuals they were?' And someone would answer: 'Who cares? They're very dead.'

Very dead. Miller took off his sun-glasses and rubbed his eyes. Very dead was what he'd be if he didn't stop dreaming. Concentrate, you bloody fool, he reprehended himself. Forget one million AD and concentrate on 1956.

They drove on.

'The Gymnasium's coming up, sir.'

'Yes, I see it. Looks damned quiet to me. Pull in here.'

The driver waved down the convoy and brought the Champ to a halt. Miller jumped out.

The area surrounding the Gymnasium was deserted except for one or two students who eyed the convoy with undisguised belligerence, and several passers-by who hurriedly disappeared down a side alley. Even for the hottest part of the day it was too deserted, and that, thought Miller, meant one of two things. Either the students were inside their white walls of learning, studying the new Humanities – Grivas on assassination and Ashiotis on sabotage – and waiting for the troops to leave, or they were in Ledra Street.

'How long will it take us to get to Ledra Street from here?'

'Ten minutes, sir, if we have a straight run.'

Miller nodded. Ten minutes. It was three-thirty now and the VIPs were due to pass Ledra Street at four-twenty-five, which would necessitate the convoy being in position by four o'clock at the latest. They could therefore stay where they were for fifteen minutes, twenty at the outside.

'Contact the SIB,' he ordered the wireless operator, 'and ask them to send a chopper over Ledra Street. I'd like to know what's going on up there. Tell them we appear to have drawn a blank at the Gymnasium.'

'Very good, sir.'

Miller walked back along the line of vehicles, stopping at each one to explain the delay to his Section Commanders.

'What about sending some men into the school?' suggested Reynolds.

'No can do, Robert. It'd take a good hour to search the place thoroughly and I can't afford to be minus a Section that long.' He paused. 'However, I'm not very keen on leaving here at ten-to-four when the Governor isn't due until ten-past. Anything could happen in twenty minutes.' He scratched his nose thoughtfully. 'Tell you what, you stay here until the VIPs have gone through, then follow us to Ledra Street as quickly as you can. Keep in touch with us on the wireless. Any trouble, call us back. Okay?'

'Yes, sir.'

Miller returned to the Champ.

'Any joy on the chopper?'

'The SIB say they can't spare one, sir.'

'Can't spare one . . . Nonsense. Get them again. I'll have a word with them. And pass me my water-bottle.'

Miller sipped the tepid water with distaste and poured some

on to his handkerchief. He soaked his short hair. Damned SIB. Anyone would think they owned the blasted choppers.

'I've got them, sir.'

Miller took the microphone and donned a set of earphones.

'Miller here. What's this about not being able to spare a chopper? Over.'

The voice at the other end was full of calm authority.

'We haven't got one, Captain Miller. I have already explained that. Over.'

'But I need one. How the hell am I supposed to know what's going on in Ledra Street? Over.'

'By obeying orders and going there. Over.'

'By obeying . . .' The veins in Miller's bull-neck stood out. 'Is that meant to be a joke? Look, who am I talking to? Over.'

'Major Kidd. And I'm not joking. You have your orders. All you have to do is execute them. Out.'

The set went dead. Miller tore off the earphones and flung them at the wireless operator. *You have your orders.* Damn the bloody man's impudence. Anyone would think he didn't want the operation to be a success. Christ, were they blind, the SIB?

'What time is it?' he snapped.

'Three-forty, sir.'

Farther down the line, in the first of the one-tonners, Webster asked: 'Can we smoke, sergeant?'

'Yes.'

'Thanks, sarge. Right, who's got a fag? Thatch?'

'Don't you ever buy any?'

''Course I do. But I didn't bring enough.'

'Bloody typical,' growled Thatcher irritably. 'Are you sure you brought enough ammo or would you like me to lend you some? Did you remember your rifle? And what about your frenchies – did you bring them?'

'Okay, Thatcher, you've made your point,' said Hayter. Then to Webster: 'Here, have one of these.'

Webster took the cigarette and lit it.

'Thanks, sarge. Jeeze, that's good. All I need now is a quart of cold beer.'

'Shut your bleedin' trap, for Chrissake,' said Thatcher.

'What's up with you?'

Thatcher turned on him.

'You're up with me. You, you bum. We'd all like a quart o' cold beer, but we can't have it, can we? We're stuck in this bloody truck, a million miles from Chris' knows where, bein' bitten to death by flies and roasted by the fuggin sun. So just keep it shut. An' don't come any closer. You smell like you been cleanin' the heads. Don't you ever take a shower?'

'I have a shower every day – not that it's got fug all to do with you.'

'It has when I've gotta sit next to you, when I've gotta sleep in the same billet. Chris', anyone 'ud think they'd never heard o' baths in Liverpool.'

'Now just a fuggin second, Thatcher . . .'

'Can it, both of you,' said Hayter. 'Save your breath for later.'

'Balls,' muttered Thatcher.

Hayter pretended not to hear him. Thatcher was cracking up, he thought, making a mental note to tell Langley if it got any worse. In fact, they were all showing signs of strain, all beginning to get on each other's nerves. But that was inevitable; they'd been in Cyprus too long. There had been too many months of shooting and getting shot at, too many days with nothing to do but get drunk, too many patrols. They were tired: tired of being constantly on the alert, of risking their necks; tired of counting the days to demob.

Demob. They were National Servicemen, of course; he sometimes forgot that. They were in for two years, not for the duration. It was worse for them. A regular got used to staying where he was put until the Marines decided to move him on. But a conscript always had one eye on the calendar. A year to go, nine months, six months. And the daily thought: Will I get out before someone puts a bullet in me? Will it be me tomorrow, or will I be one of the lucky ones?

Part-timers. Their jobs were outside, in Civvy Street: behind a desk, behind a counter, behind a barrow, behind a lathe. Writing an essay was their job, or serving half a pound of bacon. For a regular soldier getting shot at was something he'd chosen to do. He knew when he signed on that his kids would be brought up in barracks, that he'd never have a proper home, that his wife might spend her afternoons screwing the RSM. It was something he accepted. But it was different for conscripts. They watched the clock and hoped they'd soon be back in their schools, offices, shops, and factories, hoped that they'd soon be home.

Home.

Yes, they all hoped that, these part-timers. Rourke, his thoughts somewhere in England with his wife and the child he hadn't seen, hoped it. Porter, his nose peeling, hoped it. Webster, deprived of his nightly sex, hoped it. So did Thatcher, drumming away on the butt of his rifle. And Riordan, Lance-corporal Riordan, who was a pretty good Marine. And Shaw.

The truck lurched forward.

'We're off,' said Hayter unnecessarily. 'Fags out.'

From a distance the chanting was no more than a subdued murmur, a far-off monotone without form or pitch, like wind in the trees. It mingled with, and was lost among, other city noises. But the nearer the convoy got to Ledra Street, the louder the chanting became until it was possible to make out what was being said. A single word, a sinister anapaest: En-o-SIS. En-o-SIS.

The students were where Langley had seen them earlier in the day, but there were more of them now, several hundred more, many displaying gallows humour by wearing black armbands and carrying grotesque effigies of the Governor with a noose around his neck. And they were no longer orderly. They were shouting and gesticulating and leaping into the air like crazed dancers or cheer leaders at a football game. They were waving flags and banners. They were standing on low roofs, on wooden boxes, on chairs and tables pilfered from nearby shops and cafés. When they were not yelling, *Enosis*, they were singing and jeering, this sweaty, jeering, amorphous mob drunk with the sense of its own nascent power.

We have our cause, their actions seemed to say. We have numbers. We are Youth. Oppressed Youth. Tomorrow belongs to us.

Gloria in Excelsis.

Glory be to us, to our own strength, and damnation to the British.

We praise ourselves. We glorify our invincibility.

We give thanks for our magnificence.

O Lord God, O heavenly King, remove the filth from our presence, have no mercy.

O Lord God, their sins are unforgivable, forgive them not.

Receive our prayers and grant that some may die.

We sit on the right hand of greatness, of omnipotence.

We are the most high.

Glory, glory, glory.

A roar went up when they saw the convoy – an angry, defiant roar redolent of Nuremberg. Their Messiah was absent, but he was with them in spirit. He killed the British, didn't he? He was hunted, wasn't he? The British would hang him if they caught him, would they not?

'En-o-SIS. En-o-SIS.'

Three hundred throats shrieked the nostrum. Three hundred pairs of eyes shone with fanaticism. Three hundred mouths foamed and spat and cursed. Three hundred bodies shook with the glorious excitement of canalized fear. Three hundred glands experienced a new and exhilarating orgasm.

'En-o-SIS. En-o-SIS.'

The troops left their vehicles and advanced, fixing bayonets as they came. Burnished steel glittered in the afternoon sun.

The students held their ground and then, at some prearranged signal, let fly with a hundred missiles: stones, bottles, tins, Molotov-cocktails. A corporal from 2 Section fell near Hayter, a three-inch gash in his forehead. Hayter dragged him to the shelter of a doorway. The windscreen of a three-tonner was shattered, and the driver moaned as a sliver of glass pierced his eyeball. A Molotov-cocktail exploded against a wall. Burning petrol cascaded down, on to heads and shoulders, on to exposed arms and necks.

'Hold it, 2, hold it!'

'Drive the bastards back!'

'Bayonets only. Just bayonets!'

'Where the fug's that tear-gas!'

'Support!'

'No, hold it, Support!' bellowed Miller.

He saw that it was an unequal fight. He was asking his men to act as shepherds to a pack of hungry wolves who skulked behind their age and sex. He was asking them to plod stolidly forward and get cut to ribbons in the process. Well, not his men. To hell with the rules.

'Sort 'em out!' he yelled. 'Get in there and sort 'em out!'

They needed no second bidding, and once they were among the students no power on earth could have persuaded them to withdraw before they had extracted vengeance for the burns and the bruises.

Shaw smashed his rifle into a sixteen-year-old's face and whooped with delight at the look of horror and surprise the youth gave him as he clutched a fractured nose. A few yards away Thatcher, his earlier scruples supplanted by the conditioned reflexes of survival, jabbed an elbow into the breasts of a girl who was clawing at Rourke's eyes. Webster, bleeding from the mouth and cursing terribly, kicked a bucktoothed adolescent in the groin. The adolescent's agonized scream was lost as he hit the ground and a dozen boots found his skull.

The officers and NCOs were in there too.

2 Section's subaltern, a karate expert, using his bare hands against knives and hatchets.

And Langley, lashing out with the butt of his pistol.

And Hayter, back to back with the TSM, swinging punches at all and anything.

And Riordan and Porter, out of it, forced to squat by the bren in case it was needed in a hurry.

And Miller, standing on the Champ's bonnet, directing operations with the flamboyance of a sideshow barker at the fairground.

Roll up, roll up, come and see the man with the broken neck. Roll up, roll up, all the horrors of the Ghost Train, and a bit more. Roll up, roll up, best sixpenn'orth since Balaclava. Don't miss it, ladies and gents, don't miss it. Roll up.

The students fell back. Their numbers were useless against such ferocity. They were not trained killers. They had not patrolled the Troodos for twelve months. They had not seen their friends murdered and maimed. They were not thousands of miles from home.

A confused mass of twisting, snarling bodies.

A young boy crawling to safety, dragging a broken leg.

Splashes of blood in the dust.

A girl vomiting and being kicked as she vomited.

A Marine unconscious on the sidewalk, his neck curiously misshapen.

A bespectacled girl sobbing.

A lance-corporal, his shirt in ribbons, methodically punching a youth's kidneys.

'Watch out, Thatch!'

'Put the boot in, put the boot in!'

'There's one on the roof!'

'Run, you bastards, run!'

'She's got a gun, for Chrissake!'

A shot rang out. A Marine staggered and collapsed, holding his shoulder.

'Where did that come from? Where?'

'There! Look!'

A girl raced down the street, and Shaw took off after her. He caught her near the Champ and threw her to the dirt of the road. He tore at her dress.

'Stick it in while you're at it, Shaw!'

The front of the dress came away, and except for a pair of flimsy briefs she wore nothing underneath. Shaw thrust his hand inside the elastic and brought out a revolver. He waved it triumphantly.

Then Reynolds and 4 Section arrived in the second one-tonner, and those students who were still capable of running ran, leaving their friends where they lay. The Marines cat-called and spat after them, and grinned wearily at each other amid the carnage.

Reynolds rushed across to Miller. He was plainly distraught.

'They didn't turn up, sir,' he panted. 'The VIPs didn't turn up. I tried to reach you on the wireless, but I couldn't raise you. I waited as long as I could.'

Miller could not take it in. He stared at Reynolds blank-eyed. What the hell was Robert talking about? Hadn't turned up – ridiculous. It was four-thirty-five.

And then it hit him. The VIPs hadn't been through Ledra Street, either. Christ. They were fifteen minutes adrift on a carefully scheduled itinerary. Christ Almighty. They'd been ambushed somewhere along the route. Jesus, Jesus Christ.

'Get the SIB on the wireless,' he muttered hoarsely.

'I can't, sir. The set was damaged early on. That's why Mr Reynolds couldn't raise us. It's u.s.'

'Jesus Christ.'

Behind the convoy a grey Mercedes hissed to a halt. A middle-aged man in civilian clothes stepped out and walked over to the Champ.

'Captain Miller?' he said politely.

'Yes. Who are you?'

'Major Kidd, SIB. You've been having fun here, it seems. Any serious casualties?'

'I haven't checked. A few, I think. Look, for Christ's sake, the Governor's car hasn't passed here and one of my officers says it didn't show up at the Gymnasium.'

Major Kidd was unconcerned. 'I know,' he said lightly.

'You know?'

'Yes. But don't worry, the Governor's quite safe. And the Turks. They should be at the Mansion by now. You see, we changed the route and timetable this morning – thought Ledra Street might get a little warmish.'

'*You did what?*'

'Changed the plans, old man. Sorry we couldn't let you in on it. Security, you understand. However, your little diversion did the trick. The parade went off without a hitch. Well done.'

Major Kidd returned to his car and drove off. Miller was speechless for upwards of a minute, but when he began swearing he swore solidly for a quarter of an hour. Reynolds timed him.

EIGHTEEN

The rumour began in the canteen with a cook corporal who suffered from acne, and was carried to the MT Section by a Marine who had recently received a Dear John from the girl he had been sleeping with since he was sixteen. He passed it on to a driver who was about to visit Fillipedes' for an all-night drunk after seven consecutive days on the Nicosia–Platres run. It went round Fillipedes' with the eggs and chips and brandy sours, and the drinkers took it back to their barrack-rooms. Brigade told the CO officially seventy-two hours later, precisely seventy-one hours after he had been informed unofficially by his batman. Twelve hours afterwards the CO posted the Order. It was unequivocal. They were leaving Cyprus for Malta. The advance party were to sail from Famagusta on Wednesday, 15th August, and would be followed by the main party three days later. The rear party would embark on Sunday, 19th August, and sail at 0800 hours on the Monday. That was all the Order said, but it was enough, and the Marines celebrated in the only way they knew.

It was in the middle of the celebrations that someone asked: But why? We haven't finished here yet.

And someone answered: We've earned the break, haven't we? Twelve months is a bloody long time.

And others said: Break hell. Six weeks in Malta and we'll be off to Kenya or Malaya.

And yet others: Egypt.

In a cave at the edge of the Paphos Forest, a man grunted happily when the news reached him. They had given him a lot of trouble, the Marines, and he would welcome their absence.

The man was under average height, middle-aged, and moustached. He wore a stained bush-jacket over a faded khaki shirt, a pair of grey trousers and high leather boots. His cheeks were pinched, his face pale, and he looked in need of a good meal.

He pulled a sheet of paper towards him and brought the candle nearer. There was at least one piece of unfinished business to be dealt with before the Marines left. Not that it really mattered when the business was transacted, but it would be pleasant to bid them goodbye with something to remember. Pleasing to his vanity. It would demonstrate his power and how he forgot nothing.

At the top of the sheet of paper he inscribed a name, which he underlined heavily. Below the name he wrote detailed instructions. He signed himself: Dighenis.

Maria Costas entered the tiny church and knelt before the altar. She shivered, although the day was far from cold. She was dressed in black, and beneath her veil her face was lined.

It was a young face grown prematurely old: old with fear, with child-bearing, with worry, with lack of proper food. The flesh under the chin was loose and flabby, as though the muscles were yielding in concert with the spirit. But it was a kind face. The eyes were soft and compassionate, the lips generous. The face of a mother.

She was glad the church was empty. It made her feel uncomfortable to pray with the watchful and suspicious eyes of the priest on her. The priest, she was sure, knew where her husband was and what he was doing. The priests knew everything.

She prayed for her children, for her children who were growing up in an atmosphere of hatred and bitterness. *Please let them learn how to love.* She prayed for her husband. *Dear God, keep him safe.* She prayed for enlightenment. *Dear God, let me understand the struggle. Show me who is right and who is wrong.* She prayed for her family and for the village. And she thanked God for His wisdom and infinite patience, for the good harvest. Not once did she pray for herself.

She heard the door open, but she did not look up. A shaft of sunlight struck her back.

The young man in the doorway bowed his head briefly, almost ritualistically, and made his way towards the genuflecting figure. His leather soles rang hollowly on the tiled floor. He stood behind her and listened to the muttered prayers.

'. . . For my husband, who is good and unselfish, for my children, who are young and helpless, for my . . .'

The young man fired twice, aiming at the nape of the neck. The sound of the shots echoed and re-echoed around the church, and the smell of cordite lingered in the air. A wisp of blue-grey smoke curled upwards.

Maria Costas fell forward without a whimper. The young man was surprised to see how small a heap she made. He bent down and pinned a note to her bloody shawl. Translated, it read: Death to traitors.

They left the one-tonner where the road became a track, four miles from the monastery. In the distance they could see the burnt-out forest where Klein had been killed. Many of the trees would never grow again. It was somehow a fitting memorial.

Langley went over to Costas.

'This could be hopeless, you know,' he said, not unkindly. 'I mean, we're not sure, are we?'

The interpreter looked at him with eyes that were expressionless. The red swellings had gone, and so had the anger. All that remained was pained emptiness.

'I am sure, lieutenant. He was recognized. Not everyone is afraid to speak. He will be at the monastery until dawn.'

'Very well. Will you lead?'

'Yes.' Costas hesitated. He clutched the Lee-Enfield with which Captain Miller had personally issued him. 'I wish to thank you, lieutenant,' he said, but Langley shut him up with a raised hand.

'Not now. Let's go.'

The Section moved off in single file, into the grey dusk.

They marched in silence not because they had been ordered not to talk, but because conversation would have been irreverent. Costas was one of them. He had been part of the Troop for a year. There was nothing they could say to help, but there was plenty they could do. They could spill blood as blood had been spilled. They could take a life for a life.

If men strive and hurt a woman with child so that her fruit depart from her, and yet no mischief follow: he should be surely punished, according as the woman's husband will lay upon him; and he shall pay as the judges determine.

And if any mischief follow, then thou shalt give life for life, eye for eye, tooth for tooth, hand for hand, burning for burning, wound for wound, stripe for stripe.

There was no resentment at being sent on one last patrol, although Rourke believed that they were tempting fate and privately resolved to take no chances. There was his son to consider. If there was any shooting, he'd keep out of it. The others could risk their lives if they wanted to, but he wouldn't. Not at this stage of the game. Their two years were almost up. With foreign service leave and termination leave to come, they should be in the UK by November and home for good by Christmas. Christmas with his wife and son. Jesus, it was some thought.

They had been marching for forty minutes when Costas stopped suddenly. 'We climb here,' he said.

Langley groaned when he saw the angle of their proposed ascent. His ankle was giving him hell.

'Isn't there a path?'

'No, lieutenant. But it is not far – a few hundred feet. The monastery is then only half a mile.'

'All right, we'll follow you.'

They started to climb, and within seconds Costas had opened up a gap of some thirty feet between himself and Langley, who was sweating profusely and making curious bubbling noises. Twice he nearly fell, but twice he recovered before hitting the iron-hard earth. He wanted to call a halt after five minutes, but the words, whenever he thought of them, sounded like a plea. (*An officer, my boy, leads by example. There is no such thing as leading a charge from behind.* No, Father.) What Costas could do, he could do, even if it crippled him.

Higher and higher.

Loose stones and pebbles, dislodged by Costas' boots, struck him in the face. His ankle ached and throbbed, and he became dizzy with pain and weak with the mental effort it took to ignore the pain. Above him the stars danced like sparks from a bonfire. Below him the Section wondered at the bubbling noises – like a dog whimpering after a severe beating.

Of course you can do it, Brian. You're a man, aren't you? Or you soon will be. You're fifteen. Can't we rest for a while, Father? *Rest? I don't need a rest and I'm thirty years older than you are. You see that peak? Beyond that is Ullswater. We have to be there by nightfall. Don't want to be stranded on this godforsaken mountain all night, do we?* No, sir. *Well, then, best foot forward.*

Higher.

You're lagging again, Brian. Good God, boy, what are you made of? Flesh and blood, sir. *What was that? Don't mutter, boy. My God, if I'd had you in my unit you'd have been fit. My lads were the fittest in the Brigade. Prided 'emselves on it. Could outrun any of 'em. But that was during the war, of course. Too soft nowadays. Upbringing, naturally. Well, no son of mine's going to be a ninny.* I can't, Father. *What was that? Speak up. I can't hear you.* I can't, sir. My legs. *Of course you can. You can do anything you choose to do, anything you have the will to do. The will, Brian. Now let's have no more of your nonsense.* I can't, Father. I can't!

'I can't.'

Langley stumbled and fell. He slid back several yards, clawing at the earth for a handhold, tearing his fingers.

'You okay, sir?' said Hayter.

Langley turned over. Christ, it was so beautiful to lie down. So cool, so marvellous. Who was shaking him? Why couldn't they leave him in peace. That was all he wanted.

'Are you hurt?' said Hayter.

'No, sir.'

'No . . . Mr Langley! Come on, Mr Langley.'

Langley opened his eyes. 'I must have tripped,' he mumbled.

'You did. Here, I'll help you.'

'I can do it.'

'No, grab my hand.'

'*I can do it!*' snarled Langley. 'You will not touch me, sergeant! You will never touch me.'

Hayter recoiled and collided with Shaw. He flushed angrily at being waved off as though he were some kind of insect.

'I was trying ...'

'Don't. I'm not a child. I can manage. How far is the top?'

'Forty feet or so. Costas is there.'

'Then get out of the damned way. I need room.'

Slowly and painfully Langley stood up and put his weight on the game ankle. He winced. Christ, it hurt. He couldn't go much further without a breather.

Tracked by Hayter he climbed the remaining forty feet with his teeth tightly clenched. The summit was a plateau, and he sank to the grass. They could wait until he was ready, blast them. They could bloody well wait.

The monastery loomed up out of the darkness: a long, low, single-storey building with no outhouses or courtyard; isolated from time and civilization and temptation; a faded grey reminder that when the holiest of men renounce the world, the flesh, and the devil, they do it in Spades. In each of the arrow-slits it had for windows a solitary candle burned. From within came the sound of a lone voice chanting a Gregorian hymn.

'That'll never make the Top Twenty,' murmured Shaw.

'Shut up,' hissed Langley, and then to Costas: 'How many of them can we expect?'

'That is difficult to say, Lieutenant,' answered Costas, his eyes never leaving the main door. 'Four–six. I will ascertain ...'

'No, not you. This is a military operation. Rourke, you'll do.'

Rourke froze. 'Me, sir?'

'Yes, you. Do a recce. I want to know what's going on inside and if there are any exits other than that door.'

Rourke did not move. Why him? Why the hell did Langley have to pick on him? In his mind he saw himself circling the monastery and coming face to face with Maria Costas' killer. There was a shot, and his life poured out through the hole in his chest.

No.

'Hurry it up,' said Langley.

Rourke touched Thatcher accidentally, and Thatcher sensed the fear and understood.

'I'll go, sir,' he said, and disappeared into the shadows.

'Are you deaf or what, Rourke?'

'No, sir. I was just – er . . .'

'You were just er what?'

'I'd dropped my bayonet. I was looking for it.'

Dropped your bayonet, my foot, thought Langley. Scared rigid, more likely.

Thatcher was back in five minutes.

'Four of 'em, sir, four Friar Tucks. One of 'em's dressed in fancy duds – silk or somethin'. There's no sign of anyone else.'

'What are they doing?'

'Eatin', sir. They don't seem worried about anythin'. And there's another door at the far end. Leads out to a path, and the path leads down towards some trees, I think. Hard to tell. Black as Paddy's neck out there.'

'Black as what?'

'Paddy's neck. It's an expression.'

Langley deliberated for a moment.

'All right, take Rourke and watch that second door. Come in fast when you hear us.'

'Yes, sir.' Thatcher crawled across to Rourke. 'Okay, Tim?'

'Okay? 'Course I'm okay. I'd dropped my bayonet, that was all.'

Thatcher shrugged. Rourke could play it how he liked.

'Come on, we've gotta watch the far door.'

'Us?'

'Yeah. Ours is the easy bit,' he added flippantly. 'There's nothin' round there but a few spiders havin' sex.'

Langley waited until they were out of sight.

'We'll give them a minute to get in position,' he said, 'and then we'll move in. Once inside Shaw and Webster will search any ante-rooms on the left, and Sergeant Hayter and Porter will take the right-hand side. Corporal Riordan, you'll cover us from the door with the bren. If what Thatcher said is correct, our man's not there. However, be prepared for anything.'

The minute passed and they crept forward. Outside the main door Langley held up his hand. He beckoned Hayter, and pointed. Hayter nodded, took a short run, and lashed out with his foot. The door flew open with a crash, and they rushed in.

The four monks sitting at the wooden hand-hewn table were transfixed with shock for what seemed like an hour, but which was, in reality, two seconds. A tableau of dumb incredulity. They stared first at Langley and his group and then at Thatcher and Rourke, and finally, after a count of three, leapt up in unison as though controlled by the same invisible strings.

They found their voices simultaneously.

'Shut up!' shouted Langley, brandishing his pistol. He was ignored. 'Shut up!' he repeated, louder, 'and stay where you are. Tell them,' he ordered Costas.

Costas told them, and this time they obeyed.

'Right, get going, search the place.'

There was not much to search. The monastery comprised a single room whose length was approximately twice its width. Off this were six narrow, uncurtained cells, three on each side. Four of the cells contained wooden bunks and crude wooden side tables; a fifth was evidently used as a storeroom, and the sixth was a tiny chapel. The walls were icon-covered: some tapestries, some paintings, here and there an alabaster statue. The room was lit by long tapers in holders and olive-oil lamps which flickered eerily and cast tremulous shadows. There was a fireplace but no fire. The floor was uncovered and of stone.

The four silent monks represented at least two generations. The youngest was in his twenties, while the eldest, apparently the abbot, could have been anything from forty to sixty. They all wore beards and all had their long hair twisted into buns at the back. The abbot was dressed in silk vestments, whereas the habits of the others, the novices, were of coarse brown cloth. They had been eating supper, and a platter in the centre of the table was piled high with white cheese and dry bread. Several earthenware flasks of red wine were half empty.

'Nothing here, sir,' called Hayter.

'Or here,' said Shaw.

Langley turned to Costas. 'You'd better talk to them.'

Costas leaned his rifle against a chair and removed his workman's cloth cap, which he pushed under the epaulette of his bush-jacket. He looked tired and scrawny and out of place next to the abbot's silks, his ecclesiastical paunch. In Greek he said: 'My wife was murdered by an EOKA gunman this morning. She was murdered in a church. I know the gunman came here. Where is he now?'

The abbot patted his corpulence. 'You are mistaken, my son. We have seen no one but yourselves for a week.'

Patiently Costas repeated the question and received the same reply. He grunted. It was going to be very difficult.

He began again.

Across the room Langley pulled up a heavy chair and sat down. He rubbed his ankle. It was swollen.

'What do we do now?' asked Hayter.

'We wait,' said Langley.

They waited for twenty minutes and saw Costas' patience gradually become slow, controlled anger. The abbot was all unctuousness and piety, and Costas knew that such a man – a man who was ambitious, perhaps, who expected the reward of high office when EOKA finally won the day – would never talk. And his minions were too frightened to do anything but agree with everything he said.

It was time to use other, more violent, means of persuasion.

'I shall ask you again,' he said in Greek: 'where is he?'

The abbot smiled a tolerant smile. 'We have sheltered no one, my son. I wish you would believe me.'

Costas nodded. So be it.

Behind him was the cell which served as the chapel, and near the altar was an alabaster statue of Christ. He picked it up and muttered a short prayer of contrition.

'Where is he?'

'My son, why can't I make you . . .'

Costas dropped the statue. It broke into a score of pieces. The youngest novice let out a low whine of horror.

Hayter looked at Langley.

'Leave him,' said Langley, interested.

'Where is he?'

The abbot was purple with impotent fury. 'You will surely be burned in hell for what you have done. I tell you . . .'

Costas did not allow him to finish. He snatched a knife from the table and slashed at a painting of the Virgin. A foot-long gash severed Her head from Her shoulders. He slashed again.

A triangle of canvas fell limply from the frame.

'Hot dog,' murmured Shaw.

'*Where? Where? Where?*'

'My son . . .'

The youngest novice cried out in terror as Costas, losing control of his anger, went for the altar.

'I will tell you, I will tell you!'

The abbot cursed him and tried to silence him, but the novice was now more scared of his Maker than his earthly superior. Costas hurled the knife to the floor, and listened.

'Well?' demanded Langley.

'He was here,' said Costas excitedly. 'He was here until one hour ago. He took the path to Amiandos. We must leave immediately.'

Langley remained seated. He thought of his ankle, of the tortuous trail to Amiandos, of the hour-long start the killer had; and of the comparative comfort of the monastery, of the cheese and bread and wine on the table.

'Immediately?'

'Certainly, lieutenant. He cannot have gone far. He will not be expecting anyone to follow.'

Langley made no move. 'We'll never catch up with him tonight,' he said. 'He has too much of a lead. We know where he's going. Tomorrow we'll get the rest of the Troop from Platres. It can wait until then.'

'Until tomorrow! But he will not be in Amiandos tomorrow. He will have gone.'

'That's a chance we'll have to take. We'll bed down here for the night and return to Platres at first light.'

'But . . .'

'Those are my orders, Costas.'

'But he is a murderer.'

'My orders still stand.'

'Then I shall go alone.'

He made for the door.

'Stop that man!'

Apologetically, Riordan barred the exit.

'You're under my command here,' said Langley imperiously, 'and you will do as I say. Is that quite clear?'

'My wife, lieutenant ...' Costas' voice was a dispirited, hopeless whisper.

'I know and I'm sorry, but I will be obeyed. Are my orders quite clear?'

A long silence before:

'Yes.'

'Good. Now settle down. Sergeant, arrange the duty roster. A two-man guard to patrol the perimeter of the monastery until dawn.'

'Yes, sir.'

'And while you're so near the table, sergeant, you might pass me a chunk of that bread and cheese.'

It was one of those dreams where the sleeper is aware that what is taking place is a figment of his relaxed unconscious. It was compulsive, too. Not pleasant, but compulsive. He vaguely recognized the small boy playing on the deserted beach; the boy with the shock of fair hair and skinny arms and very blue eyes who laughed as the tide swept over his bare toes. He was not even afraid when the waves reached his thighs. He could swim, this boy, in spite of his size.

He floated and allowed himself to be carried out to sea. On the promenade a figure appeared. A man. The man shouted something, but it was impossible to hear what was being said. The boy was not listening, in any case. He did not want to be told that he was in danger. He wanted to find out for himself.

He dived down. The sea was dark-green. And the man was there, smiling at him, extending a helping hand. *No*. The boy swam off, but there was no eluding the man. He was everywhere. In front, behind, to the side. There was only one way out: the boy had to take a lungful of water. And another. That would make the man disappear. Everything would disappear. The beach. The promenade. The world. Everything.

Everything.

And then Hayter shook him by the shoulders, urgently.

'Wake up, sir. Wake up. It's Costas – he's gone.'

'What?' Langley blinked.

'Costas. He's gone.'

'What? *What?*' Langley sat up. 'What the hell d'you mean, gone?'

'Webster spotted it a minute ago when he and Porter came off guard.'

'Oh for Christ's sake! The bloody fool! Has he taken his rifle?'

'Yes. Do we go after him?'

Langley shook his head slowly and sleepily. 'No, sergeant, we do not.' There was no point. None whatsoever. The interpreter had made his decision.

They never saw Costas again.

Later, Webster said he thought he had heard a shot towards two AM, but as Porter had heard nothing, he admitted he could have been mistaken.

Someone asked: 'What about his kids? He had kids, didn't he?'

And someone answered: 'They'll be taken care of.'

The Section felt guilty. Costas had asked for help and they had let him down. They needed a scapegoat and opted for Langley. Langley and his bloody ankle, and Langley and his refusal to go on had caused Costas' death, for dead they knew he was. He had been in too much of a hurry to reach Amiandos. He would not have taken the necessary precautions. And now he was out there somewhere, lifeless in the tall Aleppo pine. Carrion. Only the eagles and the crows would ever know precisely where he lay.

. . . . .

The mountains receded, the black mountains. They looked harmless enough from the deck of the LST. So did the whole island, sleeping there in the August sun.

Thatcher said, 'Good bloody riddance,' and the others nodded their agreement before going below to eat.

NINETEEN

They had been in Malta for two months, and for two months they had undergone an intensive refresher course. They had practised assault landings by day and assault landings by night, street fighting, house clearing, exercises with tanks, exercises without tanks, exercises with air support, exercises without air support. They had waded ashore in the small hours and simulated the destruction of a machine-gun nest more times than they cared to count. They had raced through the cobbled streets and roused the occupants of the dozy little houses on a dozen occasions. They had sat through lectures on cover and lectures on what to do if bitten by a scorpion. They had re-fought, it seemed, every major seaborne assault since Julius Caesar decided the Britons needed taming. They had eaten hard-tack, smoked wet cigarettes, been sea-sick, and lost eight hours' sleep every other night.

And they were thoroughly fed up with it all.

It was no secret now what the training was for. The rumours, the sand-yellow colour of the newly-painted vehicles, the newspapers, the BBC pundits, the temporary retention of National Servicemen due for demob, told them where they were going – if they went, because no one believed the operation would come off. It was merely talk. Whistling in the dark. Politicians' talk. Worthless. The Gyppos were making belligerent noises, weren't they? They'd nationalized the Suez Canal, hadn't they? That guy – what was his name? – was trying to play God, wasn't he? Okay, that meant we had to shout back, beat the imperial drum, didn't it? But the shouting wasn't worth a row of beans. If they were really serious, the politicos, if they really intended to knock the Gyppos on the skull for good and all, then for Chrissake why didn't they let us get on with it? Tomorrow. Then everyone could go home.

Of course, they agreed, when they weren't throwing up somewhere in the Mediterranean from the bowels of a flat-bottomed LCA, Malta wasn't such a bad place. It was the cat's sleeping suit compared with Cyprus. It had everything they had missed for a year: women, bright lights, and the glorious sensation of not being forced to carry a rifle through the streets. There was the Valetta Gut for openers, a narrow, cobbled alley that led down to the harbour. Christ, a man could enjoy himself in the Gut. *Come in, Johnnee. Good time, Johnnee. Big eats, Johnnee. Jigajig, Johnnee.* Painted faces, flashing teeth, inviting smiles: the clarion calls and blatant advertisements of a street that sold whatever took your fancy by the vanload – from little boys to very big girls. There was even one house where, if you were so inclined, you could get flogged by two girls at the same time. Most of the women wanted paying in cash or drinks, true, but they were there and willing, that was the point. Then there were the bars that never closed. No more than dingy one-roomed shops, the majority of them, and dimly lit; but a man could get head-splitting drunk on local wine for half-a-crown at any hour of the day or night. And when he was tired of the Gut he could walk up the road to Kingsway and sip cold beer on the terrace of an open-air café. Or he could take a taxi to Mellieha Bay. There he could swim and laze for as long as he wished. There he could forget about the endless exercises, about what to do if bitten by a scorpion.

Yes, Malta was a great improvement on Cyprus. But it wasn't England.

. . . . .

'When?' asked Webster, putting on a clean white shirt.

'Tomorrow,' answered Riordan. 'We've got to be on board by ten o'clock tonight.'

'What's this one called?'

'Exercise Boathook. It looks like the big one.'

'Jesus Christ. Roll on demob.'

Captain Miller, in civilian clothes, stood in the foyer of the Phoenicia Hotel and fingered his wine-red tie nervously. He was beginning to regret agreeing to meet his ex-wife. Why the hell had she phoned him? Why had it taken her almost eight weeks to phone if she wanted to see him that much? Why did he have the uneasy feeling that her second marriage wasn't working out and that she wanted to splash about in nostalgia for a few hours? And: Why the hell didn't he do the sensible thing and vanish before she arrived.

Hello, this is Susan. Susan? Susan who? *Susan née Ross.* Susan née . . . Good God. *He is, isn't He. It's lovely to hear your voice again, Richard. I've been meaning to ring you, but somehow . . .* How did you know I was back? The Intelligence Corps? *Intelligence Corps? Oh, Bobby. Bobby's away. Something to do with this Nasser business, I think. But how are you? You haven't said. What was Cyprus like?*

So she'd been keeping tabs on him, he thought.

It wasn't bad. *It must have been awful.*

And then there was half an hour of small talk and reminiscing. Do you remember so-and-so? So-and-so's husband turned out to be a veritable bastard. So-and-so's having an affair with so-and-so. Finally:

What are you doing today? Today? Well, I had planned . . . *Can't you unplan? I was going to suggest we meet for a drink. If you can stand me, that is. I'm free from one o'clock.* Well . . . I could meet you at the Phoenicia at, say, two. *Do say yes.* Well . . . All right, the Phoenicia it is. *Heavenly.* (A pause.) *No hard feelings?* Hard feelings? God, no. All that happened a long time ago. It's forgotten. *Oh.*

The *Oh*, he thought, again touching his tie, had been an exclamation of disappointment. She did not want to be forgotten, but of course no woman ever did.

He checked his watch against the foyer clock: two-fifteen. She had never been a great one for punctuality, Susan. She considered it bad breeding to arrive as the hour was striking.

Bad breeding. God, fancy the daughter of a Yorkshire wool merchant, a man who had started on the mill floor, concerning herself with breeding. But she did and always had. Maybe that was why their marriage had failed: she had worried too much about trivialities. There was another reason, though: that crinkly, demanding Queen of Cornucopia, money. She was first generation rich and he was tenth generation poor. All he had possessed on their wedding day was ambition, and ambition didn't go far when a man's wife was accustomed to being waited on. It would have been different if he'd married her with the rank of captain, but a second-lieutenant's pay had scarcely kept her in champagne. However, that was so much water under the bridge.

'Hello, Richard.'

He turned, and there she was: slim, sun-tanned, and elegant in a short white dress. He was surprised to see how young she looked, far younger than her twenty-nine years. Or was she thirty? Her hair, though shorter now, was as fair as he remembered, her eyes as green, her nose as straight. And she had not suffered the usual dehydration of the English woman in a hot climate. She was as beautiful as ever, and he nearly told her so.

'Aren't you going to say hello?'

'I was drinking you in.'

She smiled. The same old deceptive smile: please-don't-hurt-me-I'm-fragile. 'That sounds like a compliment.'

'It was intended to be. Shall we go inside?'

He took her arm.

Porter left St Andrew's Barracks alone, and began to walk. He kept to the seaward side of the road. It was fresher there.

Outside Sliema a horse-drawn *karozzin* drew up alongside him and the driver called, 'Garry, Johnnee. Very cheap to Valetta.' He shook his head. He did not want to ride. He needed time to think, time to compose himself. There was something he had to do, something he had avoided doing for two months. But today was the day. It could be his last opportunity. When the Egyptian scare was over he and the others would be flown back to England. Pleasant, green, moral England; ambivalent capital of the world. He had to do it before then. It could send him mad if he didn't, or queer. That had happened before.

His diary entry for the previous day read: 'The mere thought of a woman makes me physically ill. Or rather I become ill with fear and apprehension. The power of reason is a two-edged gift, for the bad is as apparent as the good. Who knows, maybe Carol was the only one who could put me at my ease. Many men are unable to function with someone other than their wives, or someone very close to them. It has something to do with guilt, I'm sure. Boys are warned, when small, not to interfere with little girls. Sex, they learn – mainly from their mothers – is unclean. So the sensitive child grows up with a complex. And thinking about it makes it worse. I mustn't fail again. I can't. I must prove I can do it otherwise I'll have no future. None.'

The Gut would be the best place to go. There, in some room with the blinds drawn and a bottle of wine to give him courage, it would be okay. It had to be.

Hayter combed his hair and grinned at his reflection in the mirror. He was well pleased with himself. It wasn't every NCO on the camp who was making it with an officer's wife. And her husband a lieutenant-commander at that. None of your prissy little skinny-breasted subalterns' wives. Christ, no. This one was stacked. He was in the big league. A flat in Valetta, as much booze as he could handle, a meal on the table when he wanted one, a car if he cared to use it, and a peaches-and-cream darling ready to welcome him with open – well, open arms whenever dear old hubby was off playing sailors, which was pretty often these days, thanks to Nasser. Hell, yes, whatever happened tomorrow, life was good today.

'Just think,' said Thatcher, 'this time next week I could be sunnin' myself in tropical Manchester.'

'Dodging the rain, more like,' grinned Rourke.

They were sitting in a Floriana bar, trying not to look in the direction of a pair of teenage tarts.

'You got it wrong, Tim. It doesn't rain in Manchester. It's coincidence that the kids are born with gills and gumboots. Anyhow, after two days up there to get one or two bits o' business tickin' over for me, I'll be down in glorious Dorset, don't forget.'

'I won't. And it's Devon that's glorious, not Dorset.'

'Devon, Dorset, what's the difference? You all talk funny.'

One of the tarts, tired of waiting, came across, smiling her professional smile and revealing, in the process, a blackened incisor.

'You buy me drink, Johnnee.'

It was a command as opposed to a request, but Thatcher played dumb.

'Sorry, love, I'm trainin' to be a priest. I'm not allowed to.'

'A priest. In the Church?'

'That's right. An' while I'm here, why don't you give up your life of sin? Go to confession, my child. Tell God . . .'

But the girl, wide-eyed, had rejoined her companion.

'Pity,' said Thatcher. 'Another minute and I could've taken a collection.'

'I don't know that I'm keen,' said Langley, lying on top of his bed in the room he shared with Reynolds. 'I mean, it's not going to be much of a party if we have to leave at eight, is it?'

'Of course it is,' said Reynolds, exasperated. 'We'll have five hours, won't we?'

'I suppose so. But it seems unnatural, a party in the afternoon.'

'Oh for God's sake, Brian! They're starting it at three because most of the chaps have to leave by eight. In any case, what's the difference between a do which begins at three and ends at eight and one which goes on from midnight until five AM?'

'Nothing intrinsically.'

'Well, then.'

'Oh, I can't be bothered. Anyway, I've got a final session of heat treatment for the old ankle at four o'clock.'

He picked up a book from the bedside table. It was *The Old Man and the Sea*. He read the first ten lines.

Reynolds grimaced. He needed Langley because he had arranged to meet two Wrens at the party, and he did not want to be stuck with both.

'I hear the CO will be there,' he remarked casually, the lie springing easily from his lips.

Langley glanced up. The CO? That altered things. It sometimes paid dividends to be seen socially with one's superior officers.

'Who told you?'

'Can't remember. Someone mentioned it, said he'd pop in for an hour or so.'

'On the level?'

'Naturally.' Reynolds was a portrait of innocence. 'However, if you can't be bothered . . .'

'No, no.' The Hemingway fell to the floor in an undignified heap. 'After all, we've nothing else to do, have we? And the ankle's better. Give me ten minutes to get changed.'

He slipped from the bed and took off his trousers. Reynolds watched him. Promotion hunter, he thought.

'The Marines,' said Shaw, leaning forward on his elbows and peering drunkenly through the cigarette smoke, 'are the best goddam mob in the world. The toughest, too. The American Rangers,' he sneered, 'are crap. The Legion, crap. The Paras, crap.'

The leading seaman opposite him grinned amiably. 'As you say, Royal. You'd be nowhere, though, if it wasn't for the Navy. We get you there and we bring you home.'

'Oh, sure, sure, I'm not knocking the Navy. Good lads, matelots. Listen, the Navy and the Marines, they're like one, see. You look after us and we look after you.'

'That's it. Here, have some more screech. It's your bottle.'

'Thanks.'

Shaw held out his glass. The leading seaman filled it to the brim. Shaw drank half in one swallow, and swayed in his seat. Jesus, it was some drink, that wine.

'As I was saying,' he went on, 'the Navy and the Marines, like one. I mean, we could clear this bar here an' now, you an' me. No trouble. You an' me.'

' 'Course we could, Royal.'

' 'Course we could. Nothing to it.' He turned and yelled at a trio of soldiers, who were minding their own business by the counter. 'Hey, you bastards, we could clear you right now, me an' my mate.'

The soldiers ignored him.

'See that,' he chuckled; 'don't wanna know, those three. Hey, you don't wanna know, do you? Bastards. Pongo bastards.'

'Take it easy,' cautioned the leading seaman, who was due to meet his girl in half an hour and who wanted to arrive in one piece.

'Take it easy?' Shaw frowned. He had reached that stage of intoxication where, for him, everybody was a potential enemy.

'That's right. You don't wanna break the place up, do you? 'Course you don't. Let you and me have a quiet drink – the Royal Navy and the Royal Marines. Best there is.'

'I'll drink to that. Gonna beat the crap out of that dago Nasser, you know.'

'Sure we are.'

'Damn' right we are.'

Riordan sat at a trestle-table in the barrack-room, the bren gun in pieces in front of him. He polished the breech-block lovingly. There was no doubt about it, he thought; his weapon was the cleanest and most efficient in the Commando. Soon, though, he would have to hand it in. Soon he would be a civilian again. It would be back to the building site or the Labour Exchange. Finish Royal Marines. Finish Lance-corporal Riordan. He would miss it.

'You don't think any the worse of me because I'm married, do you, Roy?'

'Don't talk.'

'But I must. A woman has to know. I wouldn't want you to think I was cheap.'

'I don't.'

'I mean, I wouldn't want you to think I do this with anyone the minute my husband's out of the house.'

'I don't.'

'I mean ...'

'Lie still.'

'Let's take a taxi to St Paul's, Richard. I have a new swim-suit that I'm dying to show off.'

'I have to be back at eight. We embark at ten. In any case, it's too cold to swim.'

'Nonsense. I'll see you don't freeze.'

'You like to come home with me, Johnnee?'

'It's Michael, not Johnnee. I keep telling you.'

'Come home with me, Johnnee. I like you.'

Hayter pulled a face. 'But why a drive? Who the hell wants to go for a drive?'

'I do, Bill. We can have a picnic. It'll be fun.'

'Fun, my arse.'

'Don't be coarse.'

Rourke produced the latest photograph of his son.

'You haven't seen this one. It was taken on the day he was six months old. He's grown since the last one, hasn't he?'

'Hard to tell. They all look the same to me.'

'What? You're blind, George. Look at the mouth.'

'Yeah, Tim.'

'Look at the size of the legs.'

'Yeah, Tim.'

'Look at his hair.'

'Yeah, Tim.'

'I thought you said Colonel Blake would be here.'

'Give him time, Brian, give him time. Look, there are the two Wrens I was telling you about. The one with the hips is yours.'

'Say, she's not bad.'

'Not bad! If what I've heard is true, that's the misstatement of the year.'

'I don't like-a-way those three Pongos looking-us.'

'Forget it, Royal. They don't mean nothing.'

'Then why they staring? Hey, you wanna snapshot?'

'Stow it. You'll have the Shore Patrol in here.'

'Up the Shore Patrol. We'll take 'em on, Jack. You an' me. Four-and-twenty virgins . . .'

Riordan cleaned the back-sight with a pin. Give me one more chance to use this, he begged. One more before it's all over.

'Lie still, love. Lie still, for Chrissake.'

. . . . .

Early evening. It is dark now, but the streets are bright with stabbing fingers of neon; synthetic beacons that seduce. *Music. Dancing. We Serve English Beer. Souvenirs. Hot Dogs. Try Our Home-made Ice Cream.* Crowds of Maltese hurry home from work, scanning the evening papers for the results of the National Lottery. Dozens of girls, decent Catholic girls, slip into something comfortable and wait for romance.

Malta by night.

In Grand Harbour the ships' crews toil frantically without knowing why. A fisherman in a small boat far out at sea hauls in his net and shouts with delight at the size of his catch. A tearful fifteen-year-old schoolgirl confesses to a priest in an otherwise empty church that she has been made pregnant by an airman whose name she never learned. A whore in Floriana who has dealt with twelve customers in eighty minutes collapses over her supper of brandy and scrambled eggs. A member of the Royal Navy Shore Patrol gets involved in his fourth fist fight since five-thirty. An RASC captain draws his second Royal Flush of the evening and pockets a kitty amounting to eighty-five pounds. A mother of six wonders how to tell her unemployed husband that there will soon be a seventh mouth to feed. A corporal in the Catering Corps signs a chit for eight hundredweight sacks of flour and later discovers that two of the sacks are filled with sand.

And:

Behind Kingsway, in a white building, a high-ranking officer receives the codeword Toledo and cancels a dinner engagement for the following week. A rear-admiral, who has just been handed the same signal by a weary rating, crosses Exercise Boathook from his diary and substitutes Operation Musketeer.

Elsewhere other things were happening.

In the darkness of a St Paul's Bay beach-hut Miller made love to his ex-wife for the second time in half an hour. She sobbed a little and said she was sorry, but he was not sure to whom, or for what, she was apologizing.

They lay in silence when it was over. He was disappointed:

she was nowhere near as good as he remembered. She felt empty: another man, another body, another betrayal. She wondered where it would end.

'Bobby drinks, you know,' she said eventually.

'Drinks?'

'Yes. It . . . doesn't make life any easier.'

And that was all they said to one another until they left.

Porter listened to the cruel laughter. It seemed to come from a long way off. It was not in the room, in the room that smelt of other, more successful, visitors, in the room where the iron bed creaked, in the room where the window had to be left open or the occupants suffocated. It was elsewhere. In his mind, perhaps, probing like a scalpel for the weakest spot. The girl wasn't there, either. She was simply a figment of his imagination, a vaporous manifestation of his unconscious. And if she wasn't there she couldn't be hurt. If he struck her she would disappear.

'You are not a man, Johnnee. You are a woman.'

'Shut up.'

'I want my money, Johnnee. It is not my fault . . .'

'SHUT UP.'

The manifestation retreated, terrified by the look of anger and pain on his face. He hit her several times. After the first blow she did not scream again, but he continued to hit her. And when she fell he used his feet.

Like a crazy woman, thought Hayter. She drives like a crazy woman.

'Slow down, for Chrissake.'

'Frightened, sweetie?'

'No, I'm not frightened. But take it easy.'

She chuckled.

Sixty. Seventy.

He looked at her. Her lips were moist and she was breathing unevenly. It was almost as if . . . But he dismissed the idea. It was too ridiculous.

Seventy-five.

'For Jesus' sake . . . This road won't . . .'

'Shut your mouth, darling. Shut your stupid common mouth.'

He winced. She had never spoken to him like that before, never made him feel like a servant. But that, he realized suddenly, was what he was to her. For some insane reason best known to herself, she slept with him because he was common, because he was no more than an NCO. With her money and sexual appetite she could have had her pick of the officers, but she'd chosen him. Because he was dirt. Because she wanted dirt. Because he would accept, and demand, the abnormal.

'Watch out!'

She braked violently, missed the lorry, and skidded off the road. Somehow she brought the car to a halt without hitting anything.

'You're crazy! You want your arse spanked!'

'Of course I do, darling. That's why you're here.'

He got out of the car and slammed the door. 'Piss off,' he said, and left her.

The *karozzin* driver beat his horse until it squealed with pain and blood was drawn. Rourke clenched his fists and started forward.

'Leave it,' said Thatcher. 'It's not your problem.'

'But he's killing that poor bloody animal.'

'So he's killing it. They don't care about horses, these Malts. You lay into him and you get stuck in jug. You don't get home this Christmas or next.'

'Ay, that's right, isn't it.'

They walked on.

Langley no longer cared whether or not Colonel Blake put in an appearance. His Wren had made it clear that she did not find him unattractive and had even suggested that they leave the party discreetly. What was more, her uncle was a vice-admiral. Well, one never knew.

Shaw held the broken bottle by its neck and stood with his back to the wall. He grinned fiendishly – like old times, this. They would rush him, he decided. They would come in fast from three sides. Well, the first man to swing a punch would be picking glass splinters from his face for a month.

'Come on, you chicken-livered bastards.'

The soldiers hesitated.

'Aah, screw him,' said one. 'There are other bars.'

The trio went out.

Shaw roared with laughter and tossed the bottle on to a near-by table. He rejoined the leading seaman, who was by now too drunk to be of any use to his girl friend.

Riordan reassembled the bren and wiped the barrel with an oily rag. It had been with him a long time, the bren, and it had been a good friend. They had told him at the beginning of his days as a Marine that a man's weapon was his best pal. And they'd been right. It was perhaps the only real friend he'd ever had.

'Lie still, sweetheart. Shut up, for Chrissake, and lie still.'

. . . . .

'Get settled down, you bootnecks. Come on, this isn't your daddy's yacht.'

'How long does this one last for, sarge?'

'You tell me then we'll both know. What's the matter with you, Shaw? You're green.'

'My head aches.'

'Serves you right. Okay, chop-chop. Get your heads down.'

'When do we sail, sergeant?'

'I dunno, Webster. I'll get the CO to come and tell you personally, if you like.'

'Thanks, sarge. I could use a cuppa while you're at it.'

Laughter.

'C'me on, c'me on, c'me on.'

'Kiss me good night, sergeant.'

'And me, sarge.'

'Shut up. Right: Lights Out.'

'Hey!'

'I can't see.'

'Dear mother, it's a bugger . . .'

'Shut up.'

Soon the ship slept, and in the small hours of Wednesday morning the convoy slipped its moorings and sailed out of Grand Harbour.

TWENTY

Sunday.

The skies were grey, the seas choppy, and the keel-less LSTs shuddered under the impact of every wave. Below deck the hollow interiors of the ships were crammed to bursting with men, machines, and equipment. On deck those who could eat ate, those who could not were sick, and those who were not hungry played the familiar game of trying to count the number of ships in the Task Force.

They knew now that this was no exercise. They had been told that Britain and France were at war with Egypt, that British planes had bombed, and were bombing, the Canal Zone, and that the Brigade had been charged with the capture of Port Said. Some of them were enthusiastic; at least Musketeer would teach the Gyppos a bloody good lesson. Others were apprehensive: Why the hell did we have to catch it? Others were indifferent.

They had been at sea for four days, and each day had been a repetition of the previous one: an orgy of briefing, preparation, and rehearsal. They had climbed aboard the assault craft a dozen times, been swung out on the davits, lowered several feet, and swung back. They had studied maps and plans of Port Said and had become as familiar as any Egyptian with the precise location of the de Lesseps statue, the Simon Artz store, the Anzac War Memorial, the Suez Canal Company's offices, the Arsenal Basin, Navy House, the Abbas Hilmi Basin, the Sacony-Vacuum Oil tanks. They had listened to their Troop Commanders explain about the climate and the terrain, and how they would wear their green berets and not steel helmets for the assault. They were told that paratroopers would drop on Gamil Airfield on November 5th, and give them covering fire as they came ashore. They learned that they would land on the left of Casino Pier and that their beach was known as Sierra Purple. They also learned that

H-hour for them was to be 0630 local time on November 6th. And finally they learned that the landing would be opposed.

Evening.

The Tannoy was switched on in time for the troops to hear the BBC announcer say: 'Ladies and Gentlemen, the Prime Minister.'

Someone called, 'Turn the bugger off,' but he was shouted down.

'All my life,' said Eden, 'I have been a man of peace, striving for peace and negotiating for peace. I have been a League of Nations man and a United Nations man. And I am still the same man with the same convictions and the same devotion to peace. I could not be other even if I wished, but I am utterly convinced that the action we have taken is right.'

'Hot dog.'

'Big deal.'

'So you have my rifle and I'll have your briefcase.'

Eden went on: 'Our passionate love of peace and our intense loathing of war have often held us back from using force, even at times when we knew in our heads, if not our hearts, that its use was in the interests of peace. And I believe with all my heart and my head that this is the time for action effective and swift.'

'Go, man.'

'Hallelujah.'

'Hot digitty.'

'Tell us another, Ant.'

The Prime Minister was followed by the Leader of the Opposition, and Gaitskell said, of Eden: 'His policy this week has been disastrous, and he is utterly discredited in the eyes of the world. Only one thing can save the reputation of our country. Parliament must repudiate the Government's policy. The Prime Minister must resign.'

'Lousy Labour bum!' someone shouted, and this cry was taken up until it echoed and re-echoed throughout the convoy.

It was a curious paradox that they directed their anger not at Eden, who had put them where they were, but at Gaitskell. Gaitskell was turning the knife in the wound, they said to each other. Surely to Christ they were entitled to some support, no matter who was right and who was wrong. Their necks were the ones being stuck out, not Gaitskell's. They would be ploughing ashore in thirty-six hours, not Gaitskell. They were sweltering in the bowels of a flat-bottomed tub built God only knew how many years ago, not Gaitskell. And for what? To hear a politician try to make capital out of it? Jesus, no. Jesus Christ, no. Jesus Christ Almighty, no.

And that was what the troops thought at nine-fifteen on Sunday, November 4th, 1956.

'Three Queens,' grinned Thatcher, reaching forward to collect the pot.

'Nice hand,' said Shaw.

'The best.'

'Not quite. You're up against a Straight.' Shaw spread his cards fan-wise.

'You rotten sod. Why didn't you say so right off?'

'I like to see you suffer. Your deal.'

It was after midnight and they were playing two-handed poker by torch-light. Their card-table was the bonnet of a Champ. Around them, on the four-tiered bunks, others read or talked or wrote. Few could sleep. It was far too hot and humid.

'How many cards?'

'Two.'

'Dealer takes three. Dealer bets two bob.'

'Huh.'

Lying on his stomach with his head on his folded arms and watching Shaw and Thatcher assess the respective strength of their hands, Webster wondered how they could play cards so calmly. Didn't they know where they were going? Didn't it worry them?

'Your two and up five.'

'Five? You must have a bloody good hand. Okay, I'll come along. Another five.'

'That's a bluff.'

'Is it? Try me.'

'Huh.'

No, thought Webster, it didn't worry them because they were thick. They didn't realize that a guy could get killed out here. They didn't realize it. They went along with the theory that because they'd been lucky in Cyprus they'd be lucky in Egypt. Stupid bastards; you were just as dead wherever you caught it. Still, whoever else got the chopper, he wasn't going to get it. No, sir. If Langley volunteered them for anything, he'd be at the back of the queue. Mrs Webster's little lad had done his bit.

'Two pairs, Kings and deuces.'

'Hard lines, three sevens.'

'Jesus, you got golden balls, Shaw.'

'Yeah. You wanna borrow 'em?'

'Deal the cards.'

Webster debated whether or not he would be believed if he reported sick. With something like double vision, something they couldn't check on. Or he could trap his fingers in a hatch, bruise them a bit. Or he could fall awkwardly and sprain an ankle. It would be easy enough to fake an injury . . . Easy enough? No, sod it, not easy. Running with the herd was easy, ducking when they ducked, taking cover when they took cover. That, screw the Marines, was easier than opting out.

In the bunk below Webster's, squinting in the semi-darkness, Porter flicked through the pages of his diary. The pain in his head had grown worse in the last hour. It was a dull, heavy pain, as if something was pressing on his brain. It had been with him, on and off, for four days, and aspirin, the sick-bay cure-all, had proved useless.

He found what he was looking for: the entry he had made earlier that evening. It was to be his final entry. He no longer wanted to record his thoughts.

'Two years ago I would have sided with Gaitskell and been horrified at the thought of two great and powerful nations waging war on a third-rate country. Now I don't care. It is doubtless necessary to be committed to something, and perhaps

I, unwittingly, have become committed to the idea of nothingness and futility. If the world is corrupt, why should I worry? If people are essentially evil, what concern is that of mine? I won't change anything. And neither will my contemporaries, the ones who, when their National Service is done, will rush up to Oxford and Cambridge and Redbrick and stuff themselves with idealistic, and anachronistic, nonsense. Fools, all of them. Intellectual gluttons. Why bother? They would be better off digging roads. Only stupid people lust after education. The navvy is undoubtedly superior to the don, because the navvy lives and is not concerned with Life.

'We are all, I think, part of some vast and unexplained experiment. You take a group of individuals such as us and put them in a given situation. You study their reactions. You try to guess who will survive. Not merely avoid death, but survive and live. Shaw, with his strength, will survive, because physical strength is omnipotent. Thatcher, with his cunning, will survive, because cunning is omnipotent. Riordan, with his efficiency, will survive, because efficiency is omnipotent. Webster will survive because he is a survivor by nature. Rourke – quien sabe? And myself – I don't know that either. And I don't know what I shall do in England. Not, certainly, join the knowledge seekers in the useless pilgrimage to university. Not, surely, honour my father and my mother. Not anything. Blackness.

'I wonder how the girl is. Curiously her fate doesn't trouble me. What happened could have happened in a dream. Maybe it did. I don't think I killed her, but it wouldn't matter if I had. Better like that, perhaps; she would then not be able to identify me. It was her own fault, in any case. She shouldn't have laughed and laughed and laughed.'

And there the entry finished. He read it again. Some of it did not make sense. Not sane sense.

He chuckled and the pain came again. Throbbing.

'Deal,' said Shaw, who had several notes and a mountain of silver in front of him.

'Hold your bloody horses, I am dealin'.'

A few yards away Riordan listened to the laconic comments of the card players, his own heavy breathing, and the low, monotonous hum of the engines. And to other sounds: the rasping of a match; the rhythmic snoring of the X Troop corporal who had slept like a baby for the five nights they had been at sea; the colourful curse of a naked Marine stumbling over packs and boots and weapons en route to the latrines; the dry cough of a fifty-a-day smoker; the loose, liquid cough of a bronchitis sufferer; the clicking of torches; the rustle of magazines and books; the whispered telling of a familiar joke; the complaints about the heat and the humidity; the opening and closing of hatches; the lecherous and frustrated grunts over an obscene photograph; the scratching of biros on notepaper. And he smelt the smells: petrol and oil from the vehicles which were revved up daily to keep them functional; cigarette smoke from every quarter; sweat from damp bodies; bad breath, beery breath, and breath that reeked of Colgate. And he thought: Roll on the 6th.

Above Riordan Rourke was half-asleep, caught in that uneasy no-man's-land which separates consciousness from unconsciousness. Every now and then he muttered his wife's name or his son's name, and once or twice he said something which sounded like, 'Not me.' But for the most part he was quiet. Restless, but quiet.

In his cabin Colonel Blake studied a fresh batch of signals and intelligence reports. An untouched glass of brandy stood by his elbow.

The first signal was from the C-in-C. It estimated the Egyptian strength, excluding forces engaged in the Sinai Peninsula against the Israelis, as: 80 Mig 15s, 45 Il 28 bombers, 25 Meteors, 57 Vampires, and 200 other aircraft; 75,000 Infantry, 300 tanks, including 150 of a modern Russian design, an unknown quantity of anti-tank guns, and a considerable quantity of anti-aircraft guns, together with an up-to-date radar organization.

It was a formidable arsenal, he thought, and it was the height of irony that a good forty per cent of it carried the words Made in Britain.

He turned his attention to his own plan of campaign. The Sierra Purple beach, 49's landing zone, was, if anything, a tougher nut than Sierra Blue. For a start, it was nearer the west bank of the Canal, and the hard-core Egyptians could be expected to congregate in that area. The armour would have to come up damned fast if an unacceptable number of casualties was to be avoided. Then there was the question of the landing itself. He wondered if he had been hasty in nominating Captain Claire-Voysey to spearhead the assault, but eventually decided he had not. Richard Miller would have been more spectacular, but Claire-Voysey was safer. And safety had to be a considered factor. There were too many lives at stake. Too many young lives.

He sipped his brandy slowly.

In another part of the ship Miller lay, fully dressed, on his bunk and tried not to think of his ex-wife, as he had succeeded in not thinking about her for five nights. She had cried again when he had taken her home, and asked him to stay for a little while. He had refused. It would have been pointless, futile. It was impossible to turn back the clock. She had made him promise to write to her as soon as he was on board, but he had not bothered. That, too, was pointless. What could he say apart from: My dear Susan, Thank you very much for the sex.

No – no letters.

She was a slut, a grade-A slut. Beautiful, yes, but undeniably a slut. She had cheated on him, she had cheated on her Major, and doubtless she had cheated on other lovers and prospective husbands. She was the sort of woman who enjoyed keeping beds warm, who needed the constant company of a man. And if her husband wasn't available . . .

No – definitely no letters. And no further contact. The past was better buried.

'We should meet up with the others some time tomorrow,' said Reynolds.

'Pardon?'

'The others, the rest of the fleet, the Cyprus end of the operation.'

'Oh, yes,' said Langley.

They were on deck, leaning against the guardrail and watching the luminous plankton in the sea below. The convoy was in darkness, and the light emanating from the tiny marine creatures seemed incredibly bright. To their left stood Hayter and a group of senior NCOs. They were conversing in whispers, as though the occasion were sacred and the environment holy.

'I hear the French have got a battleship that can't fire a broadside without keeling over,' said Reynolds.

'An old wives' tale.'

'Probably.' Reynolds stretched. 'Well, I'm for bed. We won't get much sleep tomorrow night. Coming?'

'Pardon?'

'I said, are you ready for bed? You're in a dream, Brian.'

'Sorry, I was thinking.'

'Bad habit for second-lieutenants. Are you coming?'

'No. No, not yet. I'll be along shortly.'

'Okay. Good night.'

'Good night.'

Alone, Langley lit a cigarette, remembering to cover the glowing end with a cupped hand.

He stared out into the night, in the direction of the invisible, darkened ships, more relaxed now that Reynolds had gone. There was a time for talk and a time for silence, and this was his time for silence. For thought. Constructive thought. About the operation. It had to be a success. Not generally, but for him. He had not done too brilliantly in Cyprus. He had made mistakes, mistakes he could not afford to have on his record. Klein, Costas – although how anyone could blame him for Costas' death was a mystery. But they did, the Section, they did. Possibly Miller did, too. It was ridiculous and unfair, of course, but there must be no repetition. The landing had to go well. He had to prove he was as good an officer as . . . Well, he had to prove he was a good officer.

You're not much bloody good at anything, are you, Brian? I'm sorry, Father. *Sorry, sorry! Don't always be so damned sorry. Just concentrate on pulling your socks up. Show me that some of my blood runs through your veins, for God's sake. Try harder, that's all I'm asking. It's not a lot to ask, is it?* No.

No?

You despise me, don't you? *Despise you? Nonsense! Whatever gave you that idea. Why should I despise you?* Because . . . *Well?* Because I'm not more like you. *Rubbish! Don't ever say such a thing again. Never. Understand?*

Langley tossed his cigarette over the side. We'll see, he thought. We'll see.

'Good night,' he said, as he passed the NCOs.

'Good night, sir.'

'And dream like a bastard,' murmured Hayter.

Monday.

The fleets from Malta and Cyprus converged in the afternoon: French and British destroyers, cruisers, transports, carriers, and small escort vessels which darted like neurotic grey flies in and out of the gaps in the convoy, hunting an unseen quarry. Overhead the sky was thick with aircraft: Sea Hawks, Sea Venoms, Corsairs. From the decks of the LSTs the troops saw them form up and set a course sou'-sou'-east. It was dark when they returned.

. . . . .

The naval bombardment snarled the overture to the assault and awoke the few who had managed to sleep. Down below they could not see the white flashes that lit the sky, but they could hear the sinister howl of the shells that were softening up the defences, and involuntarily they ducked and winced at each sound. Some of them wondered, in passing, what it was like to be on the receiving end.

They ate their breakfast in silence, those who could eat at all. Those who could not smoked incessantly and stared unseeingly at a mug of tea or a slice of greasy, unappetizing bacon. They noticed that their palms tingled peculiarly with a combination of damp fear and nervous excitement. Faces pale and pinched attempted to smile confidently.

After breakfast they kept themselves occupied by checking their weapons and adjusting their packs and support straps. Their minds were filled with strange, unsummoned images and memories; people they had not thought about for years, places they had consciously long forgotten; women they had loved and abandoned; a summer cottage and children laughing and playing; an afternoon on the sand at Portsmouth; a Sunday morning drink in the local; a Christmas leave; a shopping expedition with a pocketful of money; a game of football on a piece of waste land; a holiday in Blackpool; the cry of the first cuckoo; boating on a lake. And they recalled the things they had left undone: the letter home that had not been written because it had been too much trouble; the wife who was waiting for money that had been spent on a blonde whore; the way an old pal had been cheated out of a hundred cigarettes; the child who had been born a bastard because its father was already married.

Other places, other days.

And then it was time to go on deck.

It was light now, and from the ships they saw that Port Said was covered with a pall of smoke which drifted inland like some shapeless black bird of prey and obscured most of the waterfront. The pitiless eyes of the gun-turrets had missed nothing. On the beach huts were ablaze, and to the south an oil dump had received a direct hit.

They climbed aboard the LCAs and crouched down. They looked at one another, but their brains did not register what they saw. The davits shuddered, the pulleys screeched, and the assault craft were lowered into the water. There the pilots started the engines and moved away from the sides of the parent ships, towards the beach. Spray surged over the armoured bows.

They had covered a hundred yards before they noticed, almost heard, the deathly quiet. The big guns had stopped firing. They were on their own. They reminded themselves: Keep your head down. No talking. Save your breath. Wait for the ramp to drop and then run like hell. Spread out when you hit the beach. Don't get too far ahead of the others. Don't panic. If someone gets hit, forget him. That's not your job. God's good. It'll be all right. It'll be all right.

'*Get ready!*'

They stood up.

The bow doors swung open and the ramp dropped with a crash. And there was the beach.

The front men hesitated.

'Go!' screamed an NCO.

'Go!' yelled an officer.

And they jumped.

TWENTY-ONE

The beach seemed a long way off, but in reality it was no more than thirty yards. Thirty lonely yards. They waded towards it, their weapons held high. The water was cold and waist deep. The sand beneath their feet was soft and clinging. It pulled at their legs and made a mockery of their attempts to run. All around others struggled landwards, and farther back fresh waves of assault craft disgorged more troops. From the roof of a building to their left came a burst of automatic fire, and a Marine folded like a crumpled paper bag. The weight of his equipment dragged him under.

They hit the beach east of Casino Pier and ran in the direction of the burning huts. The acrid smell of charred wood and canvas and smouldering flesh filled their nostrils and brought tears to their eyes. Their hearts pumped blood at twice the normal rate. Each of them expected to feel the sudden impact of a bullet at any second, and yet, paradoxically, none of them expected to die. It was just another war game, and sooner or later the umpires would announce the winners.

The beach rang with curses and instructions, and here and there a heap of khaki moaned or vomited.

'*Spread out!*'

'*Take cover!*'

'*Bren! Where the fug's the bren!*'

'*Armstrong's caught one!*'

'*Leave him, leave him!*'

'*Jesus, I can't stop the bleeding!*

'*Support! Where the hell's Support!*'

Behind the huts the narrow stretch of sand which led up to the Port Said–Gamil road was pitted with defence trenches, empty except for discarded weapons and half a dozen dead Egyptians dressed in bloody *galabiyehs*. One of the bodies had no head, and the maggots were already busy on the bits of red and pink vein that had been cauterized by the searing heat of the shell which had decapitated him. South of the road was a modern block of flats from which, at intervals, two or three machine-guns chattered. Farther south, an extension of the Sierra Purple zone, was the commercial area of the town, comprising shops and offices, docks and warehouses. To the west they could just make out the Arab quarter. Most of the tightly packed wooden houses were already ablaze.

'Are we crossin' the road, sergeant?'

'No, we're fuggin not. You're not Errol fuggin Flynn.'

'Don't stand there like a spare prick, Edwards . . .'

'Jesus, that was close!'

'Bren! Bren! Put a magazine through that window.'

'Captain Claire-Voysey's copped one in the leg, sir.'

'Careful with those grenades. They're not lollipops.'

The order came to dig in and hold until the tanks arrived, and they took cover on the seaward side of the road. To their rear the Sierra Purple beach quickly became a confused, sprawling, and unidentifiable mass of men and stores as the third, fourth, and fifth waves landed. Farther out at sea the parent LSTs ploughed towards the shore, while in the distance, just visible but growing bigger every second, the racing-green helicopters carrying 45 Commando winged south-east like gigantic gnats. Overhead a squadron of Sea Venoms prepared to make a strike.

It was five minutes before they were breathing normally and before they could think through the noise; before they realized they were ashore and safe. Christ, they'd made it. They were wet and cold and sore and black with smoke and sweat, but they'd made it. They were alive and kicking.

Some of them.

Miller appeared and walked the length of D Troop, oblivious of the snipers in the flats.

'Keep your eyes peeled for aircraft,' he warned each Section Commander, 'and let me have a casrep in ten minutes.'

'Anyone in 3 Section hurt?' shouted Langley, when Miller had gone. No one was. So far, so good.

Twenty yards from Langley, Porter was fascinated by the headless Egyptian, whose body was close enough for him to touch. The white maggots grew fatter as he watched, feasting themselves on the sticky coagulation. It was strange, he thought, that an hour or two ago the man had been casually sitting in his trench. Strange and somehow revelationary. He wouldn't have heard the whine of the anonymous shell which killed him. (And where was his head? It had to be somewhere.) There would have been an instant of pain, a loosening of the bowels as the muscles became useless, then blackness. And somewhere on a destroyer or a battleship a gun crew would have ejected the spent casing and reloaded, not knowing that their last shot had found a target. Probably they didn't care. Probably they were more interested in getting below to their bunks. That was the incredible thing about death: its insignificance. It wasn't, as he had believed for most of his twenty-one years, something personal and horrible and brutal and tragic. It was nothing. A blinding flash, a moment of understanding – then nothing. Into the pit. People lived their lives in fear of it, wondered how and when it would be their turn, but really their fears were groundless. How could one be frightened of nothing?

'What's so funny?' said Riordan.

'Funny?'

'Yeah. You're grinning and talking to yourself. You all right?'

'Of course I'm all right. I understand, you see, Riordan.'

'Understand what?'

'Everything.'

They ducked as the Sea Venoms swept east-west in V-formation low across the sands.

'Look, you sure you're okay?' yelled Riordan.

Porter's head no longer throbbed. 'Never better,' he said.

Like hell. Like bloody hell, thought Riordan, but put it down to nerves.

In another trench Shaw was singing softly and maliciously, and huddled at the bottom of the same trench Webster tried unsuccessfully to block out the terrifying noise of the aircraft and the rifle fire and the shouting.

'I see a wog in a window, a wog who's gonna die-diddly-ay-die-diddly-ay-die,' sang Shaw.

'Shut your goddam mouth,' groaned Webster. 'Shut it, for Chrissake. What's there to sing about?'

'Plenty. You'd see if you stopped grovelling around in the shit. There's a third-floor window in those flats and it leads into a room. Inside the room is a Gyppo with a rifle. He pokes his head out and has a bang every forty seconds. I've timed him. He's due now. Take a gander.'

'Get stuffed.'

Shaw chuckled happily. Webster was one hell of a chicken-gutted bastard.

'There he goes.'

A shape appeared at the window, fired an aimless volley, and disappeared.

'I'll get you,' sang Shaw. 'I'll get you.' He started to count. 'One two three four . . .'

Oh Jesus, Jesus, Jesus, why doesn't he shut his great clanging, ignorant mouth, thought Webster, and dug his fingers into the soft sand to stop himself from shaking. It's a game to him. A fugging game.

'. . . Twenty-four, twenty-five . . .'

Christ, Christ, let it be over. Let's quit. Nobody wants to die. I haven't done anything to deserve it. If I have, I won't do it again. Promise. Promise. Get me out of this and I promise . . .

'Thirty-seven, thirty-eight, thirty-nine, forty.'

Shaw fired a single shot at forty, and the shape, punctual as ever, fell back.

'I did it!' he exulted. 'I got one. I did it.'

'Good shooting, Shaw,' called Hayter.

'Thanks, sarge. Did you see that, Webbo? Did you see it?'

But Webster had not seen it. He was still making empty promises from the depths of the trench.

A pair of Royal Navy SBAs, carrying one of the wounded on a stretcher, ran past 3 Section's position and on down the line. Rourke tried to see who the injured man was, but the face, with half the jaw missing, was unrecognizable. Poor sod, he thought, and then: no, lucky sod. He's out of it.

'Keep your bleedin' turnip down!' snarled Thatcher, as a spray of machine-gun bullets kicked up sand.

'That's guy's getting better,' muttered Rourke. 'Jesus.'

'He's not gonna help ya, ya dumb bastard. So watch it.'

The Sea Venoms returned west-east, and the leader dipped his wings. That's the way to fight a war, thought the ground troops. Up there. Remote. No sweat and back on the carrier in time for breakfast. Yessir, none of this crawling and running and shooting crap for the fly-boys. No sudden waves of fear that come at you hot and cold when you're not expecting it. No uncontrollable bladders. No trying to bury your head where it won't be buried when a mortar goes off. No listening to the moans of the guys who weren't quick enough. No lying on your belly with your rifle stuck out like a penis and your own penis hiding in the folds of shrunken skin the way you'd like to hide if you thought no one would notice. No watching the faces of your oppos and wondering if you look as shit-frightened as they do. No staring at a house or a hut or a dead wog and your brain not registering what you see. No thinking, what the hell's that stink, and then realizing that the stink is you and if it's not you it's a body or what's left of a body already decomposing. No trying to light a fag and your hands shaking like a girl's as you try. No being put in one place and told to stay in that place until ordered otherwise. No waiting, waiting, waiting. No sand in your mouth. No remembering the lectures on scorpions and asking yourself where the hell are the fuggin scorpions, because if you could find one you'd let it bite the bejesus out of you. No remembering the other lectures and the refresher training and knowing damned well it was a load of pigs' bollocks, because the real thing's got nothing to do with training. None of that blood, sweat, and tears baloney ringing in your ears, and no telling yourself that death before dishonour was something some writer wrote when he was pissed. No asking yourself whether this is a big war or a little war or a what the hell war, because when you're in the middle of it, brother, it's the biggest, fiercest bastard ever. No, sir. Up and off into that wild blue yonder they talk about. Clean. Sparkling. Uninvolved. Well, fug the lot of you, fly-boys. Fug the lot of you.

In Spades.

It was an hour before the first of the tanks rolled ponderously ashore and up the beach. It positioned itself on the road and its big gun traversed right and left, inquisitively, before finding a nest of snipers hidden in the block of flats, behind the white walls. White because that prime colour is impervious to the heat of the Mediterranean sun. White for purity. White for a shroud.

The Marines watched coldly. And they thought: This is it, buddy-boys. You've got ten, maybe twenty, seconds. So let's see you, buddy-boys. We'd like to see you. When you choke in your own blood we want to know about it. We want to hear you yell. You don't stand a chance, buddy-boys. Not a chance. We've got the aces now. So dance, buddy-boys, and scream, buddy-boys, and pray to Allah or whoever the hell your top man is. Because this is it, buddy-boys, this is it.

The big gun coughed twice in rapid succession. A large, gaping hole appeared in the masonry, and the inside of the block caught fire. There was no further sniping from that quarter.

The Marines spat contentedly, and the lead Troop followed the tank as it lumbered off in the direction of the commercial area and the Canal.

The youth was eighteen or nineteen, and undernourished. Through any one of the many rents in his filthy brown shirt it was possible to see that the flesh barely covered the bones. On a normal day he was a labourer, but today they had given him a rifle, a new Russian rifle, and told him to help defend his country against imperialism. He had never handled a rifle before that morning, but several practice rounds had taught him how to use it, and the feel of it pleased him. It was sleek and powerful, like the hips of a girl. What was more, when the battle was over he knew where he could sell it for twenty Egyptian pounds, more money than he earned in a month. But for the moment he had to shoot it.

Beside him on the flat roof he had a heap of ammunition – enough, he estimated, to kill many of the English soldiers who were now almost immediately beneath him, skulking in the shadow of the tanks. The Englishmen had to die. Colonel Nasser had decreed it. One bullet for each soldier. None must be wasted. With ammunition, the gun would be worth more than twenty pounds.

He raised the rifle to his shoulder, took careful aim, and fired.

Porter was surprised that there was no pain after the initial burning sensation, after the impact of the sniper's bullet had tossed him to the ground like so much straw in the wind. He struggled to get to his feet, but someone – he could not see who; the face was blurred – laid a restraining hand on his shoulder and ordered him not to move. That was decent of them, he thought, letting him lie there while there was a war going on. Very decent. He was grateful for the rest. All that running and shooting was bloody hard work. Perhaps if his wound was serious enough, they would take him back to the ship. Unfortunately, though, his wound wasn't serious – just a nick in the chest. It couldn't be serious or he would know about it. That made sense. However, they wouldn't expect him to fight for a few minutes, not until he was properly bandaged.

He half closed his eyes.

The colours were beautiful: reds, greens, blues, purples, golds. Especially the golds. The golds were warm and he was cold. Odd to be cold in Egypt. Of course it was November, their spring, so the sun wouldn't be cracking the flags. In any case, it was early yet – eight o'clock, nine o'clock. The golds would keep him warm until the sun was high.

He heard a voice and attempted to focus. No, no use. The crack on the head he had taken when falling had made him dizzy. And he was tired.

Very tired.

He wasn't going to university when he got home. Determined. He wasn't going to waste his life studying dead languages and philosophies. He was going to do something. Not sure what yet, but it would come to him. Needed time. Lots and lots of time. He understood now. Understood such a lot. World needed shaking up. World needed a kick. Stupid, lovely world. He could do it. Could help. Somehow. Somehow. No more fighting. Just peace. No more pain . . .

He grunted, and gurgled like a man drowning, and when they saw he was dead they covered his face to keep off the flies.

. . . . .

Far out at sea the Planners were well pleased with the operation so far. It was going very much as they had predicted, and casualties, they thanked God, were well within the prescribed maximum. They felt they had cause to celebrate, and the sun was pronounced to be over the yard-arm.

It was a curious thing about the Planners, but were it not for the uniforms they wore one would not have taken them to be military men. Bankers, perhaps, prosperous brokers, maybe, but not soldiers. It was probably no more than the delicate manner in which they held their glasses, or the beautiful half-moons of their manicured nails, or the fact that their cheeks were plump and newly shaved, but it was easier to imagine them striding importantly along Throgmorton Street and Threadneedle Street than to accept the picture of them in the Operations Room of an aircraft carrier. Or could it be that the same people who, by some legerdemain, fix the going price of stocks and shares also run wars?

They were brilliant men, the Planners; everyone acknowledged that much. They were as familiar with the writings of Clausewitz, Schlieffen, and Napoleon as they were with the contours of their own fleshy bellies. They were a little less familiar with the teachings of Christ, Mahomet, and Buddha. And they were completely ignorant of the chemistry of Marine Jones and Private Smith. Nevertheless they were brilliant, and brilliance is a quality which allows the possessor certain licence. To them wars were simply a question of balance and counter-balance, thrust, and counter-thrust. A dance without music. Have enough men in the right place at the right time and that was success, their yardstick. Success meant promotion, success meant a KCB, success meant a place in history. It was not their function to worry about Marine Jones and Private Smith. Their vision was panoramic.

. . . . .

In the wake of their forenoon advance through the streets of old Port Said they left the excrementa of war. The shops they had looted for Leica lenses, binoculars, jewellery, and anything else small enough to be hidden with ease. The donkey the S Troop machine-gunner had sliced in two because he had not hit anything for an hour. The girl they had intended to rape – but she had screamed and they had to be satisfied with knocking her unconscious. The windows they had smashed because it seemed ridiculous for one building to have windows and the surrounding buildings to have none. The tiny boy, fezzed, who, oblivious of the shooting, appeared from nowhere to beg for alms and offer brothers, sisters, fathers, and cousins for any kind of perversion. The dogs sniffing around the dead.

Once in a while they thought of what they had seen and what others had seen and what others said they had seen. The French civilian who had been lynched by a mob, and when they cut him down his neck had crackled like dry leaves. The X Troop lance-corporal who had got cut off and who had been discovered crying because they had torn out his thumb-nails with pliers. The pilot of the Sea Venom who had been given incorrect co-ordinates for a strike and who had succeeded in shooting up and wounding seventeen Marines. The unnamed Section officer who had disappeared for two hours to return garlanded, drunk, and a woman on each arm. The room they had lobbed a grenade into and then rushed in to find a mutilated child. The official photographer who spent his time putting corpses in interesting poses and complaining about the light.

Sometimes it was quiet. Sometimes a great and wise Being decreed, for a minute or two, silence, and during the silence it was as though the war never was and never would be.

'Christ, I dropped my fags back there.'

'I'll sell you a packet.'

'How much?'

'Four bob.'

'Get lost! Two-and-six.'

'Three-and-six.'

'Three bob.'

'Done.'

And:

'When I tell me brudda about dis he'll say, shit, Ron, dat was nuttin'. It was real tough in the last war. And if he says dat, I'll smack him in the teeth.'

And:

'Get a load of her. You'd think this was a Sunday in Pompey.'

'Do you reckon her?'

'Not half. How d'you say it in Egyptian?'

'Jigajig.'

'Jigagig, love. Come and get hold of this. See, she understands.'

' 'Course she does.'

'I'm gonna have a bang. Keep watch for five minutes.'

'Don't be a mug. She's probably got half the diseases known to man and a few that aren't. You'll be on penicillin for a year after that.'

'Yeah, I guess so. Pity, though.'

And:

'Where the fug are the pyramids?'

Sometimes it was not so quiet.

There were no heroes and few cowards in the sweep down the Canal, which began in the early afternoon. There were just men. Men who had brandy and not water in their spare water-bottles. Men who limped because their feet were sore. Men who wondered when the hell the supply trucks with the hot meals were coming. Men who could not have eaten if they'd been offered a thousand pounds a mouthful. Men whose shirts were dark with sweat. Men who looked as though their uniforms had been dry-cleaned the second before. Men with warts on their noses and men who resembled film stars, carefully made-up, in a war movie. Men whose noses ran and who could not be bothered to wipe them. Men whose bright eyes showed that they were suffering from shock – or would have showed it if anyone had been interested in examining them. Men with black hair and men with ginger hair and men with alopecia. Men who whistled a popular tune. Men who hated the whistling. Men who did what they had to do because that was all there was to it. Move forward, take cover in a doorway, bring up the machine-gun or the rocket-launcher, blast hell out of whatever was in the way, run, crouch, move forward again, bring up the machine-gun . . . When a Marine was hit they waited to see if they knew him, and occasionally they did.

Oh Christ, yes, he's the guy who always drinks bottled beer; or: he's the guy who said he had it off with the CO's wife one day when he'd been assigned to clean her car; or: Jesus, I double-dated with him and those two scrubbers in Pompey or Exeter or Plymouth or Floriana – or Timbuctoo, because the place didn't matter now that he wouldn't be double-dating again for a long time.

Move forward, take cover, run, crouch, bring up the machine-gun . . . The rhythm of what some genius of a politician had already described as no more than a police action.

TWENTY-TWO

It was four o'clock and for three hours they had been advancing slowly along the dusty Canal road, clearing nests of snipers and demolishing pockets of resistance as they went. On their left, in the Canal itself, were the hulks of ships dynamited and sunk by the Egyptians to prevent passage. Beyond the Canal was incipient desert; Blackpool, as someone had named it. On their right were blocks of shops, offices, and warehouses, and separating each block, at intervals of fifty yards or so, narrow streets which met the main road in T-junctions. Each junction was covered by Egyptian fire, and it was necessary to wait for a tank to position itself at the bar of the T before crossing. Then they crossed in two stages. First from wall to tank, and then from tank to wall.

The tank commander, a blond lieutenant in his twenties, peered through one of the armoured slits and grinned at them.

'Nice day for a walk in the sun,' he called.

'Up yours,' muttered Thatcher.

The blond lieutenant grinned again. He liked working with the Marines, irreverent bunch of bastards though they were. They knew their job. There was no nonsense about them. They were as efficient now, ten hours after landing, as they had been at seven AM.

The tank clanked forward and took up its position. 'Let it rip,' said the blond lieutenant, and the machine-gunner commenced firing down the street, raking it from side to side and from end to end.

Langley tapped Hayter on the shoulder. 'Go,' he said.

Hayter went. Five paces to the tank, pause, wait for the next burst, five paces to the far wall.

'Go.'

Thatcher followed Hayter. Then came Rourke, Webster, Shaw, Riordan, and finally Langley. Langley signalled

Reynolds when he was safely across, and Reynolds repeated the whole process with 4 Section.

In the vanguard of the column Miller squinted through his field-glasses at the next objective – a small office block some seventy yards ahead. In several of the first- and second-floor windows he could see Egyptians, and he judged by the density of the fire power emanating from the block that it was held by at least twenty defenders. It would be a much tougher nut to crack than anything they had met so far.

He handed the field-glasses to his Troop Sergeant-Major.

'What do you think, TSM – twenty of 'em, thirty?'

'Easily twenty, sir, maybe more. And they've got some heavy stuff in there. Listen, that's a Browning.'

'I hear it.'

'I can't see what the hell they're shooting at, though.'

'Nothing, probably. Just letting us know they're there.'

'Nice of 'em.' The TSM returned the field-glasses. 'Pity we haven't got a few more tanks. One's not going to be a lot of use.'

'Or aircraft,' said Miller thoughtfully. 'Or aircraft.'

The TSM shook his head. 'Doubt if you'll get them, sir. Everyone'll be crying out for air support.'

'I can try. Come on.'

Two hundred yards further back, grouped with the rest of the Section amid the broken glass and ruptured woodwork of what was once a shop, Riordan checked his watch. It had stopped at three-twenty.

'What's the time?' he asked.

'You in a hurry to get to the pub, Riordan?'

'Naw, sarge, he's got a date with a Gyppo bint at five o'clock,' said Thatcher. 'Haven't you, Riordan? One of those with a ruby in her whatsit.'

'Just tell me the time, eh,' said Riordan patiently.

'I'll sell you a watch instead. A fiver to you. Made in Switzerland. Jewelled movement, the lot. Cost you twenty in the UK.'

'You haven't been collecting souvenirs, have you, Thatcher?'

'Not me, sarge,' answered Thatcher, who had two dozen

identical watches in one of his ammunition pouches. 'I bought this one in Malta.'

'Yeah, I believe you. Just don't let Mr Langley cop you, that's all. You'll get ten years.'

'Look, will some bugger tell me the time,' growled Riordan.

'Four-ten,' said Rourke.

'Thanks.'

Riordan reset his watch, gave it a shake, and held it to his ear. He tried not to think about Porter. Porter was dead. Seven hours dead. It was as well not to dwell on dead men.

A helicopter hovered overhead and sprayed the roof of a nearby warehouse with machine-gun fire. Somewhere to the north a mortar exploded. They paid little attention to either noise. Noises were ten a penny.

'What did they want to go and do that for?' said Webster suddenly.

'Do what?'

'That.' He pointed out at the Canal and at the sunken ships.

'Christ, Webster, don't you know anything?' jeered Shaw. 'If they hadn't sunk those bleeders we would have been in Suez by now. You don't use your loaf.'

''Course I do. It didn't strike me, that's all.'

'I wish something would strike you.'

'Like what?'

'Like a bloody tank. I've met some dumb bastards, but you take the Oscar. What would you have liked the Gyppos to have done – left it wide open for you to sail down in your barge? Jeeze, I can just see it. Acting Marine Webster throwing flowers at the peasants. Acting Marine Webster leads the triumphant entry into Suez. Clive of India rides again.'

'Clive who?'

'Clive . . . Oh Jesus, you tell him, Thatcher. He wears me out.'

'Not me. They're thick, these Liverpudlians.'

'Thick! Bloody nerve. Listen, mate . . .'

To hear them talk, thought Hayter, you wouldn't know that not half an hour ago they'd been mopping up the fifth or sixth warehouse of the afternoon and stacking Egyptian bodies in neat piles so that the tanks could get through. But that was how it went. A bloke couldn't stay scared permanently, not even a bloke like Webster. They learned how to switch off, forget – until it was time to go again.

Outside, on the Troop wireless, Miller received the answer to his request for air support: no aircraft available. And in answer to his second request: no spare tanks.

'They'll be asking me to walk on the bloody water next,' he grumbled to his Section Commanders. Then he shrugged.

'Okay, get the men on their feet. If we've got to do it the hard way we might as well get on with it. I'll give the tank ten minutes to soften the place up, and we'll go in in twelve. That is, at four-thirty-two exactly. Take your Sections as close as you can without exposing them. Robert, you'll lead 3 and 4 Sections, I'll lead 1 and 2. You know the rest of the routine by now.'

They knew it as well as they knew their own names and ranks. Move forward in single file, keeping as close as possible to shelter of the buildings on their right. Halt ten or twenty yards before the street which divided the last cleared block from the objective. Look at watch every thirty seconds. Wait for Miller's signal and then run like blazes for the nearest door. Lob a grenade inside and follow up with bren and sten. After that, trust that the tank had managed to kill some of them, and hope that this wasn't the day you reached the bottom of your personal barrel of luck.

They moved up. Dust rose.

It was odd, the things they thought about while listening to the tank's big gun pound seven kinds of hell out of the office block. Odd because men facing death are expected to be solemn and afraid. But they had pondered the black owl thirty times that day and their collective unconscious would have no more of it. It wanted life.

Rourke thought of the woman he'd had while in London the week before he was married. She jumped into his mind for no reason and refused to leave. She'd been some woman, paid for or not. She'd done the things he'd been panting for her to do but had not had the nerve to ask for. She'd done things he'd never done with Mary, never could do, because Mary was a wife. There had been no love in the love-making, but it had been a hell of a quarter-hour. And Thatcher thought of the meal he'd had at the end of his first week as a barrow boy, at the end of a week in which he had earned fifteen pounds. The steak had been two inches thick and dripping with butter and mushrooms; the chips soft and succulent, the peas fresh and not canned. He'd had a bottle of wine, too. He didn't recall its name, but it had tasted damned good. Shaw thought of a game of roulette he'd once played in the club where he worked. He had begun the session with two pounds, which he had left on red. Six consecutive reds had been spun by the croupier, and he had left the table a hundred and twenty-six pounds richer. He had got very drunk that night. And Webster thought about a football he had owned as a youngster. It wasn't much of a ball, second-hand with the bladder inexpertly patched, but it had been his entrance fee into many a game. The other kids had even let him score once or twice. And Riordan thought about a trick he used to pull regularly to get free eats. He would buy a large carrier-bag from Selfridges or D. H. Evans or any of the other big London stores and stuff it full of old newspapers. Then he would go into a restaurant, choose a window seat, and order, leaving the bag on the floor beside him, the store's name prominent. A minute or two before the bill was due he would pretend to see someone he knew in the street, and rush out. If stopped, he would indicate the bag and say he'd be back in a second to collect his parcel. For a couple of years there were a lot of London restaurateurs with unrivalled collections of old newspapers. And Hayter thought of the pound bet he had with Colour-sergeant Wilson. A bet which stipulated, for Hayter to win, that the Brigade would be in Suez by Wednesday. And Langley thought: Twenty paces to the street, ten paces to the block. Eight or ten seconds. Track Robert. When inside, if he goes left I go right. Careful of booby traps. Careful of grenades. And Miller thought: God, you'd think Brigade had to pay for the aircraft's fuel out of Mess funds.

And finally and simultaneously they thought: Christ, the tank's stopped firing.

They went in hard and fast from two sides, and the Egyptians opened fire as they came. The moment he heard the shooting Miller, at the head of the frontal assault group, knew he had made a mistake in his assessment of the number of defenders. The Egyptians had pulled the oldest trick in the book by concealing their true strength, and he'd fallen for it. There were many more of them than twenty or thirty. Many more. But it was too late to do anything about it. Peripherally he saw that Reynolds and the lead Section were already on top of the side entrance, and Langley and 3 Section were close on their heels.

The defenders' Browning stuttered long and loud, and Reynolds fell with a bullet in his leg. His Section Sergeant dragged him clear before being hit himself. In the confused scramble for cover that followed 3 Section found themselves in front of 4, and it was left to Hayter to hurl the first of the room-clearing grenades. Langley threw the second, and they rushed inside.

The blast had torn the clothes and most of the skin off two of the Egyptians, and a third was attempting to crawl to safety before Shaw saw him through the smoke and shot him dead from six feet.

'*Take cover!*' yelled Langley, pushing over a shrapnel-scarred desk and crouching behind it. '4 Section, take your orders from me.'

'Jesus Christ, there must be an army in here!'

'Shut that door before some bugger chucks a grenade in!'

'Watch them stairs, Riordan! Watch them fuggin stairs!'

'We'll never get up them. For Chrissake, we'll never get up there!'

'Shut up! Shut your goddam mouth, you lily-livered bastard!'

'What about Mr Reynolds?'

'Pull him in. Can you pull him in?'

'I think so.'

A 4 Section lance-corporal pulled Reynolds inside.

'Where are you hit, Robert?'

'Thigh. Can you get to Sergeant McLintock?'

'He's dead, sir.'

'Jesus wept, Miller's made a balls of this! What the hell gave him the idea a Troop could take this place!'

'Give me a rifle. For God's sake, give me a rifle!'

'Here, sir.'

'Now prop me up against the wall.'

'Listen, Robert, you keep out . . .'

'Shut up, Brian.'

'Mr Langley, we've got to do something about those stairs.'

'I know.'

'We've got to get up them before some bastard clears us with a grenade.'

'*I know, damn you, sergeant!* Riordan, shoot anything that moves up those stairs.'

'I can get up them, sir. There's no one there.'

'There must be.'

'There isn't. I don't see anyone.'

'Somebody's got to go, Mr Langley.'

'All right, all right. Go ahead, Riordan. We'll cover you.'

Riordan lugged the bren up fifteen or twenty stairs. At the top was a landing, and a corridor which led to the Canal side of the block. Off the corridor were half a dozen closed doors.

'What's up there?'

'Nothing, sir. No one. Half a dozen rooms. Doors are closed.'

'Okay, stay where you are. Sergeant Hayter, take Webster and Thatcher and see what you can do about those rooms. We've got to get some of the pressure off Miller. If the bastards aren't here, they must be murdering him.'

'Right, sir. Come on, you two.'

Hayter led the sprint up the stairs.

'You, you people from 4 Section, check what's through there,' ordered Langley. 'No, not all of you, you fools!'

'Nothing, sir. Empty.'

'Then they're all upstairs. Jesus Christ.'

They heard the chatter of the bren from the top of the stairs, and then Hayter called, '*The fuggin place is stiff with them!*'

'Can you hold?' shouted Langley.

'Dunno. For a minute or two, maybe. But we can't go forward.'

'You've got to get out of here, Brian,' called Reynolds.

'I can't go while Miller's still inside.'

'Screw Miller! Use your head. If they're coming back this way he must be pulling out. Either that or he's pinned down.'

'Can you cover us, sergeant?'

'If we're pulling out I'll cover you by pissing at them.'

'Good man.'

'I can see Captain Miller, sir,' shouted a Marine from the side door.

'What's he doing?'

'Retreating behind the tank. No, he's not, he's coming towards us – and the tank.'

'Wave him off. Tell him we'll get out under our own steam.'

The Marine bellowed Langley's instructions.

'He's going, sir. He's going.'

'So are we. Okay, move out. You and you, take Mr Reynolds. You two, grab their rifles.'

'What about Sergeant McLintock?'

'You can't help him. Sergeant Hayter, we're going.'

'Coming, sir. Riordan, gimme that bren.'

'Sergeant?'

'*Give me the bleedin' bren and do as you're told!* Now scat. Scat, I said!'

Webster, Thatcher, and Riordan leapt the stairs three at a time. Hayter emptied a magazine into thin air and raced after them.

They had been inside for less than five minutes when they pulled back, dragging and half-carrying their wounded. Thirty yards away 1 and 2 Sections and the tank gave them what covering fire they could.

'Let's get the hell out of here,' said Miller, when they reached him, and they ran.

Two hundred yards down the road they took stock. McLintock was dead, Reynolds wounded. 2 Section had lost its bren team, and 1 Section, who had caught the worst of it, was reduced to its officer and one Marine.

'The bastards!' snarled Miller, almost in tears of anger and bitterness and self-recrimination. 'The syphilitic bastards!' It was several seconds before they realized he was referring to Brigade and not the Egyptians. 'Couldn't spare any planes, the bastards. Give me that wireless.'

It took him under a minute to contact Control, and after he had identified himself and given the coded map co-ordinates of the strike area, he said: 'I don't know who's i/c aircraft up there but I want some and I want them immediately. I don't care where you get them from, but get them. Otherwise I, personally, am going to crack some skulls. Out.' He tossed the microphone at the operator. 'Now we wait and see,' he said.

They waited, and saw.

The first of the Sea Hawks came in low from the eastern bank of the Canal – beautiful and deadly, a silver Nemesis without pity. It pounced gleefully on the plump target it had been offered, released its rockets, and climbed twisting and turning into the sun. A second followed it, and a third and fourth, and a quarter of an hour after the ground troops had shot the last of the defenders who tried to escape the blazing tomb, the cease-fire order came through.

They listened in silence while Miller relayed the cease-fire order, interpreting it liberally whenever he thought it necessary. He told them that the United Nations had instructed both sides to stop fighting by midnight, but in effect the war was over as from six PM; that the United States had put heavy pressure on the British Government, because Britain's independent invasion had upset American foreign policy in the Middle East; that UN troops would be arriving in a week or a fortnight, and that when they arrived the Marines would be pulling out; that National Servicemen due for demob and Reservists recalled for the operation would be on the first available LST to Malta, and from there flown to the UK; that there was a lot more but it was too bloody complicated to go into. And when he had finished the TSM said, very quietly: 'Then it was all for nothing.'

'I suppose it was,' agreed Miller. 'It's a queer old world, isn't it.'

Later, when it was almost dark, they took to the trucks and patrolled the streets, hunting looters and irregulars. The smell of death and desolation was ubiquitous. A curious smell, a composite redolent of rooms that have remained locked and barred for years, musty curtains, cordite, old meat. On each street corner, under the glare of temporary spot-lamps, gangs of Egyptian prisoners worked at the grisly task of identifying and preparing for burial their bloated dead. From many roofs and from a larger number of shell-torn buildings came the sound of rifle fire. Some of the defenders were prepared to fight until the ultimate decision was reached.

And I saw, and behold a white horse: and he that sat on him had a bow; and a crown was given unto him; and he went forth conquering, and to conquer.

And when he had opened the second seal, I heard the second beast say, Come and see.

3 Section's one-tonner bumped northwards along the Canal road. It passed the tank which had accompanied them for most of the day, and Langley waved to the blond lieutenant. From his cockpit the blond lieutenant waved back, wearily.

And there went out another horse that was red: and power was given to him that sat thereon to take peace from the earth, and that they should kill one another: and there was given unto him a great sword.

And when he opened the third seal, I heard the third beast say, Come and see. And I beheld, and lo a black horse; and he that sat on him had a pair of balances in his hand.

They said little to one another; there was little to say. They simply looked and wondered, and marvelled at twelve short hours' devastation.

From the roadside others, Egyptians, looked back. At Thatcher smoking; at Hayter, ever vigilant, nursing his sten; at Riordan in the observation hatch of the driver's cab, the bren on the cab roof in front of him; at Shaw, bareheaded, his beret in the rubble of some warehouse or office block; at Webster scratching his nose; at Rourke yawning the big yawn of a tired man; and at Langley next to him.

The action seemed to be on their left – a burst of shooting which stopped as quickly as it had begun.

'Tell the driver to turn at the next junction, Riordan,' said Langley.

'Yes, sir.'

Christ, here we go again, thought Webster. He can't keep out of anything.

The driver honked at a group of Egyptian prisoners, and turned left, into a street half-lit by fires that would burn for days. He switched his headlamps to full beam.

International politics, thought Langley dismally. A British Government allowing itself to be blackmailed by the Americans. God, it could never have happened in Churchill's day.

His father was right, of course, when he said that Britain had gone to the dogs. There was no place in the world for a country that had only a glorious past. Tin soldiers now. Clay generals. Gutless politicians. They'd grown effete. It had taken Britain three centuries to become a great power and she'd become a second-rate one in as many decades. Emasculated.

And when he had opened the fourth seal, I heard the voice of the fourth beast say, Come and see.

And I looked, and behold a pale horse: and his name that sat on him was Death, and Hell followed with him. And power was given unto him over the fourth part of the earth, to kill with sword, and with hunger, and with death, and with the beasts of the earth.

The headlamps probed the half-light. The truck slowed to a crawl. The night had suddenly gone very cold.

So right, thought Langley. A country's greatness depended upon the greatness of its people, the will of its people. And the will had gone. The men had fought well, of course, but in their hearts they were, and always would be, carpenters, cooks, fitters, clerks, blacksmiths, salesmen, locksmiths, mechanics. A part-time army. It wasn't their fault, true, but one could not expect much from a nation of artisans. One could not expect magnificence from men whose only wish was to earn a quiet, comfortable living. One could not . . .

The first half-dozen shots from above seemed part of his thoughts. The next half-dozen removed the back of his head. A grenade exploded under the front wheels, and the truck slewed out of control. The second before he followed Hayter in jumping to safety, Thatcher saw Rourke smile stupidly and cough lumps of pink lung tissue into the dust at his feet.

POSTSCRIPT

They stood on the tarmac at Luqa Airport, watching the Viscount taxi towards the boarding point. It was raining, and the wind from the north blew the ice-cold drops into their faces. The late afternoon lights of Valetta shone in the distance.

Sometimes they talked to one another, made lewd remarks about what they would like to do to the pretty Maltese air hostess. Sometimes they allowed thoughts to replace words. Thoughts of duty-free whisky stashed at the bottom of kit-bags; of leave pay that filled their wallets; of pubs they would shortly be visiting; of people they had to see in the UK: girl friends, wives, brothers, sisters, old pals, parents; and for one of them a godson and the godson's mother.

They looked scruffy, the majority of them. Their greatcoats were soaked, their boots unpolished, their green berets stained with two years' dust and dirt. Barker, from Plymouth, and Bailey, from Leeds; Carter, Jones, A., Jones, P.; Kelland, from Dagenham, and Martin; Riordan, from London, Shaw, from Birmingham, Thatcher, Webster. Forty or more of them. A few less than the original intake.

The loud speaker crackled and they heard their flight number called. A very new second-lieutenant checked their names against his list and shepherded them across the tarmac to the waiting aeroplane. A few minutes later they were air-borne. Below them the island fell away, and soon there was nothing but sea.